Agamemnon

DHARMA Directive Book 1

RH Carver

Cosmic Inkworks

Published by Cosmic Inkworks

Cover design by Tom Edwards

ISBN: 979-8-9997820-0-7

First Revised Edition

Printed in the United States of America

10 9 8 7 6 5 4 3 2 1

To both of my dear Roberts, the big one and the little one. This book is for you.

I hope you enjoy it.

Whoever fights monsters should see to it that in the process he does not become a monster. And if you gaze long enough into an abyss, the abyss will gaze back into you.

—Friedrich Nietzsche

Acknowledgements

I'd like to thank my wife for her unwavering moral support throughout this journey—your encouragement kept me going.

To my Uncle Billy: thank you for letting me rope you into beta reading. Your support matters. To my editor, Mark Leggatt: your feedback, patience, and insight made this book stronger, and I'm deeply grateful.

And to my father—thank you for providing me with a lifetime of inspiration, starting with those stacks of sci-fi paperbacks you began lending me when I was seven. You opened the door to wonder, and I never really came back out.

Foreword

Thank you so much for picking up this book. It has been a labor of love to bring it to you. I'd like to address a few things up front, just based upon my observations of the average science-fiction reader, and the sorts of concerns they often have. I hope you'll indulge me!

A Note on Ranks and the Chain of Command

(Or, Why I Didn't Copy-Paste the U.S. Navy into the future)

In the world of The DHARMA Directive, the Commonwealth Unified Services use a deliberately streamlined and standardized rank structure. It draws inspiration from both NATO and Eastern bloc traditions—but it's also its own thing. The goal? Clarity. Simplicity. A system that tells you who's in charge without needing a decoder ring or an inter-service dictionary.

Yes, I know that in modern militaries, someone with two silver bars might be a Navy lieutenant or an Marine captain—and that calling a captain "lieutenant" can earn you a death glare. I know there are five grades of warrant officer. I even know why a major general is outranked by a lieutenant general. But most people don't. And in the Commonwealth, we don't ask them to. There are no major generals. This is the future. I did it my way.

One key example: "Captain" is a billet, not a rank. It refers specifically to the commanding officer of a commissioned warship or cutter. The actual rank of that officer might be Commander, Frigate Captain, or Fleet Captain—but aboard ship, there is only one "Captain," and it's the commanding officer. This helps avoid ambiguity in conversation and protocol alike. If you're speaking to the CO of a ship, they're "Captain." No confusion, no guessing.

The same logic applies throughout the rank structure. A lieutenant is a lieutenant, no matter what branch they serve in. Their relative positions within the military hierarchy are all the same.

So if you're a connoisseur of military sci-fi—or a veteran, period—and find yourself wondering why things don't quite work like they did in the 21st century...now you know. They finally got around to cleaning up some of those bureaucratic artifacts from previous centuries, and so a Naval Infantry (NI) company commander is a prefect, not a captain. As I mentioned above, captains command ships.

On Units of Measure

As for units of measure: I mostly use the metric system. That's just common sense in a setting with a unified interstellar polity. But where the language calls for something culturally resonant—like "missed by a mile"—I let the idiom stand. And in space, you'll notice distances are often measured in light-seconds, light-minutes, or light-hours. Why? Because when your life depends on split-second decisions, nobody's crunching meters per second squared. Meters and kilometers don't cut it in space combat when ships are moving at a tenth the speed of light or faster.

A Note on Space Magic

(Or, Why the Engines Go Vroom and the Floors Stay Down)

Yes, the Commonwealth uses faster-than-light travel. No, I'm not going to diagram the drive system. Ships can jump, translate—call it what you like—but it's consistent within the logic of the setting, and quite a bit will be said on the subject eventually. If I don't spend extensive time in this first volume explaining wormhole tension indexes or quantum tunneling, it's because this isn't a make-believe flight manual.

Same with artificial gravity. Ships have it. Your boots stick to the deck. I'm not going to make a character deliver a monologue about grav-plate harmonics just to check a box.

The technology exists, it works, and everyone takes it for granted—just like you do with your microwave.

The Commonwealth doesn't run on magic, but it does run on narrative efficiency. And that means focusing on the story, not the schematics. I once read (or heard) that fiction is just like real life, with the boring parts taken out. I have tried to write this tale by that dictum, and I hope you enjoy it!

—R.H. Carver

Prologue

The captain of the commercial vessel *Euphrates* glared at his workstation and swore, striking its beveled edge with a closed fist. It was the fourth such outburst since he'd assumed his duty station that morning.

Powell, his cargo master and first mate, smiled and made a mental note. He'd been tallying the skipper's unprovoked assaults on the adjacent console—not out of concern, but amusement. This leg of the journey, outbound toward the FTL impingement zone, was quite often monotonous. The captain's creative use of invective was alleviating the tedium, if nothing else. He regarded his old friend and commanding officer with calm detachment as the captain launched into another tirade.

"What was so damned important it couldn't go out with the regular message traffic—or at least wait a few more days?" the captain groused. True to form, the console offered no reply.

Powell assumed the question was for him. He shrugged, considered several possible responses, and chose the briefest. It was the same one he'd already given, now stripped of his usual sarcasm. The captain's mood did not invite embellishment.

"Docking fees are paid, and our charter's covered at the government rate," Powell said. "Could be worse."

The captain grunted, jabbing at his analog controls with exaggerated precision. "Yeah. Well, a few more days and we could've rotated some of the Earther engineers. Easy lift, nice payout. We're heading back to Luna practically empty. That would've made the run worthwhile. This charter fee just feels like gas money. I made that point very clear to Mr. Emerson before we left Horizon Station."

Powell shrugged again. "Wasn't in the contract. Not much to say now."

"Why the hell would I think to put that in a contract?" snapped the captain. "Who sails an entire month on a rust bucket like this, all the way from Earth to the edge of nowhere, for a two-week business trip—and then pulls the plug after two days?"

Powell snorted and feigned interest in his console. "The Government."

***

Craig Emerson, the government attaché in question, sat on the edge of the spartan bunk that occupied most of the tiny cabin, affectionately referred to by the crew as his *stateroom*. He had seen larger closets, but the cramped quarters weren't what bothered him.

He toyed with a small data crystal, running his thumb along its smooth edges before tossing it from hand to hand. His gaze was on the bulkhead in front of him, but he didn't really see it.

The walls seemed closer than they had a day ago, though nothing about the ship had changed. The lighting was steady, the air system quiet, but he still felt the pressure of confinement growing by degrees. He wiped a thin sheen of sweat from his brow and glanced at the environmental readout. The temperature was within the ideal range. It always was. That didn't help.

Since leaving the facility on Tengoku, he had grown tense, withdrawn. Meals were taken in silence. Conversation felt like effort. He avoided eye contact, kept his answers short, and spent most of his time alone in the cabin.

He told himself he just needed time to think.

I do not get paid enough for this shit, he thought, clenching the crystal until its corners bit into his palm. *This was a Category Indigo project. If they really had an inkling that it hadn't been terminated according to procedure, they should have sent a company of Gendarmes and a Navy ship, not me! I'm basically just a glorified compliance auditor, an errand-boy. My job was to get an answer to a question that was only supposed to have one possible answer. Now what?*

An announcement crackled over the address system, jerking him from his thoughts. He looked around, almost expecting intruders to have appeared during his reverie. He remained alone.

Was I supposed to walk into that conference room and declare I knew everything? Shake my finger at the Director and promise to file a report? He winced. *For all I know, everyone in that room was in on it.*

After a few moments, he stood, tugged his rumpled tunic into place, and reached for the desk drawer—then hesitated. Instead of stowing the crystal, he slipped it into his inner pocket.

Opening the door, he paused, took a breath, and left the cabin that had become his entire world.

"Captain Gathii, I regret the inconvenience," Emerson said, stepping onto the bridge. "But I've reconsidered. I must send an FTL message to my superiors—immediately."

The captain stared at Emerson as if he had just materialized out of thin air. "Assistant Undersecretary," Gathii said at last, "you could've sent that message while we were still in orbit. We could've waited, picked up passengers like we discussed, and hit the relay sooner. I told you we were sending today's burst at 0900. It went out on schedule. You know the transmission cost—"

"—Will be covered by the Commonwealth," Emerson cut in. "I understand the timing is unfortunate, but state business dictated my early departure. Now that we're well en-route, I've deemed it necessary. You'll be compensated for the delay."

Gathii sighed and raised his hand. "Mister Powell, ping the buoy. Let it know we've got another burst."

Already in motion, Powell's fingers danced over his console.

Gathii extended an open palm to Emerson. "You've got the message on glass?"

Emerson looked uncomfortable. "I'm not authorized to hand it off. I'll need to be present."

The captain glanced upward in mute appeal for patience. "Of course. Fine. But maybe, while we wait, you could explain to a humble merchant captain—"

"Skipper," Powell interrupted. His tone was enough to silence the room. "We're receiving a DSC distress signal on the emergency channel."

"A distress call?" Gathii leaned forward. "What vessel? What's the emergency?"

"That's the thing. It's from *Euphrates*. The alert says *reactor casualty*. But our reactor's nominal. And the system shows no outgoing DSC messages from us—no transmissions at all in fact, since I last pinged the buoy."

Gathii stared. "You're telling me there's a distress call—from us—about a reactor failure that isn't happening?"

Powell nodded. "I'm looking right at the analog DSC 'send' button. Safety shield's down. It hasn't been touched. That transmission didn't come from us."

"Are there any other ships in the system?"

"No contacts. Collision system's green. No anomalies within ten light-seconds."

Gathii tapped his console. "Where's the location?"

"Right on top of us. Or close enough it doesn't matter."

Emerson's breathing quickened. He understood just enough to feel dread curling in his gut. DSC messages weren't easy to fake.

Gathii's expression hardened. "Falsifying a DSC alert is a serious offense."

"It is," Powell agreed.

"If it's real—or at least sent with regulation equipment—it'll repeat. We'll get a bearing, maybe identify the source. But what then?" Gathii rubbed his jaw, deep in thought. "Pirates, maybe. But this would be new. No cover nearby, nothing to hide behind. If they are laying doggo with their systems cold, why would they blow their stealth with a fake distress call?"

He gestured at the display. "They'd have to know our departure vector in advance. We only left port early because of *you*," he added, glancing at Emerson. "Even we didn't know we'd be moving out so soon."

Powell spread his hands. "Beats me, Skipper."

"What does it mean?" Emerson whispered, trembling. "What's happening?"

"We'll let you know once we find out. For now, please clear the bridge."

"I—" Emerson began, but Powell interrupted again.

"Skipper. We never got that ping back from the comm buoy. Now the comms suite says the hailing frequency is 'unavailable due to interference.' Lindsay needs to take a look."

Gathii's face darkened. "Get her up here. Get the whole FTL watch up here. I want a full comms diagnostic. And get us out of this system the second we hit the zone. Tell Forbes to check the reactor just in case." He hesitated. "I'm not superstitious, but this is getting weird, and I don't like it."

"Aye, sir. Want me to notify Tengoku Control?"

"Forget Tengoku. We didn't send the message, we haven't broken any regs, and I need you focused. We'll debrief on Luna."

As Powell relayed orders into his headset, Emerson's chest tightened, his breath shortening without warning.

He stepped forward—too fast—and nearly tripped. His legs felt stiff, unreliable. "They're jamming us," he managed to choke out. His voice came high and brittle.

Powell looked up from his console. Emerson couldn't tell if it was surprise or suspicion in the man's eyes, but it made his skin crawl either way.

"They know," Emerson said, louder now, the words coming out in a rush. "They know about the—the data I have."

His hand went instinctively to the pocket where the crystal lay, as if that could hide it. He couldn't seem to stop touching it lately. The smooth edge. The weight.

"Nobody's jamming us," the captain snapped. "We're alone out here. Probably just a glitch. Try to breathe. What's really going on, Emerson? Is this why you had us pull out of orbit early?"

A high-pitched alarm cut him off, its staccato beep loud and insistent. The collision warning system lit up the bridge in angry amber.

Powell froze, then rasped, "Two high-speed IR contacts. Starboard bow. Distance eight light-seconds. Bearing is steady. Range is decreasing." He swallowed. "I think they're torpedoes."

That was it. The word. The shape of the thing they hadn't wanted to name.

"Torpedoes?" Gathii's voice cracked. "From whom? Where?"

There was no answer.

"Emergency burn!" the captain barked. "Now! Get us out of here!"

The bridge erupted. Emerson stood frozen, tears on his cheeks, fists clenched. Bridge officers recalled to duty, shoved past him, nearly knocking him down. At some point, a midshipman grabbed his arm, dragging him toward an acceleration couch as the ship groaned and shook under his feet, protesting against the sudden thrust.

No...no...no... a voice in the back of his mind gibbered, in defiance of the inevitable, as the men and women around him took their stations and scanned their instruments for some solution to the insoluble, an answer to the inexorable.

Gathii whirled his seat to face Emerson. "This is your fault," he snapped. "If there's something you haven't told us—if there's something in that message of yours, or in that crystal, or from whatever the hell happened down there—*fix it*. Right now. Call them off. Whoever they are."

Emerson blinked. His mouth moved, but no sound came out.

"Say something!" Gathii shouted, his eyes wild. "Who is shooting at us? Why?"

"Six light-seconds!" Powell called. "We don't have the delta-V. We've got to go to lifeboats. We can't juke them in this thing." He looked up, voice quiet, almost apologetic. "I'm sorry, Skipper. The math doesn't lie."

Gathii hesitated. Then, quietly he replied, "Do it. Secure from acceleration warning. Pass the word—abandon ship."

The bridge crew scrambled. Only the captain remained at his post. Emerson ripped off the acceleration restraints on his chest, and stumbled down the companionway, the high-pitched beeping trailing behind him like a countdown.

Though he'd never heard that sound before, he knew exactly what it meant.

1

Official Suspicion

Unity Station, The Arcturus System

"So, is it a fair characterization then, if I say your brother was more or less apolitical?"

Casimir Broz regarded the woman before him with confusion and no small amount of annoyance. As had been the case throughout most of the interview, she sat across the small table from him, apparently focused on her datapad. Occasionally, she looked up to make eye contact with her subject.

"Agent Sutton," he said, "I'm struggling to connect the dots here. Do my brother's political leanings, or lack thereof, somehow bear on your ability to catch the bastard who blew him up? I've talked to probably half a dozen of you people by now, from I don't even know how many different agencies, and I'm not getting the impression that you are any closer to getting your heads around this than you were a week ago."

Sutton looked up and met his eyes, the light levels in the compartment were dim enough for him to remove his protective eyewear. Accustomed as he was to the perpetual gloom of the planet Jotunheim, Casimir—Cass to his close associates—was sensitive to the harsh white light that Earthers considered normal.

She gave a tight smile and replied, "I am simply collecting data points that might help us create a more complete picture of events, Mr. Broz. And may I ask, exactly who it is you mean when you say, 'you people'? I assume you mean law enforcement, which strikes me as funny, given you and your brother Andre were both Territorial Rangers."

Cass shrugged. "I'm not sure I'd describe the Rangers as *Law Enforcement*. At least not in the way you're probably used to thinking about it. We were more like..." he trailed off, as if lost in a memory, before continuing, "more like search and rescue, I guess. With a little bit of game warden thrown into the mix."

Sutton's eyebrow arched, but her voice betrayed nothing except pleasant professionalism. "I see. The game in this case, being xeno-synapsids that can rip a human being into bite-sized pieces before you can say 'raw hamburger.' Is that about right?"

Cass chuckled. "Yeah. Something like that. But if we could get back to the case at hand, if you wouldn't mind?"

Nodding, Sutton resumed studying her datapad. "Did your brother mention any kind of confrontation, any strange or unpleasant encounters at the clinic in the days leading up to the attack?"

Cass shook his head. "I already told the local cops—he didn't mention anything like that. As far as I know, everything was fine at the clinic, and that part of the station is typically quiet."

"You say it's quiet. Would you say it was also generally a safe place for um—MCEs to be?"

"MCEs?"

Sutton shifted in her seat. "Modified Colonial Exomorphs. That's the official legal term we use on Earth, I hope that's not offensive. Um, is transhumans better?"

Cass frowned. "Agent Sutton, this is Unity Station, not some watering hole in the backwoods of Eurasia. I have never felt until now that there was an atmosphere of hostility here toward *transhumans* as you put it, certainly not in that neighborhood, nor anywhere on the station. It's kind of hard to be a bigot in one of the busiest spaceports in the Commonwealth, and one in the Arcturus system to boot."

"And there's absolutely nothing you can tell us about the local politics, or the local community that might shed any light on why this facility in particular may have been targeted?"

"No," Cass said slowly, "I mean you hear things, read things in the news about nativist movements and the usual corporate intrigues, but nothing that would seem to bear on the Deitz Clinic specifically." His voice became bitter as he continued, "I mean, we're only one hop from the Solar System, I guess if you were an Earther reactionary looking to blow up some bug-eyed monsters, you wouldn't want to go further out than you had to, to find a nice hospital to bomb."

Sutton brushed a stray lock of dark hair out of her eyes. She leaned back and regarded him with an unreadable expression for a moment. Presently, she uncrossed her legs and re-crossed them, pulling briskly on the hem of her skirt as if to smooth out nonexistent wrinkles. Cass's eyes lingered on her shapely, well-muscled legs. Was this some kind of subtle psychological tactic? Was he being invited to evaluate her as a sexual object for some reason, or was he reading too much into it? Was he being subtly manipulated into being more cooperative? It was a disturbing line of thought, despite the likelihood that it was simply his mind wandering into random alleyways as it sometimes did. Still, he knew very well that when speaking to internal security types, there was always a fine line between an interview and an interrogation.

Stop it, he chided himself. *She's just a step up from a street cop. Your issues with authority are making this a more difficult conversation than it needs to be. Her leg was probably just falling asleep. Get a grip.*

"Mr. Broz, let me be candid. Our interviews and other data-gathering activities have revealed little about the patients, staff, or management of the clinic that would suggest any motive for the bombing other than the one that the publicly circulated message supplied. That it was a political statement, albeit an indefensible and misguided one. I wouldn't ordinarily delve into the details of an investigation like this with a witness, but..."

She paused, and bit her lower lip, one of those nervous gestures or tells people picked up. It seemed as if she were weighing what to say next. "There are those in the government who believe that the media circus you are seeing right now, the backlash, the outrage, all of that—*that* is the real purpose of the bombing."

Cass stared at her blankly. "What do you mean?"

She raised her left hand, each point accompanied by a finger. "First, consider the selection of the target. A gene therapy clinic that was to all appearances a perfectly legitimate enterprise. It was, by the way. No colonization or discretionary gene-edit packages were being developed or sold there, illicitly or otherwise. The work being done was entirely therapeutic, on the up and up. We checked quite thoroughly. Second, the language of the message claiming responsibility. Characterizing the facility as a 'monster factory' is guaranteed to incense Outlanders... No offense."

Cass grimaced. "None taken," he replied. The term was considered derogatory by some, though it had become common parlance over the course of the last several decades. It referred to people from the so-called Outlands—worlds far outside the Core Systems, many of which were marginally habitable or outright hostile to baseline human life. On those planets, the best chance for survival might entail human genetic modification. Even in cases where Outlanders had not benefited from such adaptations, they were often considered provincial, or backward by the inhabitants of the Core Worlds.

"Third, the group claiming responsibility is a known bio-conservative extremist organization on Earth, which puts the Earth Government on the defensive—given the current political climate in the Commonwealth—and ensures that such extremist groups are front and center in a lot of people's minds, from the internal security services to the entire population of Unity Station. Word spreads, a narrative emerges: Earther extremists are killing Outlanders, and the Central Government on Earth offers little more than boilerplate condemnations and platitudes. Given that bio-conservative or at least 'Earth-Centric' politicians are on the march right now in the mid-terms, I think we can safely assume that the platitudes and condemnations will indeed appear phoned in, so as to avoid the dangerous optics of being too empathetic toward Outlanders."

Cass felt his face flush. He was getting angry and knew all too well the difficulty he had in controlling that anger, even when part of him could still assess it clinically and see it taking hold. "Dangerous optics? You know what *is* dangerous? Bombs. If they think the *optics* are tough, maybe the poor darlings should come out here and see what my brother's corpse looks like so they can form a better basis for comparison."

Pain erupted in his right hand, and Cass realized his nails were digging into his palm. Breathing deeply, he forced himself to relax. Yet even as he fell into the familiar exercise, part of him yearned to stoke that anger; to feed it as one feeds a fire, and to exult in it.

At least I know for sure I can still feel. I am not totally empty. Totally hollow. But then the familiar inner voice spoke urgently, reminding him he couldn't afford to get angry. When he became angry, significant property damage was the likely result, or something worse. His muscle mass was considerably greater than that of the strongest Terran athlete, his body attuned to a much different and ostensibly more dangerous environment than this one. Instincts that served him well in the dreary badlands of home would only betray him here. *Let it drain out of you*, the voice insisted. *Let it pass away, like the receding waters of an ebbing tide...*

For a moment, the drab walls of his economy domestic unit breathed and pulsed. Agent Sutton became distant, her voice muffled and drowned out by the ringing in his ears. He felt something akin to vertigo. He focused on his hands, clasped them on the tabletop in front of him. *This isn't real. None of this is real. It's a bad dream. I will wake up. The clinic wasn't bombed. Things like that don't happen here, do they?*

The apartment came back into focus, the cramped space he shared with his brother. Had shared. Andre's gym bag still sat where he'd left it, by the front door. His toiletries still occupied more than their fair share of the meager counter space in the head. All evidence pointed to his continued existence. All except the voices of these unwelcome strangers intruding into his life, insisting that Andre was gone. Killed. Murdered at—of all places—the cutting-edge clinic where he had been responding well to therapy.

Though rarely a concern, leaving the crushing gravity of their homeworld always carried risks for his kind. The two brothers had left Jotunheim nearly five standard years ago to live on the station, among denizens from many worlds, whose bodies were never meant to endure the almost three Earth gravities the so-called Jotuns called normal. Andre had developed a degenerative condition that sometimes afflicted those Jotuns who lived too long outside their native environment. He had grown weak, fatigued, his muscles knotting and cramping with every movement. Even the lightest activity—a simple walk—had become agony. And now, Andre had been taken from him.

Breathe. Focus on your breathing. Slow, regular. This is the real world. You need to deal with it. He's gone. Shit happens. Founders know when you're involved, shit definitely happens.

Sutton, perhaps sensing the chaos roiling within him, leaned forward and spoke, intense emotion lurking beneath her professionally cultivated calm. "How would you like a crack at the people who did this? Whatever people out here are saying, the Commonwealth values the lives of every citizen, no matter their genetic makeup or home world. There is—I suppose you could say, official suspicion in certain quarters of the government, that this act was not perpetrated by a bunch of agitators on basic income. It's bigger than that. And this attack? As *horrible* as it is, I can assure you it's only the tip of the iceberg."

Her tone grew calculating. "You have skills, Mr. Broz. Training. You have a background that allowed you to not just survive in one of the most hostile environments in known space, but to help others survive there too. You are a skilled tracker, an expert marksman, and you know how to think critically. I see you have recently been certified by your current employer for hardsuit survey work, so you are no stranger to the hazards of space and space travel. Your, um—ancestry also affords you certain advantages that might be of use in such a career. And frankly, you are highly motivated to help us find these people and hold them to account for their crimes."

Cass regarded her with puzzlement, his emotions now a swirling, amorphous storm of loss, frustrated anger, and possibly—excitement?

"Are you trying to recruit me, Agent Sutton? The questions for the witness were just the wind-up, and this is the pitch?" He queried her in a voice that sounded too calm to be his own, while he struggled internally to regain his balance, his sense of perspective. The cool self-mastery and carefully cultivated situational awareness he needed now more than ever, began slipping away again. "Aren't you worried that I'm *too* close to it? You sure you really want me storming around turning over rocks when it's my own brother they killed? Besides, I haven't represented the long arm of the law in any capacity for some years now."

Sutton grinned. "Maybe I am, in a manner of speaking. You fit the profile of certain remarkable individuals who are, from time to time, engaged to serve the Commonwealth in ways that most ordinary citizens cannot. Mr. Broz—"

"Cass," he interrupted. "I guess if we're hatching plots together now, you can call me Cass."

She nodded. "Well, Cass, the branch of service I had in mind is not one most people are familiar with. As you will no doubt understand given what you're about to learn, this is by design. You see," she began, eyes flashing dangerously as they locked with his, "due process would not exactly be your highest priority. Not for the sorts of *cases* you'd be working."

For the first time since Andre had died, Cass felt alive. He felt awake. He steepled his fingers and regarded Sutton with a steady gaze.

"Tell me more."

2

Genetic Offender

Somewhere in Nevada, Earth

E nora Anthem stood as tall and proud as one can when one is nude and holding one's meager collection of personal effects in one's arms. The dry, chill air of the bunker sent goosebumps across her deep purple-taupe colored skin. This was, she reflected, almost certainly deliberate. Doubtless, her custodians thought it was a delightfully devious way of adding insult to injury, as their charges were herded naked down the spartan concrete hallway toward whatever awaited beyond the next checkpoint.

"The genetic offender will place her items in the indicated receptacle and step forward to stand on the yellow line," droned a bored-looking guard wearing the fatigues of the Gendarmes Service, or if one preferred greater loquacity, the Commonwealth Department of Customs and Excise. Enora dropped her bundle of clothing and personal items into the stiff canvas cube indicated with a complete lack of ceremony, expression, or apparent interest in the proceedings. She found a sort of perverse pleasure in complying with her orders in the most recalcitrant manner possible, short of outright disobedience. It seemed a sure bet the guard wouldn't actually beat her for such minor displays of defiance. She was fairly sure, anyway. As the guard unabashedly swept his gaze up and down the length of her slender form, she sauntered toward the indicated line painted on the floor. Fists on her hips, she drawled, "You should really just take a holo. It'll last longer."

The guard, nonplussed, stepped toward her and scanned her head to toe with a device she couldn't identify, then gestured her onward.

After what seemed an interminable journey down the concrete hallway, stopping at various checkpoints to have her blood drawn or her retinas scanned, Enora found herself in an old-fashioned, barracks-style group shower, already occupied by three others. There was a man, presumably an Earther; a female Jotun, easily identified by her massive build, protective goggles, and ashen complexion; and another male who was obviously from her own home world of Anthemusa. Both the Jotun woman and her fellow Anthemusan seemed lost in their own thoughts, but the Earther—athletically built and almost startlingly attractive—seemed eager to make conversation. He was young, she guessed—perhaps only in his late twenties—with thick dark hair and a tawny skin tone that was aesthetically pleasing, though it told her little about his background. Only recently had she begun to recognize how Earthers' facial structures and complexions connected to the varied regions of their ancestral home. It was still a work in progress.

"Hey there," he said, his broad smile revealing perfect, white teeth. "I'm Raymond Guthrie. Everybody calls me Ray. I'd never met a Siren until today, and now I've met two." He gave her an appraising once-over but without overtly leering and asked, "What'd they get you for? Overstay your visa and get caught dealing glitter like this fellow here?"

Enora shrugged diffidently and availed herself of the packet of body wash she'd been handed before entering. "Not exactly," she responded, her expression deadpan. "I'm Enora. I'm a pirate."

Ray let out a cough that didn't quite become a laugh. "A pirate? For real? Damn. Well, at least if I end up breaking rocks on an asteroid or something, I can say I got to take a shower with a sexy pirate queen. That'll make the story better."

Enora grinned as her gaze roamed over him—bold and unhurried, before she asked in the lazy drawl she often affected, "Your story? And what exactly is your story, pretty boy?"

She had been curious what sort of reaction her forward posture would illicit from the self-assured young man and was only mildly surprised when he roared with laughter. After struggling a moment to stifle his mirth, he finally replied, "I think you got the gist of it already. You like this baby?" He made a flourish at himself with both hands, his face an exaggerated caricature of machismo, before dropping his hands to his sides, his expression becoming cynical. "This is the best physique money can buy, apparently. I didn't even know. I thought that girl was just, you know. Sniffing the cork. I mean, I work out, I watch what I eat, it never even occurred to me ya know?"

Enora quirked an eyebrow. "Sniffing the cork?" She turned her back on him to rinse herself, as she awaited his reply.

"Oh, yeah. I guess they probably don't say that where you come from. I think it comes from the old days before the Diaspora—it's a saying. Like, when you get wine service, and the sommelier leaves the cork so you can sniff it. Not that I do that—sniff wine-corks,

I mean. I guess you can sort of evaluate a bottle without really tasting it that way? But anyhow, it's just a figure of speech. When you're in one of the old families on Earth, and you hear that so-and-so is 'sniffing the cork,' that means they are trying to figure out whether someone would make a good genetic match, you know? Like, did their family have work done, back before all the laws, before the Church?"

Enora turned her head to glance at him over her shoulder. "This all going somewhere, Ray?"

The young man flashed his perfect smile at her before continuing. "Anyway, there's this girl I met at a fundraiser for my father's foundation. Well, she was really beautiful. And she was into me, or at least—I thought she was. Like, there was every reason for me be interested in this girl. She was smart, she was funny, I mean—she was gorgeous. We were talking, and she was asking about my family. I guess I thought she was considering me for something, you know—long-term.

"After my father's thing, I brought her back to my place." Ray paused, looking sheepish. "In retrospect, I guess that's when she probably got a DNA sample, 'voluntarily submitted' the lawyers called it. I guess that's one way of putting it. She wasn't four hours out the door when the Knights Chaplain came knocking. They told me I was a *genetic offender* and there was 'no excuse' for someone in my father's position, and all kinds of stuff I couldn't even process. Dad's an important guy, but I didn't think somebody would do something like this just to get to him. He has lawyers obviously, but..." he shook his head as he trailed off.

Enora drew in a long breath between her teeth as understanding dawned at last. "Your parents got you a vanity package in utero."

Ray nodded, his face grim. "My parents got me a vanity package. Vision, cognition, muscle density, immune system, bone structure, cardiovascular...hell. At least I know my pecker is guaranteed to work for the next eighty years if I last that long."

Now it was Enora's turn to laugh, and she steadied herself with a hand on the shower fixtures to make sure she didn't slip and fall on the worn and slick tile floor. "So, there's your silver lining," she said between snorts of laughter, making a concerted effort to keep her gaze on the young man's face rather than the current topic of conversation. He really was an exceptional physical specimen. "Now, if only you can find a use for the endowments bestowed upon you by your rich parents. As a genetic offender, I'm afraid your admittedly well-rounded ass belongs to the Commonwealth. I don't imagine they intend using you as a breeding stallion, now they know your dirty little secret."

The Jotun woman, who still had not spoken in Enora's presence, tittered.

Ray began to shampoo his thick mane of hair and replied, "Sadly, no. Like as not I just volunteered for the Navy. Space Rescue probably. Or maybe bomb disposal or something. And how do they plan for you to *volunteer* to repay your debt to society, Enora? I hear piracy is not generously rewarded by the authorities in the Solar system, especially not for purple people. I mean, Sirens. Or is it 'Anthemusans'? I don't mean to be rude."

Enora sighed. "Well, I do like to lure boys to their doom, and I am wet and *sexy* as you've so eloquently opined in our first ever super-awkward shower conversation, so I suppose 'Siren' is fine. Given your earnest desire not to be rude."

Ray froze, his hands still entangled in his hair, still in the middle of the act of lathering, his face a picture of mortification. After a speechless moment, he began to splutter, "oh— I'm sorry, I didn't mean to—"

"Relax, Ray. I'm only messing with you."

Laughing nervously, Ray resumed washing his hair, his face red.

Having taken pity on the poor boy, Enora continued, "to answer your question, I don't think they intend that I should pursue an exciting career in a Helium-3 processing plant. I would be...poorly suited to such work. I am not as strong as her," she indicated the Jotun woman with a toss of her head, "nor am I well adapted to the life of a roughneck. I don't even have a particularly strong constitution in one-gee environments, such as our current palatial accommodations here on the Sacred Home World of Humanity." She spoke now in an aristocratic, airy tone. "Why, my genitalia don't even have a lifetime guarantee, like yours!"

Ray, recovered from his momentary embarrassment, guffawed, and said, "Girl, you ought to talk to your parents about that!"

"Not likely," snorted Enora, "my father is the Anthemusan Ambassador to the Commonwealth, and I don't think we are on speaking terms right now."

Unable to muster a cogent response, Ray stared at her dumbfounded, water running in rivulets down his incredulous face.

There was silence after this for some minutes, and then the Jotun woman spoke, "Can you gentlemen and pirates occupy yourselves with something for a few minutes so I can wash my damn junk in privacy? I'm glad you cosmopolitan types are having a good laugh, but this is embarrassing as hell for us regular folk. Why are they doing this to us anyways? Just because we are Outlanders, some of us, doesn't mean we're contaminated or something. Do these Earther government assholes think being an Outlander is contagious? Why does this whole thing have to be like a concentration camp or something?"

Ray flushed again and turned his back to the woman out of courtesy as he spoke, "It's psychological. They have to make sure us *Übermenschen* know we aren't better than them. They mean to take us down a few pegs before they ship us off. Make us feel vulnerable. This has probably been standard operating procedure since the Great Conflict." His face took on a thoughtful expression. "I am pretty sure this intake facility was here then. It's old."

Enora turned an appraising look on the young man, but there was nothing salacious in it now. *I guess he really does have a genetically engineered brain,* she thought. "I don't feel like one of the Übermenschen. My damn back hurts."

The Jotun frowned as she turned around to face them and said, "Uber what?"

"Never mind," Ray replied, looking bemused.

They continued to shower in silence for a few moments before a guard appeared from around the corner and loudly demanded that they conclude their ablutions and exit the shower. "And hurry it up. Dry your asses off and get out here on the line. No more playing hide-the-eggplant in there!"

Enora raised an eyebrow and glanced at the Anthemusan man who had thus far remained completely silent. As he wrapped a threadbare towel around his waist, he broke that silence now to mutter under his breath, "I really hate that guy."

***

Some three days and a seemingly endless battery of psychological and physical tests later, Enora was on a ground transport, speeding over the desert.

Truthfully, she could only assume they were still in the desert, because she was reasonably sure of the vehicle's maximum speed and range. The windows were blackened so that nothing could be seen of the world outside. She shared the passenger cabin of the transport with one other person, the Jotun female she had met on her first day at the intake facility. Her name, it turned out, was Emily. The facility's name, if it had one, was still unknown and moreover of no interest to her. She had left it in the past, ostensibly forever, and what her future held was as opaque as the transport's windows.

She was fairly certain of a few things. For example, she had already known the intake facility was located somewhere in the desert region called Nevada. As the daughter of a Commonwealth ambassador, she had been made privy to some details of her forthcoming term of service that other conscripts would not have been. True, she was an embarrassment to her father and a criminal by any reasonable definition—albeit one never tried or convicted—but she was also a political landmine for any minor functionary or judge who decided to drop the boom on the daughter of the Ambassador from Anthemusa, at a time when the goodwill of that planet's government was both a valuable political commodity and, increasingly, a rare one.

Thus, she was afforded some consideration by those who had arranged this transition to a life of public service. It was not exactly respect, but some level of deference, lest this entire plan to whisk her out of the public eye and into some clandestine service should suddenly explode in their faces. Yes, she had known before she was ever taken into custody that she was indeed being recruited (or rather conscripted) into some sort of hush-hush operation, and that she was not being sent to an airless moon to be put to work in an isotope mine. Those old laws still on the books were non-specific about the sorts of duties that a person in her position could be enlisted to perform, so long as they were either military in nature or were performed somewhere other than Earth. Or both.

As a member of a diplomatic household, she had been entitled to reside on Earth for the duration of her father's duties there. However, the recent legal complications she had found herself burdened with had exposed a rather glaring flaw in her plan to seek a life of adventure here in the Solar System, free of her father's lectures, but very much charmed by his gift of diplomatic immunity. She had not considered that while she was shielded from being prosecuted for what one might reasonably deem to be acts of piracy in this system, she was not, alas, immune to being deported from it for those very selfsame acts.

This wouldn't have been of much concern to her either, except that she had already worn out her welcome on Anthemusa, having been (almost certainly) involved in a conspicuous case of (alleged) data theft within Anthemusan jurisdiction. This prior incident had, in point of fact, been a significant contributor to her father's decision to accept the ambassadorship in the first place—a point that had come up in numerous rancorous discussions between father and daughter over the last several years.

After the delicacy of her position had been impressed upon her by the lawyers and ambassadorial staff, it became clear that she had only one viable path open—unless she wished to return home, almost certainly to be arrested the moment she set foot on Anthemusan soil. That path lay through the Unified Services Command Structure (USCS), under the Special Conscription clause normally reserved for people like Ray Guthrie: those not necessarily found guilty of a crime, yet still visited by the sins of their fathers, deemed not quite human by virtue of their altered genetic makeup. Such people could visit the ancestral home, but they could not stay.

Enora, a so-called Siren, a humanoid adapted through science to life on an ocean world circling a brilliant blue sun, had found herself in the untenable position of being unable to go home, and yet unable to stay on Earth since being stripped of her special status. She could wander the Commonwealth until her money ran out, she supposed. The endorsement on her passport, however, was from Anthemusa, and it was to that world she belonged. A world that now held no refuge for her, no welcome except a prison cell.

Moreover, her father had made it clear he had no intention of subsidizing a vagabond. *His* daughter would own her mistakes and take responsibility for her actions. So, the USCS it was to be. While nothing in the law prevented her induction into the Navy or the regular security services, it was understood that genetic offenders were almost always assigned to roles matching their "special aptitudes." Which in practice, meant the kinds of duties the Government preferred not to explain to an upstanding citizen's next of kin, should the worst come to pass. It had become, she'd heard, something of a tradition to send society's debtors into harm's way.

Certainly, she expected the Commonwealth's ideas on the rehabilitation of one Enora Anthem—data specialist, free-spirit, miscreant, and aspiring space pirate—to be creative.

Yep, Enora, you really screwed yourself this time, she mused. *Well done.*

Lost in contemplation, Enora slowly became aware at some point that the vehicle had slowed. As she stirred, she saw Emily had already grabbed her rucksack from the storage rack near the front of the compartment and was making her way to the door. The future it seemed, had arrived.

3

Farewell Feast

An undisclosed location, Earth

T he auditorium was filled nearly to capacity, or so it seemed to Enora as she sat, choosing a seat toward the back of the large, octagonal room. The other occupants of the room were mostly clad in the same nondescript jumpsuit as she was herself, and came from various worlds and age groups, though none that she saw were so young that she would consider them adolescent. She did not notice Emily, Ray, or any of the other inductees she had briefly interacted with back at the intake facility among the crowd.

Within perhaps twenty minutes or so of her seating herself, the flow of attendees passing through the double doors to her right had slowed to a trickle, and presently, ushers wearing the uniform of the Naval Infantry branch of the USCS closed the doors and took up positions to either side. As stragglers sought out remaining open seats, performing the awkward, graceless steps of a dance familiar to civilized beings throughout the known galaxy, squeezing past rows of compacted knees and issuing a litany of mumbled apologies, an officer stepped out onto the stage and signaled with unmistakable body language his desire to expedite the proceedings.

Enora found herself seated next to a dark-haired Jotun, on the younger side of middle age, who shifted his considerable bulk in his just-slightly-too-narrow seat in order to give her room to sit comfortably. As with most Jotuns, his shoulders were broad, his physique densely thewed and squat. His eyes, invisible behind his dark goggles, turned to her. "Sorry, I don't think the seating was really designed with Jotuns in mind."

"Oh, no problem," Enora replied, "you're fine. So, it is 'Jotuns' then, not 'Jotnar' because I hear both."

The man's lips quirked in a faint smile. "That depends on who you ask," he replied, "and also on your ability to parse a lot of tribal politics that I don't personally give a shit about. Either is fine by me."

The man extended his hand awkwardly across his body and leaned toward her slightly. "Casimir Broz. Most people call me Cass."

Enora took his hand and shook it once, noting his grip was firm, but not crushing her fingers.

"Enora. Enora Anthem. Though I am apparently a blight upon the Anthem name, and I've been thinking about changing it. I think Grace O'Malley has a nice ring to it, but the Census and Records office will doubtless disapprove."

Cass gave her a confused sidelong glance, inviting further comment.

"Back before the Great Conflict, she was the daughter of a powerful politician, and a very successful pirate," Enora began, then with a wistful sigh she continued, "The former is definitely me, the latter—she spread her hands, "not so much.""

Cass gazed at her for a moment then chuckled, a deep honest sort of chuckle, Enora observed, before responding, "You do realize we're here to join the uniformed services, right? To uphold law and order?"

Enora grinned and shrugged her narrow shoulders. "Life is funny that way. Besides, *join* isn't really the word I would choose. I don't know about you, but I was volun-told." She then added in a meek and innocent voice, almost *voce sotto*, "on their own heads be it."

Cass chuckled again. "Actually, I did volunteer."

Enora stared at him incredulously. "Why?" She placed a hand on his enormous bicep and affecting an air of shock asked, "Are you—tell me you're not...a patriot?"

Cass looked uncomfortable, and glanced away from her as he replied, "I have my reasons. Personal reasons, I guess."

As this and numerous other sidebar conversations continued to susurrate through the auditorium, the officer at the podium cleared his throat, and the invisible microphone that was amplifying his voice alerted the audience in no uncertain terms that the feature presentation of the evening was to begin.

"Ladies, Gentlemen, and individuals that may otherwise designate themselves, good evening. I am here to advise you concerning the next steps of your recruitment. This is not your orientation. That will follow once you have accepted the conditions of your enlistment, assuming that you do so, which is not a foregone conclusion at this point. I am a Major in the Commonwealth Naval Infantry, and if you have questions after this brief presentation, you may address me as 'Sir' or as 'Major'. If it helps, think of me as Major Conundrum, because you don't get to know my name. It's better for all of us that way."

Enora turned her head to Cass and rolled her eyes. When she saw his answering smirk, she said in a stage whisper, "I bet he's been waiting all day to tell that one."

Cass murmured, "I bet he gives this same exact speech a couple times a week. He's got to spice it up somehow. I'm sure his job sucks."

The Major continued, undeterred by the audible byplay happening in various quarters of the auditorium.

"I am not in fact a member of whatever clandestine service you are about to be recruited for, I do not know it's designation, and I do not want to. With that said, I have already answered every foreseeable question that I am able to, regarding the identity or mission statement of the particular unit or units to which you might be assigned. So, now that we are hopefully clear on that point, let me tell you what I do know about your purpose in being here, and the next steps you must undertake to remain a valued government asset, rather than—whatever you were before."

The Major's gaze swept the crowd, with an obvious disdain that Enora thought might have been mere affectation. Just as likely, it was not.

"Firstly, I can tell you that each of you has already been assessed as having the necessary physical health, mental resilience, and *abilities* to perform your assigned duties, whatever they may be. You will be given a professional skill assessment later today, and most of you will then receive eight weeks of basic military training. Those of you who complete your training are very likely to be read into certain classified programs, and thus, prior to enlistment you will all be required to sign certain documents and agreements that legally bind you to secrecy concerning anything you learn at this or subsequent government facilities. I can tell you that violating these agreements is a felony and will absolutely land you in a He-3 processing plant somewhere very, very far away. I can also tell you that officially, you are to be inducted into the Customs and Excise Service, for a period of not less than ten Terran years."

At this point there was some murmuring among the audience, and before the Major could continue, a hand shot up near the front of the room. "Major, uh—sir, are you saying we're going to be spending the next ten years as...as customs agents, sir? Gendarmes? We're going to be checking cargo manifests and—"

"Yes, that's right son," the Major interrupted his voice dripping sarcasm, "See, we're going to train you as riflemen, as though you were *actual Naval Infantry personnel*, which is a better fate than you deserve. We're going to invest tens of thousands of credits into each of you; to give you a background in survival medicine, zero-gravity close-quarters combat, and cyber-warfare...all so you can hold a tablet and tick checkboxes on cargo declaration forms. Seem plausible to you?"

The young man who had raised his hand, an Earther or genotypical Core human, Enora thought, flushed a deep red and closed his mouth.

The Major went on in a brusque tone, his gaze sweeping the entire room, "then if you persevere, and don't get killed in a stupid training accident, you will be sent to the Gendarmes to get advanced individualized training in colonial law, basic astrogation, signals intelligence, forensic computing, fancy math of various specialized sorts, and a smattering of psychological crap that I don't even have a word for.

"By this point, if you haven't washed out and gone back to whatever dark corner of the Universe they reserve for people who fail at life despite having super-powers, each of you will receive additional specialized training appropriate to your unique *gifts*. Then, as members of the Gendarmerie, and therefore technically maritime law-enforcement personnel rather than military, you will be assigned a billet in some black-ops boondoggle I don't need to know about, because it's above my pay grade."

He paused, and took a sip from the glass of water he had placed on the podium before him, set the glass back down with slow precision and then asked, "Any questions?"

***

After completing the next step in his recruitment—a so-called "moral suitability" exam that ended with him signing an enlistment agreement before three staid, expressionless officials—Cass was herded with several dozen others into a dining hall for lunch. While it wasn't what he considered a *memorable* gustatory experience, the food was passable and mostly identifiable, a perk of being on a well-established Core World with extensive agriculture. On Unity Station, he'd usually had to be content with textured protein, highly refined cereals, and whatever fruits and vegetables could be affordably imported from nearby worlds like New Texas.

A brusque orderly in Naval Infantry fatigues entered after about an hour had passed, and referring to the assembled gaggle as "candidates," began a roll call. As candidates heard their names called, they were to follow the orderly's instructions to stand in one of several queues, to be marched out of the hall in an obviously well rehearsed process. Cass was never able to determine the logic that dictated who was placed in what queue—it wasn't related to name or planet of origin, as far as he could tell—but he found himself in the same group as the young siren, Enora Anthem, who flashed her infectious grin as their group was led away and deeper into the bowels of the facility.

They were issued standardized kits: plain dark gray uniforms, hygiene packs, boots that looked like they'd been designed by a prison contractor, and a collapsible duffel. Their personal belongings were boxed and tagged with printed labels they weren't allowed to read.

Thus attired and outfitted, they were led outside to an airfield, where shimmering midday heat rippled across the sere landscape of central Nevada. It was spring—sunny and cloudless. Even with protective eyewear, Cass had to squint and blink for several minutes before his eyes adjusted to the full glare of Sol. He stood with a dozen others, watching as candidates were ushered toward rows of pinnaces idling on the launch apron beyond the facility's heavy outer doors. "Off-world?" he asked no one in particular. "We going to be shipped off to some black site on Europa or something?"

One of the NI personnel who had taken charge of Cass's group, a deeply tanned and whippet-lean sergeant named Salazar, happened to be passing by and overheard.

He stopped, turned slightly, and jabbed a thumb over his shoulder. "Oh, you're going to a whole new world, all right." He paused for effect, an impish gleam in his eye.

"It's called Mexico."

4

DHARMA

Somewhere in Mexico, Earth

"Well, that was pretty bad. Beyond terrible, actually," remarked Senior Drill Instructor Salazar, his tone inexplicably chipper, as his trainees rose from their seated positions on a large fallen tree trunk. Cass looked around at the defeated faces of his fellows and knew his own face must wear a similar grim expression.

"While we all reflect on what a disaster that was, let's hump it back to the assembly area and see what the rest of the afternoon has in store." Salazar waited a beat, then turned and began walking. "For those of you wondering," he called over his shoulder, "yes, you *did* just fail the simplest land nav course I am allowed to assign you during this phase."

He spun on his heel and walked backward a few paces, still talking. "In fact, I'd like to personally congratulate Squad Three for setting a new record. Not for speed. Not for precision. No—*you* people managed to walk nearly six klicks in the wrong direction *while* holding working compasses and GPS-enabled datapads." He held up his hand as if for applause. "Stellar work."

A few trainees groaned, several others snickered. Someone muttered, "Who knew the key to being a good soldier was figuring out the quirks of Earth's magnetic field. We probably aren't even going to be deployed on this shitty fucking planet."

Cass inwardly thanked whatever divinities may be watching that he had not been assigned to Squad Three.

The six candidates of Squad Two—as they were now being called—fell into formation behind him and began jogging back toward the clearing in the woods where the next round of exercises would begin. They at least had the satisfaction of knowing they had reached their objective in the last exercise, if not quickly. Some members of the squad were in better physical condition than others, and their current environment was not especially forgiving.

The CNI Special Operations Training Complex (SOTC) Sector 14 was nestled somewhere in the Lacandon Jungle. The air was thick, heavy with heat and buzzing with life, a ceaseless chorus of insects and birds whirring in the canopy above. Cass wiped at his brow with the back of one hand and immediately regretted it, smearing sweat and grit across his face in a dark streak.

The ground beneath his boots was soft, sucking slightly with each step, as if the jungle itself were reluctant to give him up. Dense vegetation hemmed in the narrow path—thick-leafed vines and stunted trees pressing close, slick with moisture from the recent rain. Even in the shade, the heat was oppressive, trapped beneath layers of green like a dying fire beneath a blanket.

They were already drenched in sweat and tired from the day's exertion, when the priority traffic indicator on Cass's datapad chimed. He pulled it from its dedicated cargo pocket and glanced at the screen.

Mission: Escort colonial governor to LZ Alpha. Avoid loss of principal. Evac convoy departs in 20 minutes. Hostile presence expected.

Cass didn't sigh as the group slowed their jog and trudged into the base camp area. Not this time. This was round six and irritation had dulled to become resignation.

"Exercise Echo again?" Enora grumbled behind him, checking her pack. "I'm starting to feel personally targeted."

"Maybe we are," Cass muttered, eyes scanning the holographic map of the simulation area that he had come to know so well. His gaze then shifted to take in the equally familiar convoy of armored vehicles parked across the clearing from the trailhead where they had entered it.

"Same evac route, I expect." Enora continued. "Same convoy, same ambush, same ending."

Cass didn't reply. He was watching the man descending the ramp from the command skiff that had been sitting on the primitive landing pad when they arrived.

There he was again. Lieutenant Colonel Pierce, playing the part of Colonial Governor Armand Linet, Displaced Administrator of Bayeux Prime. He stood resplendent in overstated formalwear, white gloves, and a ceremonial sidearm he allegedly didn't know how to use. At least, he claimed not to when the simulated guerrillas came to pull him out of his VIP transport.

I guess I don't move in circles where that sort of getup is actually fashionable, Cass contemplated. *Or maybe it's just some local flag officer's idea of what rich Outlanders must wear? Maybe I need to check the Plexus entry on Bayeux Prime.*

Pierce certainly cut a figure in the muggy jungle setting, and as always, he was smiling.

"Candidates," he called, striding toward the convoy with his usual infuriating display of verve, "a pleasure to be imperiled with you once more. I trust that at this point, you've made peace with your tactical shortcomings." He tugged at his collar with a theatrical flourish. "Hot day. At least the groundcar is air-conditioned, so I don't have to die sweating."

Enora muttered, "Is it possible to die of smug?"

One of their comrades, a young Earther named Franks spat on the ground and said, "Only if he chokes on it."

Cass wasn't listening. He was watching Senior Drill Instructor Salazar. The sergeant had moved to stand beside the lead APC, arms folded, an unreadable half-smile on his lips. But when Cass's gaze met his, Salazar raised a single eyebrow—and gave the faintest shake of his head. That was new. *Is he giving me a hint? Taking pity on us?*

They'd failed this scenario every day for nearly a week. No matter what formation they tried or how carefully they covered the flanks, Pierce always ended up dead—blown up, riddled with simulated bullets, or "interrogated" on a livestream to their datapads.

He looked again at the militarized slate in his hand, rereading the orders. *Escort colonial governor to LZ Alpha. Avoid loss of principal. Evac convoy departs in 20 minutes.* Then he read it once more. *Avoid loss of principal.*

Cass looked to the tree line. The LZ was maybe four klicks away—rough terrain, but not impossible. He started calculating. *Maybe we've been going about this all wrong.*

Enora slapped a bug off her neck. "This place is like southern Argos on Anthemusa but with more gravity, more heat, and more bugs. I never thought I would ever have to take that puny yellow sun seriously, but here we are. It turns out, I hate Mexico. Let's saddle up and get this over with—I'm dehydrating just standing here."

"Change of plan," Cass said.

Abbot, a fit young man from Earth, and a genetic offender whose constitution had served him well during the last week's exercises, looked up, plainly confused "What?"

Cass turned to Pierce. "Sir, we're splitting the unit. Convoy's a diversion."

Pierce's eyebrows lifted. "Oh?"

"You're with me. We're taking the direct route through the forest."

Franks stood up. "What the hell, Broz? That's not the plan. The plan is to protect the convoy."

"No," Cass said evenly. "That's their plan. My orders say to protect the VIP. And there will be a convoy. My orders don't say he has to be riding in it."

He gestured toward the jungle. "They've got the road locked down. Drones. Mines. Ambush chokepoints. The only way to win this game—" He looked Salazar dead in the eye. "—is not to play."

Salazar didn't speak, but he didn't stop them either.

Enora slung her rifle with a grin.

***

As Cass and his charge set off to the north on foot, the jungle closed in fast. Thick, twisting roots and creepers tugged at their boots. Cass cut forward through the brush with a machete, keeping low beneath the canopy. Behind him, the so-called colonial governor—Lieutenant Colonel Pierce—moved easily for a man Cass had recently seen on his datapad, taped to a chair under an old style incandescent light-bulb, his expression incongruously sanguine as he was "tortured".

They traveled in silence for several minutes, broken only by the sound of boots in wet soil and the occasional hiss of a machete clearing brush. Cass finally spoke without looking back.

"So, now we're off-script, is this still part of the test?"

Pierce didn't answer immediately. He ducked under a low branch and casually swatted a mosquito from his neck. "Everything's a test, candidate."

Cass grunted. "Right. And you getting blown up every day—was that to test our small-unit tactics, or just our sense of humor?"

"Can't it be both? Or maybe, it was to test your reactions, assumptions—and most of all, your ability to adapt and learn from mistakes," Pierce said, his tone cheerful. "An ability that most of your class has so far failed to demonstrate in any appreciable degree."

Cass glanced over his shoulder. "What happens to them?"

"Some will wash out. They get sent back to a more conventional training program and career track. They may get posted to Astro-Survey, or perhaps if they've passed the criminal background checks, they go to the mainline Customs Service. The Government can always use more bodies for port inspection duty. Someone's got to check manifests and play bad cop at the checkpoints. Not everyone who volunteers or is conscripted for special duty is capable, and we will not deliberately send them to their doom, whatever they may have told you at INDOC."

"But my team, we're not those people?"

"No," Pierce said with a smile. "I don't think so. You're the ones who read the orders and asked what they meant—not just what they said. That puts you in a much smaller category."

Cass kept moving, choosing his footing carefully over a knot of roots. "So now it's just you, me, the woods, no obvious observers—what am I being evaluated on now?"

"Maybe I'm seeing how well you paid attention in basic orienteering."

"Bullshit." Cass shot a look back at Pierce, "Sir."

The older man just smiled.

Cass stopped and turned. "You're with SOCOM, Naval Infantry Special Forces, am I right? You're not just some rocket cop who always dreamed of acting. There are no colonels in the Gendarmerie. So, what is this—psychological profiling? Loyalty check? You just want to see if I really will hack a path through this jungle with a dull machete just to pass your little quiz?"

Pierce tilted his head. "Does it matter?"

"It does to me. The scenario is always the same, the guidance from the cadre minimal. We are always outnumbered heavily by the opposing force, who are actual trained special operators. I hate to think that the officers are just inflicting this crap on us for their own amusement. Honestly, the last week has felt like being a contestant on some kind of sick game show."

The lieutenant colonel considered that, then looked up through the leaves at the slivers of sunlight filtering through. His voice dropped a notch in volume but not in warmth.

"You're walking into a job where certainty is a luxury, candidate. You want to serve? Good. But if you expect clarity, you won't last. You'll get fragments, patterns, things you have to piece together yourself. The people who need simple answers tend to get eaten alive."

Cass was quiet for a few seconds. Then he turned and started walking again.

"I'll take the fragments," he said. "Just don't insult me with theater."

Pierce gave a quiet laugh behind him. "That's why you're out here, I guess. You didn't appreciate the performance. It's kind of a shame really. I've enjoyed the role of foppish planetary governor quite a bit."

"I'll bet," Cass ground out. "Let's just get Your Excellency to your shuttle, so I can go take a shower, and find some anti-itch ointment. We stay out here much longer, I *will* be eaten alive."

***

The groundcar died just as they approached a familiar shallow crossing over a small stream, its electric systems popping with a soft *whump* and a burst of ozone. Enora let out a long breath as the interior lights went dead. Outside, she heard muffled shouts. Then gunfire—short, controlled bursts.

Right on time, Enora thought. "EMP," she muttered to her comrades in the vehicle, already reaching for her training weapon.

The candidate beside her—Tak or Tark or something—stiffened beside her, face pale and intense in the dark. He was wearing the so-called governor's ridiculous formal jacket, complete with stiff collar and the shiny faux-gold fob-watch.

"Relax," Enora said, a lopsided grin on her face. "This is the part where they assume you are the principal and try to grab you—have your datapad ready. A holo of this should be worth a thousand words. Now, stay low, Excellency. I go to sacrifice my body for yours, as my solemn duty demands."

"I got nothing on the tac-net, but the flankers on the left are already down," Abbot remarked from the driver's seat, as he unfastened his safety harness.

Enora's brief survey of the unfolding situation through the groundcar windows gave her most of the important particulars. The convoy was at a standstill, every vehicle knocked out by the simulated EMP. An old petrol-burning truck, unseen until now, had rumbled out of the tree line to block the road just across the stream. On the left flank of their four-vehicle column, their dismounted escorts had been tagged with non-lethal sim rounds and sat slumped in the mud, adjudicated as "dead."

It was a textbook L-shaped ambush: attackers ahead and along one side. On the truck bed, a man rose into view, hefting a man-portable rocket launcher and swinging it toward their lead vehicle.

"Yep," she replied, as she threw open the right rear door and bailed out, crouching low to the ground. She moved to the rear of the vehicle, and peeking around the tailgate, made out a hostile in the dense foliage across the road. Shouldering her training weapon she fired, two low-velocity rubber rounds with tiny tracking chips, that would raise a decent welt on bare skin but were otherwise harmless. She thought one shot had gone home, as her target cursed and then dropped into the bushes that grew thick along the muddy track. Answering fire came from two directions, and she heard Abbot swearing fluently as at least one training round found a mark.

From her right side, she caught sight of an approaching figure, wearing a balaclava and outdated armor meant to suggest ex-corporate security. She pivoted, her carbine swinging to confront the new threat—too late. She heard the report of his weapon, and felt three impacts on her torso armor, painless but palpable.

A voice from her earpiece spoke in clipped tones, "You're dead, Anthem. Again."

Enora safed her weapon, and shrugging, found a roadside rock to perch on rather than sit in the mud. Thus seated, she watched as two members of the OPFOR threw open the door of the vehicle she had exited from, one pointing his training weapon into the back seat, as he barked an order for the governor to exit the vehicle. As her fellow candidate emerged into the daylight, his face becoming visible, they glanced at one another, then turned to face Enora.

She gave them her brightest smile.

"Surprise!"

***

Three weeks later, Casimir Broz stood at attention, eyes forward. A trio of cadre personnel—two Naval Infantry drill instructors and a senior warrant officer in gray Gendarme utilities—inspected the disassembled weapon on the metal table between them. Six of the ten recruits assigned to his pod sat behind him at old-fashioned school-desks. After eight weeks of basic training using the Naval Infantry's curriculum, these were all that remained.

The Gendarme, to all appearances a Core human in his late forties or early fifties, with close-cropped steel-gray hair and eyes to match, glanced down at his datapad before looking up to address Cass. "You were a Territorial Ranger, candidate? Is that right?" The man had a distinct drawl, an accent of some sort that Cass couldn't place. It reminded him of something he might have heard in an old cowboy holovid.

"Yes, sir," Cass replied.

The dour senior warrant officer raised an eyebrow. "We don't see too many of them hereabouts. I guess this sort of thing," he gestured vaguely around the small classroom "must be old hat to you."

Cass considered the question for a moment before answering, weighing the possible subtext of the man's words. "No, sir. I mean, we trained of course. And I do have a longstanding familiarity with firearms, and first-aid, however..."

"However?"

"The Rangers were a very different organization."

"Different than what?"

Cass hesitated, then replied, "Than whatever this organization is, sir."

The SWO smiled, his lips forming a thin line. "Delicately put. You seem quick on your toes. Let's see how quickly you can reassemble this."

Extending his arm with a crisp gesture to reveal a very old-fashioned looking analog wristwatch, the officer paused a moment to gaze at it, then said, "Begin."

Cass immediately began reassembling the pile of metal, composite, and electronic parts on the table into the complete weapon they constituted. As he had done several times already with the other recruits in the room, the officer began to pelt Cass with rapid-fire questions as he worked, periodically glancing at his watch as he did so.

"What is the designation of this weapon, recruit?"

"Sir, the K-12 pistol-caliber carbine."

"And what does this weapon fire?"

"Sir, the caseless 6.5 millimeter electrothermal-chemical round."

The officer glanced at his watch. "Ten seconds. What is the standard astronomical designation of Anthemusa?"

"Sir, Seginus VI."

" What is the highest commissioned rank in the Customs and Excise Service?"

"Sir, Commodore."

"And if I wished to maneuver a fireteam along a city street in a contested area, what formation might I consider?"

"Sir, the staggered column."

Cass slapped the last piece into place, performed a brief function check, and then placed it on the table in front of him.

The officer, already looking at his watch, intoned, "Twenty-eight seconds. Not terrible."

Cass was pleased with his performance, though his face remained impassive. That was the fastest reassembly time yet for this training session, and only one more recruit had yet to take his turn. That man, Abbot, now began the field-stripping procedure on the demonstration weapon, as Cass took his seat next to Enora. The two of them had remained in the same training pod since being handed off to the Customs Service, and over the course of the last several weeks had become friends.

"Not bad," Enora remarked, though I should point out you did it in twenty-seven seconds this morning."

Cass grinned and quipped, "You aren't a senior warrant officer, you don't hold my future literally in your hands, and you soft-balled the questions."

Enora sighed. "So, you don't find me intimidating? Give it a few years my muscle-bound friend, I'll be running this place, and you will rue your lack of respect. I have an excellent memory."

"Rue? Is that still officially a word? I thought it got phased out a while back with 'forsooth,' and the like. Is that sort of like, official pirate lingo or something?"

Enora snickered, "Verily, 'tis and thou wouldst do well to guard thy tongue, knave."

"Now you sound like a princess, not a pirate."

A the demonstration table, Abbot had finished stripping the carbine and was now undergoing a similar grilling from the warrant officer. A quiet and unassertive youth, Abbot stammered his answers and seemed extremely uncomfortable under the scrutiny of the thus far nameless man. Cass had attempted to observe the warrant officer's name tape surreptitiously and thought it read, "Garnett."

As they observed the proceedings, Enora again moved her head close to his and whispered, "Graduation tomorrow—for 'we happy few,' anyway. What's next do you think? Ole' Major Claptrap was right about one thing, it doesn't make a lot of sense for them to train us as jarheads, just to ship us out on Customs Cutters to show the flag over the benighted worlds of the barbarians."

Cass shrugged. "I don't even know why they train *jarheads* as jarheads honestly. Folks have been asking for a long time why the only sovereign power in the Known Universe needs a military at all. The Dominion worlds have real cops, the Church of Man has its chaplains, and what with corporate security forces and private fleets protecting all the big companies' *investments* out in the colonies, and the Gendarmes making sure everyone's duties are being paid, you'd think we'd have enough muscle to keep the plebes in line."

A crease appeared on Enora's forehead. "Yeah, and folks don't get an answer because the truth is unfit for public consumption. When there is only one state, the enemies of the state are all internal, and I don't see the NI being deployed on Earth any time soon. It's not too tough to figure out why we still have a Navy when you think about it."

"*Ehem,*" Garnett cleared his throat loudly. "Did you two want to share your astute political analysis with the class?"

Cass hadn't realized how loud their discussion had become. "Uh, no sir. Sorry, sir."

"Good, because you got it all wrong anyway. Perhaps someday I will enlighten you two innocents. I do hope you two don't labor under the assumption that absolute trust in the corridors of power is required to render public service. If so, I fear we've all been wasting a great deal of time here. I would expect a former Territorial Ranger to get it, at least." Cass felt a flush of heat in his cheeks. Garnett's gaze bored into him like twin lasers for a moment before he spoke again. "Class dismissed. Broz, Anthem, on me."

Cass and Enora exchanged glances, then rose and joined their superior as he stalked from the room. Their classmates, unsure what was expected of them and anxious to hear the gossip on the forthcoming conference between Cass, Enora, and Garnett, milled about in the hall outside the classroom pretending to read their datapads, or conversing in low voices.

Garnett wordlessly led the two to another unoccupied classroom, about twenty meters down the hall. Keying the door open, he indicated they should enter before him. Once within the room, the lights automatically flickering to life, the warrant officer went to the ubiquitous metal table at the head of the room and waited for the door to close behind Enora.

Once the door was closed, he rested his hands upon the table and said, "At ease."

The two recruits assumed a position of parade rest, feet shoulder-width apart, hands clasped behind their backs.

"You don't trust the Earth-side Government." It was a statement. "Fine, nor should you. Trust is earned, and that's a two-way street. But understand, if you two make it through the next phase of your training, then the Government will be placing enormous trust in you. My job here today is to figure out if that's a good bet."

Cass cleared his throat. "Permission to speak freely?"

"Granted."

"What are we doing here, sir? What is all this leading up to? Doesn't the Gendarmerie typically operate in space or at spaceports, running anti-piracy ops and such? Why are we learning about mechanized infantry tactics and cyber-warfare? I was expecting to be assuming a law-enforcement role, so going to the Gendarmes made a sort of sense but all this...I don't even understand why I'm here."

The older man turned his head to regard Cass with a steely gaze. "Yeah, I read your jacket, Broz. You got scores to settle, am I right? Okay, let me lay my cards on the table. My name is Senior Warrant Officer Robert Garnett. I am here to assess you and your class-mates for suitability as potential members of my team, which is one of several fielded by a clandestine service you have never heard of. We are unofficially known within a very small circle in the intelligence community, as 'Deniable Humanoid Assets for Reconnaissance and Military Action,' or DHARMA for short. Our purpose in a nutshell, is to protect the commonwealth from existential threats it is otherwise poorly equipped to address."

Both recruits were silent for a moment, as they digested this information.

"What sort of existential threats?" Cass finally asked.

"The sort that courts and public hearings and formal inquests are unlikely to resolve. Sedition, for one. Racketeering. I could use other strong words. Treason. Conspiracy. Insurgency. The Commonwealth has been growing for over two centuries, and even with FTL Comm relays to link the whole thing together, it's a big place. Too big, some might say. We are experiencing what one might call growing pains. Others might say we are witnessing a series of key defining moments, or inflection points, I think is the term. I'm in the latter camp, myself."

Enora spoke up for the first time since entering the room, "so you're saying we're training to be what? Intelligence officers? Assassins? Cops?"

Garnett locked his eyes on hers and simply responded, "Yes."

Visibly taken aback, Enora replied, "All of those? I may be a naïve young Outlander girl with stars in her eyes, but I feel like at least a couple of those roles are mutually exclusive."

Cass regarded his new friend with growing concern. *It just got real for you, didn't it? Girl, don't do this if it's not in you, just ask for a transfer to the Astro-Survey service. I'm getting the distinct impression that we will have fired shots in anger in this outfit before our term is up.*

"Not anymore, they aren't. Desperate times and all that." Garnett nodded at Cass, "What happened to your brother on Unity was just the beginning."

Enora whipped her head toward Cass. "Your brother? You have a brother? What happened?"

"Later," Cass growled. *Much later, Founders willing.*

"A criminal plot happened, culminating in a terrorist attack that was subsequently blamed on an Earth based bio-conservative group who almost certainly didn't do it."

Cass found himself growing angry. "They claimed responsibility!"

"Someone claimed responsibility, using an untraceable address on the Plexus. You are aware these new-fangled computer machines can be pretty tricky, right?"

Cass bit back a sharp retort, with some effort. "Who then?"

Garnett regarded him calmly. "Who indeed? These extremists may not be falling all over themselves to contradict the current narrative, because perversely enough, some of 'em are happy to claim the credit. Our intelligence estimates suggest they didn't actually have anything to do with it. Broz, if you want to set up a racket, the first thing you must do is create a problem, so you can position yourself as the solution to that problem. The problems here would seem to be growing disaffection between Earth and some of her colonies, and the perception that the Earth-based Government is conflicted and ineffectual in its response to politically motivated crimes when the victims are Outlanders, and the alleged perpetrators are not. Given these problem statements, all sorts of clever solutions come to mind, but few of them are in the long-term best interest of the Human Races. The bombing was just the opening salvo, in a campaign that is being waged largely on the battlefield of public opinion, for now."

Enora was still looking at Cass. "The bombing at the clinic...your brother was there?" Cass saw in her luminous violet eyes the compassion and sympathy she didn't wish to articulate in front of this grim stranger, and appreciated it. He resolved to open up to her about his grief later. Right now, he needed to think clearly, to get his head around all that Garnett had said.

"Sir, you're saying that there is some sort of conspiracy that is working to undermine the stability of the Commonwealth, is that right?"

Garnett nodded silently.

"And this DHARMA outfit aims to take it down, using extrajudicial means?"

Cass resisted the urge to laugh as he thought, *with any luck that's what he means.*

Garnett frowned. "Where necessary. I don't want to give you the impression that we've embraced violence and subterfuge as a first option. Your legal identities would, in fact, be members of the Gendarmerie, invested with law enforcement powers. Should the opportunity to make arrests and secure convictions for these criminals present itself, we will take such opportunities. Sadly, we have reason to believe that such opportunities will be few. Trials mean lawyers, journalists, and due process, all of which can and will be subverted if the enemy deems it worth the risk. These people are organized, well-connected, and well-funded."

"And who is the enemy, exactly?" Enora broke in.

"That is what we need to discover," the Warrant Officer replied. "They almost certainly represent powerful corporate interests. I can tell you that much. That, and that they are playing for all the marbles. The question is, have you chosen a side? This isn't a joyride, Anthem. I had decided before we ever met that you two were the first two on my list, but Abbot and Franks have potential too. I have two slots open, and I need you to understand before you sign on that the word *deniable* is part of the acronym for a reason. We take care of our own, but if you do something stupid and show your ass, you will get burned. The Government and the Service will disavow all knowledge of you and leave you to swing. Before you make this particular life choice, be absolutely sure. This is the last off-ramp right here, right now."

Cass took only a moment to respond. "I'm in."

Garnett nodded, his lips curled upward in a smile, but Cass felt that there was something almost sad in the older man's expression.

"I kinda figured you were, son."

"I am too," said Enora, her voice sounding steady and certain.

"You sure, Anthem?" Garnett asked. "Following orders is going to become a way of life for you."

She nodded. "Absolutely. Better to carry a rifle than a plasma cutter at the shipbreakers' yard."

Debatable, Cass thought. *Part of me wishes you had backed out. Only a small part, though.*

Again, the sad smile came to Garnett's face. If anything, Cass thought, it was even more obvious now that while Garnett had received the answer he was seeking, it was not evidently the one he'd really wanted. Cass found the apparent cognitive dissonance confusing and somewhat disconcerting, though he had made his choice and felt ready to live with it.

"Alright then," Garnett said, extending his hand first to Cass, then to Enora. "Welcome to DHARMA. Better head back to barracks and pack your gear. We're leaving right after the ceremony."

5

Shipping Out

Horizon Station, Earth Orbit

Captain Ada Faulkner sat at a table before a large virtual window that displayed an exterior camera view of the sprawling Horizon Transfer Station, in high orbit around her home-world of Earth. The relative quiet of the Naval Officers' Lounge offered her a rare opportunity to catch up on a lamentably large pile of virtual paperwork—a task that had occupied most of her morning. Now, however, she was gazing at the vista of Earth's gentle curvature hanging in space beyond the dull gray superstructure of the station, engaging in what her late father had called wool-gathering. Her thoughts had drifted from the minutiae of administrative work and the ache of her recent past to the more uncertain realm of the future—uncertain both logistically and emotionally.

"It's kinda nice to be back home so soon, eh, Skipper?" remarked an upbeat voice from behind and slightly to her right. Her executive officer, Thomas Aguilera, had a knack for finding the silver lining in any situation. However, in this case, Faulkner thought darkly, his optimism might be sorely tested—and more to the point, potentially annoying.

"I suppose so, Tom, though I wish it were under different circumstances. Our new mission parameters are not exactly to my liking."

Aguilera pursed his lips. "May I sit, Captain?"

"Please."

The slim, dark-haired young man slid into the padded chair opposite her, placing a cup of coffee on the glass table as he settled in.

"What in particular troubles you, ma'am? You mentioned something about picking up a Gendarme detachment for an investigation into a merchant shipping accident? Sounds routine enough. Although I would expect them to use one of their own ships if we were staying in the Core, so... can I assume we're heading to the frontier? Is that the issue?"

"Yes, and no," Faulkner replied. "Yes, the scene of the investigation is well out there. No, that's not the part that bothers me. There's more to it."

She bit her lip and tapped her stylus on the table's surface—an unconscious outlet for nervous energy. "We're not just ferrying them out there. We are to—and I quote— 'place the *Agamemnon* at the disposal of the Gendarmerie for the duration of the investigation.' Or, until they tell us otherwise. That's the subtext, basically."

Aguilera frowned and repeated the words slowly: "Place the *Agamemnon* at the disposal of the Gendarmerie—what does that even mean? Who are we taking orders from?"

"We'll be on detached duty. I retain command, technically, but we're expected to 'extend all assistance and cooperation' to some Senior Warrant Officer and his team. We're to facilitate their objectives, while still exercising 'appropriate command discretion,' and adhering to 'Naval guidelines for peacetime operational readiness,' and blah blah blah."

She sighed. "The orders came through this morning. I don't mind telling you, it made my eyes bleed trying to extract any meaning from them. Still—with the help of three cappuccinos and a thesaurus—I gathered we're to do whatever the Rocket Cops want unless we really object, in which case we're to do something else."

Aguilera sat back and took a sip of coffee before replying. "That's horseshit."

Faulkner considered a dozen colorful ways to agree, then settled on a simple, mumbled: "Mmm."

"Is there any way we can opt out?"

"Sadly, no. Not after the glowing operational status report we filed post-refit. I don't see a path out of this."

She leaned forward, resting her forearms on the tabletop. "Tom, this stinks of a black op. I don't like black ops. Neither of our careers needs this right now."

Aguilera shook his head in disbelief. "Do the Gendarmes even have black ops? That doesn't seem like their thing."

"I wouldn't have thought so either. But I've never seen orders quite like this. That, and—" She glanced around the club, lowering her voice. "I still have a few contacts in Geneva. If the rumors are true—or even if the rumors of the rumors are true—this bunch are some kind of BAMFs. And their idea of an investigation doesn't necessarily line up with standard maritime law."

"But...the Gendarmerie is pretty much synonymous with maritime law, Captain."

"Exactly."

Aguilera went quiet for a moment, then asked, "I know you were missed during your absence—and I understand why it had to be as long as it was. But I have to wonder, is this maybe retaliation? From someone at Squadron? Because this sounds like latrine duty to me."

Faulkner grimaced. *My absence. That's what we're calling it now, like I was on shore leave for a wedding or something.*

"I don't know, Tom. I've been told I still have the Admiral's full confidence. Told that by the Admiral, even. I guess it is what it is. Orders are orders."

Aguilera gave a little shrug. "True enough. Well, if there's a bright side, detached duty's a chance to prove to the brass you're really back in the saddle—if we succeed in doing... whatever it is we're supposed to be doing."

Faulkner chuckled. *Aptly put, Tom.*

"So where are we headed, and what's out there?"

"The Iota Persei system. And not much. One corporate colony and a research facility on a very unappealing chunk of rock called Tengoku."

***

By 0130 Station Time, the bar had cleared out enough that Cass and Enora could hold a conversation without shouting, which suited Cass just fine. They had chosen a place along the central concourse, figuring one spaceport bar was much like another. They'd stayed longer than either had intended, but Cass felt—and assumed his friend did as well—that the night marked a kind of threshold.

They had formally been government employees, and technically Gendarmes in the Customs and Excise Service, for several months now. But their duties had consisted only of training and preparation. They had seldom worn the uniform of their service and weren't wearing it now. However, appearances would soon begin to matter. Tomorrow at 0930, Petty Officers Second Class Casimir Broz and Enora Anthem would be required to report to the CNS *Agamemnon*, a Navy cruiser, to meet their team and assume active duty status.

As far as the officers and crew of that ship were concerned, they—and their soon-to-be colleagues—were just a routine shipborne Gendarme detachment, riding along to investigate shipping incidents or pirate activity. The real nature of the mission had yet to be revealed to them, and Cass wasn't sure under what conditions it would be.

He looked around the bar as Enora ordered another round, his gaze scanning the surroundings almost by instinct. The place had been decorated in what was evidently meant to be a nautical theme. Most of the walls featured "aquariums", which were actually holo-displays. The thousands of kilos of water and gravel required for real fish tanks of that scale were unthinkable for a dive bar on a space station.

Most of the other patrons at this hour were station personnel just coming off shift, though a few tables were still occupied by what were clearly spacers, mostly civilians. Next to their own table, a group of young men—evidently newly minted stevedores out for a night on the town—talked and laughed loudly as they enthusiastically worked their way through a variety of colorful cocktails with far-fetched names.

"So," Enora drawled as the server strode off to place her order, "there's something I've been meaning to ask you about."

Cass stiffened, a knot forming in his gut.

Please, he thought, *not now. I just want to enjoy my drink. I don't have the intestinal fortitude for this conversation.*

"What's the deal with those Territorial Rangers I keep hearing about?"

Cass relaxed.

Oh. That.

"They're an outfit on Jotunheim. I—my brother and I—were members, a few years back. Jotunheim didn't have formal planetary security forces like some of the other Dominion worlds. Still doesn't. Settlements have their own local cops, sure, but if you're out in the sticks...then there's no law. No first responders at all. Just the Rangers."

He paused, glancing at her. "I don't guess you've ever been. Jotunheim isn't what you'd call a hospitable world. Most of the settled continent is overgrown with this tangle of black brambles that hides anything smaller than a hover-tank. And some of the local fauna is—

"'Scuse me!" one of the young men at the next table bellowed, eyes locked on Enora. His face was flushed, his gaze glassy. His friends were already doubled over their table with laughter at some private joke.

"My friend wants to know if you're single," the drunk continued, barely holding it together. "He really wants to do it with an alien!"

Enora rolled her eyes, craned her neck to the left, and replied, "He's not my type. I'm not into farmhands, rat-catchers, dockworkers—you know, menials. And I'm not an 'alien.' My ancestors came from Earth. I think they covered that in Secondary School, which is why I'm assuming you and your pals legitimately didn't know."

Cass frowned. He was irritated by the boy's crassness, amused by Enora's response—but also acutely aware of how quickly this kind of thing could spiral out of control.

The drunkards groaned in mock offense—except the one who had spoken. His face had gone slack, whether in genuine confusion or feigned, and he said in a hesitant cadence, "So—you're saying all your parts are compatible with humans, then?"

"Easy, son," Cass growled. "You just get back to your party, and we'll get back to ours."

Another worker, round-faced and probably in his early twenties—the friend in question—spoke up. "Church says you're aliens. Y'all sure don't look human to me."

Enora rolled her eyes. "The Church of Man says no such thing. You haven't been paying attention. I guess that's just one more social institution that failed you, huh, Tiger?"

The first stevedore now locked eyes with Cass, who returned the stare with quiet neutrality, as amber text appeared in his near field of vision—

THREAT BEHAVIOR DETECTED

His DNI implant had kicked in—a discordant reminder of who he was now. The embedded system—questionably legal under Church oversight of human enhancement—was standard for DHARMA personnel. Wired into his nervous system, it interpreted incoming sensory input, overlaid it with contextual information, and reached out for local data networks and computer systems, including those in his battle armor.

He wasn't wearing that armor now. Still, his DNI reached outward, gathering what it could from his surroundings, and now directed his attention to the young man's elevated heart rate, which was visible to his naked eye, though he had previously not had the mental or neurological conditioning required to actually process that sort of information.

SUBJECT PULSE RATE ELEVATED BEYOND PHYSIOLOGICAL NORMS

"I ain't your son," the stevedore said, his voice hard. "And this ain't your planet, Mickie."

Cass had only recently learned the origin of that slur. But the intent behind it was clear. He focused his breathing, trying to bleed off the tension. One breath in. One breath out.

Then a hand snaked around the right side of Enora's chair and firmly cupped her right breast.

"I don't know, man," the owner of the hand slurred. "They might've assembled her in a monster factory, but these gotta be natural!"

Enora froze for the barest fraction of a second, her face a mask of shock. Then her body moved.

Her right elbow shot back. Her upper body pivoted with it. Her legs drove her upward out of the chair in one clean, brutal motion. Cass sat, motionless.

Monster factory, he thought. *That's what the alleged extremists had called the clinic in their manifesto after the bombing. The clinic hadn't even offered prenatal packages or enhancements. Just therapies. For people like my brother—people who just wanted to walk. To work. To lift weights or play racquetball without crippling pain.*

His instincts screamed for action. His trained mind pulled focus to the spray of blood that had swept across the floor and the table when Enora's elbow shattered the drunk's nose. *My brother wasn't a monster. I'm not a monster, am I? Enora's a wild child for sure, but—a monster?*

Across the table, Enora kicked her chair away and dropped into a fighting stance. The dockworker who had groped her—a young man of Asian descent, Cass thought—staggered backward, blood pouring down his face. He tripped over the legs of his own chair and went down hard.

His companions now stood—some faster than others—but all wore angry expressions. Cass didn't need his implant to know they had violence in mind.

Enora was shouting at the man on the floor, who clutched at his ruined face. "Sorry to disappoint you, buddy, but us monsters don't really have four tits. You're just seeing double. I suggest you stay down."

Five of them. One of her. Get up. Do something.

Still, he did not move. He sat, his palms flat on the table before him. Within him, hours seemed to pass as he sought self-mastery, desperate for some semblance of control over the torrent of conflicting impulses that threatened to overwhelm him, even as a mounting pressure began to pulse behind his eyes. Enora circled the other table counterclockwise, focusing on the most physically imposing of the group, the one who had instigated the confrontation.

We're supposed to protect these people, aren't we? Us expendables? Isn't that why we're here? Are they really attacking us because our skin color is outside some arbitrary norm? Because we're a bit too short or too tall? In this century? Is that what they see when they look at us? Not people. Just monsters. Born under other stars. Adapted to survive. And now...not human enough to matter.

Enora was face-to-face with her adversary now, a man who outweighed her by some considerable margin given her slight Anthemusan frame. She seemed to have reconsidered the wisdom of her tactical choices but kept her focus and remained in her defensive stance while moving laterally. A sneer spread across the young dockworker's broad, blotchy face. He moved to slap Enora with an open hand, but she leaned back, bending with the innate grace of her people, to avoid the blow. His recovery was slow, doubtless due in no small part to his state of inebriation, and Enora took advantage of this fact to step outside the man's guard and get behind him, delivering a savage strike to the region of his left kidney. He grunted in pain and turned to face Enora once again, lashing out with a savage swing of his fist that caught her in the chest and sent her sprawling.

Someone was bellowing—an inarticulate expression of rage. It took Cass a moment to realize it was him. Looking down, he saw his own hands grasp the edge of the table and fling it aside. Drinks and plates flew in all directions, as the table itself landed some distance away, careening into a column before coming to a stop, having almost taken out the server who was returning with Enora's beer.

The remaining patrons in the establishment who had paused in their conversations during the growing altercation now moved toward the exits, or stood next to the bar, mouths agape. Cass barely registered their presence. With a roar, he crossed the three meters between himself and the stevedore who menaced Enora, his stout form a blur of motion. The station had an emulated gravitational field of .9g and in such an environment, Cass possessed the brute strength of an adult gorilla on Earth. The man turned just in time to see him coming. Cass's hand shot out, seizing him by the throat. He lifted him off the ground with terrifying ease, driving him backward and slamming him into one of the faux aquarium walls. The impact sent a ripple through the display of marine life, distorting the fish in rainbow-blurred waves around his flailing limbs.

One of the man's companions, a thin, bearded man, somewhat older than the others, approached from Cass's left, fist cocked back to deliver a punch, but Cass ignored him. His adversary was pinned against the holographic wall, his feet kicking frantically some ten centimeters off the floor, his face turning purple. He scratched at Cass's hand with both of his own, but to no avail. The Jotun was like a statue, immovable and unyielding. The bearded man, mustering his courage, stepped forward and struck Cass in the jaw with a competent right hook, but Cass simply stood unflinching, contemplating in a detached way the ease with which he could choke the life from this ignorant Earther savage and use his corpse to bludgeon the other one.

The bearded dockworker struck him again, with no more effect than before, and then stepped back, uncurling his fingers and shaking his hand, like a man who had tried to punch concrete and come to regret his decision. Cass finally noticed the various flashing warning messages from his DNI regarding hormone levels and blood pressure and strung them together into a coherent picture of his current state of mind. Slowly, he regained control. He released the gasping stevedore who slumped semiconscious to the floor. Turning to his left, he gave the bearded man what seemed an almost nonchalant shove in the solar plexus, but the wiry man went flying backwards, his feet lifting entirely off the floor and arms pinwheeling, before he came down hard to slide across the smooth floor on his back and then crash headfirst into the leg of a table. His short journey ended there, with a thump.

Cass turned to face the two dockworkers still standing, only to see that Enora had drawn a flechette pistol and was holding it at the low ready position. In her left hand was a folio holding the badge issued to Gendarmes who had reached the rank of Petty Officer. One of the two remaining targets had started to pick up one of the sturdy metal chairs furnishing the establishment, with the obvious intention of using it as a makeshift weapon.

Targets, Cass mused. *The transition to thinking of people as targets again has certainly been smooth. Just like old times.*

Enora was, incongruously enough, smiling her lazy, crooked smile. "As a duly appointed peace officer under Commonwealth law, I am obliged to tell you boys that if you reach for anything other than the ceiling, I will surely gun you down, right where you stand. The shore patrol won't say shit; I'll just have to fill out a form."

Cass groaned internally. *Now you flash the badge.* The two dockworkers looked at each other, expressions somber, and raised their hands over their heads. Their fallen compatriots, now in various states of painful repose on the floor of the bar began to rouse themselves, as a chime that only Cass could hear drew his attention to another warning message from his DNI implant:

DISTURBANCE REPORTED AT THIS LOCATION, SHORE PATROL RE-
SPONDING.

"Shore Patrol are Oscar Mike," he said to his partner, glancing around the bar for any
other other threats.

"I see it," Enora responded, "I suppose it wouldn't be seemly for us to blaze out of here
before they arrive."

"Nope. I do believe that you just went and made it official."

Enora blew out a breath. "I suppose they really will have paperwork that needs filling
out. In retrospect, I should have just shot these two."

The two uninjured dockworkers paled, but Enora holstered her weapon and grinned
wickedly. "Just kidding. Have a seat, someone will be right with you."

Cass realized he was shaking. The adrenaline was still working through his system.
He drew a breath, released it, and rolled his shoulders, trying to ground himself, before
turning his goggled face to regard Enora. His serious tone belying the lightness of his
words, he asked, "How exactly did you manage to conceal a pistol in that outfit?"

Enora smirked, "Wouldn't you like to know?"

***

SWO Robert Garnett sighed deeply and leaned back in his chair to consider the
conduits and cables of the overhead as he spoke.

"One day, my children. You were on the station for one day. Thirteen hours."

He shook his head in dismay.

"I confess, I'm disappointed. I figured even you two could make it to the ship with
something resembling military comportment—once we got you steered in the right general direction."

He dropped his gaze to meet theirs, his tone sharpening. "How—I wondered—how
could even those two miscreants manage to hork up the simple task of reporting to their
first duty station? Surely—*surely*—this phase of the operation wouldn't prove to be the
hard part. All you had to do was go from the shuttle dock to your racks. Maybe stop for
chow. That's it."

Cass looked straight ahead, his face reddening.

"Instead," Garnett continued, gesturing at nothing in particular, "I find you nosing around the local bar scene—busy as a couple of three-legged cats in a sandbox."

He tapped a stylus against his datapad. "The Service is going to need to compensate the owners of that drinking establishment for the property damage inflicted on the premises during the *apprehension* of those hardened criminals you so courageously subdued. Oh, and what a band of ruthless desperados they turned out to be, too. Five dipshit hayseeds fresh from the Space Transport and Logistics Academy in Omaha." Garnett sighed and steadily regarded Enora and Cass, who stood at attention before his desk in the tiny office identified by the stenciled sign, *Cmdr GenDet*.

"Sir, if I may—" Cass began.

"You may not. Let's be clear— your duties will sometimes require you to bust heads, this is understood. Shore leave, contrary to longstanding maritime tradition, typically does not. And I've seen the toxicology reports. I think I've got a decent picture of what happened. What you need to understand is this: our unit does not—I repeat, does not—need undue scrutiny. Not now. Not when our ship is still in port. Not when we haven't run a single operation as a team. If I have to stand in front of the Commodore, or Founders forfend the General Assembly, and cover for you jackasses, it better be for a good reason. Are we crystal clear on this?"

Cass nodded sharply. "Clear, sir."

Garnett looked back to Enora, "Anthem?"

"Clear, sir."

"Excellent. I'm glad we had this little chat. Go ahead and find your billets, stow your gear, and join the team in the ready room at 1100 hours for pre-mission briefing. Dismissed."

Cass shouldered his bag and retreated gratefully from his superior's presence, feeling as though the inevitable *discussion* around the previous night's incident at the bar had gone if not well, at least less badly than he'd anticipated. As he made his way down the narrow corridor from Garnett's office to his assigned rack, Enora came up from behind him and placed her slim hand on Cass's shoulder. "Hey," she said, her voice uncharacteristically tentative.

Cass paused in his stride and turned to face her. "What's up?"

"Are we ok?"

Her face showed concern, and Cass regarded her quizzically. "Sure. Why wouldn't we be?"

She licked her lips before pressing on, obviously treading lightly. "Are *you* ok, then? You've been super weird all morning."

"Have I?" Cass replied warily.

"Look, I'm sorry I didn't find a more um—diplomatic way to handle those guys last night. I just..." she trailed off.

"I know. You don't need to explain. They were bigoted, parochial assholes. They were drunk, and the one put his hands on you. No more needs to be said. Your reaction was perfectly natural. It's my reaction that was—" he sighed and took a moment to try and frame what he was feeling. "I can't let that happen again." *Especially the part where I almost murdered a skinny Earther kid right out of tech school with my bare hands.*

"What? You were just backing up your partner. It wasn't your fault."

"I lost control. That can't happen."

Enora tilted her head and looked at him with an unreadable expression. She squeezed his arm where her hand still rested on it, and replied, "Control is an illusion my friend. Sometimes, it's necessary to maintain that illusion at least for ourselves, and sometimes"—she shrugged, letting her hand drop— "sometimes, it's not. The trick is in knowing when to let the illusion go. If that time ever comes, I'm sure you will. On an unrelated note, the next time you give me shit for my pirate lingo, I'm going to remind you of that time you actually used 'parochial' in a sentence."

She smiled, then resumed walking down the corridor. She turned her head and called over her shoulder, "I'm in 4-75-4-L, you too, right? Come on, roomie, let's meet the neighbors!"

He followed slowly, lost in thought.

6

Mission Parameters

CNS Agamemnon, The Solar System

The neighbors, it turned out, were two Core Humans: Skye Tanahill and Alfred "Ack-Ack" Avery. Alfred's nickname was apparently a play on words of some sort, but Enora didn't get it and didn't ask. He was a tall, dark-skinned man with a ready smile and an affable disposition that Enora found difficult to reconcile with his occupational specialty—serving as the team's sniper and pathfinder.

Conversely, Skye Tanahill, an athletic young woman with short, spiky hair so blonde it was nearly as light as Enora's own bone-white braids, was terse and soft-spoken, bordering on laconic. The sharp-featured young woman was assigned as the team's medic and happened to be a qualified pinnace pilot. It seemed she had previously served as a Space Rescue specialist with the Navy before volunteering for the DHARMA program.

During her own training with the Naval Infantry, Enora had come to understand just how revered the Space Rescue Corps was within that service. Space Rescue wasn't simply an analog to the old medical divisions some surface navies had maintained. Its members were recruited only from spacers who demonstrated superb spatial awareness, technical aptitude, and nerves of steel. They were then extensively trained in hardsuit operations, zero-g firefighting, survival medicine, small-craft piloting, and starship damage control. They were relied upon not just to serve as medics aboard ship but to conduct recovery and rescue operations on crippled vessels and space installations where conditions ranged from merely hazardous to outright hellish. The intensity of their training—and the dangers they faced—had even earned them grudging respect from the notoriously insular Naval Infantry. Enora found Skye's inclusion on the team both reassuring and ominous.

After introductions were made, the four DHARMA specialists found themselves with a few minutes to kill before the briefing. They settled around the small fold-down table in their shared berth.

"So, I see there are three other berths in this pod. Are those for Headhunters too?" Enora asked, using the tacitly agreed-upon slang term for DHARMA personnel. There seemed to be a general discomfort among field operatives with terms like commando, operator, or intelligence officer, though Enora couldn't have said why. Within the uniformed services—at least among those who admitted such operatives existed—they were often referred to as birdwatchers, or spooks, terms dating from dim antiquity and carrying, to her ear, a vaguely pejorative tone. It didn't surprise her that her own clandestine service had opted not to embrace them. Headhunters carried a proper air of menace. It would do.

"No," replied Alfred in a rich baritone. "Those are for real Gendarmes." He chuckled, evidently expecting his audience to catch the distinction. "Support staff. A squad of actual customs agents and a few tech specialists. We've got a dedicated armorer... and a facer."

Enora raised an eyebrow. "A facer? As in, a cosmetic surgeon?"

"You got it. 'Course, he's a real doctor too. Our DNI grayware can spoof most security systems the government can access, but you never know where duty might take us. And you can't spoof a human eyeball with safeware, so having a facer can come in real handy."

Cass frowned. "I hope they take some good pics so they can remember what we actually looked like. This face is nothing special, but I've grown attached to it."

Alfred laughed. "Big man, they already know everything about you. Everything. I wouldn't sweat it. Besides, I get the feeling for this op we're just playing the role of government employees, goin' about our lawful duty and such. I don't imagine we'll be needing face jobs just yet."

Enora cut in. "What is the op exactly? Do you guys know?"

"Investigating a merchant shipping accident," Skye said with a sardonic twist of her lips.

"What Little Sister means," Alfred continued, "is that's likely some bullshit. They don't call in an SMU to investigate a reactor casualty on a merchantman."

Enora turned from Skye to Alfred, absorbing the new acronym. "SMU?"

"Yeah. That's the outfit you just joined, girl. Special Mission Unit Sierra. It's new. Little Sister here already did a stint in SMU Taiga. I'm fresh outta the Naval Infantry. This is my first op as a Headhunter, same as you. But the Cox'n...this ain't his first rodeo, that's for sure."

"Rob-uht Garn-ayet?" Enora asked, exaggerating Garnett's drawl.

"Yep," Alfred said with a grin. "I don't know if the southern gentleman thing is just an act or what, but he's got some wear and tear on him."

"Oh?" Cass asked. "In what sense?"

"Let's just say that old son can't walk through no metal detector."

Their banter paused as Enora and Cass both absorbed the implications.

After a moment, Skye turned to Enora. "What about you, Anthem? I heard scuttlebutt that you were an ex-pirate or something. What's that all about?"

Her tone wasn't quite confrontational, but it wasn't friendly either.

Enora spread her hands in a gesture of surrender. "I may have... misappropriated some data at certain points in my past. But data can be shared without taking it from the one who originally possessed it. So how is that really theft? How do you steal knowledge?"

Alfred barked a short laugh and leaned across the table, grinning. "Did you happen to sell this data after you didn't steal it?"

Enora smiled. "Maybe? Like I said—it's not like I deprived the original owners of its use. And while I may have been armed at the time, I didn't exactly take it at gunpoint."

Alfred shook his head and made a *tsk* sound with his tongue, but his expression held no judgment. Skye raised one eyebrow—but said nothing.

"Well," Cass said finally, raising his plastic cup of Navy coffee in salute, "here's to using our powers for good."

***

Aboard the *Agamemnon*, crew quarters were divided into airtight pods. Each pod housed a department—or a subdivision of one—along with its enlisted ratings, chiefs, and, in some cases, warrant officers. Within each were offices, a head, berthing compartments, NCO staterooms, and a briefing room. Commissioned officers lived separately in what was known as *officer's country*, their staterooms often nowhere near the pods that held their subordinates.

The Gendarme Detachment stood apart from the Navy chain of command. On larger ships it might be assigned several pods, with its officers quartered alongside their own personnel.

On some missions, the Navy carried no Gendarmes at all. Shipboard security fell to the Naval Infantry Detachment; criminal investigations to the Master-at-Arms. Gendarmes embarked only when a ship expected to conduct boarding operations, inspections, or law enforcement duties in space too remote for a Customs Cutter. In those cases, the senior Gendarme officer was often a warrant officer commanding a single section—just enough personnel to crew a ship's pinnace for customs or enforcement work. That was the case aboard the *Agamemnon*. Garnett commanded the lone section and bore the honorific *Coxswain*.

At 1100 exactly, Garnett entered the briefing room in their pod, and directed the others present to take their seats. "Good morning. As some of you already know, this group has been placed on active duty and designated SMU Sierra, reporting up officially to the Special Operations Command of the Customs and Excise Service. The rest of the embarked Gendarme section are here to support us, ladies and gentlemen. They are aware that we are engaged in special operations of some sort. Nonetheless, they have not been read into the DHARMA program. Therefore, the regs around COMINT and COMSEC best practices are to be observed at all times."

Garnett glanced around the compartment.

"These are good people, and they all have Top Secret clearances. Nevertheless, for their protection and that of the program, they will be briefed on our mission objectives only on a need-to-know basis. None of the Navy people except Captain Faulkner and the XO know anything about our status or mission except that we are engaged in an accident investigation. Suffice it to say, it is optimal that that continue to be the case."

Garnett paused and looked at each of their faces in turn, and seeing that they all appeared to understand, he continued. "Here are the facts you need to know at present: About twelve standard weeks ago, this young woman released a very interesting holovid on her personal Plexus channel."

Garnett "grabbed" and "threw" a file from his datapad into the holographic projector that dominated the center of the table. The face of a woman appeared in the air above the projector, and Enora judged that it would be considered an attractive face, by many people's standards. The woman was young, but the anti-agathic treatments commonly available on rich and well-established worlds made her actual age hard to determine. She had almond-shaped eyes, dark hair, and the facial structure Enora had come to associate with the natives of the landmass of Asia on Earth, and their descendants throughout the Commonwealth. As Enora watched, the woman began to speak, though the sound on the holo had been muted.

Garnett continued, "This is Atsuko Hirayama, the only daughter of Benjiro Hirayama, founder and CEO of Hirayama Enterprises. I'm sending a company profile to your datapads now."

Garnett made another gesture on his own datapad, and a series of subdued chimes sounded around the room, indicating the receipt of the file he had just distributed. "I won't make you watch the whole vid now, but what she is telling her fans and friends, and by extension the Church and the entire planet Earth, is that she received in-utero gene modifications—and after a period of contemplation—she's decided she's proud of it. She wants the world to know that this doesn't make her or her super-rich parents bad people, and she's sure we can all come to respect and love one another for the beautiful beings we are."

Alfred snickered, then met Enora's eyes. His laughter died, and he looked away uncomfortably.

Garnett coughed and continued. "As a result of this unfortunate revelation, her father is potentially looking at an investigation for reproductive crimes, and she has become *persona non grata* on the planet Earth. Her life of ease and comfort on the family compound in California is almost certainly over, which the people in Defense Intelligence think may have been the idea all along."

"Sir," Alfred interjected, "are you saying she got kicked off Earth...on purpose?"

"No, I didn't say that. The DDI people said that may be the case. I don't know why this perky little debutante does anything she does. What we do know is that Daddy had little choice but to get her on the first available ship to somewhere safe, somewhere that would endorse her passport. The first ship available in this case was the commercial vessel *Euphrates*, an Earth-registered merchantman under a government charter, and the 'somewhere safe' was a corporate colony operated by Hirayama Enterprises in the Iota Persei system."

Garnett manipulated his datapad again, and the face of Atsuko Hirayama was replaced with the image of a murky, gray sphere.

"This is Iota Persei IV, known to the locals as Tengoku. It is a rocky, frozen world with about eighty percent the mass of Earth, too far from the primary to ever be anything but purely awful even in summer, and far too awful to ever support life as we know it on the surface. Which a practical person such as myself might conclude makes it perfect for the colony's stated purpose, which is biosciences research and development. A bunch of corporate eggheads developing who knows what in buried labs on a frozen rock in the back of beyond. What could go wrong?" This prompted a few nervous chuckles.

Enora, intrigued now, shifted in her seat. *I've seen horror vids that started that way,* she thought.

"Ms. Hirayama arrived on Tengoku, where she presumably remains, but the other notable passenger on *Euphrates,* and the ostensible reason for the government charter, is quite another matter. This is Craig Emerson, Assistant Undersecretary at the Division for Defense Intelligence."

A new face appeared in the holo display, that of an unremarkable-looking middle-aged man with dark brown eyes and a receding hairline. "Or perhaps I should say, the late Craig Emerson. The *Euphrates* departed again only two days after arriving at Tengoku, with Emerson once again aboard. That was not the plan, but it seems he insisted. Before they could reach the impingement zone, the ship evidently suffered a catastrophic reactor accident and was lost with all hands."

Cass raised his hand.

"Yes, Petty Officer Broz?"

"Sir, I heard you say 'presumably' and 'evidently,' this seems like quite a bit of supposition."

Garnett nodded. "That is an astute observation. This certainly is a lot of supposition. All we know for sure is that Tengoku Control claims they received a distress call from the ship as it was headed out-system, and then shortly afterwards, they lost contact with it. She is officially 'overdue.' Most of what we know so far is secondhand through the locals or pieced together from forensic analysis of signals to and from the ship.

"Now, here's where it gets interesting. Following Emerson's death, DDI reviewed his official message queue—standard procedure in these cases. They found a message from Atsuko Hirayama. It wasn't routed through normal intersystem traffic to the *Euphrates*; she sent it directly to his principal address at the Division. It would have been waiting for him when he arrived back on Earth." Garnett paused. "The contents are encrypted with military-grade cryptography. We have yet to crack it."

As Garnett paused, an uneasy silence filled the compartment. Presently, Cass spoke up again. "Sir, what you just told us doesn't square with a spoiled rich girl who accidentally incriminated herself in a public blog and didn't realize what she'd done."

"It does not," Garnett concurred.

Cass looked thoughtful. "There's a method here—a plan."

Garnett nodded. "And we are to determine what that plan is or was. Whatever this is all about, it has our friends in Defense Intelligence spooked. Hirayama Enterprises is a pretty big defense contractor, and the stuff they work on is cutting edge. Our own DNI implants rely on technology they developed. Emerson had been dispatched to perform some kind of audit on their security practices. I'll tell you plainly that they wouldn't give me any specifics on this so-called audit, and I'm not sure our contact at DDI even *has* specifics. If this all points to some black project going off the rails, we need to ascertain that.

"Our mission objectives are to find Ms. Hirayama, secure her cooperation, and discover the contents of her message to the Assistant Undersecretary, and any other actionable intelligence she may have that bears on the security of the Commonwealth. Our cover is that we are a regular Gendarme detachment there to interview Ms. Hirayama and others— such as ground control personnel— as part of an investigation into the loss of the *Euphrates.* To the extent that the fate of the *Euphrates* may bear on our principal mission objectives, we shall do that. If it starts to seem that the 'reactor accident' was indeed just an accident, we can offload that grunt work onto the support team, so we can remain focused on the big picture. Questions?"

There were none. Garnett turned off the holo projector, sat on the edge of the table, and regarded the team earnestly. "Just between us and the walls, this op stinks. Something is very wrong on that planet. I'd bet one of my remaining original organs, and I don't have too many.

Stay sharp, and don't let the suits and perfect hairdos down there fool you. The Iota Persei system is likely to be enemy territory, and our friends in the labyrinthine halls of government are not being as forthcoming with us as they could be." His jaw muscles tightened. "They never are."

***

Faulkner stood at the forward command interface for the holo-tank in CIC, hands braced on its curved outer bulwark as she studied the telemetry on the three-dimensional display. The ship's acceleration had ceased hours ago. They were now approaching the impingement zone—an abstract point in otherwise unremarkable space outside the heliopause, defined primarily by the absence of a strong gravitational incline or magnetic fields.

"Quantum anchor sync-arrays are online," the Officer of the Deck reported from his post on the bridge, his voice audible to all on the shared bridge and CIC audio channel. "QFD Drive field generators charged and standing by."

Faulkner gave a tight nod, though her eyes remained on the display, and spoke into her headset. "Acknowledged." She turned to Aguilera, "XO, is medical standing by for psych support?"

"Yes, ma'am."

"IEMARS, confirm local space in the jump envelope is clear."

"Confirmed—envelope is clear of contacts."

"Engineering, report readiness."

The bridge engineering watch-stander's voice was calm and steady. "Ship ready. Main drive is secured, and all lights are green."

Faulkner took a slow breath. QFD transitions weren't supposed to hurt—but they were never pleasant. The ship's AI might describe the event as "subjectively instantaneous relative displacement," and that might be borne out by the ship's chronometers—but the human body disagreed.

Something about skipping through folded spatial geometries and sidestepping time left the nervous system...irritated. The medics called it jump lag.

Faulkner had seen the effects span the spectrum. Some crew reported headaches. Some, nausea. Some just went cold and quiet for hours. Sometimes people saw things, usually out of the corner of the eye. Faces. Hands. Old memories that didn't belong. She shook the thought away and keyed the internal comms system.

"Bridge, this is the CO. Command authority is granted for Faster Than Light jump. Please set condition violet. Officer of the Deck, you may start the clock."

"Aye, ma'am, starting the clock," came the immediate reply.

The lights dimmed slightly as the ship shifted to its blue pre-jump lighting scheme. Then the rough voice of the Bosun's Mate of the Watch came over the 1MC:

"All hands, prepare for FTL jump, transition in ten minutes. Set condition violet throughout the ship."

A moment later the ship's AI intoned an automated warning of its own. "Attention. Quantum Field Drive initialized, now performing full systems sync and anchor stabilization."

On the main display, the quantum anchor map resolved into a three-dimensional lattice—tiny, flickering nodes forming the fixed points of an invisible path through folded space.

Behind her, Aguilera's voice was lower than usual. "Captain...you ever get the thing? The déjà vu?"

Faulkner turned slightly. "During jump?"

"Yeah."

"Every time."

He nodded, evidently satisfied to hear it. "Me too."

The psychologists hadn't settled on a consensus, but the working theory was that the QFD didn't just move ships, it interacted somehow with conscious minds—just enough to stir the sediment. A medical explanation remained elusive, but every spacer who'd ever made a transition knew it was real.

"Anchor sync complete," Navigation called out. "Tunnel pathway projected. Transition corridor stable within tolerances."

Faulkner watched the wireframe corridor resolve. On the floating holographic representation before her, it looked like an elongated spindle of glass, stretching off into unknowable space.

"Very well," came the smooth reply from Lieutenant Grewal, the Officer of the Deck. "Prepare to engage QFD jump sequence on my mark. Bosun's Mate of the Watch, sound five blasts on the jump alarm."

The CIC filled with the deliberately jarring tone signalling an imminent FTL transition.

This is not my favorite part of the job, Faulkner thought, for possibly the hundredth time.

As the alarm continued its atonal warble, she felt the familiar chill work its way up her spine, the skin-tightening anticipation of letting go of the universe's hand and stepping into a shadowed hallway. The alarm fell silent.

"Mark."

The world twitched. Color drained slightly from the ambient light. The floor felt too far away, then too close. Time hesitated. Then lurched.

Faulkner tasted copper. Then vanilla. Then copper again. Her mother's stern voice rang out with perfect clarity in her left ear, "stop crying, Ada, or by the Founders, I will give you something to cry about."

And then it was over. Zero seconds, ship's time. The world had reassembled itself. Faintly, she heard the not-quite-human contralto of the ship's AI, "External telemetry indicates emergence into rational space. Jump complete."

Faulkner blinked against the CIC's dim lighting, willing her equilibrium to catch up. The faint taste of something metallic clung to her tongue. Her limbs felt normal—but her thoughts lagged half a beat behind, as though her brain had to re-buffer reality. She steadied herself against the tank and took a long, centering breath. *Come on, Ada. Snap out of it.*

She focused on her console's readouts—anything to ground herself. External time elapsed... how long? Her mind reached for the formula. Something old, half-remembered from the Academy.

$$\Delta t = \alpha \times DLY$$

Distance between Arcturus and Iota Persei: 61 light-years.
QFD constant—alpha—was 0.1 days per light-year.
She did the math automatically.

$$\Delta t = 0.1 \times 61 = 6.1 \ days$$

Six days, one hour, and change. That's how much the galaxy had moved while they had been in zero-time transit. *We were ghosts for six days.*

She shook off the chill and straightened her posture. Someone exhaled too loudly, and it carried over the comms. Faulkner blinked, then opened her jaw wide until her ears popped. She checked the comm systems reflexively, then activated the 1MC channel. "CO to all decks. Once all departments have reported in, we will secure from condition violet and run post-jump diagnostics."

Aguilera spoke up at her elbow. "Captain, our emergence locus is confirmed. Six light hours out from a main-sequence star, yellow-white, 1.04 solar masses. Navcomp has completed a star fix, and it checks out. We're in the Iota Persei system. All sync-arrays recovered and stowed. Engineering reports the ship is ready to maneuver."

Faulkner glanced around the CIC. No bleeding. No vomiting. No screams. That was a win. But still... she couldn't shake the feeling that something had reached for them in the dark—

—and just missed.

7

Tengoku

CNS Agamemnon, Inbound - The Iota Persei System

The Plexus entry for the planet Tengoku noted that the name was an old Japanese term meaning "paradise"—or "Kingdom of Heaven." Nothing could have been farther from the reality that greeted Captain Ada Faulkner as she reviewed the planetary data on her display.

The frozen globe depicted there had a mass of 0.812 Earth masses and a tenuous atmosphere composed mainly of hydrogen sulfide, nitrogen, and methane. Surface temperatures during the planet's winter months could plunge to minus two hundred degrees Celsius.

Not exactly a garden spot, she mused.

"Captain?"

Engrossed in her reading, Faulkner hadn't noticed Aguilera approach.

"Coxswain Garnett and his people are on the Quarterdeck, when it's convenient."

Ah, yes. The meet and greet.

"Thank you, Exec. Please tell the Cox'n, with my compliments, that I'll be along shortly—just finishing something up."

He may be setting the agenda around here for now, but this is my ship. Let him and his commandos—or whatever they are—wait a few minutes. It might be wise to establish some boundaries now, at the outset.

Aguilera smiled, as if reading her mind. "Yes, Captain. Of course."

Faulkner sat in her command chair, situated in the center of the semi-circular bridge, which was the nerve center of the ship while it was underway. Just aft of this compartment was the Combat Information Center, or CIC, where signals, sensor data, and other tactical information were processed and analyzed for the benefit of the ship's commander. Even farther aft, behind the CIC, was a raised, railed space overlooking the cavernous boat deck in the stern of the ship, known in fleet parlance as the *Quarterdeck*. The space was often used for briefings prior to or after missions ashore and was also subject to longstanding naval traditions whose origins were mostly forgotten.

Faulkner had observed that Garnett's men and women had a habit of conducting business in casual dress, or utility fatigues, even going about in their blotchy gray utility trousers and T-shirts, forgoing the matching blouse. When contacted by Garnett about setting up the expected meeting to formally introduce his team and explain their mission requirements, she had deliberately chosen the Quarterdeck as the venue, due to the standing orders that all personnel entering that area were to be in Service Dress Uniform or the uniform of the day.

As the Gendarmes were an entirely different service within the USCS, that would mean the former in their case, and Faulkner took some relish in the idea that Garnett's team would be obliged to wear their stiff, formal uniform tunics and brass. She couldn't quite frame in her own mind why it was exactly that Garnett and his personnel evoked such near-instinctive disapproval in her. After all, it wasn't as if Garnett had written his *own* orders. Perhaps, she had to admit to herself, it was simply that his team seemed somehow…apart. Everyone in her professional sphere had a place in the military hierarchy, a position in the chain of command, above her or below. *I don't know what exactly my professional relationship with Garnett is.*

Faulkner sighed, swiping away the data-card on Tengoku. *Come on Ada, you may as well get this over with.*

"Mr. Baumgartner, you have the deck. You have the conn."

"Aye Captain, I have the deck. I have the conn," replied the second watch Bridge Tactical Officer, as she arose, and turned to leave the bridge.

As Faulkner emerged from the CIC passageway that led onto the Quarterdeck, the sentry there met her eyes and snapped out, "Ten-Hut! Captain on the Deck!"

Faulkner noted with smug satisfaction that Garnett and his tactical team were already assembled, in dress uniform, and looking very nearly military, for once. The team came to attention, and Garnett rendered a precise hand salute as he spoke, "Captain, Senior Warrant Officer Garnett reporting to the Quarterdeck as requested."

How very correct, Faulkner thought as she returned his salute. The Quarterdeck was traditionally considered outdoors for the purposes of rendering courtesies. "Cox'n, good morning."

"Captain, may I present my tactical team? These are Petty Officers Broz, Tanahill, Avery, and Anthem. I also wanted to introduce our pinnace pilot, WO Ramirez, but unfortunately, he is on sick call today."

"I see." Faulkner nodded at the assembled team but did not extend her hand. "Ladies and gentlemen, please stand at ease." At her words, the Gendarmes assumed a relaxed, parade rest posture. Faulkner took a moment to regard Anthem, whose bone-white hair, silvery-violet eyes, and dark, almost eggplant-hued skin she continued to find striking, perhaps even subtly off-putting, despite her having met and worked with sirens before. There were only three sirens aboard, including Anthem. She knew none of them well.

A person develops cognitive biases over the course of their early years, and they are hard to unlearn. "Anthem...any relation to the Ambassador?"

The young petty officer shifted as she responded. "Yes ma'am, he's my father."

Faulkner raised an eyebrow in surprise. "Really? I wouldn't have guessed." Anthem smiled faintly but made no reply. Faulkner allowed her gaze to linger on the tall Anthemusan woman a moment longer. *No cushy commission in the diplomatic service for you then? Interesting.*

"Captain," Garnett began, "As you know, my team have been directed to open an investigation into the loss of the *Euphrates* in this system. I am authorized to disclose to you at this time, that authorities on Earth have identified Atsuko Hirayama, daughter of the Magnate Benjiro Hirayama, as a possible witness of great interest to the investigation. I am to request that we approach Tengoku and orbit, so my team and I can take our pinnace to the primary corporate facility at Tengoku City, and conduct interviews of Ms. Hirayama, as well as the Harbormaster, and other potential witnesses on the ground."

You are now authorized to tell me, Faulkner considered. *What are you* not *authorized to tell me? That's what concerns me.* "Very well, Cox'n, I think we can accommodate that request. We can proceed in-system immediately. What other support are you likely to require of your friends in the Navy over the course of this investigation?" Faulkner kept her tone courteous and professional but couldn't shake the feeling that Garnett's team was working on different operative assumptions about the fate of the *Euphrates* than most everyone else on the *Aggie* was.

"I'm not sure yet, ma'am, but I can tell you that there may be resistance to our investigation among some of the personnel on the ground. It may be that this op evolves from a routine accident investigation into something less routine"—he shrugged— "we don't have all the data. If this should prove to be the case, the situation may become fluid. I wish I could be more specific, but I can't just yet."

Here it comes. "Senior Warrant Officer Garnett, may I inquire as to why the employees or visitors at a medical and biotech research facility would wish to impede your investigation into a shipping accident?"

Garnett smiled grimly. "Of course you may, Captain. I know I will."

Faulkner snorted. "I get it, Cox'n. Fair enough, I suppose the less I know about this whole business the better. We will be shaping course for Tengoku shortly. Our ETA into parking orbit is about six days. Please advise the XO if you need anything else?"

"Of course, Captain, thank you."

Faulkner dismissed the Gendarmes and returned to the bridge, where her Executive Officer awaited her, his expression placid.

"So," Aguilera asked as Faulkner resumed her seat, "how'd it go?"

"That smug son of a bitch told me to just go ahead and take him to Tengoku and mind my own business."

Aguilera raised an eyebrow. "So that's exactly how it went down?"

"Well," Faulkner conceded, "maybe not exactly."

Aguilera suppressed a smile. "So then, is there some spooky shit going on, or no?"

Faulkner sat morosely in her seat and tried to project nonchalance for the benefit of the bridge watch, whose anxious glances showed that they could sense their commanding officer's mood. "Almost certainly," she replied.

***

"Everyone strapped in?" Warrant Officer Ramirez shouted over his shoulder to the passengers on the pinnace. Cass had just finished stowing his equipment in the cargo webbing aft and sat with his shock harness locked in place. He noted that his teammates had all done likewise, and called back, "All secure back here."

He could hear Garnett and Ramirez on the flight deck exchange a few quiet words, and then Ramirez assumed the chanting, almost singsong tone all aerospace pilots seemed to have been trained in as he keyed his comm. "Agamemnon Foxtrot Oscar, this is Swordfish One-One, we're all buttoned up, requesting departure clearance, over."

"Swordfish, this is Agamemnon Foxtrot Oscar, you are cleared for departure, initiating mooring release in five seconds. Safe journey!"

"Agamemnon Foxtrot Oscar, acknowledged. Awaiting release. Swordfish, clear."

Cass felt several bumps reverberate through the hull of the small craft, and then the sudden onset of weightlessness as the pinnace was gently ejected from the Boat bay and the gravity field generated by *Agamemnon*. As he looked across the narrow aisle to Enora, he smiled, recalling the days of landing ops training, when they were quite often the only two people in the compartment not vomiting their guts out during the period of free-fall proceeding an atmospheric insertion. This time was different however, their teammates were taking weightlessness in stride, and Skye even looked vaguely bored. Alfred was humming softly and reviewing something on his datapad. Enora beamed at Cass while biting her lower lip and managed to wiggle in evident delight like a puppy, despite being harnessed securely in her seat just as he was. Cass shook his head slowly and smiled. *She thinks this is some kind of big adventure. We'll see.*

After another few moments had passed, he felt the sensation of acceleration, palpable through the inertial dampeners of the small landing craft which were much weaker than those of a starship. The gentle push grew steadily stronger, informing him their descent toward Tengoku had begun in earnest.

Following a somewhat turbulent but otherwise uneventful descent into what served Tengoku as an atmosphere, the pinnace steadied onto its final approach. Cass heard Ramirez exchanging terse words with someone on the comms, and then felt the pinnace begin to bank to the left. *We're in a holding pattern*, he realized. *That's interesting. Who would've thought a backwater port like this would ever get that busy?*

The passenger compartment lacked windows, so Cass pulled up the exterior cameras on his datapad. The view from the belly optics was breathtaking, but bleak. Gray crags stretched to the horizon, brutally sharp, their flanks sheathed in ice nearly the same color as the rock beneath. Thin rust-colored rivulets wound through the troughs between peaks—methane streams, according to his briefing materials, laced with metallic salts that kept them liquid even at these temperatures. Cass imagined stumbling into one and shuddered.

Alfred looked over his shoulder at the small display and quipped, "nice place they got here, eh?"

"Yeah," Cass responded, "maybe I'll get some time in at the spa."

Alfred smirked.

After several circuits in the pattern, Cass grew bored of the view and turned off the display on his datapad. Resolving to accept the delay with equanimity, he closed his eyes and began to doze off. At some point, he aroused into awareness and realized he was hearing another short, indistinct conversation on the flight deck, this time between Garnett and what he could only assume was Tengoku Control. Cass assumed this exchange resulted in landing clearance being granted, for he felt the craft begin to change heading, and descend further. Ten minutes later, the pinnace came to rest on a landing grid in the vast, sheltered spaceport Hirayama Enterprises had delved, obviously at great expense, out of the face of a mountain. Within moments, they had taxied into one of the two airtight docking berths that extended from the central cavern and powered down as they waited for the berth to be repressurized with a breathable atmosphere.

Welcome to Paradise, Cass mused as Garnett's brisk voice over the intercom informed them the boat was secure, and the team began to unbuckle their harnesses and rise from their seats.

As Cass exited the pinnace through the aft cargo door and made his way down the ramp with his teammates, he examined his surroundings. The berthing bay was cavernous, over three stories high, and smelled faintly of rotten eggs—traces of hydrogen sulfide that had bled in from the native atmosphere during countless depressurization cycles.

A windowed walkway ran along the opposite wall at the third level, cantilevered out over the floor. Spacers called these observation galleries "wharves," and this one connected to elevators and airlocks that would link to the rest of the port. An exposed metal catwalk and a set of stairs hung from its front edge, providing access down to the bay floor. Below, a maintenance trench ran the length of the space, covered with heavy grillwork that let a craft taxi over it while giving technicians access to the belly.

There was the expected assortment of refueling and service equipment stored neatly in niches along the walls of the bay, and several technicians had already begun a cursory inspection of the pinnace exterior. As they did so, a pressure door slid open in the windowed wharf, and a trio in business attire emerged. They were a handsome if not quite pretty dark-haired woman of indeterminate age, and two men, all wearing carefully schooled expressions of vague interest. They emerged onto the catwalk and then proceeded down the stairway toward the pinnace. As they drew to a halt at the foot of the ramp, the woman spoke first, her eyes playing across the uniformed team, now looking every bit the part of customs agents. "Good afternoon, I am Executive Director Anneka Timms, which of you would be Warrant Officer Garnett?"

Garnett strode forward and extended his hand, wearing a wide, sincere looking —and in Cass's estimation— entirely uncharacteristic smile as he replied, "I am Robert Garnett, Ms. Timms. It's a pleasure to meet you face to face, though of course I regret the circumstances."

Timms reached out and clasped his hand without missing a beat, and her warm answering smile struck Cass as saccharine and obviously fake. *Granted, I may have some biases when it comes to smarmy corporate executives.*

His eyes played over Timms's companions. The first was a portly but well-groomed middle-aged man with an unfashionable mustache, wearing a bemused expression. The second was a tall, almost gaunt man with hawkish features. His deep-set eyes scanned the environment ceaselessly, even as Timms and Garnett greeted one another. *A corporate cop,* Cass observed silently, *or a mercenary in an expensive suit. He's got the look.*

The man met Cass's gaze, as if he felt it, and Cass smiled in what he hoped was a disarming manner. Timms and Garnett, meanwhile, continued exchanging pleasantries. Timms turned and gestured to her companions. "Officer Garnett, may I introduce Gene Paulson, he's our chief legal counsel here on Tengoku, and Franz Dornier, our chief of Security."

Garnett extended his hand to each in turn. "Counsellor...Mr. Dornier." Paulson's chubby fingers were practically engulfed in Garnett's firm grip, but he pumped the other man's hand vigorously, and Cass felt his general attitude of affability was at least largely unfeigned. Dornier on the other hand, gave Garnett only a tiny, brittle smile, perfunctory handclasp, and a murmured greeting so muted that Cass couldn't be sure what he'd actually said. Garnett introduced the team, and further abbreviated greetings and handshakes were exchanged all around. Enora was introduced as the team's data analyst, and Skye as a "safety inspector." Cass noted with wry amusement that Alfred's subject matter expertise as well as his own, were not specifically raised.

Timms cleared her throat and clasped her hands before her in the attitude of someone about to make an announcement. "So, Officer Garnett, I do apologize for any delays you may have experienced en-route to us, we only have two berths suitable for a craft such as yours, and as you may have seen we have a supply ship in orbit right now, transferring cargo to-and-fro. One of their lifters was unfortunately taking up the space when your ship entered orbit."

"No need to apologize, ma'am, I quite understand."

She smiled her ingratiating smile again. "Mr. Paulson has been tasked with facilitating any interviews you may need to set up with Hirayama Enterprises employees or contractors, and of course, making sure we follow policy and procedure for these kinds of situations, while cooperating completely with the Government's investigation. He can help schedule meetings with the right people and answer any questions you may have regarding our response to the incident, from a company policy perspective."

So, Cass thought, *he's our minder. He will be sitting in on all the interviews to make sure everyone we talk to stays on script. Simple due diligence on the part of Timms and her bosses—or something more? The colony's duty to render aid to a spacecraft in trouble was laid on them when they received the distress call and rendered moot twenty minutes later from their perspective, when the* Euphrates *blew up. By the time they knew it was happening, it was all over but the shouting. The time-delayed distress signal came from twenty some odd light minutes out, and they didn't have a starship in port at the time. They couldn't have been expected to actually do anything about it; just make a record of events in case the worst happened. Their legal exposure seems minimal so far, what are these people so wound up about? Is it just because the government guy Emerson was aboard?*

"I've also asked Mr. Dornier to make himself available if you need access to restricted areas or materials. We are of course, a defense contractor, and quite a bit of our work is of a highly sensitive nature, so he can help remove obstacles, when and if appropriate."

And I'm sure he's been instructed to create obstacles too...when and if appropriate, Cass thought wryly.

Garnett smiled and nodded as if this was all exactly as he'd hoped and expected. "Understood, Ms. Timms. We look forward to getting to work. I think our first steps will be to get Petty Officer Anthem access to any telemetry you have, and to set up interviews with the Harbormaster's folks, particularly the controllers on duty at the time of the incident."

Paulson cut in smoothly, "I can help facilitate that, Mr. Garnett. Let me just reach out to a few people right now."

"I'd appreciate it."

"Great," Timms declared, "I've had rooms reserved for your team at the Cherry Blossom Hotel here in the spaceport section, it's on the main concourse, just up the wharf about two hundred meters or so, on the left. If you want to get checked in and drop off your things, go right ahead. I'm sure Mr. Dornier can have one of his people assist you with your baggage, and of course you have my contact information if you need to get in touch. Unfortunately, I do need to be moving in the direction of my next meeting, if you ladies and gentlemen would excuse me?"

"Of course, thank you," Garnett replied. Timms nodded and strode back toward the airlock and adjoining lift that linked the wharf to the berthing bay, her body language making it clear that she had already moved on mentally to her next task. As Dornier stood by, watching the group and Paulson moved off to make his arrangements, whatever those truly entailed, Cass cast his eyes once more about the facility, thinking it was one of the more sophisticated and modern small spaceports he had ever visited, especially on such an out-of-the-way colony world.

He had intended to turn back to Garnett and say as much, when his eyes were drawn back to the windows of the Wharf above, where a slender figure stood, one palm upon the glass, looking down at him. A strange feeling came over him, as he locked eyes with the young woman above, and realized in an instant that he was looking at Atsuko Hirayama. She held his gaze for a moment, and then lowered her hand from the window, and walked away.

Cass shook his head as if to dispel the aftereffect of a strange dream and then looked around to see if anyone else had noticed her brief appearance. Apparently, they had not, although he noted that Dornier was continuing to scan the berthing bay like someone on a protective detail, and Cass found himself questioning why the security officer had been included in the welcome detail at all. *We're just regular cops ostensibly here to review some sensor footage and talk to a few space traffic controllers about an accident that happened out in the black, why is this guy even here? Why is he looking around like he expects an armed robbery in the berthing bay?*

Pondering for a moment, he began to suspect he knew who Dornier was watching out for. He tried subtly to attract Garnett's attention, while the corporate lawyer, Paulson, bombarded him with names and details concerning the operators on duty in the SOC at the time of the *Euphrates'* distress call. After a few moments, he succeeded, and Garnett excused himself with a look of barely concealed relief, to join Cass a few steps away.

"I think this guy is under orders to be as *helpful* as he possibly can," said Garnett, "just so we will wrap up the investigation early to escape his help. I now know exactly when specialist Travis Thurman's Space Traffic Control license is due to expire, what kind of score he got on his certification exam, and soon I expect to know if he prefers boxers or briefs, and how he takes his coffee. I haven't even met the man yet. What's up?"

Cass stepped close and pitched his voice for Garnett's ears alone. "I just saw Atsuko Hirayama standing on the wharf. She stared right at me, gave me some kind of weird look, and then just strolled off. Not more than thirty seconds ago."

Garnett grimaced and then turned his head to gaze up at the windows of the wharf, almost eight meters above the floor, his brow furrowing in thought. When he spoke, his voice was tinged with doubt. "Are you sure it was her? You recognized her from down here?"

"It was her. No question," Cass replied, his tone level. *I mean, I have been studying her dossier for days, I know what she damn well looks like.*

Garnett studied his face for a moment and then turned to Paulson and said in a carrying voice, "Mr. Paulson? This background has been very helpful, and we're looking forward to getting to chat with some of these people as soon as possible, but we've been in space for a while, and our internal clocks are a bit out of whack. What say we reconvene tomorrow morning so my team can get settled in at the hotel?"

Paulson began to put away his datapad, nodding vigorously. "Of course, Mr. Garnett, I understand completely! We're on your timetable here, sir. Just reach out when you're ready to proceed with the interviews, I've cleared my schedule for the next few days."

Struck by Paulson's ingratiating tone, Cass tilted his head as he regarded the counsellor once again. He began to suspect that the selection of this particular lawyer as their chaperone was either a terrible mistake on the part of Timms, or a calculated stratagem of such byzantine brilliance, that they had yet to grasp the full extent of it.

Alfred chose that moment to yawn loudly, as if to lend verisimilitude to Garnett's words. Cass smiled inwardly, then realized he probably wasn't entirely acting, it *was* the middle of the "night" on the *Aggie,* insofar as starships had a day and night.

Garnett looked around at the rest of the team and asked cheerfully, "So team, shall we go get settled in? It seems we have a busy day ahead of us tomorrow." His eyes found Cass's, but if his expression was meant to convey a message, Cass couldn't read it.

***

An hour later, the team sat in Garnett's hotel room, which is to say that Cass, Enora, Alfred, Ramirez and Garnett sat. Skye sprawled on the unclaimed second bed in a most nonmilitary fashion.

Garnett had been reviewing their plans for the next day. "I will join Mr. Paulson tomorrow, Stars help me, and conduct the obligatory interviews of the SOC personnel we've identified. I don't expect to learn anything shocking, but you never know. Anthem, I want you down in the Network Operations Center, reviewing the PPI footage and taking care of that other item we discussed. Broz, take Avery and Tanahill—if she hasn't decided to sleep in," he added with a pointed glance at the somnolent blonde petty officer, "and find Ms. Hirayama. I suspect our hosts will take a dim view of this plan. Remember you're Commonwealth law enforcement officers, so play the part. We need to get her alone in a room and get the skinny."

Heads around the room nodded.

Garnett gave a satisfied nod of his own. "Let's get it done. We'll stay in close contact over comms. Do not hesitate to ping me or WO Ramirez if something goes pear-shaped, we are just running interference at this point."

Ramirez stood and motioned toward the door. "Sir, if you don't mind, I'm going to go check on the boat, see how the service and fueling is going. I'd hate for us to somehow get bumped down the priority list to number last."

Garnett chuckled. "Good idea."

The meeting broke up shortly after, and Cass sought out his bed where he lay a long while staring at the ceiling, a sense of foreboding making sleep elusive.

8

Dark Corridors
Tengoku City, Tengoku

E nora hummed to herself as she reviewed the configuration of the data storage cluster for the colony's commercial-grade radar and telescope systems. These systems were designed primarily to handle approach and departure control for the colony's Station Operations Control facility, or SOC, and were, as she'd suspected, only modest in capability. Using such systems, a ship as far away from the planet as the *Euphrates* had been when the accident occurred, would typically be detectable only by its transponder. Still, Enora thought it possible they may have picked up any unusual emissions from the *Euphrates* prior to the loss of the ship, assuming such emissions were powerful enough to register at that distance.

After orienting herself to the workstation for a few minutes and checking the operating system version, she began exploring and quickly located the telemetry log she was looking for. Cross-referencing the time Tengoku Control had reported receiving the freighter's distress call with the file's time index was a simple matter. She then flipped the data to a holo-display and watched as the icon representing the merchantman crept slowly along its plotted track, broadcasting the standard transponder data all starships carried.

This information was of course, a bit over twenty minutes delayed at this point, due to the fact that the *Euphrates* had been a bit over twenty light minutes distant from the planet at that point in time, and the signal from her transponder could only propagate at the speed of light, practically crawling along relative to the vastness of space. Enora continued to watch as the icon began flashing amber, and a new annotation popped up under the icon.

Switching to the raw feed from the passive long-range sensors—optical and electro-magnetic—she saw a single, faint blip against the darkness. That was the *Euphrates'* drive plume, caught by the telescope array twenty minutes after the fact. Then the blip distorted and bloomed outward—light and thermal radiation from the fusion bottle's catastrophic failure, the moment it lost containment. The ship had been annihilated nearly instantly. The blip became a blob, then began to fade. By the time the controllers on the ground had seen it, the crew had already been dead for over twenty minutes. *Case closed,* Enora thought. She tapped her fingers on the edge of the console before her.

The controllers had been witnesses to a rare and tragic accident. Still...

Cass is right, Timms and her attack dog Dornier and that ludicrous lawyer Paulson, all seem to be making way too much of this, Enora thought. *And the way Paulson falls all over himself to help with the investigation...he's too eager. Too eager by half. What am I not seeing?*

She returned her attention again to the virtual window that showed the configuration of the storage cluster.

Huh. The day after the accident, the IT monkeys took two storage nodes out of the cluster to upgrade the controller. Her slender hands flew over the keyboard. *They completed the upgrade eight hours later and put them back into service.*

She began to delve deep into the underlying storage system, leveraging years of experience in bending such systems to her will. After gaining the elevated access she needed, she demanded the system show her not the file from the master node, but the archived version of the file from the nodes that had been down for maintenance for eight hours.

She noted that the timestamp on this copy of the file matched that of the version she had just viewed—and nodded to herself. The timestamps matched of course, which was to be expected. If they hadn't matched, the system would've immediately updated the returning nodes to ensure consistency across the clustered quantum storage array.

As the footage began playing in her second virtual display, Enora watched as the entire, silent tableau of the ship's destruction began playing out again.

It's a shame, she mused, *I don't know about the government guy, but the crew were just working stiffs. Eighteen of them. All dead now.*

Then, as the doomed ship was about to explode on the display yet again, her eyes widened. Her hand reached out, and with three fingertips forming a spear, slammed down on the start/stop control on her holographic keyboard. Her other hand rose to her earbud and keyed it.

"Sabrehawk, this is Ghostcat."

"Ghostcat, Sabrehawk, go ahead," replied Garnett's voice after a moment.

"I need a rendezvous, ASAP. Your place or mine?"

"Mine," the cool voice replied, "1330."

Enora was already slotting a data crystal into the media slot in the console. "Roger wilco, Ghostcat clear."

***

"Run that by me one more time," Garnett said slowly, as they huddled in front of the terminal on the tiny desk in Garnett's hotel room. "What am I looking at right now, exactly?"

Enora replied, her voice husky with half-suppressed excitement, "Okay, so like I told you, the IT guys took two of the nodes in the storage system down, right? They were out of the cluster for most of the day following the accident."

"I think I got that part, these are the log entries showing that, right?"

"Right." She nodded. "So, you can see here,"—she swiped, and a new log came into view— "the timestamps match with the file from the master node, which they should. The system keeps all nodes in sync using these timestamps. And since this file is archived sensor data, there's no reason to modify it once it's closed and archived. In fact, it's illegal to do so, for obvious reasons."

She glanced at him, then pressed on.

"Now, if I wanted to fake this data—edit the file—I'd have a couple of problems to solve. First, editing it through standard means would update the timestamp, and that would raise red flags. And second, the techniques that would allow someone to make such edits *without* updating the file's metadata, well..." She hesitated, her expression becoming sheepish. "Such techniques are not widely taught in tech schools. I've heard it's possible to do it with the right tools. You know. From a friend."

Garnett sighed and rolled his eyes. "Get on with the lesson, Enora."

"Right. Okay, so the way to get around the timestamp problem, is to use a high-level AI—black-market stuff—to alter the data at the quantum-bit level and then spoof the timestamps so everything looks legit. These AIs are incredibly sophisticated, highly illegal, and designed to cover their tracks. If someone used one here, it would've cleaned up after itself and overwritten the timestamps across the whole cluster. We'd never have known."

"Unless..." Garnett prompted.

"Unless," she echoed, drawing the word out, "they did it while some of the storage nodes were offline. Due to some very bad luck on their part, they did. So, when those two nodes came back online, the system checked their file timestamps. This particular file said it was already up-to-date, because the timestamps matched. So, it never got overwritten—because the system didn't think it needed to."

Garnett's eyes narrowed as understanding dawned. "So, the archived file stored on those two nodes was supposed to be identical to the others, but you are saying it isn't."

"Exactly." Enora's voice was quieter now, her tone more serious. "Those nodes contain the unaltered version, the one that doesn't lie."

She reached for the terminal and queued up the footage. "This is what it really looked like." Enora played the final moments of the doomed ship once again, only this time two smaller, quickly moving blips of light representing intense sources of electromagnetic radiation appeared on the edge of the plot and quickly merged with the blip of the *Euphrates*.

"*Damn...*" Garnett almost exhaled the word rather than speaking it. He sat back in his chair, his face grim, but not exactly surprised, in Enora's estimation. "Those look like tracks from fast-movers. Someone torpedoed the *Euphrates*."

Enora nodded. "And someone here on Tengoku covered it up. Several people, most likely."

Garnett was silent for a moment. When he spoke again it was to ask, "did you put that backdoor in like we talked about?"

Enora nodded. "Yes, sir."

Garnett reached out and briefly squeezed her shoulder. "Good."

***

"She's in F Section, Tunnel Two," Cass told his companions, after concluding a brief comms exchange and returning his datapad to its specially-fitted cargo pocket on his battle-dress uniform blouse. "Enora got us added to Atsuko's list of known associates, so now she'll show up in the directory. It sounds like it was a really short list up until the four of us were privileged to join it—as in exactly zero names. Ergo, up until this morning nobody outside of the colony admin group was authorized to look up her address, which might simply reflect Atsuko's shy and retiring nature, but I doubt it. Apparently, Enora found out something important about the *Euphrates* too. She declined to discuss the topic over comms."

"Huh," Alfred grunted. "Wonder what that's all about."

"I'm sure we'll find out tonight," Skye interjected. "For now, let's stay on mission and find the Young Mistress before that corporate tool, Paulson, finds out what we're up to and sends an army of lawyers to intercept us. We've already passed a few security people, and they are definitely on the lookout for us. I've caught a few of them not-so-discreetly eyeballing us since we got off the tram."

Cass nodded in agreement, smiling but saying nothing. Skye had taken to referring to Atsuko only by the moniker *The Young Mistress*, in apparent reference to her family connections. Cass knew little of Skye Tanahill's background before joining the service, but he suspected it was quite different than Atsuko's.

Cass took a moment to orient himself. They stood beside a small café advertising *Authentic Continental Fare*—though he couldn't have said which continent was meant. They were in one of the wide passageways that served as avenues through the residential-commercial block housing the colony's permanent population. As with most of Tengoku City, the structure lay almost entirely underground. Only a single open atrium at the far end of the complex broke the surface—a multistory space containing the tram station and food court, where skylights above admitted a little anemic light from the system's star.

Alfred eyed the stylish façade of the café with a wistful look. "I wonder if the chow's any good here."

Skye snorted. "Pass. We eat free at the hotel. I'm not looking to line the pockets of the bloodsuckers that run this company town."

Cass filed the remark for future reference but outwardly remained diffident. "These places might be run by third-party vendors, for all we know. This charming eatery for example might be some aspiring entrepreneur's lifelong dream. It doesn't matter though.

We need to stay on mission like you said. There will be time for chow after, it's not even 1100 yet. It looks like F section is down that way."

Less than five minutes later, the team turned into a nondescript tunnel lit by dim overhead fixtures, its walls clearly hewn from native rock. The only door with a uniformed corporate guard standing watch was the one marked F-12. As they approached, the guard's expression soured. He lifted a hand in the universal signal to halt, his other hand hooking into his gun belt as he drew a breath and delivered what sounded like a well-rehearsed line.

"I'm sorry, folks. This unit is off-limits right now. If you have business with the resident, you'll have to come back another time."

Cass regarded the man for a moment, then replied in an even, pleasant tone, "I see. Why is that? We're here to see Ms. Hirayama, is she under arrest?"

The guard, appearing nonplussed, spoke slowly, as if to make sure they understood his words this time. "This residence unit is off-limits, per the colonial administration. Ms. Hirayama is not able to receive visitors at this time, unless accompanied by our resident legal representative, Mr. Paulson."

Cass cocked his head slightly. "Mr. Paulson. He's the senior legal counsel for Hirayama Enterprises hereabouts, yes?"

"You got it," the guard replied, settling into an expression of officious self-satisfaction.

"Great," Cass said. "So, may I just ask— is Ms. Hirayama, in point of fact, an employee of Hirayama Enterprises? As far as I know, she's just the boss's daughter, right? Does she represent the company or this colony in some official capacity?"

The guard opened his mouth to reply, then closed it again, his earlier confidence evaporating.

"Okay, let me try this another way," Cass continued. "Has Atsuko Hirayama retained the services of Mr. Paulson as a private attorney? Would she tell me she had, if I asked her?"

The guard said nothing. He straightened, sucked on his cheek, and attempted to look indifferent.

"Right," Cass said cheerfully. He leaned in to squint at the man's nametape. "Officer—Blake. Officer Blake, my name is Petty Officer Broz, Commonwealth Department of Customs and Excise. That's a federal-level law enforcement agency you may have heard of. These are my associates, Petty Officers Tanahill and Avery.

"We're conducting an official investigation in which Ms. Hirayama is a person of interest. She has has not yet exercised her right to decline to speak with us, nor asked for legal counsel to be present. So we're going to go ahead and knock on that door and see who answers."

As Cass spoke, Alfred and Skye moved to position themselves on either side of the guard, who eyed them warily. A text message appeared in Cass's field of view, his DNI supplying the data that proved what Cass already knew to be the case—

SUBJECT PULSE RATE ELEVATED BEYOND PHYSIOLOGICAL NORMS

Cass smiled and tilted his head toward the guard's holster. "You reach for that peashooter or try to hinder us in any way, I'll plant your fat ass on the deck and place you under arrest for obstructing a federal investigation. After that you will—without a single shred of doubt—be hauled away, right in front of your fellow rent-a-cops, to the brig of the CNS *Agamemnon*. Once you're a guest of the Navy, we'll have all manner of fun trying to figure out what possessed you to get between us and a material witness. The good news? If you choose to go that route, you'll get your wish to see Mr. Paulson today—since you work for the company, it'll be his job to try to get you out of the clink. How does that sound, tough guy?"

Security Officer Blake stood frozen, his mouth half-open, as his eyes darted from Cass to Alfred, to Skye, and back to Cass. "I'm going to have to call this in—" he began, as Cass reached out and deftly removed his sidearm from its holster, gesturing with it toward the opposite side of the tunnel from the doorway.

"Do it over there. I'm keeping this. Your boss can pick it up at the hotel later."

As the cowed and red-faced security guard shuffled away from the door, Skye snickered. "You've been hanging around the Cox'n quite a bit haven't you, Broz? He's rubbing off on you."

Cass chuckled softly. "I've always been a quick study."

***

The fit, dark-haired young woman who answered the door was unquestionably Atsuko Hirayama. She was short for a genotypical human, only slightly taller than Cass. She wore a pair of workout pants and unadorned dark blue t-shirt, an unpretentious ensemble that nevertheless flattered her slim figure. Her hair was longer than it had been in the holos Cass had seen of her, falling free to the middle of her back. Her demeanor as she greeted them was serious and reserved, but Cass perceived that her eyes conveyed welcome, and perhaps something else. Excitement? Relief?

"Hello. You are the gendarmes that recently arrived, yes? You are investigating the loss of the *Euphrates?*" Her voice was soft and musical, her tone polite. Her words, while framed as questions, sounded to Cass more like statements of fact, merely awaiting confirmation. He noted that she had used the term *loss,* but not *accident,* and a strange, cold feeling overtook him momentarily as he wondered if it was significant. *You're reading too much into things again. Don't make assumptions.*

Cass cleared his throat. "Yes. Uh, Ms. Hirayama? My name is Casimir Broz. These are my colleagues, Petty Officers Skye Tanahill and Alfred Avery. We were wondering if we could speak with you a bit about your journey here on the *Euphrates.*"

Atsuko smiled faintly, and opened the door further, making a tiny, understated gesture with her head. "Of course, please come in."

The apartment was small and neat, even minimalistic. The few decorations on the walls were mostly abstract or bore naturalistic motifs of plants or flowing water. A decorative shelf in the main living space held a few mostly porcelain *objets d'art* and several hardcopy books, most of which seemed to be on the topics of philosophy and ethics. *I'm not sure what I expected of the rogue Hirayama heiress,* Cass mused, *but this girl was certainly not it.*

"Please sit down. Would you like something to drink? Water? Or I can make tea, I was able to bring some with me on my trip here," Atsuko called over her shoulder as she entered the unit's small kitchenette.

Cass looked at Alfred and Skye, who both shook their heads in the negative. "No, thank you."

Alfred spoke up as Atsuko turned to face them once again, leaning on the small breakfast bar that separated the kitchenette from the main living space. "Ms. Hirayama, if you don't mind my saying so, I would imagine folks around here would be mighty anxious to stay in your good graces, things being as they are. You stand to inherit your father's shares of the company, isn't that right? Why was there a guard posted outside your door? I don't get the impression it's for your safety."

The merest ghost of a frown passed briefly across Atsuko's face. "As I imagine you have already surmised, Petty Officer Avery, I have been sequestered here by the order of Security Chief Dornier, so that I do not distract you from your investigation."

Cass cocked an eyebrow quizzically, confused by her response. "Distracted? How would you distract us? I see you as a material witness to the conduct of the ship's company of the *Euphrates* in the days leading up to the incident. Your testimony would seem pretty relevant."

"I can tell you little that would be of help there. The ship's master, Jonathon Gathii, seemed competent and able enough. I never witnessed any negligence on his part or the crew's, but then again, I spent most of the journey in my own quarters or in the mess. I saw little of the actual operation of the vessel, and nothing that seemed out of the ordinary." Atsuko paused, taking in a breath and then releasing it in a small sigh, as if she had quickly reconsidered her next words, and decided to say something else. "There are some observations I could share that might prove of value to your investigation, but I am not certain it is my place to do so, particularly in this venue?" As she spoke, her gaze swept meaningfully around the small apartment, then locked onto Cass. He noted how she placed a certain emphasis on the words my place.

What does she mean by her place? The venue? Her apartment? Sudden understanding struck Cass like a thunderbolt, and he cursed his own stupidity under his breath. He fished his datapad out of its pocket and keyed the sophisticated counter-surveillance suite it boasted, before placing it on the coffee table before him with an expression of chagrin on his broad features. "I think we can now assume that this conversation will be strictly confidential, if that eases your mind."

Atsuko smiled her mysterious smile. "Indeed, Petty Officer Broz, I feel much better knowing that Chief Security Officer Dornier and his associates will not be a party to the rest of this interview, should the line of questioning stray into matters unrelated to the condition of our ship, or the competence of its crew."

Cass and Alfred exchanged glances, then Cass looked at Atsuko and spoke slowly, a feeling of formless dread settling in his gut. "Ms. Hirayama, did you interact with a fellow passenger named Emerson? You may or may not be aware that he was an Assistant Undersecretary of State, engaged in reviewing certain government contracts on Tengoku."

Atsuko nodded once. "Yes. I did know, and yes, I did interact with him. He was very interested in making my acquaintance, and we spoke several times both during the journey and after we had arrived. We met in this very room, in fact. We discussed matters that I had hoped would remain between us, until his return to Earth. Sadly—" Atsuko trailed off and her veneer of quiet self-assurance seemed to crack momentarily as she gathered herself to continue. "Sadly, he never did return to Earth. Perhaps because he lacked anti-intrusion software like yours. Perhaps his fate was sealed while he sat where you do now, asking me his own questions. He asked very dangerous questions."

"What sort of questions did he ask you?" Cass was leaning forward, his eyes fixed on Atsuko's.

"He asked me what I knew about a bio-research project that the Government had initiated, with the cooperation of my father's company, a project which they subsequently cancelled. I was obliged to tell him that this project was continuing to undergo development here on Tengoku, even despite the withdrawal of funding and Government sanction."

"What was the nature of this project? Is this work still ongoing now?"

Atsuko looked at Cass, her gaze level and somber. "If I answer that, if I tell you what I told Mr. Emerson, you cannot un-hear it. You will all be in deadly danger from that moment forward, and I will very likely be guilty of disclosing classified information to unauthorized persons. Of course, my minders will almost certainly assume I have told you, regardless."

Cass sat back and realized his mouth was bone dry. "You might be surprised, Ms. Hirayama, to learn what kind of security clearance we have."

Atsuko shook her head as she replied, "Not for this."

Cass pondered this for a moment. "Do you know for sure that we lack the clearance?"

She hesitated, then shrugged. "I suppose I don't know that for certain, no."

"Then as a federal law enforcement agent, I am asking you to divulge the information to further our inquiry into possible criminal conduct, a request you can comply with in good faith, not having knowingly broken the law. If it is above my clearance, then the fault is mine."

Atsuko smiled without humor. "That is quite a legal gray area, but the fact is, I want to trust you. I need to tell someone…"

Atsuko moved around the breakfast bar and sat in one of the plush chairs in the living area, facing her visitors. She stared into the distance a moment before continuing.

"Project Seraphim; that is what they call it. The goal of the project is the creation of a highly contagious, airborne pathogen with a very specific type of disease vector. It only attacks humanoid lifeforms that possess certain genetic markers, and these markers can be specified with a fine level of granularity and imprinted on the pathogen prior to any release."

She paused, but the team merely stared at her, as they tried to process what she was saying. "In other words, the pathogen could be imprinted with the genetic markers unique to the gene-edit package provided to your ancestors, Petty Officer Broz, when they first set out to colonize Jotunheim. That particular strain would then attack Jotuns, and nobody else. The pathogen in question is, I should add, incredibly lethal and highly tolerant of any environment remotely suitable for human habitation."

Cass gaped at her, his expression incredulous. "A biological weapon. Your father is building a biological weapon that targets specific MCE populations, that's what you're telling us. You're saying this weapon was actually sanctioned by the government at one point, but now that cooler heads have apparently prevailed and tried to put the kibosh on it, your father's mad scientists are just going to go ahead and keep plugging away at their genocidal little hobby anyway? Why? To what end? They can't possibly think to sell it!"

Atsuko regarded him unflinchingly. "Yes. A biological weapon. And yes, they are still working on it. Who the buyer is, or why they would want such a dreadful thing, I have not yet been able to discover, but there are other parties involved, I am sure of it. A black-market buyer, or at least someone with a very significant interest in the project. My father and his longtime partner, Doctor Nels Lundgren were both quite conflicted about this work, I know this for a fact. Others on the Board were apparently skeptical as well. Uncle Nels told me my father agreed to bid the contract because people from the government—friends of his—implored him too. They said it was his patriotic duty. For him to knowingly allow this project to continue now that the government has abandoned it is beyond uncharacteristic for him, it is..."

"Unconscionable. That's what it is."

Atsuko's mouth tightened, and she seemed on the verge of an angry retort, then she simply shrugged. "Yes."

Skye broke in as Cass was about to speak again, "How did you come to find out about all this exactly? Does your father like to discuss this aspect of the family business at the dinner table, or...?"

Atsuko looked uncomfortable, her hands fidgeting in her lap.

Skye forged ahead when Atsuko didn't respond immediately, and her tone conveyed an admixture of incredulity, admiration, and amusement. "You're investigating this thing yourself. You didn't just make a stupid gaffe on your little holo-blog, did you? That whole scandal that got you in hot water back home—that was a deliberate ploy, wasn't it? You outed yourself as a genetic offender on purpose, so Daddy would have to get you off-world, and where better to shelter his darling daughter from the Earth's authorities than his own corporate colony here at the ass-end of Creation? Let me guess, you are the one who tipped off the State Department in the first place and landed Emerson on his final ill-fated voyage, am I right?"

Atsuko nodded.

Cass felt a strange, breathless sensation, almost a fight-or-flight response. *Things are moving too fast, I need to get control of this conversation, break this new data down into manageable chunks. We can't just chase this white rabbit down a possibly bottomless hole. Establish the basic facts, Cass.*

"Atsuko, am I to understand that you shared this information with Mr. Emerson, and that you now believe that some party subsequent to that disclosure, destroyed the *Euphrates* deliberately to prevent him from reaching Earth with this news?"

"Yes."

"Okay, let's back up a bit. You said this pathogen is very lethal. How lethal?"

"The projected mortality rate in infected subjects is thought to be somewhere around ninety percent."

Great Founders. Well, there it is. They've done it. They've ignored centuries of proscription on germ warfare, centuries of blood-soaked history. They've gone and created a doomsday weapon.

"How close is this thing to completion? How long before it could be used?"

Atsuko made a helpless gesture. "I do not know for certain. The colony administration now knows I am prying into the matter, and they have managed to block my...avenues of inquiry. Most worryingly, I think they know Uncle Nels was helping me, I came here primarily to talk to him, but he was already gone when I arrived. He resigned his position, they say. I have not been able to discover where he went, but I feel certain I know his ultimate destination. We had been in contact regarding this matter and arranged to meet on Unity Station if something went wrong, and it became dangerous for him to remain here. I, however, have been placed under *medical quarantine*, in order to prevent my leaving the planet. I was seen near the berthing bays at the spaceport when you arrived and have been a virtual prisoner since. I am certain Chief Dornier is involved in this conspiracy, it was he who arranged my quarantined status and detention. He also made it very clear it would be in my best interest not to speak to you without the company lawyer present. I am certain he knows that Uncle Nels and I have been in communication, and what the subject matter of those communications was."

"This is Nels Lundgren, your father's associate? He was helping you?"

"Yes. He contacted me some months ago, sounding very distraught. He is more than simply my father's 'associate,' he is practically the co-founder of the company, and a close family friend. When he initially reached out to me about this, he was not able to speak plainly, for fear that the security algorithms in the Colony's comms systems would draw unwanted attention to him. We had to be very careful, but after several weeks of clandestine communication, he made it clear that Project Seraphim had not been shut down, that it was going to be completed for reasons not even my father would —or could— make clear to him. He told me he had serious moral reservations about the work from the very start, but now that it wasn't even going to be under government oversight, there could be no legitimate purpose for it."

Cass scowled. "What legitimate purpose would the Government have for this abomination? It's unconstitutional!"

Alfred looked sharply at Atsuko. "Yeah...that's a good question. A *real* good question."

Atsuko assumed the mechanical tone of a person reciting someone else's words. "For extreme contingencies involving seditious threats to interstellar commerce, civil traffic, and logistics by organized enemies of the state."

Alfred guffawed. "Bullshit. That's bullshit. The government doesn't develop a secret, biological super-weapon to put down a rebellion of wildcatters or catch a pirate cartel. What contingency might arise that would signal that the time has now come for germ warfare? Who the hell are these enemies of the state? Last I heard, we *are the only state!*"

Cass spoke tonelessly, his face hard. "I think you know, Alfred. The Anthemusan Sovereignty movement has been gaining steam, ever since that decision came down that the sirens don't even have legal jurisdiction over the other planets in their own system. Apparently, Earth-based megacorps are still the highest law in the land on worlds where you can see Anthemusa in the night sky, at least as long as there is Iridium or Helium-3 to be found there. There's been rumblings on other Dominion worlds too. When you live on Unity Station and rub elbows with a bunch of spacers, you hear things. This designer-germ must have someone's idea of an insurance policy against the inevitable outcome of their own colonialism. You know the type. The sort of person who still thinks Earth is the center of the Universe?"

Alfred huffed. "Brother, that's all above my pay grade. I just have a hard time believing the Commonwealth Government would condone the use of something like this on Anthemusa, or on your planet. That's just crazy."

"Is it? You know what they say, when your only tool is a hammer, every problem starts to look like a nail."

"Man, just the idea of using a thing like this is a political third-rail. I have to think that being actually involved in developing it would be career ending, not to mention the likelihood of a life sentence on an airless moon. If word got out that the General Assembly had used taxpayer money for…" Alfred trailed off.

Atsuko smiled without humor. "Exactly, Petty Officer Avery. Credible proof that the Commonwealth had been involved in conceiving, funding, and developing something like Project Seraphim would potentially tear the fraying fabric of our society apart. I suspect that, at some level, was part of the plan all along."

9

The Knife Under the Cloak

Tengoku, The Iota Persei System

C aptain Faulkner sat at the desk in her underway cabin with her head bowed and rubbed her temples, trying to massage away the ache that was germinating there as her executive officer continued his report.

"The Supply Officer confirms there was no indication on the galley status displays that anything was wrong. They didn't know the refrigeration unit had failed until someone walked in there and found the compartment was at room temperature. Engineering and Data Systems guys are looking it over now, but the operative theory is a sensor got disconnected during the overhaul and wasn't hooked back up right."

Faulkner winced in pain as purple and green lights blossomed behind her eyelids, then spoke without looking up. Migraines had unfortunately become a part of her new normal, as had the nerve pain in her extremities that no amount of cellular regeneration therapy seemed to assuage. "You mean a sensor was disconnected on a unit that then subsequently failed, a few weeks out of drydock."

Aguilera looked pained as he replied, "yes, Ma'am. That would seem to be the case. It's rotten luck, no doubt about it."

"How much did we lose?"

"About 25% of remaining perishable foodstuffs. It cuts our endurance time down to 21 days unless we institute restricted rationing."

"I don't suppose that orbiting merchantman has anything we can requisition?"

"The *Hermes?*" Aguilera shook his head. "What she did have in her holds has been offloaded on Tengoku, we already asked."

Faulkner sat back and blew out a long breath. "I imagine the colony will be reluctant to part with any chow. They doubtless don't have a whole lot of food surplus to needs, and if they do, they won't admit to it."

"Skipper, I can call the doc—"

"No," Faulkner interrupted, then hearing how harsh her voice had sounded, continued in a softer tone. "Thanks, no. I don't want any more pills. I've had enough of pills." She grimaced.

"Of course, Captain."

Of course, Captain. Faulkner thought. *What does that even mean? I know I used to be fluent in that same noncommittal language when I was an XO, but now I've lost the knack of interpreting it. Does he mean "you are wise not to go down that road again, Captain," or does he mean "you're being an obstinate asshole, Captain, why don't you just go to sickbay"—or what?*

Something Aguilera had just said a moment before was nagging at her, and she took a moment to try and focus on what it was. "The *Hermes* is done offloading, you said?"

"Yes, skipper, seems like it."

"Are they taking on passengers, or return cargo?"

Aguilera frowned slightly, as if taken aback that his commanding officer had asked a question to which he didn't already know the answer.

"I don't believe so, Captain. We haven't seen any boats coming up today, that I recall. I can confirm with the watch—"

"It's not urgent, Tom. I guess I was just wondering what they are still doing in orbit. If they do plan to take on cargo or passengers for the next leg, they'd be well advised to be about it. If they are going back empty though, I guess I don't understand why they are wasting time and provisions dawdling around here." She grinned weakly at Aguilera. "If they have enough food for an extended stay here, it would be damn patriotic of them to share that largesse with us, but...Well, I suppose it's none of my business anyway."

Aguilera opened his mouth to reply, but at that moment, an alert tone sounded on Faulkner's desk console. Faulkner touched a control and then spoke in as crisp and professional a voice as she could muster, "Commanding Officer, go ahead."

"Captain, communications watch, the CIC Watch Officer requests your presence in the CIC, it concerns a signal we just intercepted— er, sort of intercepted."

Aguilera, listening from across the small cabin raised an eyebrow. His gaze met his captain's, his own expression curious. She keyed her controls again and replied, "Acknowledged. On my way."

***

"It looks to me like we got grazed by a terahertz tight-beam transmission, originating from Tengoku City. The weather is pretty foul down there right now, the cloud cover may have introduced some scatter in the beam, or we wouldn't have heard it at all." Chris Patterson, the *Aggie's* Communications Officer, was speaking to a small knot of officers and petty-officers near the communication section in CIC. The senior watch-stander, a young woman named Decker, was new to the ship, and it was she who weighed in next. "It's encrypted, using military-grade encryption. I don't think we can break it without tying up our Sigcomp resources for weeks, and even then, maybe not."

Faulkner grimaced. "The *Aggie* is no C2 cruiser, even after the refit, our compute resources are nowhere near as vast as we would need to crack a secure tight-beam in time for it to matter, unless the sender was kind enough to make it easy for us." She contemplated this new data for a moment. "And you're sure this ship wasn't the intended recipient? What about the *Hermes*?"

Decker shook her close-shorn head. "We just got a piece of it, Captain. I don't see how it could be intended for the *Hermes* either, she's not positioned to be able to capture the beam, she's in a worse spot than us. The beam seems to have been transmitted along this vector— Decker's hand indicated a display, with a prominent orange line representing the ultra-high frequency transmission beaming out into a sector of space that was to all appearances, quite empty for a very long way.

"That doesn't make any sense, there's nothing there." Aguilera commented, his brow furrowed. "That kind of transmission from a planetary surface would be pretty expensive in terms of energy. Who sends an encrypted tight-beam transmission from a planetary installation into the dark, where nobody can receive it? Maybe the new guy is on duty down there? Maybe they're going a little stir crazy, and—" Aguilera extended his left thumb and pinkie and raised his hand to his mouth to mime drinking from a bottle. Decker and Patterson chuckled, but Faulkner merely stared at the display for a moment and then said, "We're sure there is nothing along that vector in practical radio range of the planet?"

Decker's smile vanished. "Captain, I've confirmed with Astrogation and Tactical, the PPI is clear of traffic, no contacts in the system other than the comms buoy and *Hermes*."

Faulkner glanced at the holographic "tank" in the center of the CIC, currently projecting a spherical representation of the space around the ship for a distance of ten light seconds in every direction. Finding no answers there, she chewed her lower lip as she tried to grasp the underlying logic of the situation. She was certain that there was something important eluding her. "Chris, see if you can raise the shore party, please? I want a status update."

The Communications Officer looked momentarily confused, but then quickly motioned Decker to comply. "Aye, Skipper."

After making the appropriate control inputs, Decker began speaking into her headset in a clear contralto. "Sierra Six, this is *Agamemnon*, are you receiving, over?"

After a few moments of silence, the reply could be heard on the speakers, "*Agamemnon*, Sierra Six Actual, go ahead."

Garnett, Faulkner thought. *Good.*

She placed a hand on Decker's shoulder, who looked up at her briefly, and then spoke into her headset again. "Sierra Six, stand by for *Agamemnon* Actual."

Faulkner retrieved a headset of her own from the communications console before her, then securing it over her head, keyed the microphone. "Sierra Six Actual, *Agamemnon* Actual. We thought we would check in a little early, see how things were going."

Faulkner hoped her choice of phrasing, as well as her decision to speak to Garnett directly, would convey that it was not mere idle curiosity that induced her to contact him off-schedule. She knew he would be keenly aware that the routine comms traffic between the *Aggie* and the shore party was routed through the colony's communications system. While the actual content of their calls was encrypted per standard procedure, the signals had to travel through the local network on the ground to reach Garnett's team, and this involved a certain amount of fundamental trust in the integrity of that network, trust Faulkner wasn't sure she felt. While she didn't expect to discuss anything that would be inappropriate under regulations for such a semi-secure comm-link, she nevertheless felt the need to play things close to the vest for the time being.

As she mulled her next words, Garnett was already replying airily, "Good afternoon, *Agamemnon*. We're getting ready to wrap up here actually! As I surmised, there isn't a lot of data here that really bears on the investigation, though the locals have been very helpful, just as we had assumed they would. I am hoping to be back aboard tomorrow, as it stands now."

Faulkner felt her vague sense of unease grow. *Before you left, you made it very clear that you surmised no such thing.*

Garnett paused a moment, then continued, "We would however, like to transmit some of the salient details of this case for your review, and unfortunately regulations demand we do so over a secure link. I'd like to send one of the team outside as soon as this weather clears out, to establish line-of-sight comms so we can get that done. I don't foresee you having any problems locating the beacon, given the peaceful surroundings, it should show up on your displays like a road-flare."

Faulkner felt the constant, nagging pressure between her temples explode into blinding pain, and the feeling in the pit of her stomach grew into a hard knot. *Road-flare,* he'd said. That had been the prearranged code word that indicated a hostile or dangerous situation ashore. When Faulkner was silent a moment, Garnett spoke again. "*Agamemnon* Actual, how copy?"

Faulkner shook herself and tried to focus on the conversation. "We copy you five by five, and that's affirmative on the comms uplink, I'll hand you off to the Communication Officer to coordinate. *Agamemnon* Actual, clear."

She removed the headset and slammed it onto the edge of the console, finding herself irritated with Garnett and seeking some harmless way to obtain the cathartic effect of shooting the messenger. She sighed and pressed her fingertips to her temples. *Well, this little shakedown cruise has really gone to shit.*

"Commander Aguilera," she said after a moment, "pass the word to the Officer of the Deck, all departments are to set condition yoke."

Aguilera, showing only the faintest hint of surprise, moved to execute the order that would bring the ship to a higher state of readiness. Moments later, an announcement over the 1MC set the crew in motion. Junior personnel—"strikers"—in orange vac-suits entered the CIC, opening storage lockers and distributing additional suits to the watch-standers. Once sealed, the vacsuits would protect their all-too-fragile occupants from sudden decompression or atmospheric contamination should the ship be damaged. For now, they would wear the suits loosely and unsealed, but keep their helmets within reach in case the order came to button up.

Around the aft hatch, amber strips began to glow as it was slammed shut, metal thuds echoing through the compartment as the dogs locked home. Damage control strikers moved through the CIC, collecting coffee cups and other loose items before a sudden loss of air pressure or gravity could turn them into dangerous projectiles.

Patterson approached Faulkner as one of the all-too-young looking spacers helped her slip her legs into a vacsuit. He came to attention, the arms of his own suit tied around his waist, and stated formally, "Captain, Damage Control reports material condition yoke has been set throughout the ship."

"Very well. Please inform the Security Officer that I want a full forensic investigation into the malfunctioning refrigerator, and the related monitoring systems. He is to report his initial findings to the XO by no later than 0800 tomorrow. Oh, and advise Data Systems to initiate a full level three security audit of all systems, immediately."

Patterson regarded her with an unreadable expression. "Aye, Captain. To confirm, the Security Officer is to open an investigation...into the failed refrigerator."

"That's correct. Specifically, the confluence of events that led the monitoring system to go bad just in time for the fridge to fail completely and suddenly, without anyone knowing it for hours."

As Patterson moved away, Aguilera returned, wearing a look of concern. "What's up, Skipper? The shore party's report seemed pretty upbeat, right up until they delivered the danger code word. Can you share anything about what's going on?"

"Beats me, Tom. It seems they want to talk to us privately, and bad enough to brave the weather down there which is not something I'd want to do. I think we can assume it's bad news. The storm should be moving out a bit later in the day, I figure we'll get some straight talk then."

"And the investigation? Involving the Security Officer is coming on pretty strong, Skipper, for all we know it was just a freak mishap related to the refit."

Faulkner rubbed the bridge of her nose between her right thumb and forefinger. "That mishap made a serious dent in our mission endurance, right about the same time Garnett's team—who are investigating a fatal accident involving a big-shot government man—are being bustled out the door. Now they're flashing the danger signal." Faulkner stabbed a finger at the tactical display hovering over the tank. "We have a cargo hauler out there that doesn't seem very interested in hauling cargo, and someone down on the planet is apparently sending tight-beam transmissions with military-grade encryption to nobody at all. Make sense to you?"

"No. No it doesn't."

"Have the sensor section go active on IEMARS. If there is anything out there bigger than a golf ball that isn't already on the plot, I want to see it."

Aguilera nodded once in acknowledgement. "Active on IEMARS, volume search mode, aye."

Faulkner pitched her voice lower, so that only Aguilera could hear her next words. "Too many things here don't add up, Exec, and I don't believe in coincidence. Someone wants us gone from here, that's what my gut is telling me. And now, I find that I want nothing more in the world than to stay."

***

Enora grasped one of the metal stanchions projecting from the airlock wall and gave her companion, Skye Tanahill, a thumbs-up as she waited for the pressure to equalize. Beyond the thick outer hatch lay a narrow defile that wound between sheer cliff walls, climbing away from the base of the Admin Dome. Where it widened into open ground, about two hundred meters uphill, was the nearest spot from which she could reliably establish a tight-beam link to the *Agamemnon*.

Once there, however, she would likely be unable to reach her teammates inside the spaceport dome through its thick concrete shell—unless she routed the signal through the colony's communications network, which they wanted to avoid. For that reason, Skye would remain in the airlock, both as a safety measure should Enora run into trouble outside and as a comms relay to Garnett.

As the warm air in the airlock drained away, her visor momentarily frosted. She mentally keyed her DNI implant and instructed it to perform one last diagnostic on her suit integrity, more out of the nervous desire to be performing some action than any real concern that her suit wasn't sealed. The diagnostic check took less than a second, and the result was entirely satisfactory.

Enora grinned to herself. The only survival gear that she'd had on hand which possessed both the ability to protect her from the harsh conditions on the surface, as well as the military comms equipment required on this particular excursion, was her armored combat hardsuit. Such suits were colloquially referred to simply as battle armor, and

Enora found that while hers seemed comically overmatched to the hazards she expected to face on her brief sojourn outside to contact the ship, she was nevertheless glad to be sealed once again into its reassuring shell of integrated state-of-the-art tactical systems and protective carbon nanotube plates.

Look at you, she thought, *all dressed up in your nicest outfit, just so you can walk half a block to make a phone call.*

The tactical computer in her helmet was designed to work seamlessly with her DNI, providing the suit with up-to-the-nanosecond data on her physical state, while feeding enhanced and filtered information about the battlespace around her directly to her brain. The suit possessed infrared and ultraviolet optics, seismic sensors, enhanced aural receptors for detecting and analyzing nearby sounds, as well as advanced cyber-warfare and communications systems. On-board emergency medical gear could autonomously deliver an impressive number of life-saving and performance-enhancing pharmaceuticals, and the environmental system could maintain her air supply for upwards of forty-eight hours under battlefield conditions.

She felt like a colossus in the suit, and though that well-documented sense of invulnerability came with dangers her Naval Infantry instructors had drilled into her head—often and with relish—she was grateful for it all the same.

The last twenty-four hours had been tense, to put it mildly, bringing one revelation after another and none of them pleasant. When Cass had returned from his interview with Atsuko, he'd been furious. His report had been concise and entirely professional. Beneath the words, though, Enora had seen the rage he had almost managed to contain, as only Cass could. Alfred had looked shaken too, and the Cox'n had become downright grim—which was saying something, given that his emotional range typically ran from stoic on a good day to dour on a bad one, the variation being measurable only in degrees of wry fatalism.

Given her own discoveries regarding the fate of the *Euphrates*, an alarming picture emerged of a conspiracy reaching into the upper ranks of Hirayama Enterprises itself, one with potentially genocidal implications. Understandably, the mood of the team had soured, which was a shame, really, because Enora had just started to get comfortable in her new role as data forensics expert on the side of Good.

Most frustrating for Enora was that the team had quickly pierced the fiction that the freighter's destruction had been an accident, but couldn't confront anyone with the fact without the larger investigation grinding to a halt. The conclusive evidence that would confirm the younger Hirayama's disturbing story about Project Seraphim was naturally in the possession of the mysterious Uncle Nels, who wasn't here. It would seem that expecting Atsuko to have solid proof of the misdeeds of her father's company in her own possession was asking too much of the Universe. She had turned over a number of illicitly obtained data files that seemed to corroborate that Project Seraphim had—at least at one point—existed. How she had sussed out the rest of this sinister plot was to Enora's mind, still a bit fuzzy.

It seemed that the team's plan going forward was to go find Kindly Uncle Nels, and get him and his firsthand knowledge of the project into protective custody along with Atsuko. Then, ostensibly, all would be revealed. Step one in this plan was to contact the cruiser orbiting overhead in order to communicate the real situation on the ground to Captain Faulkner, and Enora had drawn the short straw.

As the light on the airlock instrument panel went from a flashing yellow to a steady green, the outer door slid quietly open. The atmosphere on this frigid world was sufficient to convey sound to her ears, but the mechanism was well maintained and nearly silent, making its sudden smooth motion somewhat startling. As Enora stepped over the threshold into the narrow defile beyond, she keyed her comms with a mental command.

"Archangel this is Ghostcat, radio check."

"Ghostcat, Archangel. I copy you, five by five," came the response from Skye, her voice clear and calm. "The outer door is going to close automatically in a second as a safety measure, but I should still hear you fine. Holler when you get to the top of the gorge."

Enora turned at the waist and offered a sloppy half-salute to her companion in acknowledgement, then began the ascent to the glacier above, where she should have a clear line of sight for transmission to the *Agamemnon*.

The walls of the gorge were of a grey stone that sparkled with frost, and the deep shadows they cast this close to the bottom of the incline made the already deep chill even worse. Her helmet display told her it was -168.4 degrees Celsius, and her heating elements were doing their utmost to keep her reasonably comfortable. Behind her rose one sheer wall of the Admin Dome, which was not in fact round but shaped more like an enormous loaf of bread, with a vaulted roof like an aircraft hangar. The majority of the structure was buried, and only in a few places like this one was it possible to see the full extent of its ten vertical levels.

Enora stepped cautiously, trying to assess the stability of the surface upon which she trod, which was lightly covered with some sort of dirty looking "snow" she had to assume was not composed of water. Having determined that the ground beneath her feet was not especially slippery, she began hiking up the slope with more confidence, periodically reaching out to the cliff wall on her right for support. Above her, the narrow strip of sky visible between the sheer walls of the defile was a mottled silvery ribbon—overcast she assumed—though she had a hard time imagining it ever being any other color.

She knew a storm had recently passed over the colony but had not been able to observe the weather from any of the few windows or skylights in the facility. She had heard mention of methane sleet, and fierce winds, but for her part, she had not been aware that any weather event was transpiring until someone had told her. She was momentarily struck by the strangeness of being once again on the solid ground of a planet, and yet so entirely disconnected from the natural phenomena that one associated with an inhabited world, that she might as well be back on a spaceship.

Not much of a world really. Having hard vacuum outside your walls would hardly be worse.

Gradually, over the course of several minutes, the swirling metallic band of light above became larger, and then she found herself emerging from the defile onto a broad, silvery glacier, marked by eye-catching stone arches, ridges, and pinnacles made strange by centuries of erosion. The wind, not particularly noticeable down in the defile, still gusted here and howled audibly through the grotesque rock formations dotting her immediate surroundings. Ahead of her, rising into the molten silver sky, was a communications tower, wreathed in metal grillwork stairs and catwalks. A red light flashed on a lofty antenna array at its apex.

Consulting the DNI data-link to her battle armor's communications suite, she found the indicator that showed passable connection quality to the terahertz antenna array on the *Agamemnon*, but a less favorable result with respect to laser communications. She sent a mental command to connect via terahertz tight-beam, reminded herself of the proper etiquette for communicating with a capital ship, and keyed her microphone. "*Agamemnon*, this is shore party Sierra Six Romeo, sitrep follows. Unsanctioned Indigo level project ongoing on the surface. Sierra Six advises interdiction may prove necessary. Plan is to embark Swordfish and return to base with one—standby *Agamemnon*."

Enora broke off her report and took a step toward the communication tower, craning her neck to study the enclosed maintenance shed two-thirds of the way up the structure, just as a slightly distorted female voice spoke in her helmet speakers. "Sierra Six Romeo, *Agamemnon*, we copy five by four. Standing by."

She studied the shed and the catwalks leading from it intently. Was she simply feeling on-edge because of the oppressive atmosphere of her surroundings, or had she indeed seen a brief flicker of movement through the windows? She suspected that the small metal cabin would be unpressurized, likely a basic shelter from the elements that maintenance personnel used when repairing and monitoring the systems of the sophisticated antenna arrays atop the tower. *Seems like a pretty shitty time to be out here doing maintenance*, she thought. *Maybe the storm messed something up?*

Frowning, she ordered her optics to present a zoomed-in view of the shed windows on her HUD, but studying the view for several moments, saw no one.

That's odd.

Enora bit her lower lip and pondered a moment. While it would be difficult for a nearby person to intercept her tight-beam transmissions or otherwise eavesdrop on her communications, it was not impossible. Surely in the interest of operational security, she should make sure she was not being clandestinely observed.

On the other hand, maybe her DNI was subtly directing her attention to something she hadn't even realized she'd seen? She was beginning to wonder where Enora stopped and the computer in her head began.

I'm probably just being paranoid. Still, best to be sure.

Enora picked her way along the narrow path that led from the top of the gulch to the communications tower, wary of loose rock on the path but also trying to keep the windows on the tower in view as she made her approach. *The wind probably kicked up some trash or something, and blew it around the shed for a moment,* she told herself upon reaching the foot of the tower. Still, she trod as lightly as she reasonably could in her battle armor as she began ascending the grille-work stairs that wrapped around the tower several times before reaching the maintenance shed.

In under a minute, she had arrived at one of the two doorways at either end of the elongated cabin, with the other door presumably providing access to another catwalk that climbed still higher up the tower toward the antennas and radio masts at the apex. Enora leaned to her left, to peer through a window into the interior.

The shed was essentially a slightly rounded, prefabricated box, dimly illuminated by a red light fixture, and was no more than four and a half meters long and perhaps two and a half meters wide. She saw no one inside, and no movement. The interior was quite spartan, with the wall facing the tower superstructure being covered in numbered panels, and in the center of the space, offset to provide a clear path from door to door, a single waist-high console of some sort. A hint of glistening condensation shone on the equipment, which Enora thought must be heavily insulated against the harsh environment and hellish freezing temperatures. The second door at the opposite end of the capsule was sealed, as was the one before her, although the small flatscreen display to the right of the doorjamb indicated that the interior was indeed unpressurized. *Both doors closed, so...not the wind then.*

She pressed a gloved thumb against the control that opened the door and keyed her tactical light to provide greater illumination of the gloomy interior, as the door slid aside. Instinctively her hand went to her chest where her sidearm was holstered, brushing her fingers across the grip briefly as she scanned the corners of the small room.

A faint scraping noise seemed briefly to come from the area of the floor currently blocked from her view by the console, so faint in the thin atmosphere of Tengoku, that she may not have heard it at all without the enhanced aural pickups on her battle armor.

"Hello?" she queried, her voice seeming to boom out unnaturally through the external speakers on her helmet.

Waiting a moment and receiving no response, she moved further into the capsule and peered over the console to see what may lie behind it. The first thing to come into view as she approached, lying on the floor where she could not have seen it from the doorway, was an article quite familiar to her though its presence here was incongruous; an infrared laser microphone rig, and a fairly advanced one by the look of it. Next to that, a booted foot became visible and then jerked as its owner stood, and a human form clad in a commercial-grade survival suit appeared from behind the console, clutching its edge with one hand while bringing a flechette pistol to bear on Enora with the other. Enora's implant sang out with a sub-audial alarm, and her virtual display lit with a pulsing text warning:

THREAT DETECTED

Shocked and momentarily flatfooted, Enora turned her body, shifting her stance to present a smaller target profile to her apparent assailant. He stretched a shaking arm forward, bringing the weapon nearly to point-blank range, and fired twice.

The impacts took Enora on the left pauldron, and although the pistol was not an optimal weapon for engaging a target in battle armor, it was designed to penetrate both light body armor and intermediate barriers. At a range of less than a meter it unquestionably made itself felt. A sharp sensation that might have been pain erupted in Enora's shoulder, and then a deep chill, as the force of the high-velocity flechettes drove into her like a spear-thrust, the energy dissipating into her armor rather than her lungs or heart, as would certainly have been the case had she been wearing a commercial-grade suit herself. She staggered backwards, nearly knocked off her feet.

Then recovering her balance somewhat, she pushed off her back foot skipping toward the man, for it was a man's face she saw behind the foggy face-shield of the survival suit, pale and wearing an expression of terror. She simultaneously reached out her left hand to bat the pistol aside before he continued to pump rounds into her. Her arm was slow to respond, and clumsy, and some part of her mind registered that she had been wounded. Still, she was able to rake the man's shooting hand with the knuckles of her gauntlet, and his aim swung wide and to his right as the weapon discharged again, then sailed from the stranger's hand to clatter against a transparent aluminum window.

Enora's right hand grasped the grip of her sidearm, but her attacker clawed at her forearm, then seized her wrist and yanked. Bringing his other arm around her neck, he dragged her bodily over the console, twisting his torso to flip her and gain leverage. The man was considerably larger than Enora, his frame more solidly muscled than her own delicate Anthemusan build—but she was wearing battle armor, and he was not. Rather than resisting his pull, she drove her power-assisted legs against the console, propelling herself into him. The two of them toppled; she twisted midair, landing in a crouch as her assailant crashed awkwardly onto his side.

As he scrambled to rise, she brought down her right fist onto the side of his helmet in a hammer blow, ringing his helmet against the metal floor. He screamed, a high-pitched cry that conveyed panic as well as pain, and rolled away from her. Enora planted her left hand on the floor to stabilize herself and instantly regretted it. She sat back on her haunches, wincing as pain raced down her arm, searing her nerves like an electrical current, and drew a deep breath as her vision momentarily dimmed.

As she shakily regained her feet, her attacker scrambled toward the dropped pistol and snatched it up. He stood, slapped the control plate beside the opposite door, and staggered out, pausing to fire once in her direction. Enora drew her weapon and threw herself against the wall next to the open doorway. She keyed her comms and began to transmit, struck by how strange her own voice sounded in her ears. "Archangel, Ghostcat. Do you copy? I'm taking fire, one hostile confirmed, engaging in CQB on the comms tower at the top of the gulch, time now! Get your ass up here."

As she spoke another round was fired through the doorway, striking the instrument console.

"Ghostcat, this is *Agamemnon*, please repeat, over?"

The voice was not Skye's, but that of the communications watch on *Agamemnon*.

Fuck.

In her agitated state, she had forgotten to frame the clear mental command to switch her comms suite back to the local tactical network and had instead broadcast on the terahertz connection to the ship!

"*Agamemnon*, Ghostcat, disregard."

She focused next on her desire to switch channels and breathed a sigh of relief when her implant and the suit agreed an order had been given, and her heads-up display showed she was set to transmit on the team tac-net once again.

"Archangel, Ghostcat. Do you copy? I am in some real shit."

Enora raised her left gauntlet to the door frame with some effort and activated the tiny fiber optic camera that ran along her pinkie finger. Holding her arm in this position was agonizing, and she did so only long enough to see that her enemy had retreated some way up the catwalk and was trying to take cover behind the meager shelter of a diagnostic station projecting from the superstructure of the tower. She looked down at her shoulder and noticed a yellowish, foamy substance bubbling on her pauldron.

Huh. Sealant. I suppose that isn't great.

She lowered her left arm and then swung out into the doorway and fired her weapon twice, the hoarse bark of her pistol sounding thin and strange. Both rounds struck the diagnostic station, blasting ragged holes in the outer casing of the machinery. Grunting, Enora took shelter once again.

"Ghostcat, Archangel, sitrep."

Enora almost sobbed with relief to hear Skye Tanahill's voice. "Taking small arms fire from one hostile on the comms tower up top. I'm in the maintenance shed. He's in a civilian suit and he's got a flechette gun. My um, aim sucks right now, I think...the painkillers are kicking in. Really need a hand here." Enora's tongue felt swollen, far too large for her mouth, which was, she realized, quite dry. She also realized at that same moment that she could feel a tacky, sticky wetness spreading from her left armpit down her side, almost to her waist.

Either I am sweating like a pig, or bleeding profusely.

Skye's calm voice returned, betraying only the slightest edge of anxiety. "I'm linking up to your armor to assess the medical situation. Hang tight, I am Oscar Mike, ETA five minutes."

Enora flinched as small, star-shaped holes began to blossom in the thin wall of the capsule near her. The husky report of the stranger's flechette pistol rasped once, twice, then three times.

This is very likely to be over in five minutes, she thought. As her drill instructor in Basic Training would've doubtless observed, her position offered concealment but not cover. *What else would Sergeant Salazar say about this situation? Probably something about my DNI being an extension of my own senses, and how I should work with, not against, my implant. Also, he'd probably remind me that I am wearing Battle Armor, and this guy is not. Maybe in this situation, the better part of discretion is valor?*

Enora waited for a moment, but no further shots rang out. Then, taking a deep breath, she pivoted back into the doorway and brought up her left hand to cup her shooting hand, gritting her teeth through the resulting pain, and began advancing out onto the catwalk, her weapon extended in front of her. *Just hold it together, Enora.* After she had advanced perhaps three meters, the suited figure of her adversary appeared from behind the damaged workstation that had offered him cover, his arm raised to fire. His weapon rasped, and a single round ricocheted off the door frame behind her. Enora, as she had been trained, sent the mental command to fire rather than squeezing the fallback trigger on her weapon, the electronic signal moving faster than the muscles in her hand ever could.

The recoil was modest, especially in her battle armor, but still her left arm protested the jolt that seemed to be conducted by her skeleton directly to her wounded shoulder. Her pistol barked, and the stranger's body jerked and twisted, the flechette pistol falling from the inert fingers of his hand as the projectile from Enora's own pistol ripped through his virtually unarmored upper arm, leaving gory ruin in its wake. As his weapon bounced off a guardrail and then spun away across the catwalk behind him, the figure turned, almost instinctively, after it.

"Don't do it! Get on your knees now!" Enora's voice rang out, amplified considerably by her helmet, and she felt certain the man must have heard her. Nonetheless, he staggered after his weapon, his back to her, nearly kicking it off the catwalk in his clumsy haste to retrieve it. *Don't make me do this,* she silently pleaded with him.

She hesitated, only a moment, when his uninjured left arm extended downward to grab the gun. The report of her pistol was her first conscious signal that she had fired. A second later, a second shot rang out. The man fell forward in an awkward tangle of limbs and crashed to the catwalk, a misty plume of warm escaping air marking the jagged holes between his shoulder-blades where she had shot him, and then he lay very still.

10

Just Because You're Paranoid

Tengoku, The Iota Persei System

The Security Officer fidgeted uncomfortably as he finished delivering his report to the assembled senior officers seated around the conference table.

"The Data Systems branch says they have never seen anything like this particular malware package, nor do they know how it was first introduced into the environmental control and shipboard security subsystems. The long and the short of it is, the program removed any references to Petty Officer Longfellow in the access logs that would indicate he had ever accessed any area of the ship's stores. The unaltered logs are unrecoverable at this point, but the malware is present on the neural network nodes for the storerooms and the galley. The video feed from the companionway near the refrigerated storerooms, and the unsubstantiated testimony of the night baker, are the only reasons we had to suspect he had ever been on Deck Five at all, but as per my earlier comments, the DNA evidence we recovered from the wiring harness in the cooler is conclusive. The blood we found on the rough edge of the wire harness cover is definitely that of Longfellow."

Faulkner had been watching the faces of her senior officers while the Security Officer spoke, attempting to gauge their reactions to what they were hearing. While she knew several of the senior officers quite well, a number were also recently posted to the *Aggie*, and less of a known quantity. As soon as it had become clear the stern looking young Security Officer had finished, one of those recently appointed officers spoke.

"So, you are going to stand here, and say this was sabotage?"

Lieutenant Phoebe Jones made the ostensible question sound like a statement, her habitually sharp voice somehow conveying incredulity and disapproval at the same time.

Faulkner's face remained impassive, but internally she made note of the Supply Officer's hostility. It was her department that had responsibility for ship's stores, and to Faulkner's mind, the defensiveness in the young woman's tone as well as her general lack of engagement during the investigation said nothing favorable about her competence.

Jones had been assigned to the ship during the refit, and thus far Faulkner had been singularly unimpressed with her performance. A youngish officer with an exceptionally beautiful face and raven-black tresses long enough to push the envelope of Navy uniform regulations, she was also the daughter of a serving admiral—a fact she did little to keep discreet. She had the tawny complexion of an Earthborn Pacific Islander and an athletic physique that many naval officers might have found challenging to maintain on long deployments, though Jones seemed to take it as further evidence of her own exceptionalism. Unfortunately, her recruitment-poster good looks were undercut by a near-permanent frown and a combative, aloof demeanor that had won her few friends among the ship's officers or company. Her record was unblemished but equally undistinguished, and if Faulkner was honest with herself, she had disliked Jones from the moment they first met.

"You're saying it isn't?" Aguilera retorted from his seat at the captain's right hand, his expression placid, his tone flat.

"I am saying that I find the line of reasoning tenuous. Why would Longfellow sabotage his own ship while he was on deployment in the first place? And by breaking a refrigeration unit no less? If someone wanted to put the ship out of action, one might imagine they would subvert the combat systems in some way, or maybe propulsion. Are we thinking Petty Officer Longfellow has an axe to grind with the chicken cacciatore? I am aware of some complaints among the ratings about the caliber of the midrats on this cruise, but that would be taking it a bit far."

The Supply Officer's attempts at wit evoked a few wry grins and desultory chuckles, but Faulkner's expression remained grave as she spoke.

"I'd say that would depend, Lieutenant. If someone wanted to cut short our stay in the Iota Persei system without causing any casualties, or arousing undue suspicion of foul-play, I'd say that causing a quarter of our perishable foodstuffs to spoil as the result of a plausible malfunction is a pretty shrewd play."

Jones frowned, an expression Faulkner mused, that she seemed to wear like it was part of her uniform. "I haven't heard anything yet that rules out a simple mechanical failure. The DNA evidence only tells us Longfellow once handled the wire harness, and the edge was sharp."

Lam Ming De, the Chief Engineering Officer, shook his head as he offered his opinion, his soft, almost musical voice seeming all the more understated when juxtaposed with the strident tone of Jones. "After conferring with the Security Officer, I am forced to concur that deliberate tampering seems the most likely explanation."

Jones seemed about to protest again but then subsided. Faulkner swept her gaze across the faces of her subordinates, who had grown quiet for a moment as they digested this.

Lieutenant Daniel Traxler, the *Aggie's* Weapons Officer, spoke next, breaking the awkward silence that had descended on the meeting. "Who are you talking about when you say 'someone,' Captain? I assume you mean to say that you don't think Longfellow did this on a lark, if he did indeed do it, and that he was motivated by outside parties?"

Faulkner nodded slowly. "I can't help noticing that Lady Fortune seems to have conspired to get us out of this system, just as our friends from the Gendarmerie are trying to wrap up a thorny investigation on what amounts to a private planet run by a defense contractor. As for who might ultimately have been behind such an act of sabotage... I don't have any more idea than you do, Daniel. I am just raising one possible interpretation of the available data. We will just have to see what Mr. Longfellow has to say for himself when the Master-at-arms picks him up."

The Security Officer, still standing at the foot of the table, cleared his throat. "Do you want me to have him detained at this time, then, Captain?"

"I think so, Mr. Clement. Please make it so."

"Aye, aye." The stern-looking young warrant officer, looking relieved to have duties that would excuse him from the compartment and the attention of its occupants, braced to attention before departing, being sure to dog the hatch behind him in compliance with the elevated readiness condition that Faulkner had ordered earlier.

Jones spoke again as the hatch closed, her gaze unfocused almost as if she were thinking out loud, "I suppose it may be that one of the Mickey governments paid him off to do it? It seems like they've been stirring up a lot of trouble lately, and since New Muscovy a lot of them are not huge on the Navy. Deserites, maybe."

Sitting across the table from her, Angelique Mendoza, the ship's Operations Officer, huffed and responded in chilly tones, "It's hard to even count the things wrong with that statement."

"How so?" Jones shot back.

"Well, let's see." Mendoza raised a hand and began to enumerate her points on her fingers as she continued. "First, Deserites barely qualify as MCEs. You can't even distinguish them from Core humans by looking at them, and they dislike violence, not the Navy. Second, the term 'Mickey' is rude and disrespectful; we have Outlanders serving honorably on this ship, *including* a Deserite, and I hope you don't call them that where they can hear it. Third, Hirayama Enterprises is an Earth-based corporation; why the hell would an outlander government want to protect them from an investigation? Candidly, that's just stupid."

Jones sat forward in her seat, her face reddening, a hot retort forming on her lips when Aguilera's voice cut through the air like a knife. "Enough."

Both Jones and Mendoza subsided, as Aguilera continued. "Discussion is welcome at this table, bigotry and personal attacks are not. You are both officers. Some decorum, please?"

Jones seemed to gather her thoughts, and then replied, "in any case it seems clear that we need to return to port if we suspect that saboteurs among the crew are acting against the ship. This needs to be reported to higher command authority, like the Squadron CO, as soon as possible. Not to mention our supply situation does not permit us to loiter here indefinitely. If the investigation team requires more time on site to review a couple of minutes worth of telemetry logs, I question what they've been doing this whole time, the *Euphrates* didn't crash on the damn planet."

Faulkner frowned. *First, she doesn't take the investigation seriously. Then she challenges the conclusion that we've been sabotaged. Now she wants to return to port, which is exactly what I just theorized was the desired outcome of the alleged sabotage.*

She felt another headache coming on. It was hard not to feel as if Jones was bent on undermining this mission, and it was equally hard to suppress the growing urge she felt to yell at the insufferable young woman herself.

Calm down, Ada. You're being paranoid. Jones is a bitch for sure, but you have no reason to suspect she is deliberately obstructing the investigation or the mission. The Admiral's little darling probably just thinks that a month underway in any given year is plenty. After this cruise she gets to buck for her Space Warfare badge, that's another box checked. So naturally now she wants to get back to the dating scene on Unity and run up Daddy's credit chit some more. Sometimes it is painfully obvious we are a peacetime Navy. Maybe the Corporatists are right, and we have outlived our usefulness. This girl can talk all she likes about the New Muscovy revolt, but she is too young to have been there.

She realized she had been staring at Jones silently for several moments, long enough for it to become awkward. "I disagree," she said finally. "I don't see that our mission parameters have changed at all. This is a warship of the Commonwealth Navy, not a pleasure craft. We will implement reduced rations, if need be, but we will not leave our station until the investigation is well and truly complete."

"But Admiral Blanchett needs to know—"

"—The Admiral needs to know that his subordinates are capable and willing to execute their duties as ordered, Lieutenant. Dealing with adversity is part of the job description. Founders forbid we should get into a combat situation without an adequate supply of peach cobbler, but with any luck, we will just have to orbit this nonbelligerent planet a few more times, then we can pick up the shore party and return to civilization, and all its culinary delights."

Jones scowled, and replied in an acidic tone, "If the captain feels the situation is well in hand, why have we been at condition yoke for an entire watch, while orbiting this nonbelligerent planet? I am struggling to understand how the captain can trivialize the situation and yet treat it as dangerous at the same time. Are we in danger of further acts of alleged sabotage, or are we not? With all due respect, is it possible the captain's judgement has been affected by recent trauma?"

Faulkner stiffened, and a sudden tension filled the atmosphere of the compartment, as all eyes turned to their captain.

So, Faulkner thought. *The Admiral's Daughter is that sure of her invulnerability. What game could she be playing here? Is she trying to piss me off? Without stooping to her level, how do I convey that I'm not trivializing the situation, I'm trivializing dessert.*

Aguilera slammed an open hand down on the table in front of him, anger plain on his face. "You are treading dangerously close to insubordination, Lieutenant."

"I don't see that I am, sir. I am simply pointing out relevant facts that may bear on our current tactical situation and proposed course of action to the Commanding Officer, in accordance with my duties as a department head. *Sir.*"

Faulkner, having taken a moment to wrestle control of her emotions, interjected coldly, "One good thing about being the Commanding Officer is, I don't have to propose courses of action, nor rationalize them to you, Ms. Jones. I like to think of myself as a consensus builder, and someone who values the input of her officers when it's constructive. But make no mistake, I will ultimately issue orders with respect to our course of action, and you will obey them. I trust that doesn't present a problem?"

Jones quirked the smallest of smiles, one corner of her mouth curving upward a fraction of a centimeter as she replied, "I will comply with all your lawful orders, whatever my personal view of them, of course."

Faulkner looked around the table, at the faces of the other senior officers, noting more than one clouded expression. "That's so nice to hear, Lieutenant. Ladies and gentlemen, we will remain at condition yoke pending the conclusion of the investigation on Tengoku and our departure from this system. I understand this will represent some hardship for the ship's company. We will need to ensure they are getting adequate rest and time for personal care, and that they remain focused.

"I also want ship's corporals walking all sensitive areas of the ship, Mr. Aguilera, ask Clement to see to it. If this presents a manpower problem, have him coordinate with Kamarov to get more marine sentries posted on each watch. I have concerns about the security situation—both internal and external, and until I have a clear picture of what is going on with the shore party, we need to assume that our presence here is unwelcome and may draw further unfriendly acts. The shore party signaled earlier today, using a code phrase that indicates all is not well on the surface. I expect them to re-establish contact shortly via tight-beam, and hopefully we will get more clarity then. Ms. Mendoza, please ensure the IEMARS section is maintaining a volume search program with active sensor sweeps at random intervals."

Mendoza and Aguilera both nodded. Faulkner stood then, and the assembled officers moved to do likewise. "If there are no questions?"

There were none.

"Then stand to your duties and remain vigilant. Space is never safe, and this part of space is somewhat less safe than others, it would seem. Dismissed."

***

Following the contentious briefing, Faulkner had retired to her underway cabin adjoining the short passageway that linked the CIC with the quarterdeck, presumably to take care of some administrative paperwork, but found herself lying on her bunk, staring at the overhead. Her headache was back, and of course the nearly omnipresent pain and tingling in her extremities.

This cannot be the rest of my life. It just can't.

She contemplated taking a shower, in the hope that the water would soothe her perpetually aching body, as well as her frayed nerves. That however, would be a violation of regs while the ship was at condition yoke, and she needed to set the right example. She would not luxuriate in a hot shower while her crew had to rely wet-wipes and strictly regimented toilet breaks for personal hygiene. She knew also, that no amount of hot water would salve her growing anxiety.

Was it the tight-beam transmission to nowhere? That cryptic communication from the Gendarmes? What was the key data-point that had made her feel so certain this mission had already gone off the rails? *What is it Tom likes to say? BOHICA. Bend over—here it comes again.* One or two of these things in isolation would just be weird. All of them together formed a pattern—if only she could read it. *I don't know, maybe this incessant migraine has dulled my edge. I can't see the big picture here, but this is all wrong. It feels wrong. It tastes wrong.*

She found herself smirking at the image that thought conjured. *Yeah, Ada. You're just like one of those old holovid heroes—the Indian scout who can taste blood from a rock and tell exactly what creature it came from and what happens next. Maybe you should just put your ear to the decksole and listen for hoofbeats or something. If you aren't going to be able to stay focused and analyze facts objectively, you should never have told Fleet Medical you were feeling up to active duty again.*

The comms console beeped at her left elbow, and she mashed the panel with the fleshy side of her fist. "Commanding Officer."

"Ma'am, it's Johnston, did you want me to have the stewards bring you something to eat? It's almost four bells, and Commander Aguilera says he hadn't seen you in a bit."

Faulkner sighed deeply. *I had probably best show my face in the wardroom and see if I can soothe some ruffled feathers. Founders know that eating and sleeping in a vacsuit is not something these kids had expected on this little cruise. But I can't let my guard down just to make them happy.*

"No, thank you Mr. Johnston. I think I will dine in the wardroom tonight."

"Very well, Captain."

Had her chief steward's voice conveyed concern? Or was it pity? *Concern. It was concern. Johnston has been with you and the* Aggie *for over two years, don't start in on him too.*

Faulkner straightened her uniform as well as she could with her vacsuit arms tied about her waist, checked her image in the little mirror in her private head to ensure she was reasonably presentable, and made her way to the officer's wardroom one deck below.

Approaching the entrance to the wardroom, she paused to return a spacer's greeting as he passed by and heard laughter from within the compartment. *Well, spirits can't be all that low then.*

"Seriously," one voice rang out, that of an ensign in the supply department, she thought. "She must have used her entire captain's underway weight allowance for all that baggage."

"What do you mean? The skipper's a bit intense, yeah but..." That was the voice of Chris Patterson, the Communications Officer.

"You don't know? Wow. Where have you been? So...Faulkner was on some sort of shore mission as I heard it, like two years ago? Some tiny piss-pot mining colony full of Jotuns, I guess. So, the corporate cops killed one of these Jotun miners in some kind of altercation and they decided the thing to do, was to get shitfaced on machine room moonshine and string this corporate cop up like it's the Wild West."

More laughter.

"So, the Old Lady is supposed to go ashore with an ombudsman, and talk everyone down, show the flag y'know, make peace. Only, the miner's union or whatever isn't having it, and the representatives from both sides end up drawing down on each other in the middle of this meeting. Long short, the ombuds gets shot in the pinkie finger or something, calls a Section 1120, and the *Aggie's* NI Detachment gets called in. The jarheads bust down the doors and shoot a bunch of Mickeys, including the boss miner. When it's all over, Faulkner and the ombuds are like, hiding in a closet or something."

The voice of the ensign, warming to her tale, paused for dramatic effect. "So...mission is FUBAR, right? The skipper has to evacuate the ombudsman back to the ship. But then, after they survive the Great Miner Rebellion of Planet Whatever, their pinnace gets hit leaving atmo, by some kind of homemade missile battery."

"No way," interjected the voice of Patterson.

"Yeah, wait. So, the missile sprays their boat with shrapnel, but they're okay. They got holes, but the sealant system plugs 'em, and all's well that ends well, right? They get into the slipway on the *Aggie*, and I guess after they warped 'em in to the boat deck, the pressure and temp changes made the damaged hull plates deform or something, and fuel mist starts spraying out onto the deck where—if you can believe this—it drips through the grating onto a defective power junction, and—"

"No."

"Yeah. It goes up it a ball of fire, igniting all that vaporized fuel, and engulfs the pinnace. Boom."

Faulkner leaned against the bulkhead, her breath coming short and shallow. *The fire swells through the passenger compartment, coruscating along the bulkheads, the overhead, the floor...like a flood of seawater pouring into a sinking watercraft. But this flood is made of angry hot radiance, turning the passenger cabin into a blast furnace. Alarms are blaring and the coxswain is screaming something about evacuating, but there is nowhere to go. The fire is everywhere. Each breath is agony, the smoke from the sudden inferno like a solid substance, like hot concrete that she tries to inhale. A sudden, awful blast wave knocks her off her feet...*

In the wardroom, the brash young ensign was still talking, but Faulkner had lost the thread of the narrative. Her heart was pounding, sweat had sprung up on her forehead, and her face felt strange.

"Yeah, the whole boat deck had to be gutted...so six months of cell regeneration therapy and Founders know how many psyche evals later, and they finally put her on medical inactive status, because now she's addicted to painkillers, and can't supervise the refit anyway, but the higher-ups don't want to make it look like they're throwing her under the bus, because they told her it was a low-risk ferry job..."

Faulkner staggered away from the wardroom hatch and walked stiffly to a comms panel on the wall. Pressing the necessary controls with shaking fingers, Faulkner waited for the voice at the other end.

"Chief Steward."

"Chief, this is the CO. I've changed my mind. I'll take dinner in my underway cabin."

"Aye, aye, ma'am."

"Thank you." Faulkner disconnected, and then strode down the passageway, looking neither left nor right, but at a point in space six inches in front of her nose. When she reached her underway cabin, she returned the salutes of the NI sentries outside her door and entered.

Once inside, with the hatch resealed, she sat down on her bunk, her body rigid and trembling, and allowed the tears to come.

**

She dreamed again, of fire, chaos, and noise. Something had a hold of her around the waist and was trying to draw her into the flames. She awoke to the insistent beeping of her comms console, her groggy mind taking a moment to process that she was not being entangled by the tentacles of a monster; it was only her vac suit, unsealed to her waist, in which, like everyone else aboard, she had to try and sleep while under the elevated material condition she herself had ordered. The apologetic voice that spoke on the comms circuit once she had slapped the receive button belonged to Aguilera. "Skipper, the shore party should be making contact in a few minutes, I thought you'd want to be the first to know what they have to say."

"Thank you, Commander. I'll be right there."

On the overhead audio system, the voice of the young siren from the Gendarme detachment could be heard speaking. "*Agamemnon*, this is shore party Sierra Six Romeo, sitrep follows. Unsanctioned Indigo level project ongoing on the surface. Sierra Six advises interdiction may prove necessary. Plan is to embark Swordfish and return to base with one—standby *Agamemnon*."

Faulkner frowned. *Unsanctioned Indigo project? Indigo classification by definition means a security or defense related project initiated at the highest levels of government. How can a classified government project be unsanctioned? How does that even happen?* Faulkner felt a sudden chill grip her insides, as the likeliest explanation occurred to her.

They've gone rogue. Son of a bitch. Hirayama, or some faction within the corporation has gone outside the wire with some kind of classified biotech or something, and the fucking admiralty suspected it and didn't tell me. They left me in the dark. Again.

"Interdiction?" Aguilera had sidled up to her while she was lost in dark thoughts, and it seemed clear from his tone he was burdened with his own. "What exactly does that entail in this context, do you think? Sending the MarDet to crash into some C-Level suite and slap cuffs on the executive leadership of one of the most powerful megacorps in the Commonwealth?"

Their exchange was interrupted, and Faulkner's attention was drawn back to the moment, as the speakers crackled to life once more. Again, it was Anthem speaking, but this time an undercurrent of fear ran through her voice, which sounded breathless and shrill. "Archangel, Ghostcat. Do you copy? I am taking fire, one hostile confirmed, engaging in CQB on the comms tower at the top of the gulch, time now! Get your ass up here."

The sound of weapons fire could be faintly heard in the background, among other sounds that Faulkner couldn't identify. The comms watch glanced up at her momentarily a look of confusion on her face, then she opened the channel once again and replied, requesting the shore party to re-transmit. Aguilera leaned in close to speak to her in a quiet tone, "They want to RTB with one...what? And who the hell is 'Archangel'?"

Faulkner shook her head. "One of the shore party. I don't know what their call signs are, ground-pounder protocol is different than ship-to-shore. She must have keyed the wrong channel. As far as what the 'one' thing is they plan to return with, I guess that will have to wait until we re-establish comms. Suffice to say, that transmission you heard was the sound of the investigation taking a pretty dramatic turn."

"Shall I have the MarDet standby for deployment ashore?"

"Affirmative. No action to be taken yet, just tell Kamarov to get them hot. They should be mostly suited up already, but if they aren't, get them into battle-rattle."

"Aye aye." He paused, then added, "It looks like you were right about this trip."

"Yeah, sucks being right all the time."

Aguilera inclined his head before moving off to do as ordered. Faulkner turned back to the comms watch. "Try and get her back, Miss Decker. Do you still see her suit transponder?"

"Aye, ma'am. But she's not on the tight-beam connection anymore, she must've switched to the local net and then forgot to switch back. I'll keep hailing."

"Very well. Call the bridge, have the maneuvering watch be prepared to get underway with minimal heads-up time. We may be leaving our parking spot in the near future, depending on how events unfold."

"Aye, ma'am." Decker seemed somewhat anxious but moved quickly to comply. *Good,* Faulkner noted, *falling back on her training.*

Faulkner stared into the holographic tank, as if seeking something there that was missing, not quite sure what it was. After a moment, she shook her head. She would figure it out eventually, the missing pieces would fall into place. All she knew for certain was that one of their team on the ground was being fired upon, and the situation in orbit pointed to saboteurs on her ship.

Just because you're paranoid, doesn't mean they aren't out to get you.

11

Queen's Gambit Accepted

Tengoku, The Iota Persei System

Cass knelt on the floor in front of the airlock next to Enora, as Skye's hands moved deftly over her battle armor seals, removing first the helmet, then the left pauldron. "You hanging in there, Anthem?" Skye asked conversationally, as she set the pauldron aside, eyeing the exposed shoulder joint with professional appraisal, and then set about efficiently unlatching the cuirass, and pulling it away from Enora's sweat-drenched body.

"Mmm ok." Enora mumbled in response, and swallowed several times, as if to moisten her throat.

"I should have gone with her to watch her back," Cass growled.

"Not your call, Broz," Skye replied as she worked, and glanced up at the pacing figure of Garnett, who was arguing animatedly with someone on his comm-link. "The Boss figured it was a one person job. Ours is not to reason why."

Cass snorted. "You do realize that line is from a poem about a horrific military blunder that resulted from poor communication, right?"

Skye shrugged. "Everyone's a general once the battle is over. Broz, give me a hand here." She unsealed Enora's bodysuit to her belly and peeled it away from her shoulder. The site of the wound was dark and bruised, and rivulets of tacky blood covered her left breast and her ribs down to her waist. "I'm going to cut this away, so we don't need to move the shoulder. When this crusted sealant comes away, the wound may start bleeding again. I'm gonna need you to wipe it clear, so I can see what's going on."

Enora, more lucid now but still in pain, looked up at Cass and said with mock severity, "Petty Officer Broz, I hope you aren't getting the wrong idea, now. I do not intend, as a matter of course, to have members of the unit remove my top just so you can wash me. I'm not that kind of girl."

Cass, caught somewhere between amusement and embarrassment, grinned. "Shut up, Petty Officer Anthem."

"I believe our time in rating is exactly the same down to the day, Petty Officer Broz. You don't get to give me orders."

"I'm going to give you a second Purple Heart, you mouthy minx, if you don't pipe down so Skye can fix you up."

"You two are cute," Skye said in a tone of voice that suggested the exact opposite was actually the case. "Grab that gauze and get ready." As she continued her work, she said without looking up, "Since you're the entertainment tonight, Broz, maybe you can regale the patient with one of your gunslinger stories from the old country. Those are usually good for a fractured humerus. Wipe here."

"Is it bad?" Enora asked, tension returning to her voice.

"Like I said, damage to the upper humerus, labrum is torn, you got a flechette lodged in the bone. I'll get that out in a sec. Your armor absorbed a lot of the energy, lucky for you. It's nothing a few weeks of rest and regen won't fix."

Cass looked up as Alfred walked over from where he had been in consultation with the lone security officer to have arrived on the scene, and turning to give Enora a modicum of privacy, squatted to address Cass. "Medics are on the way. The Cox'n is on the line with Dornier. I guess he's 'shocked and dismayed' by this unfortunate turn of events, and naturally he has no idea who this character could have been that attacked Enora."

"Naturally not."

Alfred stood again and moved a short distance away, clearly wishing to make himself useful but at a loss for how. When Cass turned his attention back to Skye, she was gazing into the distance, saying nothing, her hands momentarily still, and Cass knew she was interacting with the medical diagnostic features of her own DNI grayware.

"Okay," she finally said, pulling a set of forceps and a pair of small vials from her kit. "I'm going to try to remove this flechette. Enora, this is going to hurt, babe."

"Oh, good. I hope I really do get a Purple Heart."

Skye smiled curtly and glanced at Cass. "Get ready to wipe."

Enora reached out with her right hand, feeling for Cass's own free hand, and grasped it fiercely.

"I...I shot that guy in the back," she whispered, her voice quivering.

"Well, to be fair, Alfred says you got him in the front too."

Enora laughed, but the sound was forced, frenetic. Then she howled, her back arching, as Skye reached into the wound with her forceps.

"Wipe!"

Cass wiped, the gauze coming away red and sticky.

"I killed him." Enora sobbed, her voice broken and raw. Tears streamed down her cheeks. "I fucking killed him, Cass."

Cass looked down at his friend—saw the pain and naked emotion in her face, her usual bravado burned away—and his chest grew tight. He knew she'd done exactly what she was trained to do. It didn't make it any less awful. Few people understood that better. "I know, honey," Cass murmured. "I know." He held her hand until the medics arrived.

***

"We got a DNA sample, right?" Cass asked Alfred in hushed tones as the medical technicians raised the gurney that would carry Enora to the colony's hospital facility.

"We sure did."

"Good. Like as not this guy was on Dornier's payroll. That oily bastard has the eyes of a reptile, and Atsuko made it pretty clear that he's in on whatever is going down here—which I have no trouble believing. I want his ass in an interrogation chair."

"Well, I expect his ass will be right here very shortly, but getting it into an interrogation chair may prove problematic. To put it bluntly, we're outgunned right now and not in a favorable tactical position. If we run a DNA check and it turns out this guy was a Hirayama employee, we still don't have anything conclusive that says he was acting under orders. Maybe he just snapped, went space crazy. You were a Territorial Ranger, you know how extreme environments get to people. That's what they'll say."

Cass grunted. "Can't Garnett, as the senior Gendarme on the scene, provisionally invoke 1120 on the grounds that these corporate dirtbags are actively impeding our investigation?"

"What, and ask for the MarDet to come down and storm the place?" Avery whistled, shaking his head as he considered. "Man, I don't know. I'm not sure Faulkner would even go along with it—she doesn't seem like a fan of the Cox'n. Not to mention, the legal basis for that seems awful shaky. You really think Atsuko's playing it straight with us? The data she showed paints a disturbing picture—I'm not saying it doesn't—but it isn't exactly conclusive."

Cass's expression darkened as Alfred spoke. He was growing irritated with the direction his friend wanted to take this conversation, and he wasn't sure why. Alfred continued in a rush. "A bunch of inter-office mails, some video footage you can read two ways..." He shook his head and raised his hands. "I'm just saying—it takes a lot of unsubstantiated narrative from Atsuko to fill the gaps, and she comes with serious baggage. The company lawyers will have a field day with her if she winds up on the stand—Daddy's little princess or not."

Cass paused to collect himself. *Why am I so damned defensive about Atsuko?* he thought. *Alfred's right. I just met her. I'm a trained law enforcement professional; I know how to analyze witness testimony dispassionately. So why do I want to believe her so badly, when believing her means accepting something I don't want to be true?*

"Yes. I believe her," Cass said at last. "I think this attack makes it pretty clear someone's worried about what she's leveled — or plans to level — against some of the people here."

"Okay, fair point," Avery said. "But we're staking a lot on her word if we decide to push this against one of the 'Wealth's biggest companies. Maybe this Lundgren guy could put some nails in their coffin, but he ain't here, you scan me? We better have our shit carefully assembled before we do unto Mr. Dornier what we did unto his boy outside Atsuko's place."

Cass's brow furrowed in thought. "Speaking of Daddy, where is he in all of this? Do you think he knows this Project Seraphim is still ongoing? Atsuko didn't seem too clear on that. If he didn't know before, why didn't his pal Dr. Lundgren tell him at some point, since he's obviously not comfortable with all of this? And if the distinguished and wealthy Mr. Hirayama *does* know about it then what can he be thinking, letting his company get mixed up in something like this? There is a lot here that I still haven't gotten my head around."

Alfred nodded in agreement. "Like, why did our anonymous bad guy take a shot at Enora in the first place? Was it to stop us from having our private talk with the *Aggie*? They have to know we'll just try again."

Garnett, having stopped to exchange a few words with Enora before she was wheeled away, joined the two men and interjected, "I don't think he was supposed to engage her at all. Anthem says he had some kind of snooping gear up there with him. He was probably just supposed to lay low and listen in on her transmission. They want to know what we know, whoever 'they' are." He looked at Cass and added, "This is on me. I'm the on-scene commander, and I made the call to send her out there alone. It seemed an acceptable risk, given what I knew at the time. I underestimated the enemy's resolve. I won't do that again."

Cass held his gaze a moment, then nodded. "Understood, sir. I wouldn't have thought it likely something like this would happen either."

Garnett grunted. "As your CO, I do not, of course, owe you all an explanation for the orders I must give, even when such orders hazard our personnel. This is why we get paid the big bucks; to put ourselves at risk for the greater good, etcetera. I just wanted you to know that I do not hazard any personnel lightly. Try to bear it in mind, Mr. Broz. I am no happier to see young Anthem get hurt than you." He paused, then added, "And yes, I am going to put her in for a Purple Heart."

Cass repressed a grin. "You have excellent hearing, sir."

"I do. The best money can buy." Garnett turned as an electric cart slowed to a halt nearby, its occupants dismounting to approach the airlock. "Ah. Mr. Dornier has decided to grace us with his august presence—and he's brought his pet lawyer. Fantastic."

Dornier had indeed arrived, flanked by a pair of security officers and with Paulson in tow. Cass observed the security chief closely and noted how his eyes constantly scanned the area as he walked, as if assessing possible threats and avenues of egress. His jaw was set, in the manner of someone who was preparing for confrontation.

As Enora was secured in the back of the ambulance cart, Dornier seemed to pointedly survey the scene, his hands on his hips, projecting a non-verbal message that Cass read as *what's going on here?* He couldn't suppress an odd thought, that everyone present at the airlock at that moment were like performers in a drama that had thus far gone over poorly with the audience, and nobody liked their role much anyway.

Paulson strode up to face Garnett, reaching out almost reflexively to shake the other man's hand in a gesture that struck Cass as ingratiating and tone-deaf. He then spoke in his customary smarmy tone, "Officer Garnett, the leadership team is deeply concerned and saddened to hear of this incident. I just came from a meeting with the Director and she asked me to convey her best wishes for Petty Officer Anthem, and her hopes for a speedy recovery. Rest assured, our security folks will be launching a thorough investigation into this, including a review of our security protocols for screening contractors, vendors, and visitors to the facility." Dornier smirked slightly but remained silent.

"Thank you, Mr. Paulson, I'm glad to hear it, and I'll pass on the Director's kind words to Petty Officer Anthem. However, I would hope that the scope of your investigation would also extend to Hirayama Enterprises employees, as well? If there is reason to rule out the possibility that Ms. Anthem's assailant was in fact employed by your firm, I haven't been made aware of it."

"That's unlikely," Dornier broke in, his gravelly voice carefully neutral. "Employees at a facility like this one naturally undergo stringent vetting processes and background checks, and are forbidden to possess or access firearms, except when duly authorized by the Security Department."

"Yes, that was my very line of thinking too, Mr. Dornier."

Dornier's lip again made the tiniest of upward quirks, as he replied, "Whatever are you implying, Officer Garnett?"

Paulson frowned and cleared his throat. *Looks like he doesn't want Dornier going off script*, Cass thought.

"Of course, all possibilities will be considered. Mr. Dornier has the leadership's full confidence," Paulson interjected perhaps more forcefully than he'd intended. "We take security very seriously here, and we place the safety of our employees and guests at the very forefront of everything we do here." Cass wondered if Paulson had placed the smallest bit of emphasis on the word *guests*.

Behind him, Skye murmured, "Yeah, here at Gene-Splicing Incorporated, safety is priority number one."

"Pardon me?" Paulson asked, his brow furrowed.

"Oh, nothing."

Cass, growing weary of the byplay, interjected before Paulson could resume his legalistic ablutions, "You will of course notify us as soon as the perp's ID is confirmed? We got a DNA sample plus the telemetry from Enora's armor, and we will be conducting a parallel investigation, you understand."

"Naturally," came Dornier's raspy reply. "You'll be the second to know. Hope you don't mind if we send it over the comm-link, I'd have one of my guys run the report up to your rooms, but I'm afraid I'd find him disarmed and tied up in a closet."

Cass gazed at the taller man without flinching, his eyes, invisible beneath his darkened goggles but nevertheless boring into those of Dornier. "Not at all. Not unless he tried to kidnap one of us or lock us in our quarters without a warrant, and without even proffering charges."

Dornier chuckled, as Paulson's troubled face turned from one man to the other, trying to gauge the right moment to interpose himself and arrest the escalating tension. "Tough guy," Dornier remarked as if to himself before continuing, "The princess must've really tugged on your heart strings. Is that what she told you? We had Rapunzel locked in a tower for no good reason at all?"

Paulson, his face a mask of slightly befuddled, polite professionalism, bobbed once. "Yes, unfortunately Ms. Hirayama was being erm—chaperoned, for her own safety. She has been acting erratically, beginning with her ill-advised publications on Earth. Since arriving here, she has shown great emotional volatility, possibly stemming from chemical abuse and other long abiding psychological issues."

"Oh..." Cass drew in a breath in feigned shock, "She's crazy. I see. Of course. Funny thing though, we didn't notice any medical professionals or orderlies when we showed up to interview her, just one fat rent-a-cop outside her door. That's quite the twelve-step program you got her in."

Dornier was plainly preparing to speak, but Paulson interposed himself smoothly once again. "I assure you, Petty Officer, our records will show that she has been undergoing psychiatric evaluations over the course of the last several weeks, and that the results of those evaluations may cast into some doubt the credibility of any statements she may have made regarding the unfortunate final journey of the *Euphrates,* not to mention any spurious and wild accusations she may have leveled against her father's company as a result of her ongoing... personal struggles."

Cass grimaced. "There he is. The dirtbag lawyer reveals himself at last. I'm sure your records *will* show that, yeah."

"At ease, Mr. Broz," Garnett murmured. "I think this little conference has continued long past any usefulness. Mr. Paulson, we will be wrapping up our primary investigation soon, and the Commonwealth would appreciate your continued diligent cooperation with that effort, and in the matter of the criminal assault on Enora Anthem which occurred on your employer's premises. In the meantime, I need to see to my wounded, and get my team focused on preparing our preliminary findings. If y'all will excuse us?"

Paulson's head bobbed again. "Yes, of course."

Dornier watched them depart, and Cass saw the crooked half smile was back.

***

As the team exited the elevator on their floor of the hotel, Garnett motioned Cass to join him. Striding up to the door of the room Atsuko had been sharing with Enora since they had taken her into protective custody, he knocked softly. "Time to talk to the heiress again, get a few things nice and straight."

The two men stood and waited a few moments. Garnett frowned and knocked again. "Mr. Ramirez? Ms. Hirayama? It's Garnett."

Another interval passed before Garnett withdrew his datapad from its pocket and, keying in a short sequence, unlocked the door. As soon as he heard the soft click of the magnetic lock disengage, Garnett drew his sidearm, prompting Cass to do likewise. Garnett eased the door open with his foot, cautiously peering within. Cass could see that the lights were on but heard neither movement nor voices.

"Go."

Cass moved past Garnett, his weapon high at the ready, and cleared the bathroom adjoining the entryway, then the main room. The limp form of Coxswain's Mate Ramirez lay draped over a bed, his head back and eyes closed. Of Atsuko, there was no sign. Garnett moved into the room behind him, and holstering his weapon went to Ramirez. "Ramirez!" He said loudly, prompting no reply.

Garnett felt the other man's throat for a pulse, stood back and visually examined him, and then grunted. "He's alive." He placed his hand on Ramirez's chest and took on the glassy-eyed look of someone interacting with the implant display in his mind's eye. "Shallow breaths, I'd say he's been drugged. Maybe a benzodiazepine."

Cass looked around and noted the hotel water bottles that stood upon the nearby end table. Several had been opened, and one lay spilled on the floor. On the small round dining table in the corner of the room, sat the remains of a light supper. "So," Cass asked his superior, "do we report that Atsuko's been abducted? Or is that just putting the foxes back in charge of guarding the henhouse?"

"I think we have to." Garnett looked around the room. "No sign of a struggle. So...she drugged him and fled, or someone drugged the water bottles and or the food and got them both."

"You know what Dornier's bunch are going to say. The troubled heiress is acting crazy again. But there is no way she did that. She was dying for some way to get out from under the thumb of Dornier's thugs. She practically begged us to take her into protective custody; she had no reason to run from us. They grabbed her, you know they did, sir." Garnett had spoken in response, but his voice was drowned out by a sudden ringing in Cass's ears, and a momentary but intense flash of pain blossomed in his temples.

"Broz? Broz! Are you okay?"

"Yes, sir, I—I don't know I just had a—I'm fine."

Garnett eyed him suspiciously, but seemed content to let it drop. "Our DNIs should have gotten us access to the local security comm-net, at least the officially sanctioned part of it. Let's get the whole gang together and ready to move, then we're gonna phone this in and see what happens."

***

While Skye worked to revive the insensate Ramirez, the rest of the team gathered in their commanding officer's room and listened as Garnett spoke to Dornier about the missing Atsuko. The conversation had been going much as Cass had expected it would.

"So, you're saying she escaped from your custody. Maybe you should have put a guard on her door."

"Mr. Dornier, I'm not interested in bandying words with you. I'm telling you that a witness in a federal investigation is missing, presumed kidnapped, and I am reminding you of your obligation under the law to help find her."

"I am well aware of my obligations under the law," Dornier's voice growled from the speaker. "More likely in my mind, is that she drugged your pilot and took off. She has issues with authority figures, you see. I'll put out a BOLO on her. When she turns up, I'll let you know."

After the comm-link ended, Garnett activated the counter-surveillance features of his datapad and turned to the rest of the assembled team. "Alright. Young Ms. Hirayama is the boss's only daughter, our star witness with respect to both our official and clandestine investigations, and she is a huge embarrassment and liability to whoever is running this illicit bioweapon project. Let's see how anxious Dornier is to find her. Broz, what's going on the security comm-net?"

Cass used his datapad rather than his implant display to monitor the traffic on the colony's official law enforcement network. He found focusing on the internal visual interface while having a real-world interaction too difficult to manage most times, and preferred to read and input large amounts of data on a physical device.

"So far, it's all routine."

"So, no high priority BOLO on Atsuko Hirayama."

"As of now, no."

Alfred spoke hesitantly, "Sir, the habitable area of the colony ain't that big."

"Just as 'ain't' is not a word. We've had this conversation," remarked Skye from the bed across the room.

Alfred continued as if he hadn't heard her, "Maybe he just figures it's no big thing, because there aren't that many places she can really go. She's got to have some high-end civvie grayware we could track?"

Garnett sucked his teeth, then blew out a long breath. "I feel the probability that Dornier is acting in good faith here is vanishingly small at this point. As for her having grayware onboard we could potentially track, probably. But the law is very clear on such matters; we need an authorization code to track her that way, and of course we'd need to get the details on her grayware if she has any. That means bouncing an FTL message off the comms relay, and time we may not have."

Skye spoke clinically but couldn't entirely hide her feeling of dread when she interjected, "Assuming that they haven't killed her, and physically disabled it."

"She's not on the colony." Cass heard himself say.

The room grew silent.

"Explain," said Garnett sharply.

Explain. Right. It made perfect sense just a second ago. Cass took a moment to collect his thoughts. "Okay, she's our star witness, like you said, sir. So, they want to get her away from us. If they don't find her soon, we get antsy and call in more manpower, like marines. We start poking around their top-secret labs even more, turning over rocks they don't want turned. Sure, they could kill her, I guess, and throw her body in a pool of liquid methane, but that doesn't get rid of us. It leads to more questions, more scrutiny. That, and she's the Big Man's daughter, whether they like it or not. So, I don't think that killing her is option 'A,' but just hiding her in a back office only works for so long. No, they need to make her disappear, but in a way that will lead us to conclude in the proper timeframe, that we know how it went down, and that there is no point in hanging around here busting their balls about it anymore."

He focused his gaze on Garnett, sudden certainty gripping him. "We need to see if any spacecraft have left port in the last few hours."

Garnett's face grew grimmer, if such a thing were possible. "Maybe the troubled young heiress 'stowed away' on a transport, and sadly Dornier's bunch won't figure it out until she's beyond our reach, you mean. Such a shame. Yeah. Fortunately, we have privileged access to the spaceport systems as well, thanks to Ms. Anthem's efforts."

He tapped a few commands on his datapad and grimaced. "A cargo lifter departed about an hour and fifteen minutes ago, for rendezvous with the *Hermes*."

"That merchantman that was in orbit when we first got here? She's still here?" asked Alfred.

"Yes, or was, just recently. Maybe she was waiting for something."

Cass slammed his hand down onto the end table next to him hard enough that something cracked. "She's on that ship, sir! I know she is."

Garnett nodded briskly. "We'll go with your intuition, Mr. Broz. But first, I need Ms. Tanahill to get Ramirez in shape to walk. Flying seems out of the question, but I can do so at need. And you, you need to get down to the sick-bay and bust out Anthem."

Skye had just administered a hypo-spray to Ramirez who coughed loudly, rolled over and then promptly vomited. She turned her head to look at Cass as he stood to leave and said, "Let me join you. If their hospital is anything like the others I've seen, the hardest part of her recovery process is likely to be checking out. Having a medic along may circumvent some of the bullshit paperwork and save you from having to shoot someone."

12

It Sucks Being Right

CNS Agamemnon, The Iota Persei System

A knock on the hatch-coaming put an end to Faulkner's most recent abortive attempt at sleep. She paused long enough to wash her face and make herself at least vaguely officer-shaped before meeting whatever crisis awaited, then called, "Enter."

She was soon greeted by a grim-faced Commander Aguilera. "Sorry to bust in, Skipper, but I just learned two important pieces of information in about as many minutes, and I was in the neighborhood, so I figured I should report on this in person."

Faulkner rubbed her eyes and sat behind her desk, a leaden feeling in her gut. "Okay, let's hear it."

"Firstly, Longfellow copped to sabotaging the cooler. He has a kid with an MCE, living on Earth. Someone threatened to out the kid as a genetic offender unless he played a little harmless mischief with the fridge. So far, no names."

Faulkner let out a breath. "Why do I feel like that was the good news?"

"Because the other news is, we re-established contact with the shore party, and they are aboard their pinnace and inbound right now. Commander, GenDet," he referred to Garnett by his formal billet, "is officially reporting an abduction and transportation of an abductee, across interplanetary space." Aguilera used very precise, legalistic wording, which Faulkner recognized instantly, as conveying special significance. "He further reports a possible act of piracy ongoing, both of which involve the *Hermes*, which just pulled out of orbit. He goes on to accuse a number of undisclosed parties on the planet below of involvement in alleged acts of conspiracy and sedition against the Commonwealth, and requests us, and you specifically, to interdict the *Hermes* in connection with these allegations, forthwith. That last bit is pretty much verbatim."

Faulkner sat very still, her thoughts racing. She realized she'd been silent for some time when Aguilera shifted uneasily in the doorway.

Make a move, Ada. Put emotions aside—there can be no doubt this is rodeo time. And if it isn't—if Garnett is wrong—then you can throw those bullshit orders right back in the faces of the board of inquiry when they haul you up in the dock.

She tapped a rhythm on the desk with her fingernails, her face hard with resolve. "Tell Garnett, request understood. As soon as his boat is aboard, we will break orbit. Have the Quartermaster of the Watch calculate a least-time intercept on *Hermes* and advise Engineering we will be getting underway shortly."

Aguilera nodded sharply, her obvious sense of purpose seeming to energize him as well. "Aye aye."

After Aguilera left the compartment, Faulkner sat staring at the opposite bulkhead for a moment, then she rose with a groan. She pulled her vac suit all the way up and slid her arms inside, sealing it.

As she passed through the CIC, she spotted Aguilera conveying her orders. She motioned him to the holo-tank and strode forward toward the ramp that led up to the elevated area at the front of the large CIC compartment, where the communications watch sat. This mezzanine-like area was frequently called the "signal bridge" as a homage to the wet navy term for a place where seamen hung visual signal flags on ocean-going ships.

Directly behind the watch-standers' consoles, in the center of the forward bulkhead, were the sliding transparent doors that partitioned the CIC proper from the area still known officially as the bridge—another callback to earlier days—though it was now buried in the safest part of the ship. On a modern warship such as the *Agamemnon*, this space was where the Officer of the Deck, or the commanding officer if the situation warranted, would steer the ship.

Unlike its namesake from old wet navies on Earth, however, the bridge of the *Agamemnon* had no windows. Instead, it was shaped like a dome, or more precisely, three-quarters of a sphere, bisected vertically by the decking on which the bridge crew worked, a platform that seemed to jut out into the darkness of space when the ship was underway. Its smooth, curved bulkhead served as an enormous panoramic display screen that in many ways mirrored the holographic tank in the CIC, except that the display was viewed from within the sphere, not from the outside. Its layout offered a 270-degree horizontal field of view, allowing the officer in the command chair to see in almost all directions around the ship, except dead astern. The dorsal and forward sections provided a nearly 270-degree vertical view, while a concealed quarter below the command chair and watch stations remained hidden from sight by the decking.

Objects in near space such as other spacecraft could be annotated, and their courses plotted on the display, affording the bridge crew a sense of spatial and tactical awareness more natural to the human brain than relying solely on small, two-dimensional displays. NI sentries snapped to attention at her approach, and the sliding doors slid aside with a barely audible *whoosh*, as she swept past them and into the dark space beyond. *No more time for doubts now.*

As the bridge crew took note of her arrival, someone loudly spoke, "Commanding Officer on the bridge."

Faulkner strode to the command chair and addressed the Officer of the Deck, who happened to be Mendoza. "Lieutenant Commander Mendoza, I have the deck, I have the conn."

Mendoza swung her articulated display monitors aside and rose from the chair proclaiming, "The Captain has the deck. The captain has the conn." In a softer voice she spoke at Faulkner's left elbow while her superior sat and reconfigured the displays to her liking. "Ma'am, we are at 2,025 kilometers altitude. The ship is at material condition yoke. Maneuvering watch confirms we are at automatic station-keeping, propulsion reports ready for burn. IEMARS reports no new contacts, other than the comms relay, Master One, the freighter *Hermes*, designated Master Two, and our own pinnace."

"Very well."

Faulkner motioned to the Boatswain's Mate of the Watch, a veteran spacer she had known longer than almost anyone aboard. "Chief, pass the word, General Quarters, interdiction action soon to be underway."

The grizzled spacer nodded and responded with a simple, "Aye aye." He manipulated a control on the panel before him, and then the floor path lights on the bridge, as elsewhere on the ship, dimmed and turned to the foreboding red hue of combat illumination.

The sound of a simulated boatswain's whistle resounded through every compartment on the ship, followed shortly by the chief's authoritative baritone, *"This is no drill, this is no drill. Now General Quarters, General Quarters. All hands man your battle stations. The flow of travel is forward and up to starboard, down and aft to port. Set material condition zebra throughout the ship. Combat pressurization will be set to zero-point-three*

ATM. Prepare for hard acceleration and combat maneuvers. General Quarters, General Quarters. All hands man your battle stations."

A pulsing, tritone klaxon rang out, and everywhere aboard the ship, crew members were sealing their vacsuits or battle armor, donning protective gear, and preparing the vessel for action. A faintly audible hiss indicated the air in the compartment being partially drained away, leaving barely enough atmosphere to support human life. This would reduce the violence of a decompression event in combat but leave a safety margin in case crew members had their vacsuits compromised. To the left of the command chair where she sat, Faulkner heard a watch-stander sing out, "Defense-grid energized, point-defense and ECW systems green."

"Acknowledged."

A red message pulsed in time with the klaxon on the forward portion of the display dome, seeming almost to float in space.

ALERT: GENERAL QUARTERS

A spacer came by and placed Faulkner's helmet on its rack beside her left arm. She grabbed it and donned it as regulations demanded, activating its built-in life-support systems and speech amplifier. Her HUD flickered as she automatically joined the CIC comm-link network; the ship had already transitioned to general quarters.

The coarse voice of the Bosun's Mate of the Watch blasted across the bridge through his helmet speakers.

"Let's go, people—lids on! If I catch one of you passed out at your post, I'll wake you myself, and you won't like how. This is no drill!"

Almost as soon as the helmet was sealed, Aguilera's voice spoke calmly in her ears, "Captain, all department heads report battle stations manned and ready. I show condition zebra has been set throughout the ship, we are pressured at point three atmospheres."

"Very well."

Faulkner gazed at the small situational display on one of her monitors, where the icon that represented Sierra Team's pinnace, approaching from below and thus invisible on the display dome, was about to merge with that of the *Agamemnon*. "Time to recover Swordfish Flight?"

"Three minutes, Captain."

"Distance to *Hermes?*"

"Three point four two light seconds," came the reply from Mendoza, who had moved to the station reserved for the Bridge Tactical Officer, her normal position when standing watches. "She doesn't accelerate worth a damn, fortunately."

"Communications, hail the *Hermes*. Tell her...tell her we need to perform a spot customs inspection, owing to the sensitive nature of the research on the planet. Standard procedure."

A few moments later the response had arrived. "Captain, the skipper of the *Hermes* says they have no outbound cargo except mail. He wants to know why he is being 'singled out' for inspection. He sounds uh, pretty annoyed."

"Does he? How sad. Put this on the speakers in CIC, I want the XO to hear this. Give me a direct channel at my chair."

"Aye, aye, ma'am, patching you through."

Faulkner punched a control on the display mounted to her command chair. "*Hermes*, this is Fleet Captain Ada Faulkner of the *Agamemnon*. I understand there is some concern on your end about this inspection, it's simply standard procedure, I assure you."

The surly and slightly distorted reply came several seconds later, owing to the distance between the two vessels. "Standard my ass. I've made this run a dozen times, and the Navy never saw fit to interfere until now. We are practically empty, there's very little to inspect unless you people are censoring mail now. This is government overreach, pure and simple. We have places to be, you know."

Faulkner considered her reply for a moment. "Captain, you've been in orbit for days, without taking on cargo, and now I'm hearing you are both practically empty, and in a great hurry. I am having difficulty reconciling those things."

"I'll bet you are!" Came the terse reply.

Faulkner keyed another control. "Combat, Bridge. Commander, are you monitoring this?"

Aguilera's voice responded a moment later. "Affirmative. He's stalling. He knows if we want to overhaul him, we will. He's playing for time, but why?"

"Good question. Have Garnett report directly to me on the bridge when they are aboard."

At that moment, Mendoza called out, "Bosun reports we are now recovering spacecraft aft."

Aguilera, meanwhile, had acknowledged and broken the connection.

"Understood," Faulkner replied to Mendoza without skipping a beat, "helm, is your course laid in? I want a least time intercept."

"Aye, course laid in, ready to execute at the captain's discretion."

"Very well. Prepare to take us out of orbit. Maximum military power is authorized. Get us out of this damned gravity well. Bosun's Mate of the Watch, sound acceleration warning, ten seconds."

A whooping alarm filled the air, followed by the BMOW's voice on the ship wide '1MC' channel, *"Now hear this, acceleration alarm, hard acceleration in one zero seconds. Brace, brace, brace."*

The ship's inertial compensators would do their best to nullify the felt shift in gravity as the cruiser leapt forward, but at her maximum acceleration of 22 g, there was inevitable bleed-through, sufficient to cause injury to humans caught unawares. A shot clock appeared on the forward sector of the main display, as it had on numerous displays throughout the ship, and began counting down from ten. The alarm resumed and continued until the shot clock turned to red zeroes.

"Engage engines now. Ahead flank."

There was a momentary sensation of forward movement, and Faulkner was pushed back into the gel cushions of her chair.

"Signals, advise the master of *Hermes,* if I have to come run him down, I will be very ill disposed to overlook any violations of interplanetary commerce regs. He is to heave to at once, cut acceleration, and prepare to be boarded."

From the comms station, the voice of the young ensign on duty could be heard repeating Faulkner's order. *"Hermes,* from Commonwealth Naval Warship *Agamemnon,* you are ordered to heave to. Cut your acceleration to zero, remain on your present heading, and prepare to be boarded. No further discussion is to be entertained, acknowledge."

Ten seconds passed. Then twenty, then thirty, and still no reply came. "They're going to run," Mendoza said incredulously, "aren't they? Why?"

"We may have a hostage situation, and potentially a hijacking, Ms. Mendoza. I need everyone to stay frosty, I'm not sure yet where this is going, but an opposed boarding action is looking likely. This is what you all trained for. Let's earn our pay. Make sure Commander MarDet is advised, we may require his services today."

"Aye, ma'am." Mendoza, normally cool and reserved, looked uncharacteristically nervous. The Naval Infantry branch of the USCS was not formally styled Marines, but their role was nearly identical to that of their maritime predecessors. Much of the old terminology had survived in unofficial use: an individual was still called a Marine, and a shipboard detachment a MarDet. To summon the NI now—rather than leave the matter to the embarked Gendarmes—meant a likely boarding action, and shots fired in anger.

Faulkner observed the tactical display with displeasure. They had begun their burn at virtually zero velocity relative to the departing freighter, and while their maximum acceleration far exceeded that of the *Hermes,* it would still take close to an hour to catch them at the freighter's current velocity and acceleration.

A few moments later, she heard the NI sentries admitting someone through the aft-facing doors, and she turned her head in her seat to see Garnett, and his surly-looking Jotun petty officer heading toward the command pedestal. *Bratz? Broz? Something like that.*

"Senior Warrant Officer Garnett, reporting to the Commanding Officer as ordered, along with Petty Officer Broz."

Faulkner looked him up and down. "Put your helmets on, we're at GQ." Garnett had the grace to look chastised, as he and Broz re-sealed their battle armor helmets. "Want to tell me what the hell is going on here, Cox'n?"

"At the risk of getting court-martialed for talking out of turn, I think I can say that elements of Hirayama Enterprises, who may or may not be acting on orders from their executive leadership at some level, are engaged in ongoing unsanctioned research involving a biological weapon of mass destruction. Atsuko Hirayama, the daughter of Benjiro Hirayama, has critical information regarding this, and she is very likely on that freighter, and not voluntarily."

Faulkner stared. After a moment she chuckled, without humor. "Well, isn't that just dandy. Can I assume this is what you and your team of commandos, or whatever they are, have really been sent here to investigate?"

Garnett said nothing for a moment and then spoke quietly. "Oh, we investigated the destruction of the *Euphrates,* I assure you, Captain. She was torpedoed. I couldn't mention it before due to OPSEC."

Faulkner felt a sudden chill grip her. "By *whom?*"

"Unknown. No other vessel was in evidence on the telemetry logs, until the torpedoes went active. They seemed to come out of nowhere. Even that limited data was sanitized in a comprehensive hack job in order to make it look like an accident. It wasn't easy to suss out. Captain, my team needs to get onto that ship and ascertain the whereabouts and condition of Ms. Hirayama. It is not an exaggeration to say it is a matter of Commonwealth security."

"I have the Marines suiting up for a boarding action, Lieutenant Kamarov was planning to run the op, I believe."

"Captain, I'd like to handle this one. The NI could back us up, but I assure you that my section has been selected based on their qualifications for such an action. I think the available members of Sierra team, plus one of our two support squads should be sufficient."

"So, the whole section are actually secret commandos then?"

Garnett smiled. "No, only the Sierra Team SMU are secret commandos. The rest of the section are veterans of the Customs Service with a badge in anti-piracy ops. They have been hand-picked for their ability to keep their firearms aimed in a safe direction, and several can even walk and chew gum at the same time. Suffice to say, they are all high-speed, low-drag."

Faulkner snorted. "I'll assume that's really good. Very well Cox'n, overall operational command of this shitshow is yours, but the Lieutenant will be accompanying you, with half a platoon. I believe you will all fit in one pinnace, and it's not negotiable. His folks will provide support if needed and liaise with *Agamemnon*. They will not participate in any sort of illegal bloodbath, and they will provide an accurate accounting to me, of just what transpired during this operation. Understood?"

Garnett nodded gravely. "Understood, Captain."

"Your bad guys show no sign of slowing down. Do we think the crew of the *Hermes* is in on this sinister plot, or do they all have guns to their heads?"

Garnett shook his head. "Also unknown, I'm afraid."

Faulkner pursed her lips in thought for a moment. "I'm going to speculate that it's the former. They've been hanging around in orbit doing a whole lot of nothing since we got here, and for a freighter like that, time is money. They seemed to have finished loading and unloading days ago. They haven't taken on more reaction mass either, so they aren't heavy. If I were you, I'd assume the crew is in league with your kidnappers, and they were just waiting around for this one special shuttle."

Garnett nodded slowly. "Makes sense. All that being said, I tend to concur."

"You have about forty-eight minutes, until we are within optimal intercept position. Before you go, I want whatever intel you got on this torpedo incident, so my tactical people can have a look, and see what they make of it. This news concerns me greatly."

Garnett nodded, glancing at Broz.

"Will do, Captain. I'll see that Ms. Anthem runs that data down right now. Also, I was hoping she could have a seat in Combat somewhere, so she can help us with SIGINT and technical support from here, she was wounded as you may recall, and her shoulder is no good for a boarding action. Also, I erm — I actually would like to request the services of an NI command pilot, mine was drugged down on the planet by parties unknown and isn't fit for duty."

Faulkner raised an eyebrow. "You mean Coxswain's Mate Ramirez? He seems to spend a lot of time in the sickbay. It sounds like he has a delicate disposition. Isn't that a bit odd for an aerospace pilot?"

"He's having a rough week, yeah."

"Mmm. Very well, that's fine on both counts. Now, go. Good hunting. I'll have the NI notified of the new command arrangements."

"By your leave then, Captain."

Garnett braced, then spun on his heel smartly, and made to leave the bridge with Broz in tow, so Faulkner turned her attention to other matters. *Best to leave the haunting to the spooks,* she thought, *on the other hand, if this situation on Tengoku is somehow related to an attack on civilian shipping, then this whole mess has just taken on a new complexion.*

She reviewed the data on her command console, which showed the time to intercept *Hermes* slowly ticking down. After several minutes alone with her racing thoughts, she spoke in the general direction of Mendoza, "any aspect change on the *Hermes?*"

Mendoza conferred with the Astrogation watch-standers and compared their readings with hers before replying, "Negative. No change in aspect. Master-One is still on the same out-system heading, zero-one-two by positive zero two-five true, she's still accelerating at one gee. They seem happy to just pretend we aren't here."

Faulkner nodded. In space of course there was no magnetic north as there was on Earth, so by widely agreed-upon convention "true bearings" used Galactic North as a reference—specifically, the radio signal emitted by Sagittarius A*. The *Hermes* was beating a path toward the impingement zone surrounding the so-called "hill sphere" of the star system, where the gravitational incline of Iota Persei and its attendant bodies would flatten enough to permit use of FTL jump systems.

A few moments later Mendoza spoke again, "Swordfish flight is away."

"Time to target?"

"Six minutes plus or minus."

Faulkner grunted acknowledgment, her eyes now on the tactical display forward. "All stop. We're going to pull ahead of her pretty quickly, let's not leave the boarding party in the dust. Let's give them some time to see how things are going to play out over there. Be prepared to flip the ship for deceleration burn."

"Aye, aye."

Almost as soon as the order had left her lips, the sound of Aguilera's voice crackled to life in her helmet. "Conn, Combat. We just picked two anomalous electromagnetic field events starboard, Navcomp doesn't know what to make of it. Two short blips on one magnetometer, then gone. Possibly artificial."

Faulkner considered a moment. "Run it through Battlecomp. I'd like—" her chest grew tight, as realization dawned on her "—Wait, two short-lived, artificial looking magnetic fields? Were they about 60,000 gauss each?"

She heard Aguilera inhale sharply before replying, as his train of thought caught up to her own. "Mag catapults? But how?"

"Maybe. I don't know. Standby."

Muting her comm-link connection, she spoke to the helmsman, trying to keep any hint of a tremble from her voice that might betray her fear. "Helm, belay that last, ahead standard, *now.*"

Switching back, "Tom—"

"Skipper, Battlecomp concurs, high probability that the events were cycling missile launchers, recommend we go defensive immediately."

As if to underpin his words, another voice blared over the 1MC, "*Conn, IEMARS, contact! Two high-gee detections starboard, contacts are four point six light seconds out and CBDR, assess as hostile fire. Vampire, vampire, vampire!*"

"Conn, Weapons, I concur," came the voice of Traxler on the voice network.

"Tactical concurs," came the brittle sounding voice of Mendoza, "vampire threat profile suggests they are milspec anti-shipping torpedoes. Earliest time to intercept, one-eight-three seconds. Recommend we go active on ECM."

"Do it."

Faulkner gazed at the main display dome, where two red, caret-shaped icons had appeared where nothing should be, and moved toward the position of the *Agamemnon.* Callouts next to each indicated their increasing speed and acceleration. Having been propelled from their tubes by electromagnetic catapults at a force of 50g, they had now engaged their own motors and would accelerate relentlessly toward their target at a rate no manned spacecraft could match.

Faulkner swore under her breath, as she contemplated who or what the hell could have fired them, and how best to evade them and neutralize future threats, when their enemy seemed able to remain invisible to some of the most sophisticated integrated detection systems the Navy possessed. She knew that there were a few ways a spacecraft could achieve a degree of stealth, but each had very serious limitations and none seemed applicable here.

One problem at a time, Ada. We need to pick up speed.

She made a quick assessment of the situation on the display, which showed the torpedoes approaching from starboard-high on a tangential intercept, already moving toward *Agamemnon* at 138 meters per second squared, and coming on hard. "We don't have enough V to juke them at this range. Helm, maintain heading but bring us to flank speed in ten seconds and begin anti-missile evasion with maneuvering thrusters. Weps, program PDC grid for maximum density fire, launch countermeasure drones at your discretion."

"Aye aye," came the responses. The acceleration alarm whooped again. Faulkner was vaguely aware of the BMOW's voice on the 1MC announcing torpedoes inbound starboard. On the plot, she saw the ship's previously predictable trajectory begin undulating like the path of a snake through sand, making tiny lateral changes to complicate the targeting logic being calculated by the torpedo AIs. As both hunter and quarry began moving at ever increasing fractions of light speed, the targeting picture could become complicated by time-late sensor data, and the helmsman of the *Aggie* was doing his best to make it even harder to determine the cruiser's exact position in space at any given time.

"Ms. Mendoza, I want you keeping a close eye on every torpedo launch and get ready to draw me a picture on the plot, there's going to be a lot of them, I'd bet. They have to rely on torpedoes if they want to stay invisible."

Mendoza looked momentarily confused, then nodded. "Of course, to make a gun run worth it they would have to paint us with active targeting sensors to get a good lock, and then we would see the radiation."

"Unless their passive IR and optical sensors are really good," muttered the watch-stander next to her. "Forty-five seconds to impact, mark."

"ECM?" queried Faulkner.

"No joy," responded the electronic warfare officer, his voice cracking. "They keep burning through!"

"Point-defense firing," Lieutenant Traxler sang out, "maximum density program." Sensing incoming targets in their effective range, clusters of high-powered lasers on the outside of the ship's hull with overlapping fields of fire, were laying down an invisible torrent of sizzling ultraviolet beams in an attempt to knock down the incoming torpedoes.

Faulkner realized someone on the voice net was quietly weeping. A moment later, Mendoza spoke again, the timbre of her voice rising with excitement, stress, or both. "First inbound vampire down! Hard kill! The other is juking—it's getting awful close."

"Helm!" Faulkner commanded, "come port now, hard over, and continue evasive. Bring us to two-seven-two by positive zero-two-zero."

"Helm, aye, new bearing two-seven-two by zero-two-zero."

The ship lurched, and Faulkner could hear her structure creak and groan as the inertial compensators struggled to negate the devastating effect such a violent course change would ordinarily have on equipment and personnel. She was slammed hard into the right side of her harness and knew anyone who was moving about the ship unsecured at that moment had almost certainly been hurled into a bulkhead or other solid object with dangerous force. Somewhere, she heard a structural alarm plaintively beeping.

"As soon as she steadies out, give us ninety degrees port yaw on the thrusters so our broadside PDCs can come to bear."

"Steady out, then nine-zero degrees port yaw, aye!"

"Probable impact in one-five seconds!" Someone was shouting.

"Kill! Second vampire is down; debris spray might get us... incoming!"

"Sound collision!" Faulkner shouted, but before anyone could reply, she felt her chair tremble and quake violently, and a shudder ran through the entire compartment, everything in her field of vision began to jump and vibrate. A sound like gravel being hurled into a steel trashcan reverberated through the air, and then the collision alarm was blaring.

13

Boarding Action

Commercial Vessel Hermes, The Iota Persei System

Cass watched with wry amusement, as Alfred once again checked the bindings on his K-80 Mjölnir designated marksman's rifle where it rested in its storage bracket, seeming to take all the fastidious care of a new father strapping his infant into a car seat for the first time.

"This kind of sucks, don't it?" Alfred asked nobody in particular.

"Doesn't it," replied Skye Tanahill.

"Yeah, man. I'm tired of the inside of this damn boat. I'm tired of spaceships, honestly. And that hotel bed was real nice. Better than my rack on the *Aggie*."

"Doesn't it," Skye reiterated, "this kind of sucks *doesn't it?*"

Alfred shook his head, his broad, expressive face the very picture of patient, long-suffering umbrage. "Girl, I don't know why you gotta be that way."

Cass chuckled. "You afraid somebody's going to steal your gun, Alfred?"

"Never hurts to triple check. This bad boy is a hell of a rifle, but it makes a decent club too. You don't want to find out the hard way. I once saw a kid get nailed right in the melon with a full ammo pouch that belonged to his buddy. It was during a deployment just like this. Well," he amended, "kind of like this. Pilot had to accelerate all of a sudden, guy's gear wasn't squared away...pow." He illustrated by punching his left fist into his right palm. "Knocked his ass out cold. Pretty sure it damaged the relationship too. Loose gear on the float is no joke."

Cass grunted. A moment later, Garnett appeared at the flight-deck door, braced himself with a stanchion and called out loudly, "All right, all hands give me your eyes and ears."

Twenty-seven pairs of eyes turned to regard the Senior Warrant Officer. In addition to the three healthy operators of Sierra Team, they had brought along a full squad of Gendarmes from their support section, and two squads of naval infantry, all in battle armor and with full combat loadouts. The *Hermes* ostensibly had a crew of ten, but Garnett apparently wasn't taking any chances.

"Sorry, there wasn't time for a briefing before we mounted up, but events are unfolding rapidly. Situation; the heiress to the Hirayama family fortune, Atsuko Hirayama, has been abducted from the colony on Tengoku, and we have reason to believe she is on the *Hermes*. She is in possession of information vital to Commonwealth security, and we believe she was abducted by unknown actors, to ensure she and her information cannot become an asset to the Government. I will be sending her picture out on the tac-net shortly.

"We do not know if the crew of the freighter is abetting her abduction willingly, or if the vessel has been hijacked, but assume the former. The manifest says ten crew but there may be additional tangos, number unknown. How they are equipped is also unknown. They haven't tried rolling the ship or pulling any other hijinks to foul up our approach, so we are going to grapple a port-side airlock and use the docking collar for a speedy ingress.

"I will exercise overall operational command of this action. The Gendarmes will stick their noses in first and, if these people want to be civilized, we will present them an order to submit to inspection. Needless to say, I'm not holding my breath."

There were a few nervous chuckles, and no few smirks. The NI were used to being the sharp tip of the spear, and Cass suspected that going aboard a potentially hostile vessel behind the Gendarmes was not exactly how they were accustomed to doing business. The fact that Kamarov technically outranked Garnett probably didn't help either, though Garnett, he had recently learned, did actually hold a reserve naval commission and Kamarov himself seemed sanguine about the arrangement.

"The NI under Lieutenant Kamarov will follow on. First Squad will proceed forward, Second Squad aft. Your objectives will be to secure the conn and the reactor room, respectively, as per standard procedure. The Gendarme squad will carry out a search of the vessel. Sierra Team will function as a reserve and will assist in the search once the vessel has been secured.

"A schematic of the *Hermes* has been pushed out to you, please review it. If our ingress is contested, we will be in a pretty tight spot, so we may need to push out aggressively fore and aft, to establish a secure perimeter around the airlock before we proceed to clear the rest of the ship. Questions?"

"Rules of engagement, sir?" One of the NI squad leaders queried.

"We will be weapons tight. If you're fired on, or see unarmed civilians about to be, respond with appropriate force. And bear in mind—this looks like an abduction. It may become a hostage situation. Treat it as a rescue and don't shoot the person we came to save."

The sergeant nodded.

"Ok, three minutes, boys and girls. Lock and load."

Cass was reaching for his own K-12 carbine, when, through his helmet audio system he heard the familiar voice of Enora Anthem on the Sierra Team tactical channel. "Sabrehawk this is Ghostcat, do you copy?"

Garnett had closed his visor, but Cass heard his voice on the comm-link. "Ghostcat, Sabrehawk. Go ahead."

"Sir, the XO wanted me to tell you not to count on the *Aggie* for cover right now, we—we're under attack."

"Specify."

"I can't, I'm not sure what's going on, but we have two torpedoes inbound and the ship is ducking and weaving, I don't think anyone knows who is doing the shooting. It's just like what happened to the *Euphrates*, sir."

There was silence on the channel for a moment, then Garnett's voice returned. "Copy that. Keep us advised, over."

"Will do. Be careful, I mean um, good hunting. Ghostcat out."

Cass keyed his own comm-link to address Garnett, "Sir, I find the timing of this attack most...inauspicious."

"Inauspicious?" Garnett asked dryly. "Son, you sound like a southern boy sometimes. Is that your way of saying you smell a rat?"

"Affirmative."

"Me too," Garnett replied. "Keep your head on a swivel. I don't know of an auspicious moment for one's mothership to come under fire, but I concur with your assessment. Much as these folks on *Hermes* seemed to object to our company, they haven't done much of anything to delay our arrival. A suspicious man would say they'd prefer to have us in there than out here, and that does not bode well. I'm sure that by now, Kamarov has heard the latest news through official channels. I'll let him decide how best to broach the subject to the grunts but, just between us, if you see anyone over there doing anything at all naughty, assume the trap is closing and act accordingly. I get paid to explain things like this to the higher ups, and I don't mind doing so when I'm still riding that high from not getting killed."

"So, you're saying shoot first and let God sort 'em out?"

Garnett chuckled. "You a theist, Broz? Now you really sound like a southern boy. I think you know perfectly well what I'm saying. When the feces impacts the air circulation system, there will be no doubt in your mind. You're going to smell it. When that happens, just do your job, and don't overthink it. You scan that?"

Not knowing what else to say, Cass just nodded and gave the only response that felt appropriate, "Yes, sir."

***

"We're in. Cycling airlock now!" Petty Officer Schilling pressed a control on her datapad, and the outer airlock door began to slide open. The Gendarmes hovering behind her raised their weapons to cover the entryway, as a swirling mist began to billow into the docking collar.

Cass, hanging on to a stanchion in the second rank, tensed, awaiting his turn to push down the tube of the docking collar and into the waiting ship. The decision had been made to maximize speed of ingress over safety, by pressurizing the docking collar while the airlock of the *Hermes* was open, thus allowing the entire length of the flexible tube plus the airlock chamber itself to equalize in atmospheric pressure with the environment inside the freighter. When this was done, the NI troops and Gendarmes would deploy into the tube, and then the hatch on the pinnace behind them would be sealed, to minimize danger to their own vessel.

Then, the cyber-security specialist with their support squad would override the inner door of the airlock, allowing the entire boarding party to breach the *Hermes* at once, without risk of depressurizing the inner compartments of the freighter, and without waiting for the airlock to be loaded and cycled multiple times. There would still be an awkward moment when each member of the boarding party passed within the artificial gravity field of the freighter, and this would slow their entry somewhat.

As he watched the environmental readout on his HUD, he could see the pressure in the tube increasing with agonizing slowness, and realized he was fidgeting. *Just like old times. Stay cool, stay loose.* Unbidden, another thought intruded into his silent mental preparations, and he keyed his comm-link. "Ghostcat, this Lawman, do you copy?"

He waited in anxious silence for several seconds, receiving no reply. "Ghostcat, Lawman do you copy?"

Finally, a strangely distorted and staticky reply came, "Lawman, Ghostcat, go ahead."

Cass cleared his throat, his sudden relief at hearing his friend's voice quelled when he recognized the fear in it and then tried to think of something sensible and pertinent to report, to rationalize what he now realized had simply been his own desire to make sure she was still there. "We are in position here, about to breach the inner airlock door. We haven't heard a peep from *Hermes*. What's your status?"

"We...we're hit. I don't really know how bad, I don't want to get in the way and ask someone, and the damage control system is still getting updates. I think a torpedo blew up next to the ship."

A third voice abruptly cut in, and hearing it was Garnett, Cass realized belatedly that he had been talking on the team tactical channel, and of course Garnett, and his other teammates would have heard.

"Ghostcat, this is Sabrehawk. If we can get a hardwired connection to the freighter's central network, can you patch in via the pinnace and do something on your end to express our displeasure with the caliber of hospitality we've been receiving from our hosts?"

There was a moment's silence. *I wonder if he has a plan here,* Cass wondered, *or if he's just trying to give Enora something to do.*

"What did you have in mind, over?"

Garnett's voice returned, "Can you shut off the artificial gravity on my signal, over?"

Another pause, then, "Probably, Sabrehawk. Call me back when you have a hard-link, I'll see what I can do. The security measures on that bucket can't be all that great, unless the bad guys have been doing some renovations."

"Understood. I'm sure their network-security is in no way ready for you, Ghostcat. Standby, we'll be in touch. Sabrehawk out."

Cass, sensing that this exchange was now officially over, switched back to the platoon channel, and soon heard the voice of Schilling, the cyber-security specialist who crouched only a few meters ahead of him in the doorway of the airlock, "pressure is about equalized, I'm ready on the inner door, sirs."

"Sierra Six Actual, this is Alpha Six Actual, we're a go back here."

Ah, that would be Kamarov.

"Do it."

Cass braced himself to move, and a moment later he felt Alfred's hand slap his right shoulder, in what he assumed was encouragement. The airlock lights went from dirty white to amber, perhaps in some visual form of protest against Schilling's interference in its proper functioning, and then the inner door slid open with surprising speed.

"Third squad, go, go, go!" bellowed the voice of the petty officer in charge of the Gendarme support squad. The Gendarmes having already been staged in the airlock itself and subject to the freighter's artificial gravity field, poured quickly through the inner door, their carbines leveled, targeting lasers visible in the dim light of the airlock and the storage area beyond. As they did so, Cass and Alfred pushed forward in the zero-gravity space of the collar, grabbing onto the stanchions mounted on all sides of the airlock door, and swinging their legs inwards to allow gravity to capture them and pull their feet to the deck, before hauling the rest of their bodies through the aperture.

Garnett's voice, amplified by his suit's audio system, could be heard to boom through the narrow space, "Commonwealth Customs Service, get down on the deck! This is a lawful interdiction action! Resistance is a violation of Article Five of the—"

The rest of Garnett's announcement was cut off by the harsh rasp of automatic gunfire, and not the kind that came from pistols, Cass noted. He immediately spun and plastered himself against the forward airlock bulkhead as near simultaneous callouts began coming in on his comm-link, "Contact Left!" followed by "Contact Right!"

Alfred's amplified voice came from across the airlock, where he had taken cover in the corner opposite Cass, "Welp, guess they plan on doing this the hard way."

"It would seem so." Cass peered around the coaming of the inner hatch, and raised his carbine, seeing flashes from across the next compartment and to his right. From his vantage point, he could see several shipping crates stacked up in front of a cargo elevator, and next to it, what he knew should be the top of a stairway that led down and aft into the cargo holds. The stair itself, as well as the lower half of the elevator, were obscured by the crates which had no doubt been positioned in such a manner as to provide cover.

The Gendarme squad was splitting up and moving forward and aft along the bulkheads, keeping in motion and plastering the crates and anyone foolish enough to present a body part with withering, full-auto fire, very much aware they were in a precarious tactical position, and with no viable fallback point, save the airlock itself. Falling back to the airlock meant the enemy would be firing right through the open hatches and into the docking collar, which would have dire consequences both for the mission, and the personnel in the long, articulated tube, which was only about a centimeter thick and now pressurized to one atmosphere.

Cass had a sudden flashback to his anti-piracy training in Norfolk, where the instructors had referred to the docking-collar as a "people sausage". The image was disturbing but apt, and he had been thoroughly drilled on the naval doctrine in these situations, which said that once they opened the inner airlock door, the first and only real option was to get it behind them, at all costs. While the boarding party all wore sealed battle armor, a significant breach or several breaches in the fabric of the tube could cause it to rupture violently, spewing its occupants into the void of space as the atmosphere within the collar and the freighter sought to escape.

Cass added his own carbine to the weight of fire being poured into the makeshift fortification he could see, knowing full well that on the left (or rather forward) side of the utility compartment, there was another hatchway he couldn't see, and doubtless more enemies positioned to ambush the party as they exited the airlock. Several hostiles were in partial cover directly across from the airlock, hiding behind the bulk of a cargo loader, and doubtless positioning themselves to get good tactical data on the boarding party as they came through the airlock. Out of the corner of his eye, Cass saw Skye and Garnett swing through into the airlock, move apart left and right, and squat to bring their own weapons to bear.

"First and second squads, move up," Garnett barked into the platoon channel, "all hands go to infrared, I'm popping smoke in three. Ack-Ack, give me smart rounds on target ASAP. We need to get out of this kill box."

Sending a quick mental command via his DNI link with his armor, Cass switched his helmet visor to infrared mode, anticipating the grenade that would fill the area with a cloud of thick smoke. Already the local tac-net was populating the HUD in his helmet with identifying icons that designated known or putative enemy positions. Alfred, wielding the Mjölnir, would select targets and illuminate them with his armor's targeting system and fire his counter-defilade 'smart' rounds, effectively small self-propelled grenades that had the ability to alter course and track a target even around cover and through the smoke.

Moments later, as the NI Marines began to swing into the airlock, Cass saw the smoke grenade sail past him and activate, gray billowing clouds erupting from behind the parked cargo loader, where the grenade had struck something and rolled to a stop. Mere seconds after the smoke began to appear, Cass heard the integrated grenade launcher on the Mjölnir *chuff*, and a tiny light like a firefly trailing dark wisps of vapor arced into the compartment beyond, curving downward and to Cass's right before disappearing behind the stack of crates. An authoritative bang marked the detonation of the 25 millimeter munition, and Cass saw the crate stack shift slightly from the resultant blast wave.

Third squad, meanwhile, had borne the brunt of the ambush bravely, but not without consequence. Cass saw two flashing MEDICAL EMERGENCY overlays on his visual overlay, hovering over the crumpled forms of Gendarmes on the deck, and saw an icon indicating a third, hidden from view by the hatch coaming, was dead.

The boss was right, these guys have good guns, good gear, and they wanted us right here where they could meet us on their own terms. I guess this constitutes the shit hitting the fan.

Cass waited until the last NI Marine from first and second squads had passed him, and then, seeing that Garnett and Skye were still providing covering fire with their own weapons, Cass dove through the hatchway, heading toward the aft bulkhead of the compartment, crouching low. His center of gravity was naturally lower than that of most Earth-born human males, and he moved with what others often found to be surprising speed when sprinting.

He saw a spark, and felt a slight shiver run through his body as a round ricocheted off his left pauldron. It didn't slow his charge. As he reached the stack of plasteel cargo crates that had concealed Alfred's target, he made no effort to pull up short but instead pumped his powerful legs to propel him directly into the crates, leaping into the topmost layer of the stack at the last minute with his legs folded up under his arms, and his chin tucked into close to his armored chest.

His body slammed into a crate, knees and forearms first, and while the crate he'd struck was too heavy to be empty, it was not so heavy that the mass of his armored body propelled by the power of his Jotun physique, couldn't push it over. Man and crate toppled over the wall onto the side where their adversaries still took cover, even as one of the Marines moved around the wall of obstacles to flank them.

Cass somersaulted headfirst into an armored enemy he had seen on his display, crouching nearby the one whom Alfred's round had struck. Cass kicked his stunned and off-balance adversary in the hips with both his feet, while still prone atop the tumbled crate. The (mercenary? Smuggler?) flew backward and fell hard onto his rump. His weapon, jarred loose by the impact with the decksole, spun away from his grasp. Cass was dimly aware of the flashes and muffled reports of carbines to his right and saw a vicious close-quarters gun-battle developing between shadowy figures marked with bright tags in his HUD, but his focus was on the challenge directly before him.

He rolled to his feet and saw through the roiling smoke with his infrared enhanced optics that the prone man he'd kicked was reaching for a pistol strapped to his chest harness. Without conscious thought he raised his carbine and fired twice into the armored figure's torso, and once into the hardened, aluminum oxynitride visor. The recoil from his carbine was barely perceptible in the armor, but the figure of his enemy jerked violently, and then became still. *I should feel something right now,* part of Cass's mind told him. *Fear, or regret maybe?*

Later.

Cass turned his attention to the other hostiles on this side of the makeshift barricade, found them overwhelmed by the flanking Marines and marked COMBAT INEFFECTIVE by his sensor suite.

The one targeted by Alfred's smart round was dead, his armor in pieces on the deck and spattered with emergency sealant and gore. The one he'd shot himself was likewise dead, and three others lay sprawled on the deck unmoving. Skye had advanced to one of the wounded Gendarmes and knelt by her trembling form, obviously accessing the wounded woman's medical data feed, as her hands found their way to the trauma kit she carried. Across the compartment, he saw the Marines had likewise cleared the barricade that blocked the hatchway leading forward, noting that the tac-net indicated at least two hostiles had retreated through that hatch and sealed it behind them.

They fought, if not to the last man, then pretty damn close. Not typical for hired goons who kidnap rich kids for financial gain. Who are these people?

A female voice Cass didn't recognize spoke on the platoon channel, and his DNI identified the speaker as the squad leader of the second NI squad. "Clear aft."

A moment later another voice, male this time, responded, "Clear forward. Two tangos got out and sealed the hatch. It's powered, we're gonna need to hack it, or crack it."

"Hack it," spoke Garnett's voice in his ear. "I wanted a hard link anyway, and airtight interior hatches are typically wired right to the environmental control system."

"Aye aye."

As the cyber-warfare specialists set to work on the sealed hatch, Garnett addressed Cass, his voice still coming over the platoon channel. "Broz, you take Avery, and Dawson's Gendarme fireteam, head aft behind second squad. While they secure the power room, I want you to clear everything else abaft of frame forty, compartment by compartment. See if you can find the girl. I'll take the rest of the gang forward once we're past this whole door kerfuffle and do the same. Get some peepers out, the cargo hold is a big space probably full of obstructions, so you may get some use out of them. If you get into a shitty situation, call me and if needed, do not hesitate to draw on second squad for support. Questions?"

Peepers? Cass was momentarily puzzled by the nomenclature before it clicked. *Ah, recon drones. Right.*

"None, sir."

"Very well, then git. Good hunting."

Cass nodded, then motioned to Alfred Avery and Petty Officer Dawson to join him before seeking out the squad leader of the second NI squad.

He found her leaning against a bulkhead, slapping a fresh magazine into her carbine, while her squad kept a wary eye on the aft stairway. The tag floating over her head in his HUD read *RAWLINGS, T.*

"You heard, Sarge?"

The Marine NCO nodded, her armored helmet giving the gesture an uncanny, robotic quality. "Yeah, we're gonna clear a path to the heart of the castle, you guys will be following along to poke in all the dark corners and maybe find the captured princess. Or possibly, just a shit load of empty cargo containers."

Cass guffawed, "Yeah. That would be just my luck, honestly."

Rawlings straightened, glanced to her right, and pointed toward the grillwork stairway—the ladder, in spacer parlance—that led down into the belly of the freighter. "That's problem number one. The cargo hold. Taking the elevator seems like a bold move, and the ladders go down to a raised catwalk, and then another exposed ladder. We'll be completely visible and hanging our asses out the whole way down. Looking at the plans, I don't see any other way to move further aft without going through there. The crew spaces and work areas are mostly forward. There's nothing back there but the engineering spaces, dry stores, and the boat deck. The main hold takes up the whole width of the ship, and there's nothing above it but reaction mass tanks and other inaccessible bits of spaceship gubbins."

Cass nodded, as he peered carefully through the open hatchway into a cavernous space, containing tall storage racks and pallets of containers. He considered the tactical situation himself. *We can send in peeper drones to get an overhead look at the whole compartment, but if the bad guys are in there and they have anti-drone tech, they'll quickly disable them. They may have put everyone they had on the airlock defense, but maybe not. If they do have an ambush prepared for us down there, we need to present them with more than one problem at a time.*

Cass looked across the loading bay, to see that the cyber-ops specialist, Schilling, was crouched by the access panel next to the sealed hatch leading forward, and bundled fiber optic leads ran from the panel to her kit.

"Well, I guess we are gonna have to see just how good their gear is. Our comrade on the *Aggie* may be able to help level the playing field. Standby one."

He switched channels, and then spoke, fervently hoping he would receive a reply. "Ghostcat, Lawman do you copy?"

A long moment passed and Cass's anxiety began to build, then the shaky voice of Enora Anthem came on the channel, "Lawman, this is Ghostcat, affirmative."

"Ghostcat are you into the freighter's systems yet? We could use some technical support if you catch my drift."

Enora seemed to perk up at this, her voice taking on some of its characteristic ebullience, "oh yeah? You want I should turn off the gravity?"

"No," Cass replied quickly, "no, no. That would be a bit precipitous at this time, and the bad guys all seem to be in combat armor anyway. How about the lights?"

Several seconds passed before she replied, "the lights?"

"Yes, all the lights in the cargo hold. Emergency lights, everything. I want it pitch black in there."

Another delay followed. "Ghostcat, do you copy? How are you hanging in?"

"Sorry," she finally replied, I think we are getting pretty far from the *Hermes*, and it feels like we are running hell-bent for leather. I think there's a time delay, wait..." her voice seemed to fade momentarily before returning, "we are almost half a light minute from your present position and accelerating hard, away from you. I don't mind telling you, it's getting awfully intense around here."

Cass licked his lips as he sought for some reassuring response that wouldn't seem trite. "Well, that's the life of a space pirate, I guess."

"Yeah," came the delayed reply. Enora's voice seemed distant. "Security protocols overridden, I had a script from when—um, I had a script already that took care of it. I almost wish it had been more challenging because it might have taken my mind off things. Sending the command now, give it a minute or so to get there. Lights out in cargo area. Be careful."

"You too, and thanks. Lawman out."

Cass took a deep breath, then switched to the tactical channel his ad-hoc team would be using. "Okay, Enora's going to switch off the lights in there in about a minute. They'll switch to IR or UV or something, but it will still make it hard to spot the peepers. I figure we can get an idea of who— if anyone—is down there and where, before they find a way to deal with the drones."

"Sounds outstanding," Rawlings drawled, "armed with that information we can assess our tactical options. Unless...you're taking charge of this band of adventurers, Petty Officer Broz?" She looked the question at Cass.

Cass shook his head in the negative. "No, Sergeant, I do not share my CO's penchant for subverting the chain of command, I'm perfectly capable of following your lead, within the constraints of my orders."

Rawlings laughed, a pleasant almost girlish laugh. "I hope you aren't suffering any insult on behalf of Kamarov. The Lieutenant is only slumming it with us grunts on the *Aggie*, because he heard a rumor in the officer's club that heading up the MarDet on a deep space cruise is a sure-fire way to get his ticket punched. People have started calling him 'Buck Dodgers' when he isn't around. With him, the buck stops somewhere else. He's probably thrilled your boss is willing to take accountability for this op. If it goes bad, it won't be a black mark on his record, and his trajectory toward a sweet desk job somewhere on Earth remains unaffected by any unpleasantness, like dead civilians."

Cass, momentarily taken aback, cleared his throat and replied in his best deadpan, "I appreciate your candor, Sergeant."

"Don't worry," she replied cheerily, "that wears off pretty quickly. It's been about 45 seconds, let's get our peepers out, and see what we see."

Alfred and Petty Officer Dawson, having silently observed the interaction up until this point, looked at each other. Both chuckled audibly, before activating the tiny drones concealed in the gauntlets of their combat armor. As Cass moved to do the same, Rawlings addressed the marine squad, "NCOs only for now. The rest of you, keep your peepers in reserve, we may need them later."

As Cass unsheathed the cassette of tiny drones from his own armor, two bumblebee-sized robots stirred to life at his mental command and took to the air. In that same moment, a metallic snap sounded from the direction of the cargo bay. The lights beyond died, leaving the space beyond the wide hatchway in total darkness.

Rawlings moved up next to the hatchway and placed her back against the bulkhead. Cass, examining his virtual display, saw that his two peepers, and those deployed by his comrades, had already identified three infrared signatures. They appeared to be subjects in combat armor, covering behind a large cargo container. The tiny drones were equipped with acoustic echolocation technology that allowed them to "see" obstacles in total darkness, provided there was an atmosphere to propagate sound waves, and they moved with very little noise to survey the entire cargo hold from above. Cass heard Rawlings speak in a booming voice both in his helmet and from outside it, and realized she had employed her voice amplification system, making herself heard throughout the entire area.

"Hello, criminals! This is the Commonwealth Naval Infantry Corps. Article Five of the Interstellar Commerce thing, blah blah blah. Surrender immediately or we will happily kill you. Please signal your understanding by throwing down your arms and stepping into the open. My interpersonal skills are underdeveloped, and you guys shot one of my best friends, so please make this interaction short and sweet, or we will proceed immediately to Plan 'B'."

Cass snorted. *I'm betting it's going to be Plan "B".*

"Maybe you should have let me deliver that speech, Sarge?"

Rawlings looked at him, her expression bland through her visor. "Why?"

Cass opened his mouth to reply, but a sudden eruption of intense pain behind his eyes made him forget his words. *Again? What the hell?* His head swimming, Cass put his hand out, feeling for the bulkhead to stabilize himself. The pain began to fade, and he realized belatedly that Rawlings had been speaking, but couldn't seem to recall what she'd said. He felt as though just momentarily, he'd been somewhere else. *A narrow space, between shelves with labeled bins, boxes and cartons strapped down with cords...the familiar flimsy packages that O2 scrubbers were usually stored in. A parts room?*

"Broz!"

A strange, high-pitched squeal filled his ears, and he shook his head trying to clear it, but the squeal remained. "Gah, what the hell is that noise? Is it just in my head? I feel like I just got hit in the cranium with a hammer!"

"Check your HUD," Rawlings advised, concern clear on her face. "SADS. They deployed SADS to kill our peepers. I've never seen it do anyone in like that before, though. Seems like they've chosen not to view my surrender demand favorably. Such a shame."

SADS? Yes, of course. Sonic Area Denial System.

Rawlings was speaking again, "are you good to go?"

"Yeah," Cass responded, shaking his head one last time and taking a deep breath. "Good to go."

"Well, without the telemetry from the peepers, I guess smart rounds are a no-go."

"Wouldn't have been a sound idea regardless, Sarge," Alfred chimed in, "The deck of the cargo bay is right over the ventral inner hull plating. With our luck, we'd blow a hole through it with HE rounds and decompress the whole section. Little holes we can assume will get plugged with emergency sealant; big holes are a problem. On the other hand, the frangibles wouldn't do great against that battle armor anyway."

"Oh, yeah. Right. So, we throw some Roman Candles in and go in hard. Bounding overwatch?"

Cass nodded. "Bounding overwatch. We can cover from the first catwalk if you want to go in first with your gang."

"We're the NI, of course we're gonna go in first. This time." She grinned. "Did everyone copy that? Flash bangs out, then we're taking the stairs. Rocket Cops have the overwatch. Set optics to UV for now, and activate illuminators, sound off."

A chorus of "aye, ayes" acknowledged her order and she nodded in satisfaction. "Okay. Sparky, Green, Roman Candles on Infrared. Wait for my command then we go in three."

The marines Rawlings had called out, began to position themselves to throw.

"Are we sure they aren't using UV themselves?" Cass queried.

Rawlings shrugged. "It's a coin toss, I guess. They obviously have some top end gear, but infrared is by far the more common low-light band in civvie stuff, even law enforcement stuff, so it seems a good bet."

The so-called Roman Candle Cass was intimately familiar with, having used it in his time with the Rangers. An evolution of the basic flash-bang grenade, it had been engineered as a compact, deployable device that, when triggered, emitted powerful radio-frequency noise and rapidly cycled through intense bursts of light across various spectra, including visible and infrared or ultraviolet, creating a dazzling and disorienting effect. These bursts were designed to overload sensors and temporarily impair the vision of those relying on enhanced optics without causing permanent damage. Also, like its namesake, it emitted a single long, loud, unnerving, high-pitched shriek. The difficulty here lay in determining which optical band the enemies were using and how best to deploy the grenades to cause maximum confusion among their adversaries while leaving their own forces unhindered.

"Yeah," Cass concurred slowly, "seems like. Good Call, Sarge."

"I'm so glad you approve," she replied. "Okay. Ready boys and girls? Roman Candles out! Go in three...Two...One... Now."

14

Don't Give Up The Ship

CNS Agamemnon, The Iota Persei System

C *alm. First and foremost, be calm.* Faulkner took a deep breath, before keying the comms unit in her helmet. "DCC, Conn. This is the captain. Report. What's broke?"

The voice that replied was unfamiliar to her, one of the newer, junior petty officers that had joined them at Unity Station, she assumed.

"Captain, debris strikes have compromised one of the starboard He-3 tanks. We've got containment breaches. He-3 leakage is causing significant thermal anomalies in the environmental control and gunnery compartments on the starboard side, amidships. It's going to strain our life support systems, and lead to potential overheating and air filtration issues. Additionally, that tank normally serves as reserve reactor fuel, and that cross-feed to the reactor had to be closed. No immediate impact on power generation or propulsion, but we've lost a lot. We have outer and inner hull penetrations obviously, still assessing the extent."

Gunnery spaces? Not good. "How are the starboard point-defense clusters?"

There was a pause before the voice returned, "Uh–"

Only to be interrupted by another voice, one she recognized as a senior chief that usually worked the first watch. "Captain, this is the Damage Control Assistant. The tank rupture is going to impact the cooling of the starboard point defense lasers, no question. We're working on it, but it's going to take some time to get everything back online."

Spectacular, Faulkner thought her mouth twisting into a grimace. "I don't think I need to tell you how bad we're going to be needing those PDCs, Chief."

"No, ma'am, you do not."

"Good. Get it done. I'm going to be increasingly busy over the next few minutes; coordinate damage reports with CIC."

"DCC, aye. Coordinate with combat, fix the PDCs. Most rickey-tick."

Faulkner cut the connection and then addressed Traxler, who had responsibility for the operation of the PDCs, "Weps, how do the temperatures look on the PDCs right now?"

"Not terrible, but in the yellow. We ran them hard," came the reply.

Faulkner sat back and exhaled slowly, viewing the curved expanse of the bridge display. *Where are you, you bastard?*

She considered the fact that BuShips, the Government, not to mention uncounted armies of engineers and assorted eggheads had been trying for decades, if not centuries, to solve the equation of true, workable stealth in space warships. It couldn't be done, they said, not really. That was the consensus. It certainly had been her whole adult life, as far as she knew.

Yes, you could paint a ship in light and radar absorbent coatings. Yes, you could "lie doggo" and remain hidden from most sensors, by controlling the emissions of your comms equipment and such. But you couldn't keep your power plant hidden completely from infrared, not forever. You couldn't mask the electromagnetic field required to screen ships from dangerous cosmic rays and high energy particles while traveling at meaningful fractions of light-speed, and you couldn't *maneuver* without giving yourself away. That was the kicker. The laws of thermodynamics were firmly against the idea. And yet...

"Conn, Combat."

Aguilera's voice on the command channel was even and calm. His voice was almost always calm, Faulkner reflected as she keyed her helmet microphone to respond. It was one of his more admirable traits. "Combat, Conn, talk to me."

"We got nothing down here. BattleComp doesn't have any idea how to plot the bogie, nor frankly do I. What is the game plan, if I may ask, ma'am?"

"The plan is, do what every warship does when the CO is caught *in flagrante delicto.* We come up with something on the fly. We don't give up the ship."

"Ada," Aguilera's voice was gently chiding now, "the only reason we aren't dead right now is that you had the ship at general quarters already. Comparisons with any historical defeats at sea may be a bit premature."

"We could still be dead right now, the night is young," she returned with a grim smile that her friend couldn't see. "I need a target, Tom. Five billion credits in equipment on this barge, there has to be—"

"Vampire, vampire, vampire!"

Faulkner saw almost as soon as the terse warning cut across her private channel, the two red, caret-shaped icons appear on the display.

"Two inbound hostile fast movers!"

Moments later the voices of Traxler and Mendoza chimed in as procedure demanded. "Weapons concurs."

"Tactical concurs! Inbound tracks are hostile anti-shipping torpedoes!"

Ada thought quickly, knowing her next orders would potentially mean the difference between life and death for her ship. *Do I want to juke these torpedoes even if I can?* She wondered. *Make some erratic course changes, follow the book, and I may evade them. But it also forces our unseen enemy to break off and try again later from some other intercept angle. They will still be invisible, and I'll have the same problems then that I have now, but I won't even know when or from where the next attack will come. No. I want them to have us right where they want us. I want to know one of their vectors, maybe two. Steering and velocity, if I can get them to show me. They are on our starboard quarter right now, coming in behind. Not ideally placed for a T-bone intercept, they may not have decided to commit to battle until something we did made that decision for them. Maybe when we boarded the freighter?*

Faulkner keyed the Bridge channel with a mental flick and delivered the orders in clipped tones. "Helm, maintain acceleration, steady as she goes. Tactical, make sure we are capturing all the data we can on each weapons release, we're going to need it in a bit."

As Mendoza and the helmsman acknowledged their orders, Faulkner addressed the ECM officer, "countermeasures at your discretion, Mr. Eddings, do your best..." she trailed off as something tugged at her mind, an idea trying to be born, and she finished belatedly, "countermeasures at your discretion."

"Countermeasures, aye."

Countermeasures. Pixie Dust. The hard countermeasures employed by the Navy were largely comprised of canisters of nano-reflective particles, a form of chaff colloquially known as 'Pixie Dust.' These particles were designed to reflect and scatter electromagnetic radiation and light. Normally, such countermeasures were used to help shroud the ship against intelligent weapon systems like missile AIs, but, in this instance, mightn't they serve another purpose?

The nervous voice of the quartermaster of the watch broke into her thoughts, having grown increasingly agitated as the inbound torpedoes approached, and his captain didn't order any alterations in their course. "Orders from the Conn?"

"When I have orders for you. mister, you will know, I promise. Now, shut up and drive."

The young petty officer visibly flinched in his seat. "Aye, aye!"

"Weps, I need you to shoot them down. I'm not going to be maneuvering until almost the moment when we rotate the ship to give them our broadside."

"Aye Captain, but...the starboard side defense clusters—"

"I know," Faulkner broke in, "they're working on getting them fixed. We'll rotate to the port side, that's the best I can do right now, put the lion's share of the work on the port batteries. We're holed on that side too. At least the point defense clusters still work."

"Yes, Captain."

"Good man," she said in what she hoped was a jovial, comradely tone. *You need to manage these kids' emotions better; that's part of the job. It's not their fault they were sold a pleasure cruise to the Commonwealth's many exotic ports of call, where they could wear themselves out with casual sex before the Navy sent them home, and covered them in college money and the adulation of their peers. You need to be able to lead them better than this.*

"ECM, I want you to reserve four, no—six, canisters of Pixie Dust, and set them to delayed deployment, let's say a thirty second delay. Hold on to those until I tell you."

Before he could respond, another watch-stander called out, "projecting forty-eight seconds to impact, mark!"

"Point-defense firing," Lieutenant Traxler's voice cut in immediately, "maximum density program, as ordered."

"Acknowledged," Faulkner murmured, her mind entering a state of hyper-focus. "Helm, anti-missile evasion maneuvers on this track, now. Tactical, you see what I see? They are coming in high and astern, and quickly. But, not quickly enough to overtake us anytime real soon. I'm going to start shaping our course down and port, directly away from them."

Mendoza took a moment before answering. "Yes, Captain, but...that will leave them in our baffles, they will pull in right behind us. We won't have good point defense coverage, or good sensor coverage."

"We can't leverage our sensors worth a shit anyway. As for PDC coverage, that's very true. But this course will make their next couple of moves obvious. We can talk about that as soon as we take down these missiles, which Mr. Traxler's team is about to accomplish with their customary style and verve, isn't that right, Mr. Traxler?"

"Conn, IEMARS. Kill!" shouted a nervous watch-stander in the CIC, "one vampire down. The other is, twenty, that's two zero seconds from impact and CBDR."

"Chief," said Faulkner with all the calm she could muster, "sound collision, just in case. Helm, all stop on the mains, give us ninety degrees port yaw now!"

The starfield on the display dome lurched vertiginously as the ship spun to the port to present her full inventory of port side defensive batteries to the single remaining oncoming torpedo. The high-powered excimer laser clusters poured invisible yet lethal coherent ultraviolet light into the vicinity of the enemy weapon, refining their targeting data as it drew ever closer.

"Incoming multiple projectiles, it's canister shot, brace, brace!"

Faulkner, tensing against the coming blow, grabbed the arms of her chair in a white-knuckled grip, and unconsciously closed her eyes.

So-called "canister shot" warheads deployed a burst of small, high-energy metal projectiles on their terminal approach, akin to a blast of ball-bearings. While less precise than a single kinetic-kill weapon, the spray of depleted uranium slugs covered a wide area and was still potentially lethal, if enough of them hit.

Once again, alarms wailed, and the reverberating sound of pinball-sized slugs spraying the *Agamemnon* like a shotgun blast assaulted her senses. Willing herself to open her eyes, she saw the entire compartment around her vibrating as if the bridge crew were inside a bell being struck. As she tried to focus and scan her displays for meaningful data, a voice spoke with authoritative calm on the 1MC, "Now hear this, this is the XO. All department heads make reports to Damage Control Central."

Moments later, another more tremulous voice reported, "Decompression casualty, Portside at Frame seventy-one! Power distribution and life-support systems on decks three and four, port-side aft at frames seventy-one and seventy-two are inoperable, medical assistance requested. Away the Flying Squad, away!"

Damn. That doesn't sound good. Deploying the Flying Squad most likely meant compartments badly holed, and crew members in total vacuum. The Flying Squad would be lending support to standing rescue and repair parties as the situation warranted. For now, her focus needed to remain on the big picture.

"Combat, Conn. Are we still in the fight? Are pieces of my ship falling off, Tom?"

The voice that answered, however, was not Aguilera's, but Traxler's. "Conn, Combat, standby one."

What felt like a very elongated moment later, but was in actuality mere seconds, Traxler's voice returned, "Skipper, the XO just went below to take charge of the Flying Squad. It sounded pretty serious, DCC advises that Space Rescue are cutting through bulkheads on Deck Three to effect rescue of personnel. They have reports of spalling injuries, and electrical hazards. From what I can tell, our combat effectiveness is still good, with the caveat that the cryogenic plant on the starboard side is packing up, it's fragged worse than we thought. The ChEng says, and these are his words, 'It's full of holes.' That last hit also took out both port-side slipways into the boat deck, and some auxiliary life support systems. I have the Watch in CIC."

"Very well," she replied. "Helm, bring the bow around to our previous heading, and resume acceleration, ahead flank. I want a gradual change in our heading to bring us down and port, directly away from their approach vector." Without waiting for an acknowledgement, she addressed Mendoza next, "Tactical, given the point at which they last fired, and the distance from the first launch, assess the approximate range to the bogie. I know we don't have a lot of data, best guess."

Mendoza took a moment to punch the requested calculations into her console, before answering, "let's say, four light seconds or a bit less, and closing at about 0.01c. It's hard to say with more certainty, but they will surely be in optimal missile launch range in less than one minute, and they will be in optimal gun range in a little over five minutes if we just keep running. Given the limited data set, they have the velocity advantage certainly, and the acceleration advantage possibly. They are going to run us down from behind, and sooner rather than later, ma'am."

"Okay. I want to bring that moment in a little, actually. They will be reloading their tubes already, and I don't want to do this all day." She studied their course and positional data on her chair mounted displays for a moment more, then issued her next orders. "Helm, cut acceleration to zero, all stop."

The helmsman seemed momentarily stunned at the order, but his hands moved jerkily to comply. "Aye, aye. All stop."

Hopefully, they'll think they hurt us worse than they really did, and we shut the drive down due to damage. We're just a helpless, fleeing rabbit. Feel free to close for the kill now. Faulkner flexed her fingers insider her gloves, then shook her hands reflexively, as if to shake out the tension she felt there.

"Okay, people. Here's the plan, I want those countermeasures I asked for ready to deploy, we're going to drop the whole lot of them at once."

"But Captain—the ECM officer interjected, "I've been pumping the Pixie Dust out like crazy, it doesn't seem to do much to slow them down. Those missile AIs are so damn good, I don't..."

The round-faced young man seemed on the edge of tears, and Faulkner suspected he was the one who had been sobbing on an open channel earlier. Looking around the bridge at the faces she could see from her command chair, she saw similar expressions of anxiety, and in some cases hopelessness.

"I'm not concerned with slowing missiles down," she said. *Time for everyone to get with the program.* "I want to pump that stuff out astern, down our track, clouds of it. Thick enough to walk on."

Mendoza's face lit up with sudden realization. "That's why we've minimized evasive maneuvers—you're drawing them into a stern chase on purpose! After their second salvo, we've established their general bearing and a recent position, and you turned us away to make them chase us. If we maintain our current heading, and they remain on our six..."

"Correct. We narrow their approach options down to essentially one. Right up our tailpipe. Unless we give them a reason to break off this run and try again later, which we don't want to do. We can assume their angle of approach with confidence, just need to see if we can firm up our guess on distance. On my order, dump the pixie dust. Then we're going to rotate ninety degrees to bring the guns to bear and see if we spot any footprints in the dust. If we do we see any, that telemetry will be time late due to light-speed sensor lag, and we won't have a target lock to feed the fire control computers. So, we'll need to lead our shots carefully. Are those countermeasures on a thirty second delay?"

"Yes, Captain!" came the shaky reply.

"Very well. Prepare to deploy countermeasures astern. Weps, get ready to engage with guns. Helm, if they get off another spread of torpedoes, we *will* maneuver so stay frosty. They may hold them until the range comes down a bit, to try and be sure of a kill, which suits our purposes fine, but we don't really know. Things are going to get really interesting, real fast around here. Is everyone clear on the plan?"

A chorus of staggered assents flooded the CIC channel.

"Good."

Faulkner checked her chronometer. *They might be reloaded now, but if I were the enemy commander, I'd hold my wad a bit longer. We took down three out of four missiles from not much further away than this, and the fourth only winged us. Why not increase the odds of a good hit next time? He or she has got to be smelling blood, and seeing we are showing our stern like this, they must be thinking it's just a matter of time.*

She waited an agonizing two minutes, then five minutes, and still there was no third torpedo attack. "ECM, dump the Pixie Dust now. All of it."

"Countermeasures, Aye, Captain."

As the canisters of reflective particles were launched astern, Faulkner watched the display dome with mixed apprehension and anticipation. *If this doesn't work, I have no idea what Plan "B" is, so here's hoping this crazy ass idea works.*

She waited thirty seconds before giving her next command. "Helm, engines all stop. Rotate the ship, ninety degrees port yaw. IEMARS, I want all eyes on that cloud, set sensors to track-while-scan and report detections of any kind."

Now, we wait.

Seconds dragged by, then a minute. Drumming her fingers on the arm of her chair she frowned, then finally spoke, if only to diffuse the tension on the bridge. "Do we have good dispersion on the countermeasures?"

"Aye, ma'am. It looks good to me; the field covers almost five cubic kilometers now and expanding."

"There!" someone shouted, "possible bogie sighted, distance three point eight light seconds."

Faulkner saw that indeed, an anomaly was highlighted on the display dome, indicating something had been silhouetted against the light-scattering dispersion field of the Pixie Dust. She focused on the display, her eyes narrowing, and saw something there in the computer interpolated imagery—little more than a distortion in the dispersing cloud of counter measures, like the vague outline of a hand moving beneath a bed sheet. Then it was gone.

"Okay, that had to have been our bad guy. Ms. Mendoza, provide Mr. Traxler with a firing solution based on our best projection. Mr. Traxler, commence saturation barrage."

Traxler, with a tone of resolve, keyed into the gunnery net, "Gunnery teams, Combat. This is the Weapons Officer. We have a target reference point in the tank, low confidence. Stand by for saturation barrage with all dorsal and ventral mounts, duration two-zero seconds. On my mark..."

There was a brief pause, the tension palpable on the bridge and through the gunnery decks alike, as the crew awaited the order.

"...Mark!"

The coil guns roared to life, and a thunderous vibration was felt throughout the *Agamemnon* as they unleashed a torrent of tungsten projectiles towards the point in space where the ghostly silhouette they had seen in the dust cloud was projected to be when the shots arrived.

"Rounds out," Traxler announced, his voice steady now as he fell back on years of drilled responses. "Time to target, three-seven seconds. Stand by for battle damage assessment."

Faulkner's grip tightened on her chair's armrests; her focus locked on the expansive display dome. Nearby, Mendoza leaned intently over her console, exchanging rapid, hushed analyses with her team, while Traxler, ensconced in the Combat Information Center behind her, was doubtless engaged in his own consultations.

"Wait one!" Mendoza's voice, tinged with anticipation, cut through the tense atmosphere. "IEMARS is picking up something...hold on, the interference from the Pixie Dust is complicating the picture. Let me clarify this." Her fingers danced over the controls, a concentrated furrow marking her brow. Moments later, she inhaled sharply, "We've got a hit! Detecting an oxy-nitrogen gas plume, Captain. They're venting atmosphere!"

A pinkish icon appeared on the display dome, labeled UNKNOWN/*TENTATIVE*. Mendoza once again spoke animatedly into a channel Faulkner couldn't hear, her fingers flying over her station. As Faulkner watched, her heart in her throat, the pink icon deepened in hue to magenta, then to an angry red and then flickered, the tag now reading, *M-3 CONFIRMED HOSTILE.*

A breathless voice burst out on the CIC channel "Conn, IEMARS! Detection at three point six niner light-seconds. New Contact bearing one-eight-zero by positive two relative, assessed hostile. Contact looks like a blacked-out light combatant, maybe a frigate. Designating contact Master-Three!"

Faulkner grinned, a thin humorless grin. *By the Founders, I've got you now.*

Her ebullience was short-lived, as the same CIC watch-stander then called out, "We are being painted with targeting sensors—incoming ordnance, gunfire!"

They know we can see them, Faulkner realized in dismay. "Evasive!" she just had time to shout.

15

Wounded

CNS Agamemnon, The Iota Persei System

E nora Anthem sat at her console in CIC, her eyes darting between the tactical display of the ongoing space battle and the dwindling signal from the fleeing freighter. Her left shoulder throbbed, a dull ache radiating from the wound she'd taken. The medics had patched her up, but the pain persisted, a constant reminder of her limitations. As periodic shudders seemed to grip the mighty vessel, and the terse conversations around her took on a more urgent tone, she tried to focus on her primary responsibility in CIC, which in her judgement was, and had always really been, to stay out of everyone's way.

Her mind kept drifting back to the boarding party—Cass and the others were out there, risking everything to secure Atsuko and stop whatever this Project Seraphim was about. But the freighter was getting further away, the time-late nature of their communications worse, and every second that passed made it less likely they'd be able to establish anything like a real-time conversation with the boarding party—at least not in a time frame that would make any difference in the outcome of their mission. The main CIC channel crackled with updates from the bridge, but the messages were becoming increasingly fragmented.

The XO had left the CIC a few moments ago, to personally assume command of the damage control parties, and his relief, Lieutenant Traxler, bent over one of the ancillary displays attached to the holo-tank, his shoulders hunched, his overall body language conveying extreme unease.

Cass had connected with her some minutes ago to ask her to sabotage the lighting in the cargo bay of the *Hermes*, but since then, the *Agamemnon* had accelerated like one of Deseret's famed sabrehawks and was now well over a light minute away from the freighter and heading away from her fast. Enora pursed her lips and considered the likelihood that any request from the boarding party addressed to her could be construed as time-sensitive at this point, given that all she could really do was carry messages to people on the same ship. Hacking the freighter's systems any further was a doubtful prospect at best; under the circumstances, a data linkage would be far too slow to be useful.

Having so concluded, Enora routed her incoming comms to her personal datapad, unbuckled her safety harness and approached Traxler, not knowing what the chain of command really dictated in her case, and when his eyes flicked up from his display, his expression was taut and strained through his visor.

"Permission to go below, Sir, and assist in damage control operations. I've got a Level 3 Damage Control qual. With voice comms between us and the *Hermes* being better described as correspondence at this point, I can be of more use with the damage control teams, than just sitting here on my ass. Sir," she concluded lamely.

"Granted," Traxler ground out, before raising a finger to forestall further conversation as the captain addressed him on the CIC channel.

Enora nodded, sketched a salute for good measure, and then departed through the aft hatchway, which NI sentries dogged shut behind her.

Enora had descended two decks and was making her way aft, when the entire ship seemed to heave, the deck disappeared from beneath her feet, and she found herself flying backwards down the passageway she had just traversed. She landed with a grunt, wheezed, and felt the deck sole vibrate and undulate beneath her back and buttocks. The lights above her flickered and went out. After a moment the shuddering ceased, and Enora lay on her back in total darkness, gasping for air, her palms pressed to the deck as it to reassure herself of its continued existence, her heart pounding. Presently, emergency illumination activated, bathing the passageway in a dim orange light that made it strange and unfamiliar. She rose shakily to her feet and noted that her helmet display was flashing an amber warning.

PRESSURE DROP DETECTED

"That can't be good," she breathed to herself, and flinched as she tried to steady herself against a bulkhead with her left arm, drawing a complaint from her injured shoulder. A different, staccato judder shook the ship again. *Coil guns. We're firing at something.*

She steadied herself a moment, then resumed her journey aft, toward the starboard point defense operations center that her data pad told her was the current location of Commander Aguilera, encountering nobody else in the passageway except a single fireman who came out of a compartment behind her at one point, and bolted past her without a word, vanishing into a damage control locker.

When she found Aguilera, he and a small team of firemen, ratings from various departments and a few space rescue men were in conference over something they were observing on an environmental display near a sealed hatch.

"It's fluctuating but not gone," he was saying, "and the pressure differential isn't that bad. I'm leaning toward going in."

She began to salute, then decided it might be perceived as lubberly and instead simply addressed Aguilera without preamble, "Petty Officer Anthem, I've got a Level 3 DC qualification, can I help?"

The XO looked up from the display, his face hard to read in the dim emergency lighting. "Good timing, Anthem. We've got spalling in the bulkheads, electrical junctions out all over the place, and He-3 leaking into the fire-control compartments all along this side of the ship. We're working to contain it, but now we've got more and bigger problems. We've got injured crew near missile tube two. I need you to go forward and assist Repair Two with stabilizing the environment, and evacuating casualties to the infirmary. Maris here will go with you," he indicated one of the naval firemen standing nearby. "You take direction from him, okay?"

Enora nodded. "Okay. Yessir."

"Good. The route is hazardous, you two be careful and keep in touch on the Flying Squad tactical channel. Dismissed."

The fireman, Maris, brushed past her and began moving down a lateral passageway, not looking to see if she followed. Enora moved after him, taking long strides to first catch up, then move abreast of him. For several minutes, they strode along the passageways of the ship in silence, before her companion finally spoke.

"Anthem, eh?" came a voice in her helmet, a voice with a faint yet familiar accent...an Anthemusan, the first denizen of her own home world she had encountered since coming aboard. In the dim ochre light, she hadn't been able to see much of his complexion or features through his survival suit visor. "*Petty officer* Anthem. Funny, I reckon you're practically royalty. How are you not an officer?"

"I'm—I'm with the Gendarmerie," she replied awkwardly, having been caught somewhat off-guard by the subject of her family connections, especially under such circumstances. Still, the other siren's tone was not hostile, merely curious.

"Yeah," Maris replied, "I've spotted the uniform once or twice before."

Enora flushed. "Yeah. Sorry, look this is my first real space battle, okay? Can we just maybe save the reminiscences about the old country until after it's over? I'm kind of on edge right now. Let's just say Dad didn't really get a vote on my career choice, and leave it at that?"

"Dad?" Maris echoed, incredulity evident in his tone. "That must make you...you know what, you're right. Let's stay focused on the mission. I didn't mean to pry. I guess I'm nervous too. I just— shit."

As they turned a corner to enter a compartment labeled, *5-32-G-2 /LAUNCH-2,* the lanky spacer came to a sudden halt, and Enora took a few more steps before doing likewise. They were confronted with a sealed hatch, and next to it, an indicator on the nearby wall panel flashing an angry red that indicated vacuum on the other side.

As the two paused to consider the situation, they were joined by two additional crewmen, who skidded to a halt next to them. The senior, a chief petty officer and bosun's mate by his insignia, quickly took charge.

"Don't just fucking stand there, Leroy, seal this zone and depressurize. It's obvious Space Rescue and the medics haven't made it up here yet, and shit on the other side of this hatch is likely to be FUBAR. You two," he pointed at Enora and Maris, "head into launch-prep and fire control once the pressure equalizes. We'll check out the starboard magazines. Get walking wounded out here, into the passageway. If you find someone in a bad way that you can't move, call the XO, and he'll have the rescue guys expedite. Aid kits are on the interior bulkheads every ten meters."

The Chief's voice dropped an octave. "If you spot an officer, do what they say. Otherwise, don't touch any buttons unless you know what you're doing, and don't worry about repairs unless it's required to address an immediate hazard to life or ship safety. The Chief Engineer and his people are on the way. This tube's fragged, but they might still get it working again, and we don't want to start yanking on wires just yet, and cock something up. Triage and evac—nothing else unless directed. Clear?"

Enora and Maris nodded, while the other spacer moved to obey the chief's command. The passageways on a naval vessel were divided into segments or 'zones' by evenly spaced sets of double airtight hatches, each capable of being sealed to isolate a segment, effectively turning it into an emergency airlock. Once sealed, this zone would be depressurized to match the vacuum on the other side of the hatch, allowing them to open it in relative safety.

"Check your suits, get ready for vacuum," warned the junior fireman, whose given name Enora assumed was Leroy.

The hissing sound of escaping air filled the corridor as the zone depressurized, and the party gathered near the hatch to the missile loading spaces. The ambient noise of the ship—a low, steady hum that had become background to their every moment—faded away, leaving an eerie silence in its place. The indicator on the wall panel flickered from red to green, signaling that the pressure had equalized.

The Chief gave a nod, and the hatch slowly creaked open under the guiding hand of Maris, revealing the scene on the other side. A thin haze of smoke or vapor drifted through the opening, carried by residual wisps of atmosphere escaping into the void. Beyond the hatch, the passageway was a wreck. Bulkheads were scorched and warped, the telltale signs of rapid decompression and spalling obvious in the twisted metal. The area beyond was lit only by flashing alarms and the dim, sickly illumination of emergency lights. The first body was only a half meter away from where Enora now stood, a female form, sprawled face down in the companionway on the other side of the hatch, next to a ladder that led to an elevated catwalk over the loading rollers for the ship's weapons. Her neck was bent at a horrifying and unnatural angle, and Enora couldn't help but think she was glad she couldn't see the woman's face. Maris knelt by her side and made a Li-Fi data linkage with her suit. He studied his data pad for a moment and then stood, shaking his head. "We can't help her."

The chief followed him in followed by Leroy, and his voice growled on their local comms, "Okay, let's go. You guys forward, me and Leroy here go aft, we'll be monitoring the Flying Squad channel, keep in touch. It ain't gonna be pretty in here."

That, Enora later reflected, had been an understatement. The space beyond the companionway was tall, long and narrow, and the inner bulkheads had been lined with holo-displays and works stations. These were burnt out junk now. The cylindrical, cage-like structure that housed the loading rollers in order to keep weapons on track in zero gravity conditions, was warped so badly it was doubtful that ordnance could pass through it into the tube beyond, even if the tube had been operational. Virtually all the equipment Enora could see was blackened as if by fire and comprehensively smashed. Debris littered the deck sole, and cable runs had been dragged out as if to restore some measure of power, then forgotten.

On the deck between the roller-cage and the companionway hatch, three ordnancemen were busy taping the survival suits of several wounded comrades, some of whom were moving, while others lay ominously still. When they noticed Enora and her companion approaching, the senior of the three giving aid, an ensign according to his suit insignia, waved them past, and toward another hatch in the forward bulkhead. He seemed to be speaking, but was apparently on the wrong channel, as his words were inaudible in the vacuum that filled the compartment. A moment later he seemed to rectify his error, for his voice crackled to life in their helmets. "Check on the fire control center," he shouted, his voice both unnecessarily loud and squeaky with stress. "There were two techs in there, and we can't reach them. They aren't answering on comms, and we can't get through the hatch, the environmental computer locked it down when we got hit, and now it's screwed up. It was taking too long to bypass. We were about to load another bird when—these guys..." He gestured at his patients as his voice trailed off, and Maris broke in soothingly. "We got it, Sir. If you can get anyone who is mobile out into the passageway, Space Rescue will be along ASAP. We'll work on the door."

Enora had already advanced to the specified hatch, which was recessed into the bulkhead a few meters away from the dilating iris that covered the inner aperture of the missile tube itself. Her datapad in hand, she established a Li-Fi connection to the wall panel and set to work. *At least I'm able to make myself useful where it concerns computers. They haven't invented the AI yet that can match me for pure stubbornness.*

Enora's fingers flew over the surface of her datapad, bypassing the security protocols with a speed that spoke to both her skill and desperation. The hatch to the fire control center finally yielded, sliding open with a reluctance that boded ill for what lay beyond. Ripping an aid kit from its bracket on the bulkhead, she stepped forward, but the moment her boots crossed the threshold, she froze.

The compartment, what was left of it, was a nightmare. The forward bulkhead was torn open, jagged edges of metal framing a gaping hole that led directly into the void of space. Through it, she could see the cold, indifferent stars staring at her in the distance. The vast emptiness beyond seemed to pull at her, a silent reminder of the dangers that lurked outside the fragile walls of their ship.

To her right, the equipment lining the wall was nothing more than a twisted, charred ruin, wires hanging like the entrails of a gutted animal. Indicator lights occasionally flickered from the wreckage, the last remnants of power bleeding out of shattered systems. Burn marks and melted slag traced the path of the deadly barrage of projectiles that had hammered through the *Agamemnon's* armor and peppered the area, blackening the walls and turning once-smooth surfaces into rough, cratered scrap. Pieces of the inner hull and equipment lay scattered across the floor, torn free by the kinetic energy of the impacts. In some places, the metal of the opposite bulkhead had been punched clean through, leaving gaping holes that exposed the vulnerable innards of the ship's systems.

Enora dragged her gaze away from the abyss that yawned just meters from where she stood, and down, toward the sprawled form of a suited spacer, slumped against the jagged remnants of the forward bulkhead, his back pierced by a sharp fragment of melted infrastructure, which now jutted out through his abdomen and between his weakly clutching hands, like a blackened, twisted spearhead. Of his partner, there was no sign at all. Willing herself into motion, Enora moved stiffly forward, one leaden step at a time, toward the carnage, every instinct in her screaming that she looked into the face of Death, that she should be running as fast as her feet would carry her in the other direction. *Cass worked a salvage yard; he should be the one doing this shit. We hit another bump like that last one, and I'll be doing an unscheduled EVA.*

"Holy shit," remarked the voice of Maris, who had slipped in behind her, and now held on to the shattered remnants of a chair, as if to anchor himself to the ship.

Enora crouched down before the wounded crewman, and could see his mouth was moving, yet nothing of his words reached her over the local comm net. Turning on her helmet light, she leaned forward, letting her helmet touch his. The face behind that visor, now inches from hers, was young, pale and terrified. "Hey," she tried to pitch her voice to be reassuring, and yet loud enough to carry through her helmet into his, "we got you tough guy, just hang on. The medics are coming." Her words sounded like tired clichés in her own ears, and she tried not to grimace.

"Please..." his voice sounded distant in her helmet, high, raspy and thin, "I've been calling—nobody could hear me. I think my suit is broke. I almost went—his head turned feebly as if to indicate the rent in the ships bow.

"It's okay—" Enora looked down at his chest where the spacer's name tape, now visible in the garish light read, CRAWFORD, P. "—Crawford? What's the P stand for?"

The young spacer's eyes were unfocused, and for a moment she thought perhaps he hadn't heard her.

"Peter..." he finally answered, and she saw now his lips were flecked with blood, "It's Peter. Please, Mommy, I just want to go home. I'm cold, and I want to go home."

Enora drew back, sucking in a sharp breath, and keyed her comms, her vision blurred by welling tears. "We need the medics, we need to get him out of here, right now."

"They're already coming, but I just called again." Maris had begun to say more, but whatever he'd meant to say, his words died in a mumble, as a sudden tremor ran through the deck and into their feet, and the comms channel set aside for the Flying Squad began pulsing an urgent demand for attention. "What was that?" Enora queried.

"Fucked if I know," came her comrade's terse response, "checking in with Mother Duck."

Enora, momentarily confused by Maris's response, wracked her brain to put context to the fireman's words, before remembering that "Mother Duck" was the call sign automatically associated with the leader of the Flying Squad, the person in overall command of damage control teams and emergency response aboard ship. She switched comms channels with a mental command and was met with chaos.

"...back, get back, I got him! Get everybody back. There's halogen in the air, just stay there!"

Now she heard the voice of Maris, trying to cut through the gabble of voices and strange background noises, "XO, you there? Mother Duck, this is Maris, how copy, over?"

"Mother Duck is down," replied an unknown and unidentified voice, "clear comms! Charlie Team, report status by the numbers..."

What followed seemed to be a roll call of sorts, interrupted frequently by garbled shouting, and Enora quickly became lost, unable to make sense of it.

"I better get back there." Maris's priority signal on the local net overrode the noise momentarily so he could make himself understood to Enora, "Something has obviously gone terribly sideways. You stay with him until Space Rescue gets here. I'll make sure to light a fire under 'em."

Enora nodded. "Okay. Don't let them forget about us."

"I won't," Maris replied over his shoulder, "don't fall out of the spaceship."

"Hah, funny. I mean it, he's in shock and he needs to get to the infirmary soon, or it won't matter."

"I know. We got a lot of people need to get to the infirmary," Maris was already out of sight. "Do what you can for him, try to keep him calm and don't let him move. Give him one ampule of Syntherol if there's none in his system already. Chief Martin is down the hall."

As Maris disappeared through the hatch, another unfamiliar voice overrode her comms with a terse announcement, "*Fire, fire, fire!* Fire in compartment 5-57-2-L, amidships. Available repair teams to compartment 5-57-2-L. All other stations maintain readiness."

Enora swallowed hard, realizing her mouth was very dry. Outside the ship, through the jagged hole in the wounded vessel's skin, Enora saw the stars begin to slew to the left, in an awe-inspiring but nauseating display. *We're turning,* she thought. *To run, or fight?*

Doing her best to ignore the gorge rising into her throat, Enora knelt by Crawford's side and connected to his suit computer. The medical data it transmitted was confirmation that his condition was every bit as bad as it looked. He had not been given any pain medication, so she removed a dose from the aid kit that she'd forgotten she was holding, and loading the specialized injector, pressed it against Crawford's thigh and depressed the button. Once again, she placed her helmet against that of the young spacer. "Pete, you hangin' in?"

He mumbled something incoherent in response. Enora squeezed his gloved right hand in hers, her eye on the distressing medical feed. She decided basic human companionship might be the only thing she could offer him at this point and so really, no topic was too inane given the circumstances. "It's okay buddy, they're coming. We're gonna get you all fixed up. How long have you been on this tub anyway?"

She got no answer. The deck beneath her began to resonate, the vibration transferring through her boots into her body. Outside the hole in the hull, she saw that the sky was filled with fire.

***

"Target reference Master-Three. Engage with guns—short burst only. Fire for effect!" Faulkner snapped out the orders without thinking. Her head and neck ached, and her ears were ringing. She knew her ship fared worse. This time, a lucky shot had demolished one of their forward-facing missile tubes. She needed to strike a killing blow now, while she still could. Her eyes riveted on the new icon that had just appeared on the dome, Faulkner slammed her palm down on her armrest and barked, "Weapons, prepare to load Helios shots in all remaining tubes."

"Helios shots, aye!"

Faulkner had almost ordered the loading of the standard kinetic anti-shipping torpedoes typically seen as a mainstay in ship-to-ship engagements in open space but had quickly reconsidered. The Helios warhead was an ingenious adaptation of the ancient

Casaba Howitzer concept, a weapon born from the theoretical arsenals of 20th-century Earth. It was a nuclear device in essence, but unlike most such weapons, the Casaba Howitzer was designed to focus the energy of an atomic explosion into a narrow, directed beam of plasma, effectively turning the explosive force into a projectile of searing hot ionized gas. Upon detonation, the Helios torpedo would convert a portion of its own mass into a directed energy jet, channeling the explosive force forward in a tight cone. This made the Helios not just an area-of-effect weapon, but one capable of delivering a devastating, high-energy punch at a specific point, albeit with a broader margin for error than kinetic projectiles.

Faulkner understood the trade-offs. Her kinetic weapons afforded a deadly precision attack, but precision presupposed visibility, a solid lock on the target. The Helios, on the other hand, were the cosmic equivalent of horseshoes and hand grenades—a less precise but more forgiving option when the adversary might vanish again any time.

"Mr. Traxler, initiate firing point procedures. Prepare tubes one, three and four for a salvo fire mission, target Master-Three. I want those birds ready to fly on my mark."

"Aye, Captain. Initiating firing point procedures for tubes one, three, four. Targeting Master-Three for salvo fire mission."

"Helm, bring her about ninety degrees port, give us a least-time intercept on Master-Three, ahead Flank. Astrogation, these folks have been in a huge hurry to meet with us, but they may be reconsidering the wisdom of that now. If they veer off, be ready with a new course to give me a good intercept. As of now, you have the conn."

"Aye-aye, I have the conn."

As her orders were acknowledged, Faulkner gave the tactical situation further thought. The *Aggie* was now facing the mysterious vessel and counter-burning, slowing her progress away from the enemy. This caused the distance between them, which they had been trying to maintain to some degree, to begin shrinking much faster than it had been.

They hold the velocity gauge, and if they want to use it, they can veer off and disengage, run, do whatever they want to do. If they don't flinch though, if they keep coming, that won't help them at all, the high relative velocity just means they'll fly right into my birds. They can rethink this. They can run. But will they? Is ceding that freighter and the system to us an option for them? Let's find out. We're going to play chicken and see who blinks.

She glanced at her displays to see four flashing indicators spring to life. They signaled that the electro-magnetic catapults that hurled the *Aggie's* missiles from their tubes had begun charging. The fire control technician began speaking a well-rehearsed litany in response to Traxler's prompts, moving crisply and with a steady cadence through a program of practiced steps that helped provide order to an otherwise chaotic situation. "Charging mag-catapults, sir. Capacitors ramping up to full charge for optimal launch conditions."

"Open outer covers for tubes one, three and four. Confirm tubes are clear and prepped for missile loadout."

"Outer covers opening. Tubes one, three and four are clear and ready for missile loading."

Traxler now provided the prescribed next order, while Faulkner stared at the contact on the display dome, willing it to remain steady. "Load Helios torpedoes into tubes one, three and four. Run diagnostics to confirm all systems are nominal."

"Helios torpedoes loading into designated tubes. System diagnostics underway... All systems green across the board."

Mendoza pressing a control on her console, recited her part of the ritual, "finalizing firing solution for Master-Three."

Traxler, his voice dead calm now, addressed Faulkner directly, seeking authorization to release the devastating weapons that were the *Agamemnon's* most advanced ship-to-ship armament. "Captain, I have Tactical's firing solution. Tubes one, three and four are loaded and ready in every respect. Awaiting final go for salvo launch."

Faulkner felt certain she knew the answer to her next question but wanted to be sure. "Any change of aspect on Master-Three?"

Mendoza responded promptly, "Negative. No aspect change. She's coming ahead. Range to target now three light seconds."

Cry havoc, Faulkner said to herself, then out loud, "On my mark... Shoot."

"Executing salvo fire. Tubes one, three and four, engage Master-Three."

The deck shuddered slightly, and on the main display three blue, caret-shaped icons sprang to life, and then seemed to ignite into incandescent flares, as the torpedo motors engaged.

"Torpedoes away. Confirm torpedoes are on-track to Master-Three. Tubes one, three and four are now reloading."

"Time to target?" Faulkner asked, her eyes still locked on the display dome.

"Battlecomp says sensor lag is negatively affecting confidence, but about two-seven seconds."

Surprise, Faulkner thought with a tight smile. *Now, what's your next play? If I were you, I wouldn't bother trying to juke those torpedoes, too late for that. I would—I would close to within knife-fighting range, trust my defensive weapons to save me, and make a gun run as I went past to try to salvage something from this mess. Shit.*

"Weps, I think she's going to double down. Weapons free on the guns, fire as you bear."

Traxler began to reply, but whatever he meant to say was drowned out by sudden urgent callouts on the CIC channel.

"Inbound ordnance, gunfire!"

"Aspect change on Master-Three!"

Both announcements came almost on top of each other, and Faulkner heard as though she were a bystander to the action, her own voice bellowing, "Counter battery fire now!"

A mere second or two later, a shockwave rippled through the atmosphere of the bridge much like a blast of warm air on a hot summer day, when an outside door is opened onto an air-conditioned room. Faulkner was slammed forward violently against her chest harness, as kinetic energy was transferred into her body, and realized dully that alarms were blaring around her. The combat lighting on the bridge flickered, and her next thought was that her neck hurt.

Just as the reverberating cacophony began to fade, it was replaced by the rumbling thunder of the dorsal and ventral gun mounts firing again. Then finally, as the enemy vessel passed out of their coil gun engagement envelope, merciful respite and quiet. Faulkner became dimly aware of someone speaking.

"...penetrations, crew berthing forward of Frame fifteen, decompressions on Deck Two. Repair parties responding."

Faulkner mentally took stock of herself, and the evolving situation, feeling herself sliding into a reverie about another day, another disaster. *No, keep it together, be right here, right now. Check with Tom, make sure we're still in the fight. No, Tom is dealing with the repair parties, I need to talk to...to Traxler.*

"Mr. Traxler," she heard herself saying thickly and realized her lip was bleeding, "operational status?"

"We're losing a lot of atmosphere, Skipper, we took several rounds on our bow armor, I'm trying to sort it out with DCC. Main propulsion is one hundred percent, guns showing green. Missile tube two is out of commission for the long-term though, the mag-catapult is fragged. The ChEng is heading forward to take a look, but it sounds like a total loss. I'd say we're lucky we didn't have a bird already in the tube. We have—we have fatalities. Not sure how many."

"Understood. Post fire-mission assessment on Master-Three?"

"Standby one," came the terse reply, the stress from his increased workload evident in Traxler's voice. Faulkner looked up at the main display to see at that moment, one of the two remaining blue carats on the dome seem to merge with Master Three, and blink out. The other continued past the target.

"Two birds destroyed. One bird detonated and may have hit. Tactical can you confirm?"

Mendoza's voice sounded distant at first, then seemed to regain strength and composure as she spoke, "Registering something, it's..."

Her voice trailed off for a moment then returned, this time jubilant, "debris and atmosphere, and a big heat spike! We hit her! Good hit. She went into a turn to our starboard at the last second, but her track doesn't look right, it's very um—wobbly. I think we hurt her bad, Skipper. I'm not sure she has maneuvering control."

"Conn, IEMARS," came a report from the sensor watch section, " we confirm, target is trailing gasses, and lots of reflective debris. We observed what looked like a secondary explosion, something under pressure blowing up. She is no longer accelerating."

Faulkner sat still for a moment, gazing up at the dome that was her window into the space beyond the fragile bulwark of her ship's hull, watching the icon representing the enemy vessel continuing in a wide erratic turn, as if slowly doubling back on its previous course. "Communications Watch, hail the enemy vessel and put me on."

After a momentary pause, Lieutenant Patterson replied, "You're on ma'am."

Faulkner took a moment to compose herself, and make sure her voice was steady. "Unknown vessel, from the Commonwealth Naval Warship *Agamemnon*, this is Agamemnon Actual. You are ordered to heave to, deactivate weapons systems and surrender your vessel. Prepare to be boarded. Respond."

Several seconds passed, long enough for her message to reach the enemy vessel and for them to feasibly respond, but no reply had come.

"Astrogation, be ready with an intercept as soon as she steadies out. Assuming she does steady out."

"Aye, ma'am," came the prompt response.

"Okay," Faulkner breathed. Get us moving that general direction." Faulkner switched to her external channel and repeated her demand but still received no reply.

"Oh, Founders!" Mendoza blurted, as the icon marking the mysterious vessel on the display dome was washed out in a brilliant, expanding sphere of white light.

"Tactical?" Faulkner inquired as calmly as she could.

"Hard kill," Mendoza replied after a moment, sounding slightly dazed. "Target Master-Three destroyed."

Faulkner sat still for a moment, sweat streaming down her face, staring at the spot on the dome where the enemy ship had been, and then it dawned on her that she heard a rising commotion on the main CIC channel, like echoing, distant waves crashing onto the shoreline. After a moment, her mind identified the sound.

It was the sound of cheering.

Faulkner blew out a breath and took a moment to take stock of the situation. She surveyed the display dome briefly, and then turned her head to face Mendoza, earning a muscle spasm followed by a twinge of pain that spread from the back of her neck to the space behind her eyes. "Tactical, I see nothing out there now but the comm-buoy and *Hermes*, report contacts."

Mendoza gave her superior a look of concern, but then answered dutifully, "Confirmed, the buoy of course, and Master-Two, the *Hermes*, still on her previous course, but no longer accelerating. Swordfish flight is still docked to her. No new contacts."

Mendoza, Faulkner observed, wore a somber expression and did not seem to have been among those cheering. "Well done, Tactical, and good shooting, Weps. Well done, everyone. Let's put the ship to rights and get back to the *Hermes*. Our troubles aren't over yet. Ms. Mendoza—"

A quick burst of digital noise interrupted her, as a new voice joined the CIC channel, "Captain, this is the CMO. Requesting a private conference."

Doctor Halsey? Faulkner assumed this could only be the casualty list or 'Butcher's Bill' being presented and dreaded having that conversation with her longtime acquaintance at this exact moment. "Doctor Halsey, I need to make safe the ship, is this urgent?"

"It's urgent, Ada."

Ada? The breach of military protocol in front of the entire Bridge and CIC watches was unlike the normally staid and buttoned-up ship's surgeon. "*Doctor,*" she replied, emphasizing his title in gentle rebuke, "I'm pulling you into a private channel."

Once her HUD indicated she and the doctor had switched channels, she resumed in a rush, "Nathan, we aren't out of the woods yet and the ship is full of holes. I have a lot going on at the moment. What's up?"

"Ada," the older man's voice was soft, and unusually reedy.

"It's about Tom."

16

Some Princess

Commercial Vessel Hermes, The Iota Persei System

"Push in, push in! Green, watch our left. They're gonna want to flank us. New-boy, eyes right!"

The darkened cargo bay had been transformed into a stark tableau of chiaroscuro under the glow of their UV illuminators. Shadows clung to the edges of the towering stacks of containers, deep and impenetrable, while the areas bathed in the Marines' ultraviolet lights were washed out into ghostly monochrome. The Roman Candles had turned the visual and IR spectrums into a chaotic, flickering light show as had been the intent, rendering traditional optics all but useless. Cass could hear the eerie wailing sound their countermeasures produced, even through his helmet with its sound dampening hardware, and hoped the situation down on the floor was as unnerving for their nameless adversaries as it looked from his vantage point.

He absently listened to Rawlings' steady but excited stream of instructions to her people on the squad channel as he scanned the cargo bay from above, watching for any sign of movement from behind the containers that partially blocked the stairway and catwalk from the enemy positions further in. There was a sort of central aisle between the pallets of containers, as well as potential pathways between the outermost port and starboard container stacks, and the walls of the cargo area.

Cass concurred with the sergeant's assessment, that their outnumbered adversaries would likely seek to move around the walls of containerized cargo to the left and right, to escape the sensor noise caused by the Roman Candles, and gain a favorable position from which to ambush the advancing Marines, who may be tempted to move in a straight line down the much wider center aisle. It was the most obvious avenue of approach, and for that very reason, possibly the most dangerous.

Rawlings herself, as well as two of her Marines, had taken cover behind the cargo containers that flanked the opening to the center aisle, and were using their gauntlet optics to peer around the corners for hostile activity.

Cass spotted a flicker of movement toward the left edge of the first rank of containers, only dimly visible in the UV illumination provided by his armor, and possibly invisible to his comrades who lacked the visual acuity in low-light conditions that his Jotun heritage afforded him.

"Contact left!" He warned, and immediately selected triple-burst mode on his carbine and fired.

Within seconds, the already surreal atmosphere in the compartment was pierced with the staccato drumbeat of automatic weapons, as his own team of Gendarmes began laying down covering fire, and some of the Marine team began blind firing down the alleyways between the front rank of containers.

He fired another burst at the same shadowy target, now highlighted in his display, as the networked computers of his team's battle armor shared data at the speed of light, collectively ascertaining more about the tactical situation. Green, the Marine who had been assigned to watch the left flank of the advance, had knelt and fired as well, almost as soon as the words had left Cass's mouth.

The shadowy figure, struck by multiple shooters, slumped against the side of a cargo container and remained still.

I think we've done what we can from up here, that ambush didn't go well and they lost a gun. If they're spreading out...may be best to go right down their throats, Cass decided. "We're coming down, Sarge," he announced on the squad channel, and then paused to await her acknowledgement.

"Affirmative," came the reply.

He keyed his comms again and spoke now to his own team, "Gendarmes, get ready to move, we're going to go right down the middle, and then disperse one row in. Ack-Ack, Meeks and I go left, everyone else goes right, check your targets, Marines are expensive. Let's go."

With that said, Cass stood from his crouched position and descended the metal stairway. He had no need to look back to make sure his troopers had followed, the sound of their armored boots clanging against the grille-work was audible behind him. The team stormed down the stairway, and without pausing, Cass plunged into the central alleyway in between the shipping containers where Rawlings and her comrades held position. The sound of automatic gunfire slackened momentarily as Cass's team charged through the opening.

As Cass passed through the first row of containers, he pivoted smoothly on his back foot to face left, down the first aisle where two of the hostiles had been covering when they'd first entered.

It took Cass less than a second to process that two figures confronted him now, one almost right in front of him, the other about six meters further down the aisle. Cass saw a flash and then felt something strike his armor on the left pauldron, knocking him forcefully back a step. Cass returned fire instantly, a triple burst of armor-piercing rounds striking his battle-armored adversary dead on, right above the solar plexus.

At this range, not even the metal foam cuirass encasing the vaguely feminine form of the presumptive pirate could withstand the repeated impacts of the high-velocity 6.5mm rounds that Cass had pumped into it. As his adversary stumbled backwards, Alfred, making the pivot right behind him, fired only a half second later, hitting her in the right shoulder and arm, spinning her around and ripping an advanced looking heavy pistol from her hand as she fell.

Cass looked beyond the stricken woman just in time to see the second armored enemy behind her toss what appeared to be an EMP grenade down the aisle, which landed right behind the crumpled form of his comrade, and bounced toward Cass. Reacting purely by instinct, Cass kicked the grenade like a rugby player and sent it sailing back toward the man who'd thrown it.

The device hit the side of a nearby cargo container with a soft clank and ricocheted, landing almost directly behind its thrower, who twisted at the waist to look down at it as if dumbfounded by this unfortunate twist of fate. It emitted a flash, and then a brief, intense burst of electric blue light rippled outward in a circular wave, accompanied by a sharp, crackling sound. The pulse created a visible corona, making the air shimmer and nearby objects seem to distort as if in a heat haze. The moment the effect washed over the armored figure, his movements grew halting and froze. While most military-grade combat armor was insulated to some degree against electro-magnetic attack, at a range of only half a meter, the EMP grenade had certainly fried some or all of the tango's systems and shut down his power-assist servos.

Cass considered demanding the man's surrender for a brief moment. But just as the thought crossed his mind, young Guardian First-Class Meeks acted. Another shot rang out, striking the now helpless enemy in the side of his helmet.

Guess not. The man dropped, dead or unconscious, and hit the deck with a clatter.

"Clear the next row, Go, go, go!" Cass heard Rawlings shout and saw a flash of movement out of the corner of his eye, as she and several members of her squad stormed through the gloom to clear the next aisle. They had seen only the three hostiles in their initial reconnoiter of the cargo bay, but that didn't mean there weren't more they hadn't seen.

"PO, you're hit." Meeks pointed to Cass's pauldron, where sealant foam oozed from a hole about the diameter of an index finger. Cass rotated his shoulder, feeling a twinge of soreness now that the adrenaline was waning. His hardware HUD and DNI cortex display showed no terribly alarming messages; the armor had held up. "Just sore, the armor did its job."

Meeks shook his head. "Shit. That was—I've never seen anything like that. PO, you are a machine, pure and simple. That grenade..." He barked a sharp, unsteady laugh." We fragged those tangos good, didn't we? We—"

His voice faltered as he bent over, his armored gauntlets bracing against his thighs, the earlier triumph gone from his tone. "Oh shit, I think I'm gonna be sick."

Quickly, Cass activated the command override function on Meeks' suit to administer an anti-nausea drug before he could vomit inside his helmet. "You're okay, Meeks," Cass reassured him, giving a gentle slap on the back. "We did what we had to do. What they forced us to do."

He scanned the aisle where they stood; the other Gendarmes had cleared the port side without encountering hostiles and had again assumed overwatch positions. Alfred had moved adjacent to the last containers on the starboard side of the aisle and was using his finger camera to carefully look around the corners. From the comms chatter, it seemed that the Marines had met no further resistance in the next row.

Noticing that something about the environment had changed, Cass scanned the area around him, and it took him a moment to come to the realization that the Roman Candles had ceased their shrieking and flashing, leaving the cargo bay dark and quiet. His helmet had already begun to allow visible spectrum light through the visor filter. He patted Meeks' shoulder again. "Take a second, buddy."

Cass activated his comms to speak to the other members of the fireteam, "Dawson, take your guys and advance up the port side, clear the next aisle. We're going to go around this side, we'll meet you there."

They acknowledged and moved to do as ordered, while Cass gently drew Meeks after him toward the starboard side of the bay and the narrow passage that offered a way around to the final row of containers. "C'mon Meeks, I need you to watch my back."

The Marine squad and Cass's detachment methodically cleared the remainder of the cargo bay, discovering no one else. The male enemy combatant encountered by Cass and Meeks was dead, as was the one who had tried to slip around the side of their assault and flank them. The female, a stocky woman perhaps in her thirties, with the physical characteristics of a Terran or a genotypical human colonist, was alive but grievously wounded.

Cass called for a medical evacuation. After confirming that Skye would join them as soon as she was able, he turned to resume clearing his sector—just as Garnett's voice came over the Sierra Team channel. "Lawman, this is Sabrehawk, sitrep."

"Sabrehawk, Lawman. We just had a highly kinetic disagreement with three tangos, two of which are KIA, one wounded and awaiting evacuation. No significant casualties for the Good Guys. We have secured the cargo bay, and we are now proceeding aft. No sign yet of any hostages."

"None up here either. Hopefully that changes, soon. We have taken the bridge, it looks like an actual merchant crew and skipper running the boat, they claim the ship was seized by pirates. It seems that since then they've been forced to go along with some criminal scheme at gunpoint, and they've never heard of anyone named Atsuko Hirayama. It sounds a lot like bullshit, but we'll sort it out later. *Aggie* is out of effective comms range and busy, so don't bother trying to raise Ghostcat right now. Carry on, Sabrehawk out."

Cass clicked his tongue in irritation. *What if she's not even on the ship? What if I am a complete moron, and she's locked up in a storage room back at Tengoku City, or frozen solid on the planet surface somewhere?*

As he stood ruminating, he was joined by Rawlings. "What did your boss have to say? Shall we resume our quest to save the princess?"

Cass couldn't help but grin at the Marine's irrepressible sense of humor. "We shall."

***

Moving through a longitudinal gangway, the squad quickly arrived at a four-way junction. According to their schematics, the power room was located at the end of the main passageway, while the cross passage led to several storage rooms and the ship's machine shop.

"We'll secure the power room," Rawlings declared, "while you guys search the rest of the castle. Hopefully, you don't awaken any more dragons."

"Yeah," Cass averred, "dragons bad."

As the Marines moved out, the Gendarme fire team began methodically searching the compartments on the port side first. Cass had decided not to divide his small team for this portion of the mission, opting for safety over expediency.

Nearing the end of the lateral corridor, having already cleared a machine shop and a tool storage area, the fire team heard a sudden sharp yelp from ahead. A figure in a green cleanroom coverall lurched into view, followed shortly by a partially visible man in paramilitary fatigues awkwardly moving through a hatch coaming. Cass heard weapons coming up and saw the green glints of ranging lasers dancing across the torso of the man in the coverall, as he seemed to stagger down the passageway toward them, his hands invisible behind his back.

Cass raised his hand in a quick signal to hold fire. "Hold your fire! Identify targets," he ordered, his voice calm but firm. The team's weapons stayed trained on the stumbling figure, their ranging lasers still dancing on the man's chest, but no shots rang out. "Wait! Don't shoot! Help me!" the middle-aged man shouted, his voice cracking as he stumbled forward. "I'm not armed; I'm not with them!"

As Cass tried to process the situation, the man in fatigues fully emerged from the hatch where he had apparently been wrestling with some burden, which turned out to be Atsuko Hirayama, her wrists bound and wearing what could best be described as pajama pants and a sweat-stained athletic bra.

"All of you, on the deck, now!" Cass barked. The man in the coverall, some sort of medic or lab technician perhaps, dropped to his knees, then fell forward onto his stomach, his face pressed against the cold deck plates, a whimper escaping his lips. Cass could now see his wrists had been zip-tied behind his back.

As the man in fatigues stepped fully into view, it became clear that he was using Atsuko as a human shield, pressing a gun firmly to her temple. She looked frightened but composed.

"Back off or she dies!' the frightened pirate— or mercenary, Cass assessed—shouted, his voice filled with desperation. He pulled Atsuko closer, the barrel of his gun never wavering from her head.

Cass took a step forward, his expression hardening. His instincts screamed at him to act, to save Atsuko, while another part of his mind urged caution, and careful consideration of all his options. Before he had even made a conscious decision, he spoke. "Never mind the girl. You and your former confederates have committed an act of piracy in interplanetary space, in a naval jurisdiction, your big worry now is how not to get put down like an animal," he said, his voice dripping with menace, allowing his gut to take over, pushing aside the urge to overthink and over-analyze. The guard's eyes widened in anger and fear, and he swung the gun to point at Cass.

Atsuko's face in that moment became blank, almost vacant. Then with a swift, practiced movement, she struck the guard's wrist with the edge of her hand, knocking the gun from his grasp. The weapon clattered to the floor as she brought her heel down hard on his foot.

The guard yelped in pain, his grip on her loosening. Atsuko twisted her upper body, using the momentum to drive her elbow into his solar plexus, knocking the wind from his lungs. Her lithe form a sudden blur of motion, she struck the doubled-over mercenary with an open palm, landing the blow on the bridge of his nose, which caved in with a sickening crunch. Blood sprayed as the man stumbled back, clutching his face.

Cass opened his mouth to speak, but the surreal tableau before him was still playing out. Atsuko had taken a single step toward her former captor before her hips rotated in a smooth motion, and then her leg uncoiled like a spring, expending its force on the hapless mercenary's pubic bone directly above his crotch. His legs buckled beneath him, and he sat down hard, before rolling over onto his side, moaning.

The gendarmes moved in swiftly; weapons trained on the mercenary. Two of them grabbed him, forcibly flipping him over facedown, and securing him with zip-ties. Cass picked up and made safe the pistol lying on the deck, before proceeding to peer cautiously into the compartment from which the three had emerged. It was an unremarkable storeroom, and apparently now unoccupied. Unremarkable except...

I've seen this room before.

Cass shook his head unconsciously. *No, that's not possible, it's just deja vu. That's all.*

He entered and glanced around the compartment, just to make sure it was indeed empty of prisoners or personnel, and then returned to the passageway and approached Atsuko, his expression a mix of incredulity and admiration.

"Well, looks like you didn't need much rescuing after all," he remarked, tilting his head to regard the slender woman before him.

Her placid face remained so for a moment, then finally the corners of her mouth curved into one of the delicate smiles Cass remembered. Her voice when she responded was quiet and calm. "On the contrary, your intervention is most welcome. I merely did my part to aid in my own rescue. My education has been quite thorough, and of course, I try to stay fit."

"You...try to stay fit," Cass echoed, voice thick with disbelief.

Atsuko nodded, her expression remaining serene. Cass began to compose his reply, but then the man in the green coverall who had remained face down on the deck during the altercation, cleared his throat and squirmed, his hands still bound behind his back. He lifted his head slightly, peering around. "Uh, excuse me? Hello? Still tied up here."

***

"His name is Dr. Eliot Vance," Cass said in answer to Rawlings' unspoken question, "and he's a scientist who works for Hirayama Enterprises down on Tengoku, well—was working for them— I guess. His employment status is no longer clear."

"And this must be Atsuko Hirayama," the sergeant replied, nodding in Atsuko's direction, her expression hard to read through her helmet visor.

"Yes, they were both abducted around the same time."

"Why?"

Cass blew out a breath. "That's a very delicate subject, Sarge."

"Ahh. Above my pay grade, you mean?"

"Something like that."

"Couldn't have anything to do with the highly scientific shenanigans those guys are rumored to be getting up to down there on that ice ball?"

"I couldn't say," Cass replied blandly. They were standing outside the hatch to the reactor room with several of Rawlings's squad members, waiting for a verdict from the technical specialists who now probed carefully within the sensitive heart of the ship.

"Of course it does," Vance interjected bluntly. Rawlings placed her fists on her hips, stretched her back and then muttered loud enough for the whole group to hear, "shocking."

"Well," Cass said with an exasperated gesture, "there you have it. Can we please not get into this right here, right now?" He turned to the truculent scientist, a tall, thin man in his mid-fifties—perhaps early sixties, though modern anti-aging therapies made it hard to tell. Graying and sharp-tongued, he'd already been forthcoming about his role at Hirayama Enterprises and just as eager to air his grievances with its leadership. In fact, it had been difficult to keep him from doing so at length during the walk to the reactor room. Still, he had corroborated Atsuko's allegations that the labs on Tengoku had continued developing Project Seraphim—if that could be considered good news. "Hold on, Doctor. Let's save the details for a secure debrief. Shall we?"

"Right," Rawlings drawled, "OPSEC and all that. Hold one." She held up a finger, and tilted her head in the near universal manner of someone trying to focus on a comms call while others are talking, and then after a moment nodded then looked up and spoke, "Okay, New-Boy says the Reactor is secure, no booby traps in evidence, and the ship's systems are more or less functioning normally, except there are holes in the dorsal hull plating where we shot it up. Seems to be sealing ok. We laypeople may now enter the inner sanctum, if you want to know what a fifty-year-old Spheromak reactor looks like."

"Not especially," Cass replied. "I'll tell the Cox'n we have rescued two hostages, including Atsuko, and see if there are new orders. I have no idea what's going on out there with the *Aggie*, and now that we have things mostly mopped up here, it's making me nervous."

"Yeah," Rawlings replied, "about that, you only encountered the one tango, guarding these two?"

Cass snorted. "Well, I'd say he encountered Atsuko before we got to have a proper encounter ourselves, we just sort of cuffed him and helped stop the bleeding."

Rawlings regarded the sullen prisoner standing between two armored Gendarmes. He had not yet been interrogated at any length. In fact, they did not yet even know his name; that would be a conversation for later. He carried no identification, nor bore any insignia that might mark him as a corporate mercenary, though Cass felt he had the bearing of one. While he tried to affect an attitude of defiance, he wobbled unsteadily on his feet, and his face was puffed up and purple.

"Is that right?"

"Yeah, she kind of disarmed him and then broke his nose, and a rib or two. And maybe some other stuff."

Rawlings was silent for a moment, and then guffawed, her uninhibited, girlish laugh inspiring mirth in Cass too.

What would this girl do if she couldn't be a Marine? Cass wondered to himself.

She looked at Atsuko who fidgeted, finally showing signs of discomfiture, and then slowly shook her head. "Some princess."

17

Eleven Flags

CNS Agamemnon, The Iota Persei System

F aulkner stood in the medical bay, her face a mask of controlled emotion. The sharp, antiseptic smell of the room did nothing to calm her nerves. Dr. Halsey was removing a stained surgical smock for disposal, his lined face haggard and showing obvious fatigue. The sick bay on *Agamemnon* was only accessible through its own internal airlock, the only section of the ship where the crew currently went about their duties without survival suits and helmets.

"Ada," Dr. Halsey began somberly, his usual professionally detached demeanor somewhat threadbare, "I know you have a lot on your plate, I just—

Faulkner cut him off. "What happened, Halsey?"

The doctor took a deep breath, gathering his thoughts. "During the battle, Tom and his team were in a gunnery compartment just forward of the damaged cryogenic plant. The plant was leaking He-3 as I'm sure you've been told, but I guess the situation appeared manageable."

He paused, seeing the growing anxiety in Ada's eyes. "Go on," she urged, her voice barely a whisper.

"The atmosphere in the next compartment had become dangerously thin due to hull breaches, and we had fire control technicians who were unaccounted for in there. From what I understand, it was also accumulating He-3 which of course, is inert and has less molecular weight than oxygen. This obviously wasn't clear to Tom, or the personnel with him. It was probably streaming out through the holes in the hull almost as fast as it was coming in. His team saw the pressure level was unstable but not all that far off from the pressure level in the passageway, and decided to go in. It seems the defensive lasers had been damaged in the first attack, and as a result there was volatile krypton difluoride gas from those damaged systems leaking into the compartment as well. It's normally inside a shielded and closed system, you know."

The older man paused for a moment to let his words sink in, before continuing. "Recall that when we go to combat pressurization, we increase the oxygen fraction to maintain partial pressure. When they opened the hatch, the oxygen-rich air from the passageway flooded in—at about seventy percent O_2 at that setting. There must have been a spark... and the mix went up."

Faulkner's eyes widened, as she processed the implications of his words. "The gases reacted with the oxygen."

"Yes," Halsey confirmed, his voice pained. "The sudden introduction of oxygen must've caused violent exothermic decomposition. The He-3 leaking into the compartment had actually created a buffer of sorts, preventing ignition of the krypton difluoride, but when they opened the hatch..." the rest of his words died on his lips.

Faulkner clenched her fists, fighting back tears. "And Tom?"

Halsey shook his head, his blue eyes reflecting the leaden weight of the loss that he knew was settling upon Faulkner's chest as he spoke. "I'm sorry, Ada. Tom was caught in the explosion. As were two of the team with him. The techs in the compartment were probably already dead. He was exposed to the full force of the blast."

Ada closed her eyes, a single tear escaping down her cheek. The well-meaning old surgeon continued to speak, almost babbling about toxic fumes and craniofacial trauma, but she barely heard him.

Fire all around her, closing in on her like a shimmering curtain of agony...like the wrath of an angry spirit, a demon escaped from its phylactery, to visit pain and suffering on those foolish souls who ventured into the Void, where humans were not meant to intrude...

Faulkner shook, a sob almost escaping her lips, before she steeled herself to ask the next question, the question that a commanding officer must ask, even one who had just lost her best friend. "What about the other casualties?"

"We've treated twenty so far, mostly burns, spalling injuries and blunt force trauma, a few with compromised survival suits are in bad shape. The Space Rescue teams are still trickling in with more. We have eleven dead. Including Tom."

Ada closed her eyes, the weight of the words crashing down on her. *Eleven dead.* Her mind raced, a whirlwind of emotions and thoughts. This deployment had always felt wrong to her. Escorting Garnett's team of supposed Gendarmes on what had felt like a black op, had unsettled her from the start. She had voiced her concerns, but duty had compelled her to follow orders.

Now, here she was, with eleven of her crew dead, including Tom, a man she had trusted and relied on, even when trustworthy and reliable people had been a scarce commodity in her world. The price of this mission had been far too high, and for what? What could possibly justify this attack on her ship, her people, in a supposed time of peace?

Her thoughts spiraled as she replayed the events leading up to the deployment. The briefing, the vague orders, the secrecy. She had never been fully on board, but now, whoever the shadowy enemy was who had necessitated their presence out here at this backwater corporate colony, had drawn blood. The precious blood of people who had trusted her judgement, and her leadership, to bring them back home alive. Had she failed them somehow? Had there been some way she could have circumvented this?

What is going on in this system that could possibly rationalize all this? What shady corporate dealings can explain the eleven folded Commonwealth flags that I am going to have to send home to grieving loved ones?

"Garnett and I are going to have a long, candid talk."

"Who, Ada?"

Unaware she'd spoken aloud, Faulkner shook her head. "No, nothing. I need to get back to CIC, please keep me apprised of the situation down here, and send the files of the souls that we lost to my message queue, with your notes. If you need anything urgently, and I am unavailable for any reason let—"

She'd almost said to let Tom know.

"—phone Mendoza in Combat if you need anything."

As she turned to leave, Halsey called after her gently. "Ada, take a moment for yourself. He would want you to be strong, but it's okay to grieve."

Faulkner paused at the large, sliding airlock door, her back to the doctor. "I will, Halsey. I will. After I've gotten to the bottom of whatever is going on here."

***

Enora pressed her back to the bulkhead to allow the captain to pass through the med bay airlock unhindered. The expression on her face had made it clear, the CO was not someone she wanted to engage with right now, for any reason short of, well—no qualifying reason came to mind. Having taken a few moments of relative calm to flush the sanitary systems of her suit at the appropriate station, she had re-entered the receiving area of the med bay, to find none other than the ship's master stomping out, and the Chief Surgeon sinking wearily into a chair behind the compartment's dominant feature, a long check-in counter. All around her, nurses, Rescuemen, and other personnel continued to work tirelessly triaging new arrivals, and moving them into and out of operating rooms, exam rooms, or aid stations as the situation dictated.

I never thought I would look forward with such giddy anticipation, to the moment when I can just sit down, and pee in a traditional setting, she reflected wearily. She didn't really want to disturb the obviously tired and troubled Dr. Halsey, but the other emergency responders and nurses all appeared very busy, and she had an important inquiry to make before she returned to the CIC.

"Doctor?"

"Ah, Petty Officer Anthem. Is your shoulder bothering you?"

"No," Enora replied quickly, "well yes, actually, but it's okay, that's—There was a fire control tech, Rescue brought him in a few minutes ago? Peter Crawford? I was hoping you could tell me how he's doing? I was sort of the one who found him."

The surgeon gazed at her somberly for a moment as if deciding whether to answer. "Enora, isn't it? Enora, I'm sorry, Peter didn't make it. He had simply suffered from too much trauma. I promise, we did everything we could for him, as I know you did."

Enora nodded stiffly.

"I'm sure there was nothing else you could do under the circumstances. Did you need any pain medication for your shoulder? I can ask one of the nurses..." Dr. Halsey trailed off.

Enora had already walked away.

***

When she had returned to CIC, Faulkner went to the holo-tank, where Traxler was still standing watch, his body language signaling his fatigue, his face drawn and tired through his visor. *They're exhausted. We're all exhausted. Do I dare let my guard down though? Do*

I dare not too? These kids can't go on much longer without some real rest, and neither can I, if I'm being honest. If Tom were here...

Well, he's not.

"IEMARS, Commanding Officer, report contacts."

The answer came promptly, but the voice that reported was undercut with weariness. "Detection at 30.5 light minutes, Master-One, the comms buoy. Detection at four light seconds, Master-Two, the *Hermes*. No new contacts."

Faulkner let out a slow breath, then keyed the channel reserved for the Bridge. "Bosun's Mate, pipe down from General Quarters. Secure from battle stations, set condition x-ray throughout the ship."

As her order was repeated over the 1MC channel that broadcast through the entire vessel, a palpable wave of relief could be felt. No sooner had the announcement concluded than everyone in the CIC began unlatching their helmets, scratching itches that had been maddeningly out of reach until now. The combat lighting was replaced by the normal bright white underway lights, as normal watches resumed, and weary watch standers, some of whom had been on duty for close to eighteen hours without a break, could now seek out their bunks or a shower.

"IEMARS, continuous deep scans."

"Aye, aye," came the dutiful reply.

"Comms, please prepare an FLT burst transmission, include our logs and most recent operational status report. Send to Commander, CruRon 7, Third Fleet. Transmit when ready. Oh, and have Senior Warrant Officer Garnett report to my underway cabin as soon as he comes back aboard," Faulkner said to nobody in particular, and then strode from the CIC.

***

About an hour later, Faulkner sat drumming her fingers on her desk, regarding the man before her with a deepening frown as he spoke.

"Atsuko Hirayama and Dr. Vance are material witnesses to several very serious crimes, not least of which are acts which may amount to sedition, and which I must assume are ongoing on Tengoku, right now. I would say the attack upon *Agamemnon* only underscores the seriousness of the situation we uncovered during our investigation. In terms of the resources that have been brought to bear in order to keep these crimes under wraps, I am as surprised as you are. I certainly would not have knowingly placed your ship or crew in danger of attack from a vessel like the one you describe and not told you about it. When we last spoke, I was candid with you, that the *Euphrates* had been attacked, and her assailant's identity unknown. That is as much as I knew about this stealth ship, until the moment I heard you had been attacked while we were aboard the *Hermes*." Senior Warrant Officer Garnett's gaze was level, his expression earnest as he continued, "I don't presume to tell Navy captains how to handle their business, but I assure you that we're on the same side, ma'am."

"You can lay off the Virginian gentleman routine, Garnett. I'm not in the mood for your folksy charm right now. I want to know just what kind of shitstorm your outfit has gotten *my ship* into."

"With respect ma'am, it wasn't my outfit that got your ship into it, and I think the captain is well aware of that."

Faulkner grimaced. "Ah. 'Just following orders,' Senior Warrant Officer? Or can I call you Lieutenant?"

Garnett sighed. "My reserve naval commission is hardly a closely guarded secret, Captain. I served three years of active duty in the Naval Infantry. And yes, to answer your question, I am subject to orders just like you, and like you, I carry them out faithfully as duty requires."

Faulkner glanced down at the file she had been scanning on her datapad, prior to the meeting.

"Yes, I see. NISOC in fact, the 2nd Reconnaissance Battalion, 330th Special Operations Regiment. You were involved in the pacification of New Muscovy. Many of the details, shockingly, remain classified."

Garnett, apparently having decided her recital of his record didn't constitute a question, gave no answer. Raising an eyebrow, Faulkner continued. "Commonwealth Distinguished Service Medal, Naval Infantry Commendation Medal with V device for valor, Purple Heart with Oak Cluster...Goodness, Mr. Garnett, I'm looking through here for something that might qualify you to be a transportation safety investigator, and that's about the only credential in the galaxy you *don't* have. Your dress smock must weigh ten kilos by itself. Where do you find room in your locker for all those medals? You're a hero, Mr. Garnett, and therefore incredibly suspect, in my view. How does a hero like you"—she paused for a moment for effect—"land a gig as a glorified traffic cop?"

"Captain," the older man began, "As I said, I serve the Commonwealth in the time, place, and manner my superiors deem best. I observed operational security protocols on this mission, that's true. Yes, I was given to know by my bosses that the so-called shipping accident may have been somewhat less than accidental."

Garnett stood at parade rest and looked straight ahead as he spoke stiffly, "I can assure you however, that were I at liberty to disclose everything I had been briefed on before coming aboard the *Agamemnon*, none of it would have ameliorated the situation you faced with that stealth frigate. Not only have I not encountered anything like that, I've never even heard of anything like that. Not a whisper. If such a vessel were known to be in operation, and not by us, I'd assume you would know about that long before I did."

Faulker had to concede, he had a point there, but Garnett continued to press the point home. "As far as I know, when I report in to my superiors, I will be in the unenviable position of having to break the news to them. And Captain, I assure you, my superiors and yours hang out at the same parties. They're all going to be pissing their britches, unless I miss my guess."

She sat back with a deep sigh and regarded Garnett in silence for a moment. He endured the scrutiny as he had the entire private audience thus far, with courteous, carefully schooled aplomb. *You certainly are a cool customer, Garnett.*

"You know," she said at last, "when your team first reported aboard, you struck me very unfavorably. You were decidedly un-Navy-like, in my estimation. More so than the average Rocket Cops."

Again, her words met with no reaction.

"But that's not really who you are, is it? Now it seems you have more combat experience in a Navy uniform than anyone in my crew, including the NI detachment, and I am re-evaluating what's really been bugging me about you and your team this whole time. I'm not ready to discuss my conclusions just yet, but let's just say for the moment, I agree, we both just work here, and we both need to play the hand we've been dealt. I am going to call a staff meeting as soon as you leave this room, and you will be expected to attend. We are going to discuss the tactical situation, the ramifications of all that's happened, and our further course of action. I will need complete transparency from you, within the constraints of your orders, starting now. I need to ask about your current mission parameters. Do you intend to invoke Section 1120? Do you intend under that authority to request my people and assets to assist in a raid on the labs?"

Garnett seemed to show human vulnerability at last, his face telegraphing frustration. "Do we have a choice? They're making a bioweapon that can wipe out targeted populations in huge numbers, and they—or someone in league with them anyway— killed a government envoy and attacked a Commonwealth warship to cover it up."

Faulkner nodded. "Right, so I'm not yet entirely clear on all that. I need a full report on this alleged superweapon, with my CMO present, and I'd like to have Doctor What's-his-name and Ms. Hirayama present. I want all the key players to sit down at one table, and we're going to talk this through. Does that present an issue for you?"

Garnett shook his head in the negative. "No, not on my end but, Captain, some of the information I have to share is highly classified. Normally, I'd need to get clearance for everyone involved, but that's not going to happen in any useful timeframe."

"What about a COC? We're all directly involved in this situation. Can we use that to expedite clearance on a need-to-know basis?"

Garnett considered for a moment, then nodded, "That's a good idea. The Contingent Operational Clearance is designed for exactly this kind of scenario. Since everyone here is already involved and aware of parts of the operation, I can grant temporary clearance to discuss the sensitive details under COC guidelines. We'll need to document it afterward, but it should allow us to move forward without delay."

"Fine, then that's settled." Faulkner's voice took on a sharper edge. "I'm glad we can move forward as partners on a more equitable basis—especially given that the 'operation' as you put it, now potentially involves the armed takeover of a civilian colony using military personnel."

Garnett chuckled softly.

"Something amusing, Lieutenant?" Faulkner's eyes narrowed.

"Nothing, ma'am. Just—Garnett hesitated, a slight grin on his face. "I was just thinking— that stealth frigate never had a chance."

18

Hell Is Empty

CNS Agamemnon, The Iota Persei System

The steady hum of the *Agamemnon's* life-support and electrical systems provided a low, constant background noise in the ship's gym. The lighting was dim in the long compartment, but bright enough to illuminate the rows of equipment and a few scattered crew members who had come in to relieve some tension after several very stressful watches. Cass sat on a bench, unwrapping his hands, having finished his routine at the heavy-bag. His eyes scanned the room, and fell on Atsuko, as she entered through the airtight bulkhead hatch, her posture upright, a familiar look of calm determination on her face. Dressed in form-fitting workout attire, she seemed unfazed by the stares of a few off-duty crew members. They quickly turned back to their own routines as she made her way to a vacant exercise station. Cass noticed she moved with a controlled grace that was hard to ignore.

He approached as she adjusted the settings on a resistance machine that looked like a cross between a Pilates reformer and a hydraulic press. Old-fashioned free weights being a poor idea in a variable gravity environment such as a spaceship, such machines comprised the bulk of the exercise equipment. "Need a hand with that?" he asked casually.

Atsuko looked up, offering a brief smile. "Sure. I'm not familiar with this model. I could use some help making sure it's set right."

Cass nodded, moving around to the machine's control panel. "Yeah, they're tricky if you haven't used them before. Let me check the resistance settings." He adjusted a few controls, then gave her a nod. "There. That should be good for a start, adaptive tension, level 5. Sound right?"

Atsuko nodded, and Cass positioned himself behind her as she mounted the machine and got ready to lift, and he found his gaze lingering on her form—strong, athletic, a mix of determination and grace. He mentally shook himself. *Focus, Broz.*

As she began her first set, he kept his hands ready, spotting her as she lifted, though the danger of injury on such a machine was minimal compared to traditional free-weights. The machine responded to her movements, the digital readout fluctuating as she pushed forward against the resistance. Her muscles flexed with each controlled extension, the tension bands stretching in response, then recoiling as she brought her hands back in a smooth, steady rhythm. Her face was focused, a thin sheen of sweat forming on her brow as she moved through her repetitions. Cass could see her muscles working beneath her skin, the machine's advanced sensors adjusting slightly to compensate for any changes in force or angle.

She's stronger than she looks. But then, you already knew that.

She paused, inhaling deeply, then pushed through another rep.

"Good, good." Cass murmured encouragingly.

She exhaled sharply, her breaths controlled and measured, as she continued her set. After a few more reps, Atsuko's movements slowed. She finished the set with a final, determined push, and the machine's tension bands retracted smoothly. She released the handles and took a moment to catch her breath, her chest rising and falling as she calmed herself.

Cass waited until she was finished, giving her a moment to breathe and relax her muscles. Then, once she seemed settled, he stepped a bit closer. "How's that feel?" he asked, keeping his tone light.

Atsuko nodded, wiping a bead of sweat from her forehead. "Good. Feels like I needed it." She glanced up at him. "Thanks for helping with the setup."

Cass smiled. "No problem. Figured I'd make myself useful." He paused briefly, then continued, "I've been meaning to check in, see how you're doing after all that chaos."

Atsuko sat up and regarded him with large, liquid brown eyes. "I'm fine. I've been through worse, believe it or not."

Cass raised an eyebrow, then sat beside her on the bench. "Worse than being drugged and kidnapped by mercs?"

"Different kind of worse," she replied. She wiped her brow and looked at him thoughtfully. "So, Petty Officer Broz, my savior," she began almost playfully, "have you lingered here to question me further about that matter we discussed in my living room?"

He chuckled, rubbing the back of his neck. "Maybe a little. You're the one with the insider's perspective." He glanced around to ensure nobody was in a position to overhear them, but the gym was growing quiet as the change of watch drew near. "I still don't get why anyone would create something like Seraphim unless they were planning on using it. What's the endgame?"

Atsuko set her towel down and took a deep breath. "The endgame? We can only speculate, but I would imagine that such a weapon is being viewed as an equalizer, a way to narrow the hard power deficit between the Commonwealth government and other, non-state actors. I think some people are beginning to realize the days of the General Assembly on Earth ruling all they survey are coming to an end. Some see themselves as the future. Corporate elites, technocrats—people who can move faster and adapt quicker than any centralized government. If you stop to think about it, the Earth is not really central in our galaxy, not topographically. And while the birthplace of our species has long been economically and culturally central of course, that becomes less the case every passing year." She pursed her lips here for a moment, "unfortunately, the citizens of Earth will likely be the last to come to this realization. You as much as said so yourself, when we first met in my quarters."

She leaned forward, her face growing earnest as she continued, "Commonwealth politicians imagine Earth as Rome, with the galaxy as their Europe. But the galaxy is not Europe. Your world is not Gaul. You may know, your planet produces over thirty percent of all the lanthanum and yttrium mined in the entire commonwealth. The Galaxy is huge. The Universe beyond it incalculably vast, and our fleets will never be able to sail all the way around it, showing our flag. The Commonwealth is an empire in all but name, and every previous empire in our history has come to a turning point, a moment when its reach finally exceeded its grasp, when it went from too big to fail, to being too big to function. Such a moment presents opportunities, for those who seek...a new paradigm."

Cass frowned, and taking a moment to get his mind around the metaphor. "And this is such a moment? You're talking about secessionists? Rebels?"

Atsuko considered. "In a sense. I am talking about the real ruling class in our society, and the fact that they seem to find the Commonwealth to be increasingly obsolete. I have heard such sentiments more than once. There is an assumption among many people I think, that the value proposition of the Commonwealth is clear to all, including the elite. I am not certain this is a safe assumption."

"The *Ruling Class*?" Cass repeated, his tone dripping scorn. "The Commonwealth has its flaws, but we are still a democracy, I don't think I'd characterize a bunch of corporate fat-cats and captains of industry in quite that way. I'd call that social stratum *influential* for sure, but not a ruling class."

Atsuko hesitated a moment, then reached out and placed a palm gently on his cheek. "Casimir, that's only because you are not a part of it."

Cass grunted, wishing to argue but also acutely aware of the warm press of Atsuko's hand against his face. "That's a pretty cynical view of things, Atsuko."

"It is just reality as I see it," she replied. "You are a soldier. You serve the State. But people like my father, they see the world differently. They see the State as a tool, and when a tool stops being useful, you discard it."

Cass felt a twist of unease in his gut. "That sounds like zero-sum thinking at its worst. Just because the Government isn't perfect doesn't mean it needs to dismantled completely. And what about you? How do you see it?"

Atsuko's hand dropped from his face into her lap. She leaned back, as if considering how much to reveal. "I see things changing. I see old systems breaking down, and new ones being born. I just don't know if the new ones will be any better than the old."

Cass nodded slowly, taking in her words. "You know sometimes you sound like Garnett."

Atsuko gave a small, almost sad smile. "Your Warrant Officer Garnett is a shrewd man."

"I guess," Cass allowed, "but these cold hard truths about the Universe seem to be a bit easier to take, coming from you. He's not as pretty."

Atsuko glanced away, and Cass sat there frozen, staring at her, momentarily mortified by his own audacity. He must have been studying Atsuko's reaction more intently than he realized, for his DNI awoke and flashed a message on his cortex display:

SUBJECT HEART RATE ELEVATED BEYOND PHYSIOLOGICAL NORMS

Cass struggled for the proper words to relieve the sudden awkwardness he felt. "I just meant—"

Atsuko turned her face back toward him, and her smile was back. "You are very kind to say so, Casimir."

"I am? Oh, that's good," Cass mumbled.

Now she laughed, a musical sound that Cass didn't recall ever having heard until now. "We have a few hours before the Skipper's big confab," he said, "Have you eaten yet?"

***

The atmosphere in the conference room was tense, a palpable weight of unanswered questions hanging over the gathered officers, Gendarmes, and guests. Faulkner sat at the head of the table, her expression inscrutable as she listened to others giving their input. The room was dimly lit, with the tactical display on the wall casting a cold, bluish hue over the proceedings. Her senior officers were present, with the exception, Faulkner noted, of the supply officer, Lieutenant Jones. Garnett, and his senior NCOs were also in attendance, as were the rescued civilians. The latter sat at the farthest end of the table from her. One, the young heiress, sat quietly and calmly, seeming to look at nothing. The skinny, and she thought rather eccentric scientist, Doctor Vance, looked around curiously during the proceedings.

It was Mendoza who was currently giving her report. "As most of you already know, the stealth ship exploded with significant force. Based on the sensor readings of the debris field, the chances of finding any pieces large enough for a detailed analysis are next to nil. Whatever remains of that ship is scattered across light minutes of space."

Mendoza, her brow furrowed, paused to collect her thoughts, before she proceeded. "Our biggest concern, tactically speaking, is understanding how it managed to evade our sensors so effectively. We detected the magnetic field build-up from her missile launchers, which is why we knew it was preparing to fire, but nothing else. Its navigational shields—if it had any—never showed up on our sensors. The same goes for its emissions while it was under thrust. The ship masked its IR signature so completely that we couldn't pick it up, even at relatively close range. The telemetry we analyzed after the action indicates a very maneuverable vessel with good acceleration, better than ours in fact, and yet we picked up no drive plumes, no radiation at all that would be characteristic of a vessel that size accelerating with reaction engines. Their propulsion systems may be using a completely different principle than those we are familiar with." Here she paused again and shrugged. "Frankly, I have no idea how they could mask their drive emissions otherwise, that is beyond anything we've seen before. It defies everything we know about current stealth technology."

Faulkner tilted her head and asked a question, "What sort of different principle?"

Mendoza glanced hesitantly toward Lieutenant Commander Lam Ming De.

When Lam seemed hesitant to speak, Faulkner prompted him using the venerable nickname of chief engineers in the Navy, "ChEng?"

Lam cleared his throat, "I hesitate to speculate at this point Captain. Gravitonics perhaps? The idea would be to harness gravitational fields in much the way we do for shipboard gravity generators. Gravitonic engines, if they were fully realized, could propel a ship without the traditional exhaust signatures we associate with fusion or ion drives. This would allow a vessel to move at high speeds while essentially 'slipping' through space, making it nearly impossible to track using standard methods. We've long toyed with the idea within the military, of gravitonic catapults for missile tubes, or graviton thrusters for sub-light drive applications, but the power consumption numbers have never been attractive enough to warrant anything more than experimental prototypes. The energy demands are astronomical, far beyond what our current reactors can sustain for extended periods. Every prototype we've tested either burned out too quickly or required a power source that would take up half the ship."

"Why didn't our gravitic sensors pick them up in that case?" asked Patterson, the Communications officer.

"They aren't really that sensitive," Lam replied, "their primary function is simply to detect dangerous gravity inclines in local space, to ensure safety when using the Quantum Fabric Drive for FTL jumps. They aren't tuned to detect something like that." The chief engineer gave a little shrug and raised his hands in a gesture of uncertainty. "Or maybe I'm wrong. Like I said there isn't enough data to really say one way or the other."

As the group processed this, Traxler cleared his throat and spoke hesitantly. "We do think these people are human, right? I'm just asking the question."

Faulkner tilted her head in consideration of the question which she knew others had been thinking about as well. "If they are aliens, they have a peculiar interest in the situation unfolding in this system. Either that, or their arrival here and their attacks on both us, and presumably, the *Euphrates*, are incredibly difficult to rationalize. What we're about to discuss casts the actions of that vessel in a fairly comprehensible—and very human—light."

She glanced at Garnett.

Garnett for his part, stood and announced, "Ladies, gentlemen, I need to advise you that the rest of this briefing must be conducted under a Contingent Operational Clearance, as per the relevant regulations. Everything we are about to discuss must be considered classified and is not to be discussed with anyone outside this room. This is binding on civilians as well, I must add."

Garnett addressed the only two civilians in the compartment directly, "Ms. Hirayama, Doctor Vance, I must ask you to now state for the record that you understand and will comply with Commonwealth law regarding non-dissemination of classified materials."

Vance rolled his eyes, his characteristic bemused expression becoming if anything, even more droll. "I do so solemnly swear!" He uttered with mock seriousness, his hand in the air.

Atsuko nodded her expression opaque, and affirmed, "I do."

Garnett, apparently satisfied, continued. "As most of you know, my team had embarked on this ship in order to conduct a routine post-accident investigation into the cause of the destruction of the freighter, *Euphrates*. I am now ready to disclose what may have become apparent to some of you since then, which is that our skillset is not strictly limited to accident investigations, nor was the investigation necessarily expected to be routine."

He flicked a command at the holo-display which now showed the face of a slightly balding, middle-aged man.

"This man is Craig Emerson, Assistant Undersecretary of State for Defense Intelligence. He died aboard the *Euphrates*. His job was to perform an audit on the labs on Tengoku, to ensure that they had properly disposed of all materials pertaining to a defense project the government had awarded them, then cancelled. Suffice to say, they had not done so. One assumes he was on his way to report this fact to his bosses on Earth when an apparently invisible assailant torpedoed his ship. I think we all know now how that was accomplished. The larger question is 'why?' To answer that, I think we need Doctor Vance here to explain a bit about Project Seraphim."

Dr. Vance shifted nervously in his seat, glancing around at the attentive faces. "Well," he began then licked his lips, continuing with little of his accustomed impertinence, "I only put the whole thing together quite recently myself. Project Seraphim, in simple terms, is a bioweapon program. The idea was to create an aerosolized virus that can target specific genetic markers—genetic edits, to be precise. The goal is to selectively target and eliminate populations of Modified Colonial Exomorphs—MCEs—without affecting unmodified humans."

A susurration made its way around the table as the naval officers turned to each other with looks of stunned disbelief. Faulkner glanced at the Jotun, Broz, sitting next to Garnett. His face was anything but surprised. He was silent, thick cords of muscle knotting in his neck and jaw. To his right, she observed, the Siren, Anthem, stared at the tabletop in front of her, unusually sedate.

Vance had paused, gauging the room's reaction before continuing. "The virus is highly contagious, and the data I saw indicated an expected mortality rate among the infected subjects of possibly ninety percent. It has an incubation period of roughly eight Terran hours. It's ability to attack only those carriers with certain genetic traits makes it a precise but wide area weapon for... well, for genocide. The kicker is, it's designed with a built-in clock—after a set number of generations, it goes dormant. Theoretically, this gives the affected population a window to surrender or comply... or face extinction."

Dr. Halsey, quiet up until this point, slammed a hand down on the table loudly enough to make several people jump. "And of course," he said, his voice dripping sarcasm, "being that viruses never mutate, I suppose this clock is guaranteed to work without a hitch, is that right?" The grandfatherly surgeon's eyes bored into Vance. "What the hell sort of monster have you people created down there? What were you thinking?"

Broz's deep baritone quietly cut through the agitated conference room, "Hell is empty, and all the devils are here."

All eyes turned to regard the Jotun, whose goggled countenance gazed impassively around the table. "William Shakespeare. The Tempest."

Vance seemed to gaze into the distance for a moment, then cleared his throat and resumed his briefing. "My team weren't involved in creating the pathogen. We were tasked with developing an aerosol delivery mechanism—one that could efficiently disperse a payload over a wide area, half a kilometer or so, not accounting for wind, and ensuring the contents remained stable and viable in different atmospheric conditions. I'm a chemical engineer by training, so to me, it was just a complex challenge: optimizing particle size, achieving maximum dispersion, making sure the carrier medium wouldn't degrade the payload."

He gulped and took a deep breath, his voice wavering. "At first, I thought it was for something like agricultural use, maybe even terraforming applications. I mean, they talked a lot about 'targeted biological factors' in vague terms, which isn't uncommon in my field—pest control, disease vectors, that sort of thing. I was focused on the technical side: how to keep aerosolized particles suspended long enough to ensure maximum coverage without them breaking down. It wasn't until these last several weeks that we began to suspect the real nature of the project."

Vance shifted in his seat before continuing. "It was all very compartmentalized, you see. When the project lead, Dr. Lundgren disappeared, I started doing some snooping. Even after I learned that our work was indeed intended to be weaponized, I figured it was just theory-crafting, another black-budget experiment that would go nowhere. Then, when Atsuko reached out to me and told me Dr. Lundgren had fled in fear for his life, some of us started asking pointed questions. One of my colleagues, Mark McNeil, made it clear he wasn't going to be a part of something...something like this, and they later found him outside the dome with no suit. Suicide, they said."

Vance was shaking now, with some powerful emotion. "Word started to spread around the lab, that it was that Dornier character. Imagine that! He essentially put a hit on one of the project team to get us back in line, as if we— the engineers and biologists—were a bunch of street thugs, and he a mob boss from some old holo. It became pretty clear at that point that Dornier was really nothing more or less than our jailor, and his so-called security forces the prison guards. When I started making a racket—well, I suppose you could say I was put on ice— that's the right phrase isn't it? I went to bed one night and woke up in a storage room on that freighter. I didn't see who did it, I don't remember how I got there. Drugged, I suppose."

The other participants had grown silent.

"Mark had a wife back home. A teenaged daughter and a baby on the way."

"Venerable Founders," somebody muttered, "what if they set the fucking thing off in a spaceport or something?"

Faulkner found herself speechless. This was entire scenario was hard to accept, and yet all the evidence pointed to it being true. Her thoughts were interrupted by the quiet voice of Atsuko.

"Seraphim isn't just a weapon. It's a political tool, a means to control entire colonies by holding their very survival over their heads."

Faulkner decided now was the time to begin directing the flow of the conversation. This was getting to the heart of her most burning questions. "Why?" she asked. "In service of what goal?"

Atsuko shrugged, the barest hint of frustration visible in her body language. "Revolution?"

She sighed and began again, her voice calm and deliberate. "I think it's important to frame this question in the context of the broader difficulties the Commonwealth faces in maintaining control over such a vast colonial network. As many of you already know, the Dominion worlds and even the smaller, newer colonies have grown increasingly self-sufficient in recent years. With that self-sufficiency has come a natural momentum toward autonomy—nativist movements gaining ground, a questioning of Earth's right to dictate their futures."

Atsuko paused, acknowledging the dawning understanding in the room, before continuing. "We've all seen the recent news from Anthemusa, the growing resistance to centralized control, the push for more local governance. These aren't isolated incidents; they're part of a larger shift. As this independence grows, the effectiveness of Earth's traditional methods of governance and enforcement diminishes. Military spending is already under constant scrutiny, and against a backdrop of constant and growing expansion by humans into a vast galaxy, the administrative problems inherent in colonialism grow in scale, exponentially."

She leaned forward slightly, her expression thoughtful. "It's against this backdrop that I think we must consider Project Seraphim's purpose. My uncle, that is, Dr. Lundgren, felt this project was not conceived as a visible deterrent in the conventional sense, but as a hidden measure—a last resort, meant to be revealed only at the most critical juncture, perhaps a full-scale revolt by a dominion world like Anthemusa or Jotunheim. The idea was simple, if ruthless: threaten to use a weapon that could wipe out entire population centers based on their genetic modifications, leaving infrastructure intact, and you have an undeniable leverage point. The weapon was meant to be held in reserve, unknown to all until the moment it was needed, when it could be used to force a rebellious colony into immediate compliance. Its existence was to be revealed only when all other methods had failed—a final, decisive option to maintain Earth's control."

Into the brief silence that followed, Mendoza's words rang like hammer blows, her tone harsh, "and if the colonists in question have no genetic edits? What then? How would they coerce mostly genotypical human colonies like New Texas into obedience?"

Atsuko replied dryly, "I imagine that thinkers on Earth, especially among the mothers and fathers of the Church of Man, assumed they could draw upon the shared wellspring of genetic heritage to engender a sense of communion between the inhabitants of any such colony, and Mother Earth."

An audible snort announced Skye Tanahill's sudden entry into the discussion, "Perfect messaging there, you even know how to talk like them."

Atsuko's lips formed a tight smile. "Yes. I'm very familiar with the rhetoric. I am also well aware of the political power that can be generated by fear of the Other."

Faulkner again took control of the discussion, needing clarity on certain points, "I need to stop you there for a minute. So, your father knew about all this? He took this contract, and then funded the continuation of the research after the government tried to pull the plug?"

Atsuko shook her head. "My father was not forthcoming on this matter. After the Government terminated the program, he refused to speak further about it even to me. And remember, the company is quite large. There are many important stakeholders and decision-makers beyond just our family. A board of directors, whose input carries significant weight in its governance. I learned of this only from Dr. Lundgren, who shares my concerns over the ramifications of creating such a thing. We were benevolent co-conspirators, the two of us. My father left Earth on urgent business shortly before my own contrived departure, and I have not spoken with him in some weeks. I needed to figure some things out— first."

Skye, her junior rank among the assembly seeming in no way to discourage her from active participation, broke in again, her tone one of vindication, "She didn't give daddy a choice—she got herself banished here on purpose, to look into this whole mess."

Atsuko's only answer was a slight inclination of her head, as every face swiveled to look at her curiously.

"That was a bold move," Traxler remarked, his expression and tone warming to something bordering on admiration, "now you can never go back."

"No," Atsuko agreed simply. "I cannot."

This is all very interesting, Faulkner mused, *but I'm not ready to lionize this girl just yet. We need to know who has access to this super-weapon, and what they plan to do with it.* Faulkner steepled her fingers and regarded the young woman at the end of the table with a measuring gaze. *Still—* she allowed grudgingly— *Her sacrifice means something. She thought blowing the whistle on this horror show was the right thing to do, and now the Church is going to make sure she pays for that principled idealism with permanent exile from her home-world. Daddy and Mommy had already ensured she would have money, status, and a fine education. They had to make sure her privilege was total and throw perfect breasts and a brighter smile into the deal. Or maybe...something else? What was your birthday gift really, Atsuko Hirayama?*

Faulkner asked, "So, the Government decides to cancel the project. Maybe saner minds prevail, or they decide the juice just isn't worth the squeeze. But Hirayama Enterprises goes ahead and keeps at it, trying to create a usable super-weapon. For whom? As you pointed out, Atsuko, your family business is a for-profit enterprise. I have to imagine this research project has been fantastically expensive."

Dr. Vance was nodding his head in agreement. "Yes. I can tell you my department's budget alone was a staggering figure."

"So," Mendoza picked up where Faulkner had left off, "where is the return on investment? Who could be the ultimate customer for something like this if not the government? The ethical and legal ramifications of possessing such a weapon are dire, I think we all can agree. One might imagine that's why the government abandoned it in the first place. Any way that you slice it, it's a PR disaster waiting to happen—for both the buyer and the seller. So, who would want it? And who could afford to own it, or risk being caught with it?"

Vance barked a dry, humorless laugh. "That's the twenty billion credit question, isn't it?"

Heads around the table nodded in agreement. Faulkner turned her head toward the grizzled warrant officer and asked, "so what do we know about the *Hermes*, her crew, and these alleged pirates?"

Garnett looked a question to Casimir Broz, who promptly responded in his usual professionally brusque tone. Cass leaned forward, flicking a file on his datapad to the holo-display. A series of portraits appeared, along with the vital statistics of the persons displayed. "The *Hermes* is officially registered to a small outfit called Orion Logistics. But when we dug into their background, turns out Orion is just a front company buried under layers of legal and accounting tricks, all designed to hide who really controls the ship. Even determining true legal ownership of the vessel is no simple matter."

He glanced around the room, ensuring he had everyone's attention. "The actual crew of the *Hermes*—the ones on the payroll for Orion Logistics—are alive and insisting they were just caught in the crossfire. According to them, the hostiles we encountered were pirates who stormed the ship while it was docked at an emergency repair station and seized control."

Cass paused, his expression hardening slightly. "The captain of the *Hermes* won't say anything more without a lawyer, which makes sense if he's worried about getting dragged into whatever mess this is. But here's where it gets interesting—the pirates themselves are mostly dead, except for three we captured, all wounded in the boarding operation. Two of them are clean—no criminal records, no connections to anything suspicious, they claim to be passengers and won't say anything else. But the third, Mr. Purnell here, the individual who had been guarding Atsuko? He is a 'former' employee of the Darkstar Mercenary Company."

He emphasized *former* with a skeptical tone. "Darkstar has a reputation for taking on jobs off the books. It's likely they were hired to secure something—or someone—valuable enough to justify taking over a civilian vessel, assuming they did take it over, and the mercs and crew weren't in this together all along. Our current best assessment is, the tangos were all incognito Darkstar people, and the piracy story is a cover to give the crew plausible deniability."

"They were," Atsuko interjected, then looked nonplussed, as if she'd spoken aloud without meaning to, "I heard them talking."

Cass looked at her steadily for a moment, waiting for her to say more. When she did not, he resumed. "We're still trying to extract more data on who the client is, what they know about the stealth frigate, and where they planned to take Atsuko and Dr. Vance. One more really interesting point though—" Cass selected another file and flicked it to the display— "Someone else we know in this system has a former employer in common with Mr. Purnell. Mr. Franz Christoph Dornier, the security chief at Tengoku City."

Faulkner raised an eyebrow. "He worked for Darkstar too?"

Cass smiled grimly. "Yes, ma'am. Small world, isn't it? That doesn't get us any closer to finding out who the buyer really is, Darkstar just provides muscle for corporations, typically. They don't have the kind of deep pockets required to back something like this, nor is it likely they developed a stealth warship by themselves. It does however draw a dotted line from the gang on the Hermes, to the security team planet-side, and from the security team to Madame Director Timms, at least in my mind. So, we have at least some number of the leadership team for Hirayama Enterprises here in this system and maybe the main office too, Darkstar mercenaries, and Orion Logistics, all working at the behest of someone to get Project Seraphim delivered. It looks like a well-funded and far-reaching conspiracy."

Atsuko placed her hands on the table before her, as if to study them as she spoke. "Whoever wants this weapon would have to believe its value far outweighs the risks. The most obvious answer is a nascent rogue state—someone who either has immaculate information security discipline, or who lies outside the Commonwealth's sphere of influence and who wants a decisive tool to level the playing field."

"Are we talking about a secessionist colony like New Muscovy, here?" Traxler asked of nobody in particular, "I mean, what really is outside the Commonwealth's sphere of influence? There is nothing else, right?"

"Only the rest of the Universe," Vance responded dryly.

Faulkner felt a cold chill pass through her, as Vance's full meaning hit home. There were the rumors of course, of "lost" colonies, independent branches of Humanity that had broken off contact with Earth before the Diaspora had begun in earnest. Moreover, with FTL technology continuing to improve, there were more star systems now accessible from the Core Colonies than the Navy could hope to patrol. *Let's not get lost in idle speculation, Ada.* She cleared her throat. "How long do we think we have until this thing is complete?"

"Two weeks. Perhaps three weeks. No more, unless there is a major unforeseen setback," Atsuko replied, just as Vance had opened his mouth to speak. The elder civilian lapsed into quiescence, his expression troubled.

Faulkner gazed around the room, trying to gauge the responses of others, and her eye lingered again upon the empty chair where Lieutenant Phoebe Jones should have sat.

"Does anyone know where Ms. Jones might be?" she inquired irritably, "maybe she has a more pressing engagement?"

Mendoza cleared her throat. "I will see that she is located, Ma'am."

"Do," Faulkner responded absently.

This is a can of worms, she thought, a pulsing throb springing to life between her temples. *What am I to do with this?*

"We need more information, and we need to contain this thing before someone opens Pandora's Box," Garnett was saying in a clear, slow cadence, "Captain Faulkner, as the senior Gendarme officer in the system, I wish to advise that I have found evidence of a conspiracy to violate Commonwealth sovereignty, which requires intervention per Section 1120 of the Colonial Emergency Powers Act. I hereby request military assistance in quelling the insurrection."

Faulkner massaged her temples with her fingertips. *And there it is, the sound of the other shoe dropping.*

19

Failure of Imagination
CNS Agamemnon, The Iota Persei System

Faulkner stood with her back to Garnett, gazing at the holographic display that mirrored the larger tank in the CIC. Following the meeting, they had adjourned to the office area adjoining her underway cabin. "So, what do you think of young Atsuko, and her tale of daring and intrigue?"

"I think," Garnett said in careful measured tones, "that she is charismatic, highly intelligent, physically attractive, and adroit at manipulating situations to her advantage. She is educated, analytical, a competent investigator in her own right, and her upbringing has taught her how to fade into the background when needed. I imagine her abductors were completely fooled by that 'timid Japanese girl' routine, whereas I am not."

Faulkner raised an eyebrow but for the moment said nothing, so Garnett continued.

"I do think the moral outrage is sincere, though. I should add, she is an expert in hand-to-hand combat it turns out —I found that little tidbit interesting—and she is most certainly hiding something."

"More than one something."

"Yes," Garnett conceded after a pregnant pause, "more than one something."

"Anything in particular you'd like to highlight?"

Another pause, "Nothing I'm at liberty to discuss."

"I see. So, you can't shed any light on how this admittedly charming and intelligent young woman with no official role in the company came to unearth so many details on this top secret weapon program while under what amounts to house arrest?"

Garnett said nothing.

"You're going to be keeping an eye on her."

"Oh, yes, ma'am," Garnett chuckled, "you know—maybe I should recruit her. She's very intent on finding her 'Uncle' Nels Lundgren, a man I very much wish to have words with myself. I feel that helping her in that endeavor is likely to be a much more profitable course of action than trying to hinder her. I think of it as killing two birds with one stone."

Faulkner's underway cabin grew silent for a moment. It was Garnett who broke that silence first. "Ma'am, regarding my request, do you intend to kick it upstairs? I feel time is not on our side here."

Faulkner sighed, finally turning to regard him. "No, Mr. Garnett, I don't think so. And I don't think I'm meant to, actually."

"Ma'am?" Garnett asked, frowning.

"You said earlier that our bosses go to the same parties. You were right, of course. They do, and they all have their illustrious careers to think of. I imagine the admiralty would prefer...what do you call it in your line of work—plausible deniability."

Garnett inclined his head in understanding. "So, we're on our own."

"So it would seem."

"What do we plan to tell Tengoku Control regarding our precipitous return to their lovely little private world?"

Faulkner gave the matter some thought. "What would you suggest?"

"I think I'd advocate for a strategy of strategic ambiguity. Dornier's team were almost certainly behind the attack on Enora Anthem that your CIC got to listen in on, the perp was a veteran of Earth's planetary security forces, and was dishonorably discharged a while back, seems like Darkstar material to me. He was trying to intercept our communications with the ship. The whole confrontation with Enora was probably unintended, a result of him panicking when he got caught. However, when you consider that someone down there thought our report was going to be interesting enough to listen in on, then factor in our team dropping everything to find Atsuko, plus all that's happened since..." Garnett shook his head ruefully. "It seems impossible at this point to think they don't know that *we know* about their dirty little secret."

Garnett ran a hand through his steely gray hair, his eyes gazing into the distance. "Now that we have *Hermes* in tow, the only safe assumption they can make is that we recovered Atsuko and Dr. Vance, and the jig is up. You can be sure that they will instantly see through any sort of pretense that we are just dropping in for a quick conference, and it's all business as usual. On the other hand, we don't want to lean into them with threats and give them reason to feel cornered. I don't imagine they are eager to destroy all the evidence at this late stage, now they are so close to the finish line. That wouldn't sit well with their mysterious partners. Still, we don't need to escalate the situation right away. Let's split the difference."

Faulkner put a finger to her chin, then spoke slowly, "We have encountered hostile forces en-route to inspect *Hermes,* resulting in a confrontation. They must've seen that much even on their civvie space-traffic control gear. Atsuko Hirayama, a person of notable importance to their firm, is now under our protection. Additionally, we have identified significant security concerns and require immediate debriefing of key personnel on-site."

Garnett nodded, his expression thoughtful. "Yes. We make it clear we're suspicious of their involvement to some degree, which is only natural at this point. But we keep our actual intentions vague, keep them on the back foot until we can establish orbit."

"And when we do?"

Garnett smiled. "I had Enora prepare a little subterfuge of our own, while we were ashore. She installed a backdoor for us, into their systems. We cannot access or take control of the computers in the research dome; they are on a separate network with carefully monitored landline disconnects. We can, however, access the systems of the space port and hab domes. Once we are close enough to make a data linkage we can lock down the space port facilities, and the comms systems. Having done so, the marine detachment will secure key points around the colony, while my team moves into the lab dome and secures Seraphim and all personnel on site."

"And if Dornier and his people resist?"

"Then, Captain," Garnett replied, "we drop the hammer on them with zero hesitation."

Faulkner blew out a long breath. "You have enough people? It's not a tiny facility."

"We do," Garnett confirmed. "Our intel says the security team numbers around twenty armed effectives right now. I'm not saying it will be a walk in the park. We will need to move fast, be aggressive, and, if they resist, we will be relentless. There is no room here for pussyfooting around. Their gear is good, ours is better. At least on the ground we won't be outclassed. If it comes to violence, I feel certain we will prevail."

Faulkner nodded, sighing in resignation. *You're going to get my face on the fucking news, aren't you, Garnett?*

"Your plan is approved. I'll inform the MarDet, the command arrangements are as before. You seem to have won Mr. Kamarov's confidence."

"As an old jarhead myself, that's nice to hear."

Faulkner grunted. "I suppose I don't need to underscore my earnest desire not to become famous as the woman who ordered a massacre of civilian scientists. Armed mercenaries are one thing, but I don't want to see pictures of a bunch of dead lab coats sprawled on the floor. I especially don't want to see them on the Plexus, while I am sitting at home trying to enjoy dinner. It's bad for the digestion."

Garnett inclined his head, and the grim little smile had returned. "I share your concerns completely, ma'am. We will do our very best to minimize collateral damage of all kinds."

Faulkner studied the older man for a moment and had a sudden moment of clarity. *You've become cynical,* she thought. *You've been heaping all your own anxieties about the Service, about the mission, about the future, onto Garnett and his team. We've both sworn an oath to protect and defend the Commonwealth, and now it's time to earn your paycheck. You've let yourself come around the view that after the Jotun miners' strike, the fire, and the rehab, you were entitled to some slack. Well, you're not, Ada. You had your chance to walk away, and you didn't. Time to go all in, you're either ready to sit in the big chair or you're not.*

"Well," she finally said, the word almost a sigh, "I was a few days from a medical discharge before I landed this gig, anyway. At least now, worst case, I will have a really good story to tell about how my naval career ended. Possibly at my court-martial, but nevertheless a good story. How did we get here, Robert? How did this creep up on us like this?"

Garnett thought for a moment, then shrugged. "Failure of imagination, I guess. We've been thinking in terms of known threats, predictable responses, assuming that people play by the rules. I think maybe we've been going through the motions for a while. We've grown complacent."

Yeah, she thought, *I know that you meant our society as a whole, but if the shoe fits, I suppose I'll wear it.*

Garnett had paused a moment for effect, and now continued, "This stealth technology we've encountered...look, the Commonwealth has always relied on a tight list of approved defense contractors, right? Supposed to ensure quality, keep things under control. Those contractors are forbidden from selling to anyone else, which means they've got a guaranteed customer in the government— but only one. Sounds good on paper, but the unintended consequence? They get complacent too. They don't have to think outside the box because they know whatever they develop will have only one buyer, the Commonwealth. It's a milk cow. No incentive to push boundaries or innovate much.

Meanwhile, all those manufacturers and R&D shops who didn't make the list? They're left fighting for scraps, competing with each other for corporate and colonial clients, driving innovation and competition in ways we never anticipated."

Garnett was warming to his topic now. "The central government's strategy was meant to secure our weapons tech advantage, but it might've done the opposite—created a whole underground arms race we've been blind to. Now, we've got this stealth tech out there we can't even detect properly. We've got a bioweapon that can target specific humanoid genotypes, and by the way, I confirmed with Dr. Vance, it can absolutely be made to target non-modified genetic characteristics. If someone wanted to turn this weapon on genotypical Earth humans, it's only slightly more difficult than tuning for Sirens, or Jotuns. Maybe our illustrious leaders were slow to realize that, but I'm sure the idea eventually crossed their minds."

Faulkner felt a chill run down her spine.

Garnett's voice had hardened with thinly veiled anger. "When we figure out what the real endgame is here, I think the audacity of it is going to rock the intelligence community, the military, and the central government up to the General Assembly."

Faulkner found herself pondering an old saying from Earth; *May you live in interesting times.*

"Yes, about that stealth ship. We have no guarantee that that was the only one of her class. While it seems unlikely there would be another nearby, given that nobody else joined in the attack, we can't assume that will continue to be the case. The crew needed rest and time out of the suits, but every hour that goes by now and we don't return to General Quarters...it's making my skin crawl. I've already passed the word that we will be returning to Condition yoke shortly, and that everyone should assume we will be at Battle Stations as soon as we make orbit. I see no other sane choice."

The comms panel behind her desk beeped sharply, cutting through the silence. "Captain, Comms watch, Ensign Watley. The acting XO asked me to advise you; Lieutenant Jones has locked herself in her cabin and refuses to come out. The Master-at-Arms tried to override the door, but it's been physically jammed somehow. She sounds agitated, possibly intoxicated. The Security Officer is in sick bay with a bad concussion, and the MAA wants to know if he should call the Gendarme detachment. Medical is on the way, but we're not sure what's going on."

Faulkner glanced up at Garnett.

"By your leave, Captain?"

"Go."

***

As Cass and Atsuko made their way through the small crowd that had gathered in the berthing module in Officer Country where Lieutenant Jones had her quarters, Cass had a moment to wonder how exactly Atsuko had managed to attach herself to this matter of shipboard security, and was considering how to suggest she return to her own stateroom for now, when his companion spoke warmly to someone entering the lateral passageway from the other side. "Alfonzo!"

His eyes followed hers, finding the still somewhat pale countenance of Warrant Officer Alfonzo Ramirez.

"Present," the normally jovial pilot replied with a weak grin. "How are you hanging in, Atsuko?" Ramirez nodded to Cass in greeting.

"Good to see you up and about again, sir," Cass offered.

"Thanks, Broz. Sorry to leave you in the lurch on that boarding op, but it sounds like it all worked out."

"Yes sir, well enough. What's going on here? The Cox'n said something about the Supply Officer barricading herself in her stateroom? Do we know what that's all about?"

"You probably know as much as I do. He'll be down soon, I think he was hobnobbing with the CO in her office when the call came. Let's chat up the Master-at-arms here, get his take."

While the group had been talking, Enora, Skye and Alfred had entered the module using the same entrance as Cass and Atsuko, and now joined their comrades, with back-slapping and kind words for the recently recovered Ramirez. "You missed a hell of a confab with the scientists and ship's brass, Fonzie. We'll have to tell you all about it. Broz here quoted Shakespeare, it was really something," jibed Skye.

"Casimir has the soul of a poet," Atsuko put in with apparent seriousness.

"Yeah," Skye agreed, "and shit for brains."

Cass, rather than dignify this with a response, chose this moment to scratch his nose in a manner that resembled a rude gesture, as Enora and Alfred sniggered.

Ramirez looked first at Skye, then Cass, and chuckled awkwardly. "Okay, you can brief me later, right now try not to make me laugh— it hurts." He turned and led the small group to the door where the Master-at-arms, one of his assistants, and two medics were gathered outside Jones's stateroom.

"Hey there, Chief," Ramirez greeted the senior NCO with his customary smile and relaxed demeanor.

"Warrant Officer Ramirez." The other's look was appraising, his tone polite, but reserved.

"Can you bring us up to speed here? We'll see if we can be of any help."

The chief petty officer who served as the ship's Master-at-arms cleared his throat and clasped his hands behind his back as if preparing to deliver a lecture, "Lieutenant Jones failed to report for duty during her last watch, sir, and had recently been absent for an important meeting. The XO—rather the acting XO, I guess—asked me to check up on her. She's in there, obviously, and won't open the door panel. I could hear her moving around inside, pacing I'd say. We were able to talk with her a bit through the door panel, she sounded... off, like she'd been drinking—slurring her words a bit. But it wasn't just that. She was paranoid, kept asking who I was, and why I was there, even though she knew it was me. Kept saying she couldn't trust anyone."

He paused, glancing at the others accompanying Ramirez, as if trying to gauge their reactions. "I told her I just wanted to talk, maybe help her out if something was wrong, but she got agitated really quick. Started ranting about people watching her, spying on her. At one point, she said something about 'being betrayed by her own blood,' which made no sense to me. I tried to use the security override on the door lock, but she's done something to it on the other side, shoved a shim into the frame or something."

Cass glanced at Ramirez, who was nodding as the other man spoke, his hands on his hips in an attentive posture, his expression the very picture of polite, professional interest.

"Okay, why don't we try to talk to her?" Ramirez suggested reasonably.

"Be my guest," the chief replied.

"Okay, Broz, it's you and me for now, you've had experience in this sort of thing I imagine, my negotiation skills are mostly employed in sleazy nightclubs for nefarious purposes, so keep an eye on me."

Cass raised an eyebrow. *I feel like your people skills are actually pretty on point, but okay.*

"Sure thing, Sir."

Ramirez stepped closer to the sliding door panel, and knocked twice, softly. "Hello, Lieutenant Jones? It's Alfonzo Ramirez from the Gendarmes, I have Petty Officer Broz with me, I guess the captain thought we could help sort out what the trouble is down here, can you tell us a bit about what's got you upset?"

When Jones responded, her voice sounded thick, slurred, and more than a little caustic, "The Captain. That's what the captain thinks, is it? That I want to talk to a couple swinging-dick rocket cops about all my problems?"

"Well," Ramirez replied philosophically, "we are trained for these sorts of situations, by which I mean, angry people on the other side of locked doors. Now, I'm not saying I excelled at that part of the training, I'm just a pilot. But I did show up, and I did pass."

On the other side of the panel a derisive snort could be heard. "Barely, I'm guessing. Go away." There was a moment's pause, then the lieutenant's voice came again, louder, "I have a sidearm, and I'm not in the mood for your bullshit."

Broz glanced sharply at his superior's face, and saw it crease with worry. There was the sound of sudden quiet conversation behind him, and Broz turned to see Garnett in a huddled consultation with the Master-at-arms. Garnett gave the NCO a comradely pat on the upper arm, then turned from him, to join Cass and Ramirez at the door. He said nothing, but merely moved to stand against the bulkhead, when Ramirez looked at him over Cass's head and silently mouthed "gun."

The pilot then turned to once again place his mouth near the door panel, "Uh, that's great Lieutenant, but I don't have mine because I just came from the sickbay, where I've been puking my guts out for what feels like weeks. I'm still too shaky to pose any threat to anyone, let alone have a shootout. The medics aren't packing either, needless to say. I'm sure you could take me unarmed at this point, so I surrender. Can we just, you know—talk this out? Pretty soon I figure the captain is going to send someone in here with a plasma cutter and slice through the door. Then they'll have to chuck sedative gas or flash-bangs in there and drag you out, and then everyone's going to be all pissed off. Why don't we just skip that part? I think the main concern on the Skipper's end is you not showing up for work. It's not worth getting your eardrums perforated over, and you don't want any part of that sedative gas either, trust me."

For several moments, there was silence, then the sound of something scraping against the inside of the doorframe. Cass tensed, his muscles bunching. The panel slid partly aside, and as Cass grabbed the edge and forcibly slid the panel fully open, as the muzzle of a 6mm military-issue pistol appeared in the opening.

Garnett slid smoothly in from the side, grabbing the unsteady hand that held the weapon, and with his other arm, reached across his own body, grasping the barrel of the pistol, and twisting. The nano-titanium alloy of the gun barrel crumpled like an empty beverage bottle in Garnett's fist, and Jones let go her grip on the weapon in shock. Cass launched himself forward and wrapped up the slight figure of the supply officer in a bear hug.

I'd heard the Cox'n had some cybernetic work done, but damn.

Jones squirmed, crying out and cursing. Garnett and Ramirez piled into the small stateroom and performed a cursory inspection. Cass also looked around the compartment, noting a mostly empty bourbon bottle on the small desk that must have been liberated from ship's stores. Jones, continuing to struggle futilely in his arms, smelled of body odor, alcohol, and something else he couldn't place. Her hair was disheveled, and she wore only her utility trousers and a sweat-stained tank top. Her bunk was unmade, the sheets and zero-gee webbing hung over the edge and had partially fallen onto the deck, and the cabin was in most un-military disarray.

Ramirez turned to face her, and spoke, his tone soothing, "settle down LT, Broz will turn you loose if you just settle down, we just don't want you hurting yourself— or myself, I told you, I'm delicate right now. Take a breath and try to relax."

The faces of the medics appeared at the doorway, their expressions a question directed at Garnett, who shook his head, forestalling them with a finger.

Atsuko also appeared, and undeterred by Garnett's fierce expression, walked in and placed a hand on Jones's shoulder. "Perhaps a woman's voice?"

Cass glanced at Ramirez, who in turn looked to Garnett.

The elder warrant officer shrugged. "You're here now, Ms. Hirayama, go ahead."

"Lieutenant Jones," Atsuko said softly, "it's okay. We're here to help."

Jones's struggles lessened slightly, her gaze flickering to Atsuko. "You don't understand," she muttered. "None of you do."

"Then help me understand," Atsuko replied. "Sometimes talking about it can make things clearer."

Atsuko gently stroked the other woman's upper arm, as one might soothe an upset child.

Jones shook her head, her voice tinged with desperation. "I can't trust anyone. They're all watching me."

"Who is watching you?" Cass inquired, but Jones did not immediately answer.

"Phoebe, tell us about this New League," Atsuko coaxed, her eyes fixed on those of the now quiescent Jones.

The who? Cass wondered, his brow furrowing in confusion. *When did she say anything about a new league? League of what?*

Jones sagged against his body as if stricken, and Cass realized that if he let her go now, she would simply slump to the floor. *Did I just check out for a second and miss something? And since when is Atsuko on a first name basis with the supply officer?*

After a moment, her body seemed to convulse, and Cass realized she was weeping. He gently steered her toward her bunk and sat her down. Tears were flowing down her face now, and she struggled to suck in air to speak.

"I don't know who they really are," she whispered. "My father—he said they were the future of the Commonwealth. That we had a chance to be on the right side of history. All I had to do was look the other way when the coolers went down. We would return to port early, and everything would..." She trailed off, overcome with emotion, her breathing quickening into shallow gasps.

"Your father...Admiral Tamatoa Jones? He ordered you to abet sabotage of a Navy vessel?" Garnett's tone was incredulous.

Cass grimaced, dismayed at this revelation but apparently not as surprised as his commanding officer was. *A high-ranking mole in the Navy...The Deuce, you say?*

Jones nodded but still seemed unable to speak. "Okay," Garnett said to the waiting medics, "you'd better come on in."

"They tried to kill us!" Jones wailed, her anguished voice cracking.

The Navy medics moved into the stateroom around Atsuko and the Gendarmes who occupied most of the available space, and one unrolled a kit onto the deck sole, while another knelt before Jones, and began shining a penlight in her eyes, one at a time.

Jones turned her tear-streaked face toward Atsuko, her eyes filled with a mix of fear and relief. "He said it was for the greater good," she whispered. "That sacrifices had to be made."

Atsuko nodded understandingly. "Sometimes those we trust can lead us down dark paths. But you don't have to carry this burden alone."

Cass exchanged a glance with Ramirez, who gave a subtle shake of his head, indicating they should let Atsuko continue.

"Phoebe," Atsuko continued softly, "can you tell us more about what your father asked you to do?"

20

Riding a Tiger

CNS Agamemnon, The Iota Persei System

C ass paced back and forth in the cramped area afforded to him in the berth he shared with Enora.

"It's not enough to take to the brass, you know that. They're not going to investigate, let alone take any punitive action against a two-star admiral based solely on the ramblings of his own daughter—a troubled junior officer so drunk and so high on tranquilizers at the time, that she wouldn't need an FTL drive to travel among the stars. She's never going to repeat that stuff in an interrogation chair, or in front of a board of inquiry."

Enora had been uncharacteristically quiet since returning to their quarters with Cass. Now she looked up from where she lay sprawled on her bunk. "Do we believe her? I mean, normally, corruption among the powers that be isn't difficult for me to imagine. I've met too many of them at my father's little get-togethers for that to be an issue. Once you've had a few ambassadors and governors run their hands over you while your parents are literally in the room—well, very little surprises you on that front anymore. But an admiral ordering his own kid to sabotage the ship she's serving on?"

Cass grunted, and scratched his head. "It does seem far-fetched, but if any of what Jones told us is true, this conspiracy has deep pockets, and more than a few contacts in government circles. It's staggering in scope, but the stealth ship was definitely real, and Project Seraphim is real. The guy who shot you was real. Occam's Razor would seem to apply. Given what the Cox'n told us before we signed up, about corporate sponsored insurrections, I have to think she's telling the truth about this cabal— or league or whatever. Certainly, Atsuko believes her."

Enora sat up, swinging her legs over the side of the bunk. "Atsuko knows lots of things she shouldn't," she said thoughtfully. "But that's a discussion for another time."

"What do you mean?" Cass demanded sharply.

Enora regarded him for a moment, her oval face impassive. "Cass, seriously?"

"What?"

"You didn't notice her pull that 'New League' business out of thin air? It's like she'd heard the phrase before. And I refuse to believe that she walked into that top-secret lab complex, batted her eyelashes at a few scientists, and they all started just pouring out their most guarded corporate secrets. I'll grant you she's a good-looking girl, but she's not that good looking. I know you like her, but you can't be that naive."

"You mean scientists like Vance? He probably spilled his guts as soon as the daughter of the CEO expressed an interest. He obviously has moral objections to what's been going on, plus he resents authority on general principle. If you look up 'eccentric scientist' in the dictionary, there's probably a picture of his face."

Enora raised one eyebrow doubtfully but said nothing.

"Spit it out, Enora."

She sighed, running one hand through her ivory-white hair. "Like I said, she sure does seem to be in the right place at the right time, an awful lot of time. But I don't really want to go down this road right now. I just want you to give a little thought to the matter of how she always seems to come up with some critical piece of missing information right as we go looking for it."

Cass stood still for a moment and stewed. *She's got a point, so why am I so resistant to even considering it? Atsuko has been a slow but steady spigot of information since we met her, never gushing— but always trickling.* He decided to acquiesce to the change of subject Enora obviously wanted. This one bore careful consideration when he could be alone with his thoughts.

Cass leaned against the bulkhead and regarded Enora with a measuring gaze. *She looks tired, and even thinner than usual,* he mused. "How's the shoulder?"

"Hurts. Regen is going okay, though, it'll be fine."

"You going to be good for this next op? Enora, this may be where the deniable part of 'deniable humanoid assets' comes into play. If you don't feel up to it, tell the Cox'n. I'm sure he'd excuse you from this one so you can heal up. And..." he hesitated before continuing, "it may be advisable if you want to make it to your mandatory ten years. We may come back from Tengoku in one piece, but I wouldn't lay odds that our careers will. These people are not a hated terrorist cell or gang, they are one of the most powerful medical research firms, not to mention prime defense contractors in the explored galaxy. We have to assume they are among good company in this New League."

"You're gonna need me. I have to have a good signal without a lot of attenuation to run the worms I planted in their systems."

Cass had to concede this was true. While Garnett could certainly find his way around a neural network, he was going to be very busy, and the backdoors they had deployed were code that only Enora understood well. "Yeah. How are you doing otherwise? You seem kind of off these last few days."

Enora sighed and examined her hands. "I don't know, Cass, I fatally shot a stranger earlier in the week, and then during the battle with that invisible warship, I found a kid who didn't really look old enough to enlist, skewered by a piece of the hull and practically hanging outside. He died. I tried to help him but—" she shrugged. "As usual my efforts were better spent sitting in front of a terminal, far away from firearms, sharp objects, and the void of outer space. At least on this mission I will have ample adult supervision."

Cass studied her for a moment; concern etched on his face. "Enora, you've been through a lot lately," he said gently. "What happened with that guy...it's not your fault. You were defending yourself. You can't predict how someone will react when they're discovered doing something they shouldn't be doing. He made the choice to escalate."

"Nathaniel Reed," Enora replied softly, her voice trembling. "That was his name. That's the guy I killed."

Cass nodded. "It's good that this burden weighs heavily on you, Enora. I know it feels bad. It's not supposed to feel good. But I want you to remember, when I lost my shit back on Unity Station, and almost mopped the floor with a few of those dockworkers after they assaulted you. Do you remember what you told me?"

Enora hesitated a moment, her brow furrowed, then nodded wordlessly, her silvery eyes glistening wetly in the harsh overhead lighting.

"You told me," Cass continued slowly and deliberately, "control was an illusion, and the trick is in knowing when to let the illusion go."

"Yeah, that Enora's a genius," she replied bitterly, "She should write a self-help book. If I had a time-machine, I'd go back in time about thirty days or so and kick that pretentious little bitch in the crotch."

Cass straightened, suppressing a grin, then moved to kneel in front of her. "You sorted me out, that's for sure. Now I want you to remember, control in those situations—the comms tower, the young spacer who died—it was an illusion. You never had it. You just played the hand you were dealt, and you did exactly what I would have done, what a lot of people would have done in your place. You tried to be a good shipmate; you did your job. You're feeling way out of your depth right now, I get that, so am I. Don't think for a second that I'm not. This situation is FUBAR, and we just do not have control, Enora. We *do not have control*. We just need to power through. We have to remember we are on the side of righteousness, at least as far as it pertains to this Project Seraphim business, and just try to ride this tiger without falling off."

He reached out and gently grasped her right hand. "I trust you. I told you to consider sitting this one out because I'm your friend, and I know how you hurt right now. Believe me, I do. But I'm actually glad you're set on going, because frankly, I didn't want to set foot on that frozen hellhole again without you backing me up, and that's a fact."

Enora smiled then, and some of her old ebullience began to return. She squeezed his hand, hard. "I got your back."

"I know."

"They don't have tigers on Jotunheim do they?"

"No, but riding a nocturnodon is even dumber, and doesn't have the same ring."

Garnett chose this moment to stick his head into the compartment and interrupt, "you two had better try to get some rack time, you have about four hours to lay down in real sheets, then the Skipper's going to have us suit up again. She's not willing to bet the farm that there aren't more stealth ships laying doggo out there somewhere, and I don't blame her."

"Right," Cass answered, standing up. "Sir, can I have a moment first?"

"Walk with me," Garnett replied, and turned to move off down the central corridor of the berthing module.

***

"Sir, Enora and I were talking, and she raised a concern I want to share with you." Cass paused, uncertain quite how he wanted to proceed.

"Atsuko."

Cass stopped walking for a moment, taken aback, and Garnett stopped too, turning to face him across the passageway.

"Yes, sir. Enora feels that she may know more than she is letting on, and that I may be getting too close to her to see it. I have to concede, she may be right. I have a hard time believing that Atsuko would have anything to do with this criminal conspiracy or a super weapon, but she does seem..." Cass trailed off. "I'm not sure. She's very intelligent, she must have been able to intuit or figure out a lot listening in on her father and this Dr. Lundgren. Certainly, Vance could have told her much to confirm her suspicions once she arrived in this system. I don't know if Enora is just being paranoid, or I'm not paranoid enough."

Garnett sighed. "If you are asking me if I think it's possible you are sometimes thinking with an organ other than your brain when it comes to Ms. Hirayama, the answer is yes." He held out a hand to forestall Cass from responding. "That said, it's encouraging that you have enough self-awareness of the fact to come to me with this, and in turn I'm going to give you the benefit of the doubt, as a grown-ass man, that you will recognize when and if your personal life is having a detrimental effect on your work. I will also submit to you this possibility, that there are other explanations for her insights into our enemy's actions and motives, besides bad-faith or complicity."

Cass frowned, replying slowly, "do you have one such explanation forefront in mind, sir?"

Garnett met Cass's gaze steadily. "I do," he replied. "Consider that Atsuko might have access to information channels that aren't exactly conventional."

Cass's frown deepened. "Information channels? What are you implying, sir?"

"I'm implying that the Universe is a big, and strange place. I can't really say more about this. On the other hand, if Atsuko wishes to open up to you about it, there's not much I can do about that."

Cass's frown deepened. "I don't understand."

"Cass," Garnett began carefully, using his given name for possibly the first time Cass could ever recall, "I cannot say more. Do you understand? I'm not telling you I am unwilling to continue the conversation, I'm telling you, I can't."

Cass stared at Garnett, confusion and concern etched across his face. "I...I think I understand, sir," he said slowly. *He's under orders not to talk about this? Why? What the hell is going on here?*

Garnett gave a subtle nod. "I knew you'd catch on. Just remember, some things are need-to-know, and for now, that's all I can say."

Cass took a deep breath, trying to process the implications. "Understood, sir."

"Good," Garnett replied, his tone softening. "Keep your eyes open and trust your instincts."

Cass hesitated before speaking again. "Sir, do you trust her?"

Garnett met his gaze steadily. "Trust is a valuable commodity these days. I trust actions more than words, son. So far, Atsuko's contributions to this operation have been invaluable. Keep that in mind."

"Yes, sir."

"Now, unless there's anything else, we have preparations to make, and you will benefit from getting some rack-time while you can." Garnett said, signaling an end to the conversation.

Cass nodded. "Of course, sir."

After Garnett had moved along down the corridor toward his office, Cass turned and walked in a different direction, but not toward his berth. Instead, he found himself standing outside the small officer's stateroom that had been set aside for Atsuko.

He raised his hand, making a loose fist poised to knock, when the door panel slid aside, and Atsuko stood before him in her borrowed military issue sweatpants and tank top, her familiar faint smile in place.

"Good evening, Casimir. I am delighted to see it is you lurking outside my quarters, and not another nurse or yeoman come to diligently make themselves of service."

"Lurking?" Cass answered, a small smile quirking his lips.

"A figure of speech," she replied, her smile widening. "Come in."

She stood aside to let him enter, and he found the layout of her modest quarters were essentially the same as those of Lieutenant Jones, a bunk, a fold-down desk, a locker, and a small refresher unit. He entered, and she slid the panel closed again.

"What's on your mind?"

"Yes, I just uh—"

She cocked her heart-shaped head to the side, prompting him to continue.

"I just wanted to get your take on something. I was talking to Garnett earlier, about the investigation, and—" he waved his hand in a vague gesture, "—everything. He suggested that you might have, some kind of special access to information that could be of help, and I was just wondering, I mean..." he found himself gazing into the deep, molten bronze pools of her eyes, flustered and uncertain how to continue.

"Special access?" Her tone was cool now, her expression guarded.

Cass felt momentarily dizzy, for just a moment the strangest sensation came upon him, and then he recalled a moment during the boarding of the *Hermes...*

A feeling of vertigo, like his feet had lost contact with the deck. There's a large space around him, but he can't see it, all he sees is a dingy storage room, shelves lined with boxes and cartons. But that isn't where he is, it's where Atsuko is.

"You know what's weird?" he said, his words tumbling out before he even knew what he was going to say, "You know when you were on that ship, and we were coming to find you— I was so sure we'd find you there— I was in the cargo hold with the marines, and I had this sort of...I don't know, seizure? I guess?"

Atsuko was looking at him with concern, her face becoming grave. "Seizure?"

"Yeah, I almost feel like it had happened before too, but what's crazy is, I can't remember when. But it was on this deployment, I'm pretty sure about that. Maybe seizure is the wrong word."

She regarded him now with an expression he couldn't identify. Was it concern? Dread?

"Atsuko, is this about some classified new cybernetics or something? I'm not going to say anything if so, I just want to understand."

"You just want to understand what?" Her tone when she responded was mechanical, emotionless.

I just want to understand you, he thought bitterly, *I just need to know if you really are the person I think you are— or that I want you to be—that is probably closer to the truth.*

"I am who I am, Petty Officer Broz."

Cass opened his mouth to reply, but his words died on his lips. *No,* he thought. *This is too surreal.*

His thoughts began to race, and he felt hot, his uniform collar was too tight, and too itchy. He tried to slow down the tumult of emotions and thoughts competing for prominence in his mind, and focused on a single idea, like a mantra, as he stared into Atsuko's eyes. *Can you read my mind?*

Atsuko turned away, concealing her face with her long, straight hair.

Can you, Atsuko?

"Yes," came the reply, her voice quiet and taut with some emotion Cass couldn't decipher. "And it is becoming easier."

"I—" Cass blew out a breath he didn't realize he'd been holding. "I don't know what I was going to say if you could. That's the one possibility I did not prepare for, coming into this conversation. I was ready to hear that you had a network of spies in your own family business, or that you were—" Cass stopped. *You were what?*

"Complicit in the conspiracy?" Atsuko finished for him.

"If you can really read minds," he shot back angrily, "then you know that's not what I was thinking."

She turned to face him once again, brushing her hair aside with one delicate looking hand. *The same hand she used to break a guy's nose not long ago,* Cass reflected. Atsuko's expression softened, and she reached out the same hand to touch his face, in that same gentle, almost hesitant gesture she had used in the gym. "I am your friend, Casimir, and I am on your side."

"Okay, but you have psychic powers and didn't feel that was something you should mention before now?"

Atsuko tilted her head and regarded him seriously, her hand still lightly caressing his cheek. "I wouldn't phrase it quite that way. And I did not raise the matter, because you were not ready to hear it. Are you feeling well now? I am concerned that my efforts to—to connect with you—have somehow harmed you."

"Well, forgive my imprecise language, but I'm fine now, and I'm ready to hear all about it. At least I think I am. I feel this is probably a pretty important topic, actually."

"Later," she replied gently her hand dropping to press lightly upon his chest for a moment. "There is the raid to prepare for, and you need rest. This is not the time."

"I'm getting a lot of that lately, apparently it is not the time for any meaningful exchange of ideas right now."

Atsuko quirked one corner of her mouth up in a tiny gesture, that faint ghost of a smile that he had come to find so expressive, "What do you mean?"

"Forget it," Cass replied ruefully, "just something Enora was saying in quarters, along roughly the same lines."

Atsuko's hand fell from his chest, and he found himself wishing that she would resume the physical contact.

"So," she said, her face earnest now, "you and the lovely Enora Anthem...bunk together?"

Cass stared at her for a moment, flustered yet again. He wished that he could in that moment, reach out and read *her* mind.

As he could not, he took a few seconds to process then recovered a bit of his poise and said with exaggerated patience, "in separate bunks, Atsuko."

She laughed now, a full-throated, musical laugh. "I am sorry, I should not tease you."

"Especially given that you already knew that."

Atsuko's expression grew serious once more. "I am not sure it works the way you think it works," she replied, and then seemed struck by an idea. "Perhaps Enora and I need to spend some 'girl time' together? She has a fascinating background, I feel we should get to know one another better."

Cass groaned. "Founders and the Prospect of Unity forfend."

Atsuko leaned in abruptly and hugged him, pressing her left cheek against his right. Neither were especially tall, and Cass found it pleasing that they were of nearly the same height. His senses drank in her warmth against him, her clean scent filled his nostrils. "Goodnight, Casimir. Be careful tomorrow, know that I am with you."

Fifteen minutes later Cass found himself standing outside his own berth, his hand on the door panel control pad, and his thoughts a jumble. Telepathy? Could it be true? It was difficult to accept, and yet the evidence seemed indisputable. The existence of such abilities certainly did answer a few questions, while at the same time, presenting new ones. As he keyed the pad to open the door, he heard Enora mumble something.

"Go to back to sleep," he murmured, as he stepped into the narrow space within, removing first his goggles then his uniform blouse, and throwing both onto a chair he could easily see in the partial darkness. He stood there a moment more in the shadows, scratching the back of his closely shorn head. *So, we will talk later,* he mused. *Later. That's a hell of a word to say to someone, really.* His mind wandered, vacillating between his frustration with the two women who had somehow become central to his new life, and thoughts of his brother, Andre.

What should I have made sure I told you, Little Brother? Did I leave something unsaid? Something to raise later, at the gym maybe, or over dinner? Am I here right now, on this stupid ship, because it is what my sense of duty dictates, or because I feel guilty? If I choose to assume that the people on the planet below represent the same group that had you killed, I imagine it will help me stay focused. I know that it will unquestionably make it that much easier to keep pulling the trigger. I wonder if you would approve. Maybe Enora still knows something I've forgotten?

Cass removed his boots and began climbing into his bunk, and in his mind's eye, floated the face of Atsuko Hirayama, smiling that secret little smile. He remembered her warmth and the smoothness of her skin against his. He could almost recall the scent of her.

All I know for sure right now is, I'd better not fucking die tomorrow.

21

Shore Party

Tengoku Orbit, The Iota Persei System

Senior Warrant Officer Garnett stood at the front of the briefing room aboard the *Agamemnon*, his eyes scanning the assembled team with a stern intensity. Cass, Enora, and the rest of DHARMA Team Sierra sat attentively in the first row, armor donned and helmets resting beside them. Behind them sat the Gendarme support squad, and the NCOs and officers of the ship's marine detachment. The air was thick with tension.

"Good morning, everyone," Garnett began, his voice cutting through the silence. "We have a critical situation on Tengoku. As some of you already know, our recent visit to the colony below has confirmed that elements within Hirayama Enterprises are covertly developing a weapon of mass destruction. This cannot continue, and we cannot allow any related materiel to leave the planet. Time is not on our side, and failure is not an option."

He pressed a control on the lectern, and a holographic display materialized behind him. The schematics of Tengoku's colony appeared, highlighting the spaceport dome, tram lines, executive dome, Residential areas, and the isolated lab facility suspected of housing Project Seraphim.

"Our mission will proceed as follows," Garnett continued. "The Gendarme detachment, designated Shore Party Sierra, will depart the *Agamemnon* aboard our pinnace, approaching under normal procedures to avoid suspicion. Upon landing, Petty Officer Anthem"—he nodded toward Enora, "will infiltrate their systems using our pre-established access points. She'll initiate a full containment lockdown: halt all trams, seal the domes, and secure control of the spaceport doors. Movement within the colony will be frozen."

Cass exchanged a glance with Enora. She gave a slight nod, her expression focused and resolute.

"Having done so," Garnett said, "Team Sierra and the Gendarme squads will deploy directly onto the landing grid in full armor the second we are wheels down. The grid will still be open to the lower pressure native atmosphere of Tengoku, so the enemy can't play any games with us by depressurizing the bay while we're disembarking. We will keep the inner berthing bay doors closed, so we can get all our boots on the ground and in a state of full combat readiness before we greet the locals. Our primary objective is to secure the Spaceport Dome—neutralize any immediate threats and prevent any escape attempts. From there, we'll advance to the Executive Dome to apprehend Hirayama's senior leadership and secure any and all related evidence."

He allowed a brief pause, ensuring the plan was clear. The holographic display shifted to emphasize the lab facility.

"At the moment we begin our final approach, a second pinnace carrying the marine detachment, designated Shore Party Bravo, will launch and execute a combat landing on the surface outside the Lab Dome. Their orders are straightforward: infiltrate via the emergency airlocks, arrest all personnel, and secure all computers, equipment, and materials. Prevent any destruction of evidence until it can be thoroughly examined. Lieutenant Kamarov will command that boat."

Garnett's gaze hardened as he surveyed the room. "Expect resistance. Hirayama's regular private security forces are run-of-the-mill, but they are being augmented by incognito Darkstar mercenaries, well-trained and equipped. We don't expect they will hesitate to engage. Our advantage lies in surprise and decisive action."

Petty Officer Dawson from the Gendarme squad raised his hand. "Sir, what are the rules of engagement?"

"Use of lethal force is authorized only if you face an immediate threat," Garnett replied. "Our goal is to apprehend suspects alive for interrogation, minimize collateral damage, and avoid harm to noncombatants." Garnett gazed around the room to include everyone, "That means we try not to blow away anyone in a lab-coat unnecessarily. As I said, the idea here is to get the eggheads into custody. That said, consider any armed civvies including Hirayama staff as enemy combatants to be disarmed peacefully, if possible, or forcibly, if required. Given what we know as of a few days ago, there are as many as two hundred family members, vendors, guests and support staff on-site, apart from the research staff and security team. You will be drawing riot-control gas grenades in addition to your normal combat loadouts; they may come in handy. If hostiles attempt to use civilians to their advantage, you must assess the situation carefully. Non-lethal methods are preferred in such scenarios. Petty Officer Anthem will assist by providing identification and tracking of known hostile personnel."

Kamarov, the Marine Detachment commander, was frowning as he spoke. "Do we have any protocols in place to manage potential panic among the civilians once the lockdown begins?"

"Yes," Garnett said. "A lockdown announcement will be broadcast, explaining that a security drill is in progress. This should reduce panic and keep civilians in designated areas. Ground teams will be responsible for directing any civilians they encounter to the safe zones."

Cornet Chen, Kamarov's second in command raised her hand next. "What if they attempt to destroy evidence before we can secure it?"

"Petty Officer Anthem will work to prevent remote data purges originating from the executive suite, but her access to the lab networks is severely limited," Garnett said, acknowledging Enora again. "On the ground, prioritize securing data storage and servers. If necessary, cut power to prevent data loss. Speed is essential."

Cass spoke up. "Do we have intel on their security measures or any potential cyber defenses?"

"Limited," Garnett admitted. "We know they have advanced systems, but specifics are unclear, Petty Officer Anthem didn't have many opportunities to delve into that area. Be prepared for electronic countermeasures of all kinds, and improvised defenses. Director Timms and her team are up against a wall here, and they will not be excited to see us. Bear in mind, that once their security forces fire a single bullet to prevent us from apprehending them, they may as well have fired a thousand. They will have taken up arms against the Commonwealth and thus, will have very little left to lose at that point. Desperate people do stupid things."

He took a moment to meet the eyes of each team member. "This mission will demand adaptability and coordination. I know this group excels at both. Trust in your training and in each other."

A heavy silence settled over the room. The enormity of the task ahead was palpable.

"Any further questions?" Garnett asked.

No one responded. Cass craned his neck to look around the room. He was met with resolute expressions.

"Very well," Garnett concluded. "We deploy in two hours. Use this time to review mission details and prepare your gear. Dismissed."

As the team dispersed, Cass stood and collected his helmet. Enora joined him as they headed toward the armory.

"Looks like we're in for a long day," Cass remarked.

Enora managed a faint smile. "Bad news is, we don't get paid overtime."

He glanced at her. "You confident about accessing their systems?"

"I've thoroughly hidden the access points. Unless they've overhauled their entire network since yesterday, we should be fine," she replied.

"Let's hope they haven't," Cass intoned. "Otherwise, I expect this little excursion is going to become exceptionally interesting."

***

"Ladies and Gentlemen," came the voice of Ramirez over Cass's helmet comms, his tone pitched in a creaky, exaggerated parody of the singsong lilt used by aerospace pilots everywhere, "we are beginning our final descent into Tengoku City, where the local time is 0946. Our lovely flight attendants will be coming through to make one last check of the cabin prior to landing. Please remain seated, with your seatbelts securely fastened for the remainder of this very short, and possibly doomed flight. We recognize that you have many options when it comes to combat landings on hostile planets, and we thank you for choosing Customs and Excise Starlines, where your safety is priority number three, or—maybe four."

Cass heard low chuckles around him and shook his head. *Glad he's feeling better.*

Alfred's warm voice immediately piped up on the local channel, "Man, I know you ain't talking about the crew chief. He's a good-looking man, but even his momma wouldn't call him lovely."

Next to him, Cass saw Skye's helmet slowly begin shaking side to side in wordless reproach, as more and louder laughter burst out in the cargo cabin of the pinnace. The crew chief had crossed his legs primly and, with an exaggerated sigh, began fanning his helmet as if he were a starlet in a holo-drama on the verge of swooning. Cass snorted. *Another lesson in proper grammar, incoming in three...two...one...*

But Skye held her peace this time, and the nervous banter in the hold died out as quickly as it had begun.

In the quiet that followed, Cass could feel the nimble landing craft banking, and hear the hostile, rarified atmosphere beating against the skin of the pinnace as it descended toward the waiting landing grid, and by extension, whatever manner of welcome party Timms and Dornier had arranged to meet them. Cass felt sure they would be coldly received. As much as he dreaded the looming confrontation ahead, he could not imagine it being resolved amicably. The *Agamemnon* would be communicating with ATC on Tengoku, and he knew Faulkner would be on hand to offer platitudes and noncommittal assurances that the Gendarmes enroute to the surface were simply there to conduct interviews, or other non-specific investigative activities etcetera, but he felt sure everyone involved already knew the time for deception on both sides was past. Timms had two fundamental choices; resist— or do not. While resistance ultimately seemed foolish, he knew that failing to resist too had far-reaching legal and extralegal consequences for her and for her associates. Cass couldn't imagine that her shadowy allies—or employers, as the case may be—would look well on her giving up Project Seraphim or destroying it and thereby denying it to the New League, without even putting up a fight. *No*—he had conceded even before boarding the pinnace— they would resist. No criminal entity willing to countenance the use of something like Project Seraphim would tolerate the arrest, interrogation, and eventual trial of the people behind its creation. Names might be named, and dark secrets exposed to the light of day. Cass felt a tight knot forming in the pit of his stomach, as he tried to do the mental calculus on the most likely outcome of their mission, but the short-term future remained a nebulous maelstrom of terrible, vague potentialities.

Just ride the tiger and don't let go, he admonished himself. *If someone points a gun at you, you shoot first and let the lawyers ask questions later.*

His ruminations were interrupted by Garnett's voice in his ear. "Alright people, get loose. You are authorized to lock and load. We hit dirt in five."

Cass removed his weapon from its storage bracket, checked that it was safe, and charged it. He glanced around the cabin and verified that the others were doing likewise, so he opted to say nothing. He would be officially assuming the role of Leading Petty Officer for the shore party, even though his permanent rank was too low for such a billet. Garnett had quietly breveted him to the temporary rank of Chief Petty Officer. Oddly, Cass found himself uncomfortable with this formality, even though he had led teams of this size before.

With a mental flick, he summoned the colony's schematic to his HUD and reviewed it one last time. The so-called Executive Dome was the administrative as well as the topographical center of the facility, with other buildings linked directly to it—and sometimes to each other—via tunnels and tram lines. By design, the Lab Dome could only be reached through the Executive Dome.

This presented them with tactical challenges as well as opportunities. By seizing the Spaceport Dome and then the Lab Dome, they could flank whatever security forces the colony leadership had doubtless assigned to themselves as a protective detail. Cass and Garnett agreed that these forces would most likely be the more seasoned and better-armored Darkstar mercenaries, of which they had identified nine, including Dornier himself.

Garnett spoke again, on a private channel this time. "Agamemnon Actual conveys her felicitations and wishes to inform us that the other boat is launching now. Everything squared away back there, Chief?"

Garnett's use of his brevet rank was a pointed and somewhat unwelcome reminder of the importance he placed in Cass's new role as his ranking NCO, a role that placed him roughly on par with an NI platoon sergeant.

"Yes, sir. Squared away. I'm about to get them up."

"Do so. Once we're wheels-down, timing is everything," Garnett continued. "We need to move swiftly to secure the Spaceport Dome and facility staff, before we can push for the Eagle's Nest."

Cass nodded, though Garnett would not be able to see it from his seat in the cockpit. He took some amount of grim amusement from his superior's characterization of the Executive offices. "Understood. We'll execute the plan as briefed—First Squad secures the berthing bays, Second Squad covers the perimeter around the boat. Third Squad—the SMU will secure the harbormaster's station up top."

"Good. Make sure we watch our spacing and keep alert for sabotage or other nasty surprises on the grid. Those last few seconds before we touch down will be dicey. Ramirez and Anthem have been watching for anything alarming during the approach and haven't spotted it, but that doesn't mean much."

"Understood," Cass replied, "at least there hasn't been any anti-air."

Garnett's voice was quiet when his reply came. "True, but that fact doesn't give me much comfort. It feels like the *Hermes* all over again. From where I am sitting, that landing grid looks like a carnivorous pitcher plant, and we're the dumbass fly."

Cass took a moment to process the metaphor then grunted his agreement. "My head will be on a swivel, Sir."

"Good. Two minutes out, now. Saddle up."

Cass switched back to his local channel, and spoke in what he hoped was a crisp, authoritative tone. "All right, gang, show time."

As he spoke, the cabin lighting dimmed and turned red. The crew chief, already unbuckling his safety harness, stood and moved to the rear cargo door. Cass felt the ship bank sharply, her engines whining shrilly as Ramirez goosed them for power. His guts made a perfunctory protest, but Cass ignored them. He gripped the stanchion over his head for stability and barked, "Get ready. Final weapon and suit checks. Squad leaders sound-off when ready."

The occupants of the cabin began their checks, acting on muscle memory gained from repeated training. A moment later he was met with two terse replies.

"First Squad ready."

"Second Squad ready!"

"Roger," he droned, "Sierra team ready. Prepare for depressurization." Cass changed channels again and reported to Garnett up front, "Sir, ready for aft cabin depressurization."

Garnett's cool voice acknowledged, and a moment later the cabin pressure indicator began flashing amber. Cass's suit HUD reported the pressure in the small craft dropping, so it would match that of the open landing grid.

The deck of the pinnace evened out, and a moment later there was a resounding thump that reverberated through the craft. The crew chief spoke into a channel Cass could not hear, then after a moment's pause, the red deployment light over the door blinked and flashed green. The crew chief hit the release on the aft door, which began to drop with a faintly audible hydraulic whine.

"Go, go, go!" Cass barked. "Sierra One and Three on me, Sierra Two—once we are out, deploy and disperse, you know the drill."

The hatch to the flight deck had opened as Cass spoke, and now Garnett appeared, watching the proceedings from behind his closed visor. Ramirez and Enora would remain on the boat, the former to keep it ready for a hasty dust-off, and the latter to operate their cyber-warfare systems from her console. Garnett would assume personal command of the shore party once they had deployed.

Cass nodded at his superior, then turned and rushed down the ramp, which had just reached the concrete of the landing grid. The already thin atmosphere in the cabin had become foggy, as the much warmer environment of the pinnace was exposed to the frozen one of the planet's surface. Enora had overridden the outer doors of the landing grid to ensure they remained open, and they would continue to do so if all went well, until the entire party had deployed and secured the perimeter. Then she would close it and re-pressurize the area, before opening the taxiway doors that lead deeper into the spaceport. The pressure differential would hopefully deter the enemy from opening the taxiways doors before Garnett's people were ready, and pouring in. Unless they had depressurized the berthing bays as well, in order to equalize...

"Ghostcat, Lawman. Confirm you see pressure on the other side of those taxiway doors?"

"Affirmative," came Enora's voice, sounding confident and crisp now, "I show one atmosphere in each berthing bay. Someone opened an airtight door in Bay One a few seconds ago."

Cass glanced around has he advanced toward the specified door, a broad expanse of glistening steel that parted in the middle, to allow spacecraft to taxi off the landing grid into a hangar. He saw no ground crew, nobody but his own party spreading out to secure the area. The huge artificial cavern was lit by bright lighting panels on the ceiling, and the tarmac by colored LED fixtures recessed into the pavement. They were red, indicating an unsafe landing grid. The lighting combined with the feeble sunlight and thin atmosphere of Tengoku created a strange, twilight ambience. Cass looked up toward the back of the cavern, where the elevated windows of the harbormaster's control room looked out over the grid. He knew the leader of Second Squad would be keeping a watchful eye on those windows, but it made him uncomfortable to turn his back on them. He saw no movement there, but of course that meant little. He smiled faintly, as he tried to imagine what the conversations between their boat and ATC had consisted of, then he cleared his mind of such distractions, and focused his mind on the task at hand. Real-time data from other team-members and the pinnace began streaming into his HUD. Second Squad had fanned out around the craft, and now knelt or stood, their carbines at the ready, scanning the environment in all directions.

"Sabrehawk, Lawman. No resistance encountered, no personnel other than ours on the grid. Initial perimeter secured."

"Roger, I am conferring with Ghostcat on a few matters, then I'll be right behind you. Let's go ahead and start with Bay One as planned, it sounds like our hosts are in there anyway, so we can go ahead and get the party started. We'll be closing the outer doors and re-pressurizing momentarily."

"Affirmative. First Squad, I want a firing line here. Sierra, stack up. When the doors open, we'll have about twenty meters of tunnel before it opens out into the berthing bay, and then there will be the wharf up top to consider. That would be fantastic spot to set up a defense. Ack-Ack, you'll be counter-sniper, Archangel, you and I hang here and wait for the Cox, then on his command we'll push in with First Squad behind us. Copy?"

He was met with curt acknowledgments and nodded. "Good deal." He was joined at that moment by the armored form of Garnett, who moved to place his back against the rough wall next to the huge doorway, and glanced at Cass. A faint sound alerted him to the fact that the main sky-doors were closing. A klaxon had sprung to life, indicating an imminent change in pressure.

"Okay, we have two minutes until equalization."

"Any good gossip from Ghostcat, sir?" Cass inquired.

"None yet," Garnett replied. Enemy comms are all being encrypted using keys that weren't in the spaceport's computers. Probably Darkstar cyphers. There was some chatter between the *Aggie* and the Director's office earlier, but all it amounted to was Timms protesting about some obviously fabricated contamination emergency, and the Skipper telling her it was a fascinating story, but we planned to land anyway. Since then, they've gone quiet. Signals intelligence is sort of thin right now, we can't get through all this rock and steel with IR, and the security cameras we can access aren't showing us much. The place looks like a ghost town right now, but the cameras in the executive offices, berthing areas and wharfs are turned off. They must've figured their systems were compromised when we held the sky-doors open and busted on in, and that we might be able to spy on them. They've probably physically destroyed or unplugged the ones that would show us anything useful."

Cass nodded. "Makes sense."

Garnett looked about them for a moment and then spoke, "large open areas, high ceilings, let's get some peepers out. They may be of service, at least for a while. I expect the bad guys are even now working to figure out what Ghostcat did to their networks, and how to undo it, so we can't assume we will retain the keys to the kingdom for much longer."

Cass relayed the order, and a swarm of tiny drones began to coalesce in the air over their heads, drinking in data and awaiting a chance to swarm through the immense door into the areas beyond, and thereby expand their masters' bubble of awareness.

"Okay," Garnett asserted a moment later, "we're pressurized. Ghostcat, open the doors. Let's see what we've got."

As the massive doors began to split and open with a metallic groan, sliding back into the rough-hewn walls of the landing grid cavern, they did indeed see, and whatever Cass had expected, it was not this. A sea of faces stared back at him—dozens upon dozens of civilians packed tightly in the broad passageway. Maintenance workers in oil-stained coveralls stood shoulder to shoulder with hotel staff in crisp uniforms, their eyes wide with confusion and fear. The harsh overhead lights cast a pallid glow on their faces, highlighting the anxiety etched into every line. As the doors to the landing grid opened wider, a blast of frigid air flowed into the passageway, and the civilians crowded there without the benefit of survival suits, far less battle armor, could be seen to flinch and huddle together in even more abject misery.

"What the hell—" Skye began, and then someone started firing.

***

Enora sat at the compact signals station in the cockpit of the pinnace, observing as her comrades outside arrayed themselves to push into Bay One, and then heard Skye's truncated communication end abruptly in pandemonium.

Enora sat forward and stared. A crowd of possibly a hundred or more people, mostly low-level workers by the look of them, was jammed into the opening to the berthing bay, and as the doors opened wider to reveal the entire passage beyond, the sound of gunfire could be heard reverberating in the cavernous space outside. The crowd of civilians predictably panicked and began surging forward, their terror palpable even from here.

"Oh, crap." Enora's fingers flew over her console, as she took direct control of the swarm of recon drones that had been operating on an automatic program. She directed them over the heads of the frenzied crowd of dockworkers and technicians, down the passage into the berth itself. As she did so, she heard voices emerge from the momentary cacophony that had overtaken the platoon channel.

"Contact front!" Alfred's deep baritone bellowed in an effort to cut through, and then Garnett's voice, sharp and obviously stressed, "Clear comms! Check your damn targets, they're being driven into us from behind, someone's firing into the crowd. Pass them through to Second Squad, get them out of the way!"

More shots could be heard through the open cargo door now, and then Cass's familiar voice boomed, "Hold fire! They're just regular people, pass them through! Sierra Two, get up here and get these people corralled against the other wall! Check for weapons, and do not gun down unarmed civilians."

Enora heard the NCO in charge of Second Squad acknowledge, and saw his detail begin to move into the mass of humanity that stampeded through and around First Squad and Sierra Team onto the landing grid itself. As she maneuvered the aerial drones over the crowd, she was able to get a picture of the berth itself. There was no vessel docked there, the open space was occupied by terrified workers, and ground service vehicles lined up to form an ad hoc barrier between the door, and the elevated wharf at the opposite end. The wharf itself was a long, glassed-in structure that hung above the berth and ran its entire length, and fronting it was an open metal catwalk and stairway. On the catwalk, crates and tankage of various sizes and shapes had been shoved against the guardrails to form a second, elevated barricade, and she could see muzzle flashes there. Several bodies lay still on the concrete floor, sprawled out where they had fallen after apparently being shot in the back. *Human shields,* she thought silently, appalled beyond anything she had ever experienced. *They fired on their own people to drive them out into the landing zone and cause chaos. So much for the damned announcement.* As Enora considered what and how to report, in order to prioritize the most important information, one of the service tugs in the berth began moving, turning toward the access tunnel and gathering speed.

"Sabrehawk there's a ground vehicle on the move toward you—remote controlled, I think. We have hostiles on the elevated catwalk behind cover and firing, how copy?"

"I copy five by five," came her superior's cool tone, his command override cutting through the chatter and crowd noise being picked up by the team's helmet microphones. "Ack-Ack, make it stop. Anti-armor rounds, right now. It's going to make for the boat."

The robot tug had begun speeding down the access tunnel, and to Enora's horror, rammed into a fleeing woman in a technician's coverall who hadn't been aware of its approach, hurling her to the pavement and nearly running over her.

Ramirez had risen from his seat and now leaned over Enora, watching her display, his face aghast. "What is this? What in the name of Unity and all the Founders...is this?"

"Move!" came Alfred's amplified bellow over both comms channel and through the air, and Enora switched her display quickly to his helmet cam, just in time to see him shoulder his bulky Mjölnir rifle, and fire directly into the oncoming machine's stubby nose.

***

Cass grabbed the person who had staggered into him, a middle-aged man wearing the white coat of a food service employee. Jerking him away from the path of the oncoming tug, Cass wrapped him in his armored arms and threw them both to the deck. Just seconds after he slammed into the pavement, there was a white-hot flash of light and then the concussion wave hit. His helmet audio system tried to dampen the sound of the explosion so he wouldn't be deafened, but the noise was still nothing short of cataclysmic. The two men were seized as if by a giant fist and rolled away from the center of the blast. When Cass felt sure enough of his motor control to try and raise his head and survey the scene, he saw carnage.

The tug had exploded violently less than twenty meters from him, and perhaps thirty from the pinnace. What remained of it was a smoking, blackened pile of ruin roughly rectangular in shape. Around it, the pavement had been scorched for several meters in every direction, and the immediate area beyond that was littered with corpses, and recognizable body parts. As the protective systems in his helmet relented and allowed outside sound to once again be passed through to his ears, he heard the shrieking wail of some kind of alarm, blending in discordant symphony with the voice of a woman, howling in agony as she rocked back and forth on the ground near Cass, clutching her head. Blood streamed from between her fingers.

Alfred sat on the floor, apparently staring at the results of his work, his rifle laying nearby, forgotten. Another armored figure, one of the Gendarmes from Second Squad, was sprawled on his back between the destroyed vehicle and the pinnace. Cass's HUD informed him the man required urgent medical attention, and also that Skye was making her way toward them. Cass released the man he realized he was still holding in a bear hug, and whose eyes were closed tightly, tears rolling down his face, his hands balled into fists.

"Are you okay?" He shouted, cognizant of the fact that the poor fellow was probably nearly deaf. The man opened his eyes and blinked several times.

"I— I don't—I don't know?" His reply ended in a note of confusion, as if he looked to Cass for his own assessment, and Cass could do nothing but nod and give him a perfunctory pat on the shoulder. "If you can, you need to get over against the wall, next to Bay Two." He indicated the far side of the landing grid with a vague gesture of his hand. "There's going to be more shooting. We'll get you looked at when things calm down, okay?"

The cook, if that was indeed his profession, stared at Cass with an uncomprehending look, but then made a jerky nod, and slowly got to his feet. Cass also rose, and looked around him, his awareness expanding to again encompass the larger situation. He saw Skye moving in his direction and waved her toward Alfred and the other wounded man, Park, who was now struggling to stand. Cass saw on his HUD when he focused his attention on Alfred, that his blood pressure was dropping, and he had been administered pain killers and clotting agents. Cass frowned but knew Skye would attend to him in due course. He needed to get his arms around the tactical situation. He became dimly aware that pot shots fired from within the berth continued to ricochet dangerously off the concrete.

"Lawman, you operational? Sound off."

Garnett's voice was gravelly and hoarse. Cass looked around to locate his superior among the confused mass of shaken and wounded civilians wandering about, and knots of overwhelmed Gendarmes vainly trying to restore order to the situation. Spotting him near the door to Berthing Bay One, he nodded. "Yessir. I'm okay, Ack Ack is wounded."

"I know, we'll attend to that. Right now, we need containment on this goat rodeo, the plan's out the window. Ghostcat, close these damn doors, all we need is for them to find their courage and decide to send infantry in here just this moment, to capitalize on this confusion. Chief, we need to talk options."

The steel doors to the Berthing Bay began sliding shut almost immediately. As Cass considered his reply, Enora's voice came over the channel, "Guys, erm— Sabrehawk from Ghostcat, somebody just tried to open the doors to Berth Two."

Cass frowned. "Well, I was going to say we could see what's behind door number two, but that may not be such a great idea. If they want those doors open, we probably want them closed."

"Agreed. What about that service hatch?" Garnett pointed to indicate a small, man-sized metal door set into the wall beneath the control room windows. "We need to get these people out of here sooner rather than later, and the solution to that problem may provide us with an alternate route to the concourse level. They're forted up in there, and maybe the other berth too. I think the truck bomb was phase one of a two phase ambush, and we allowed phase one to move forward when we opened the doors to Berth One."

Cass nodded. "So, phase two is waiting in the other berth—the second slice of bread on this shit sandwich—but they can't make the sandwich if they can't open the doors."

"Succinctly put," Garnett remarked.

"Okay, schematics say that service hatch leads to a system of service tunnels for infrastructure access, and a sort of central hallway that leads to a secure elevator up to the Harbormaster's control room. At the far end of the tunnels, there are access points in the parts warehouse, hydroponic gardens and hotel sub-level."

Garnett nodded his head slowly. "Okay, possibilities. Enora, do you still have eyes in the berth?"

"Affirmative," came her immediate reply, "I don't think they've seen the peepers, I have them in the overhead lighting truss. I see maybe, six armed security personnel in hard-suits, with carbines. Their cover is pretty good. They seem to be talking things over, no real movement."

Cass studied the schematic of the spaceport in further detail and frowned. "Thing about the service hatch is, it's actually an airlock, for obvious safety reasons, and it only fits a few people at a time. I don't feel good about having our people waiting around in that potential kill-closet, when we don't know what's on the other side yet."

Garnett spoke again to Enora rather than responding directly to Cass, "Ghostcat, can you hack the airlock to get both doors to open at the same time?"

There was a moment of silence before she replied. "Negative, it's hard-wired to prevent that from happening. We would need to cut through."

Cass spoke up, "Boss, I can take one or two people through there, find a path for the civvies into the hotel, where they can shelter in place. Then we can take the bulk of the shore party through those tunnels, up and out through the hotel lobby into the Guest Services Atrium, and then out onto the concourse. You know that big hallway that connects to the upper loop around the berths and control room? They can't have enough manpower to effectively barricade every approach. We can get behind them the way they tried to get behind us, sweep the wharfs clean without having to charge those fortifications."

Garnett considered that for a moment. "You don't want to use the elevator?"

Cass shrugged. "Seems like another good way to get gunned down before you even have time to ask for directions to the restroom."

Garnett chuckled. "Concur, let's break it so they can't use it either."

Before anyone could respond, there was the snapping sound of high-load circuits opening, and the overhead lighting went out, plunging the huge cavern into near darkness. Civilians predictably began jabbering, crying, and yelling, renewing the sense of pandemonium that their NCOs had just been on the verge of containing.

"Quiet!" Garnett's voice rang out through his helmet amplifier. "I know this is all confusing, and you're cold and scared. You have experienced some terrible things, maybe you've lost colleagues today. We don't have time to talk you through everything that's been going on. I need you to remain calm. If you are hurt, we will have our medic take a look at you. We're going to get you to the hotel to shelter, while we sort everything out. I am Senior Warrant Officer Garnett, with the Gendarmerie. You're going to be okay. Now, please gather up next to that wall over there, listen to these folks, and we'll all get through this."

As Garnett finished his brief speech, Enora's voice spoke over the comms, "They've shut down the whole network. They're probably going to try a system restore, and reboot."

Emergency lights sprang to life around them, doing little to illuminate more than the tarmac itself, and the pensive faces of the terrified civilians.

"Alright," Garnett decided. "Lawman, grab the Mjölnir from Ack-Ack. Ghostcat, what are you doing right now?"

"Very little," Enora said with a sigh. "Once the systems come back up, they will have control of the doors and such again. It will take a while, thirty or forty minutes. For now, I'm dead in the water. I may be able to infiltrate the main networks again after they come up, but for now..."

"Alright, you're with Lawman. You two clear the way through, let me know when we can send the civilians. There may be saboteurs or bad actors among them, and even if there aren't, I can't leave them here unsupervised with the boat and I can't have them milling around in the line of fire when the systems come back on."

"Aye, aye," Cass acknowledged, walking over to Alfred who still sat, legs splayed out on the tarmac and his helmet off, while Skye ran diagnostics on his condition via their tac-link.

"Can I borrow your gun, brother?"

Alfred smiled weakly, his expression barely visible in the gloom.

"It's all yours. I think I just got promoted to supervisor," he replied then grimaced in obvious pain, his voice upbeat but shaky.

"Slacker," Cass said and shook his head, "I always knew you were cut out for management."

"Lawman, double time, we're on a schedule here. Shrike," Garnett continued, using Ramirez's personal callsign, "you're good at the psychology bullshit, get out here, and help get these civilians squared away."

Cass nodded to Alfred as he bent to pick up the hefty DMR from the pavement. "Get well soon. If the gift shop is open, I'll stop and grab you a card."

"I appreciate that, that's very considerate of you. I knew I made the right choice coming to this outfit," Alfred called after him as he moved toward the ramp of the pinnace to meet up with Enora. "Hey, if they got any of them roasted almond-shaped protein nuggets, could you pick me up a bag?"

Cass snorted and kept walking.

22

Trajectories

CNS Agamemnon, Tengoku Orbit

Captain Faulkner drummed her fingers on the arm of her chair—a habit her bridge crew had come to know all too well. It meant one of two things: deep concentration or profound irritation. At this moment, it was unmistakably the latter.

"Director," Faulkner began, keeping her tone measured, "I'm struggling to understand the issue. The senior Gendarme in this system has found credible evidence to suggest your facility's personnel may be involved in illegal activities. By law, he has every right to conduct an inspection in person."

On the display, Director Timms narrowed her eyes and pressed her lips together, emitting a silent, exasperated huff. "Captain, I've already informed you that we're under a Level Three quarantine. No one may enter the facility, for any reason, until this situation is resolved."

Faulkner studied Timms for a long moment. Whatever game these people were playing, it was already in motion, and Faulkner had no intention of wasting more time on this call.

"Director Timms," she said, her voice turning cool and deliberate, "this is you, correct? Not an AI avatar standing in for you? I ask because you don't seem to be absorbing and integrating new data in a natural, human manner. Let me try one more time. The *Agamemnon* happens to be equipped with a rather sophisticated device known as a *telescope.*"

She paused, letting the word hang in the air before continuing. "Using this advanced piece of technology, we've observed no lab personnel standing on the glacier outside, no sign of any evacuation protocol in effect—nothing that supports your claim of a hazard.

Your actions in this 'crisis' do not align with your own standard procedures, such as opening the Lab Dome to the outside, to vent contamination and freeze the interior."

Faulkner leaned forward slightly. "In short, Director, nothing we can see suggests that your disaster is anything other than a work of fiction. I suggest you prepare to continue this conversation with Officer Garnett in person when he arrives. *Agamemnon* Actual, out."

With that, Faulkner cut the link, leaving Director Timms to stew. She sucked in a breath and blew it out loudly. "What an odious woman. I sincerely hope she's implicated in all this. Watching her get frog-marched into the brig would be downright cathartic."

Standing next to her, Lt. Commander Mendoza smirked. "I agree, ma'am."

"Any word from Squadron?"

Mendoza frowned. "Just the standard acknowledgment, so far, Captain. Nothing that addresses the content of our last report. Do you think they'll send us some relief once the brass have had a chance to review it?"

Faulkner considered the question for a moment. "I rather doubt it," she replied heavily. "I imagine this operation will be viewed as something of a political third rail now that it's all gone sideways. That, and we are subject to the Tyranny of the Three."

Mendoza raised an eyebrow, but said nothing, waiting for her skipper to elucidate.

"It means, for every ship deployed forward, there is typically one returning to port, and one being refitted or doing training. We'd just undertaken a major refit when you came aboard, had the wonderful luck to be reactivated in time for this whole mess. We were deploying just as the *Ajax* was heading in for post-deployment refit, and I happen to know that the *Nike* and *Vigilant* are in the Seginus system, breaking in a bunch of kids right out of Basic. Out of the rest of the squadron that leaves us, the *Perseus*, and the *Warspite* to hold down the fort. *Warspite* is on patrol light years away from here, and she's heading to the breakers soon, she's old. She may already be on her way to be decommissioned as we speak. *Perseus* was parked at Unity when we left, but the bosses wouldn't want to leave the system undefended, with only a few Gendarme cutters to keep the peace. Unless they want to take it upstairs, call in a task force from Sol, I don't know who they could send in a timeframe that would do us any good. And that's assuming they want anyone else to have their names attached to this mess —which they probably do not—until they know more about how it's going to play out on the ground."

Mendoza looked taken aback. "That's...a somewhat dark view, isn't it Captain? Surely Fleet wouldn't really let political expediency stop them from taking a firm handle on a situation like this?"

Faulkner held up a finger, her tone thick with sarcasm. "*Potential* situation like this. The facts of the matter are still far from certain."

Mendoza simply stared at her, speechless.

"Lt. Commander," Faulkner continued softly, "when a military force has nobody at whom they can point and say to their civilian bosses, 'there is the enemy', it will inevitably start to come under certain pressures. Public opinion becomes increasingly important, and it will, of necessity, become a political entity until such time as a clear and present danger again presents itself. I can testify to this fact. Many politicians and social elites on Earth already view the Navy as a self-licking ice cream cone. They have an unpleasant, visceral response when we end up on the news. Usually, the bigger the story, the greater their annoyance with the Navy Brass."

Mendoza's expression turned somber. "You're talking about the mining colony?"

Faulkner nodded, her voice dropping. "That—among other brutal lessons I've received over the years, in how the sausage is made at Fleet HQ. If I were you, Angelique, I wouldn't count on the cavalry riding in until the shooting's already done."

A watch-stander's voice cut through the brief silence between the two women. "Conn, IEMARS. Emergence event detected, bearing one-five-zero by three-one. X-ray burst measured at X-4 magnitude, time-delayed five hours. Assessing telemetry now."

Faulkner and Mendoza inhaled sharply, bracing for whatever came next.

"Conn, IEMARS—new contact! Signal is weak, fading fast. We assess it as a stealth frigate, similar to the one encountered before. It's—contact lost. It moved too far from the emergence locus."

Faulkner tapped the comms switch on her chair's control panel. "Did we get enough for a plot, any trajectory data?"

Chris Patterson, the current CIC Watch Officer, answered first. "Not much, Skipper. Looks like they're shaping up for an in-system course, but no telling if they've settled on a heading yet. My guess is they're coming our way."

"I concur, ma'am," Lieutenant Baumgartner, the current Bridge Tactical Officer added, his tone steady.

A throb of familiar pain bloomed behind Faulkner's forehead, and she grimaced. The medication she'd been prescribed for these headaches supposedly wasn't psychoactive, but she still hesitated to take a dose just before possible action—and the attendant life-or-death decisions she would have to make.

"XO," she said very deliberately, catching Mendoza's dark eyes with her own, "pass the word. We'll go to Condition yoke in a few minutes, and I expect we'll call battle stations not long after. Everyone needs to prepare accordingly."

"Aye, aye," was her reply, and she left Faulkner's side to carry out that instruction. *She's not you, Tom, but Founders know, I hope she still has your job when this is all over. She's whip smart, and a good officer, but she's still just a kid. I'm tired of seeing bright young kids end up in med-pods or floating out the airlock in metal coffins. Eleven dead in the attack, two from the boarding party. Twenty-nine in the sick bay in serious condition. I wonder how many kids we've lost on that damn planet by now? How many more will die before we return to port?*

Faulkner exhaled a weary sigh and glanced toward the display dome overhead. Out there—unseen—another threat was moving, like a shark closing on prey that paddled cluelessly on the surface. *Assuming we get back to port at all,* she added silently. That glum train of thought was interrupted by another call from Patterson.

"Con, Combat, Patterson here. Captain, we've continued monitoring the colony below for signals intelligence, and something interesting has just occurred. The main comms array for the colony and the auxiliary comms towers have gone dead, as has the landing grid ILS. The whole colony seems to have gone dark."

Faulkner frowned. "Contact Sierra Team leader, and see if this is their handiwork, please."

"Aye, aye."

Faulkner pondered this new wrinkle. Regardless of the cause, the outcome was one she considered fortuitous, as the colony could not send or receive transmissions as long as the comms gear remained powered down. This meant, no ship-to-shore communication from the new bogie, and no chance the enemies below could send fresh data regarding the Seraphim weapon to the new arrival in the system. Presently, Patterson reported again.

"Skipper, Sierra Actual says it is not their doing, the enemy powered down the colony computers to initiate a reboot. They estimate forty minutes until everything starts coming back, at which point they will have lost control of those systems."

"So, at that point, the Director will be able to communicate with the stealth frigate via laser, and we will be unable to jam or intercept such signals."

"That is...essentially correct."

Faulkner turned her head to address Traxler, who currently sat at the auxiliary weapons station on the bridge, rather than in the CIC. She had been fighting and maneuvering the ship more aggressively than was the norm in recent naval operations and had been frustrated with the inability to communicate with the weapons officer directly, using simple voice or eye-contact. "Mr. Traxler, feasibility of a coilgun strike on the comms center and antenna towers. Can we take them out without risk of depressurizing the colony domes?"

Traxler gave the question a moment's thought before replying, "Captain, the risk is certainly non-zero, but very low. I would caution that whenever heavy equipment violently explodes near a pressure vessel, there is always the risk that something penetrates and violates that pressure vessel, should something go perfectly wrong."

"Mr. Traxler, you know what is at stake. We cannot, under any circumstances allow that stealth ship to communicate with the planet below. Can we do it without undue risk to civilians and our own shore parties, or not?"

Traxler hesitated but a moment, then nodded. "Yes, ma'am."

She next turned to her Bridge Tactical Officer, "Tactical, what is your best projection on the new bogie's time to intercept?"

Baumgartner was fairly junior and had joined the ship post refit. Faulkner had seldom been on the bridge with the earnest, redheaded young man, but he seemed capable enough. "Captain, given that we are at station-keeping and more or less at a standstill relative to them, I estimate they will be in torpedo range in approximately thirty-seven hours, assuming a least-time intercept course, and an acceleration of thirty gee, which seems well within their ability. Given that we know little of their actual main propulsion system, I am also assuming a flip and decelerate maneuver halfway along their path which is standard for a vessel using a reaction drive like our own. This makes the most pessimistic estimate for their time to engagement about 24 hours, which means we must be leaving orbit in six hours to avoid being overtaken before we can reach the impingement zone."

"Thank you," Faulkner replied. "Okay, people we assume the worst case. We have six hours, tops, to conclude this operation, recover our boats, and be on our way. I'm not looking to tangle with this intruder in our current state, and still without any reliable way to see them."

Faulkner swept her gaze over the bridge watch, then looked once again to Traxler. "Weps, get with Mr. Baumgartner on a firing solution using the ventral guns, I want to ensure their laser and radio comms are completely knocked out. We don't know what they've already transmitted to their mysterious friends about this colony's activities, but no further data leaves those labs."

She again addressed the entire bridge speaking slowly and loudly so that the ship's automatic log would be sure to capture her words, "This is a matter of Commonwealth security. If we cannot secure the data our teams went down there to find and neutralize those lab facilities within that six hour window, I may be forced to order an action I really don't want to order. I need you all to understand, we will not leave that facility functioning, and in the hands of the intruder. I will, on my authority, order the destruction of the entire colony by orbital bombardment, if it comes to that."

As she expected, the expressions on her bridge watch-standers' faces were shades of shock and horror.

"Let's not let it come to that. Carry on."

***

High above the partially buried Tengoku City, the CNS *Agamemnon* rolled like a colossal metallic whale to present her belly to the frozen surface of the world she orbited. Silent in the vacuum of space, her coil guns fired a pair of 120 mm tungsten-jacketed, depleted-uranium penetrators. Hurled to fifty kilometers per second, they crossed the thin upper atmosphere and seconds later punched into the targets. The central comms relay near the spaceport and the secondary tower where Enora had struggled with her assailant both erupted in iridescent fire as hundreds of millions of kilojoules of kinetic energy tore the structures apart. Shrapnel fountained skyward before raining back down in a hail of molten slag. In the span of an instant, the colony's sophisticated communications equipment had been reduced to two blackened craters, littered with unidentifiable bits of twisted wreckage.

23

No Plan Survives Contact

Tengoku City, Tengoku

C ass grabbed a stanchion mounted on the interior wall of the small airlock, bracing himself against a sudden tremor that ran through the floor beneath his feet, and caused the structure around Enora and himself to shudder for a brief moment, before all was once again still.

"What the hell was that?" Enora queried. Her voice was steady but her silvery-violet eyes were wide with evident concern.

"Unknown," Cass replied before turning to look at his superior, whose armored form was still visible through the jagged rectangular opening they had made in the outer airlock door that led to the spaceport apron.

"It's just the Navy doing their part to ensure that what happens on Tengoku stays on Tengoku," came the voice of Garnett on their squad channel. "Nothing to worry about. You two get a move on, make sure we're clear to the hotel lobby and then holler back."

"Aye, aye." Cass sketched a salute, and then the pair turned and proceeded around a first corner, and down the darkened service passage that led deeper into the bowels of the colony's infrastructure. As they moved cautiously into the gloom, the pair switched their optics to IR enhanced mode, and Cass noted the significant and growing thermal differential between the cold walls and floor of the tunnel, and the overhead pipes that dripped periodically, forming steaming little puddles on the slightly uneven floor. *Those pipes must carry steam for heat*, Cass mused, *crude but effective, I guess.*

"Schematic says, go past this first junction," Enora's voice brought his mind back to the matter at hand, "to the left is a parts warehouse, and right leads to a machine shop.

We need to go right at the next intersection after this one, and up a couple of flights of stairs."

Cass nodded, taking note of the upcoming intersection, his electronically enhanced gaze scanning the dim expanse of the passageway that stretched before him into murky shadows, eying the corners of the crossing passage for any sign of an ambush. Dim red emergency lighting cast anemic, evenly spaced pools of light across the floor, providing little actual illumination, instead contributing to the eerie, surreal ambiance of the subterranean space. Cass quietly muttered, "Sharp tip of the spear, Cass. Sharp tip of the spear."

To their right, a shallow alcove came into view. Most of the space within was occupied by a pipe chase that stretched from floor to ceiling. It produced a small cloud of steam and a peculiar whistling and ticking noise. Cass swept the area with the barrel of his borrowed marksman rifle but found nothing threatening. It seemed like a normal mechanical function of the pipework, and he swung his weapon back toward the four-way intersection, which was now just five meters away.

Cass motioned Enora to the left, while he placed his own gauntleted hand on the edge of the wall on his right, and deployed his fiber-optic finger camera to get a view around the corner and down the right-hand branch. Seeing nothing untoward, he said, "Looks clear right."

"Clear left," came Enora's reply.

Cass began moving again, turning his head to once again scan the main passageway before them, when his HUD flashed:

WARNING: THERMAL ANOMALY

A schematic of his armor blinked onto his visor, with the right pauldron illuminated and flashing amber. Cass looked down at his shoulder and swore as his IR enhanced optics showed bright red beam trained on him—sliding up toward his visor as he moved.

'Cover!" he yelled, flinging himself backward, seeking to get clear of the intersection. At the same moment, his tactical computer began wailing an alarm in his ear, and a new urgent text alert pulsed:

THREAT DETECTED: ENERGY WEAPON

"Contact right—laser!" Cass bellowed, seeing that Enora had momentarily frozen, her helmet swinging around to seek the source of the threat. He wanted to scream at her to move, but she was already diving.

She threw herself to her left and as she did so, the bright beam of laser light playing across her combat armor flared, becoming for an instant sun-bright as the near-infrared laser Q-switched to a deadly directed energy pulse, which seared the left side of Enora's helmet black as she dropped to the floor and rolled out of the intersection.

Cass immediately keyed his command interface to connect to Enora's armor, as he snapped out, "Ghostcat, sound off!"

"I'm ok," came her trembling response. "My optics are messed up though, I don't have IR anymore. Where are they?"

Cass crept back to the corner, his rifle at the high ready, and knelt, while he pondered their position. "I didn't see the shooter, they might be behind a pipe chase down that way, there's a bunch of them all along here."

His mind raced. *This is a terrible place to stop for a confab, Cass. Make a call and execute it before you both get burned down.* Briefly checking the readout on Enora's armor, he found it agreed with her self-assessment. They needed to move.

"Back," he said, "fallback to that alcove back there and cover."

"Okay, roger." Enora replied, and together they slowly eased back the way they had come, their enhanced senses reaching out for any data that could help them. A moment later, Cass heard a mechanical whining sound, followed by the clack of what sounded like multiple articulated mechanical limbs on concrete. His blood ran cold. *He knew that sound. The passage of years could not erase it from his memory.*

"Expedite, go!" he shouted, and with a thought, selected *anti-armor* on his Mjölnir rifle's self-guiding munition launcher.

As they pivoted to slip into the scant cover of the alcove, a figure straight out of Cass's nightmares emerged in the intersection. Four slender, metallic limbs ending in elongated hooves supported a compact, armored torso topped by an upright trunk—essentially a turret. Its shoulders bore a rifle assembly on one side and an anti-armor laser emitter on the other. Where a flesh-and-blood creature's head would be, the automaton had a lopsided sensor array, with a huge electronic eye on one side, and on the other a series of small, integrated range-finding and ambient sensors. As it moved, its hooves clacked on the hard flooring, and the effect was one of a giant metal arthropod that had sensed prey entering its burrow.

The trunk pivoted toward Cass, prompting him to duck back into the alcove as the telltale staccato of automatic gunfire ripped through the air. A deluge of small-caliber caseless rounds ripped through the tunnel and carved gouges out of the far wall of their tiny refuge, piercing the pipes leading up and into the overhead, unleashing jets of hissing steam that obscured their view, and would have been scalding at this distance had they not been wearing armor.

Cass waited for a lull in the torrent of high-velocity rounds. Then, yanking a grenade from his harness, he armed it and hurled it through the billowing clouds of water vapor in front of him at an angle—so it bounced off the far wall and ricocheted down the corridor toward their mechanical adversary. A moment later, the weapon detonated with a reverberating bang, and Cass heard to his dismay the sound of robotic limbs retreating down the passageway. *Shit. I guess it would be asking too much for the grenade to have rolled right under its undercarriage.*

"Lawman, Sabrehawk. Sitrep." Came the voice of Garnett in his ears.

"Sabrehawk, we have at least one Centaur autonomous weapon platform in here, looks like a Mark One. We are pinned down, over."

"A Centaur? Are you sure?" Garnett sounded incredulous. Truly autonomous robotic weapons were forbidden for police or military use, and generally illegal to operate under any circumstances—though a few loopholes in the law did exist, which some private security firms were rumored to have exploited.

Cass glanced at Enora. Making sure he was on the local audio channel so only she could hear, he muttered, "Am I sure? Maybe we should take a vote on it. What does that even mean—*am I sure?* Of course I'm sure, asshole—that's why I said it."

Keying his comms to the squad circuit again, he spoke in a more professional tone. "Uh, that's affirmative, Sabrehawk. After reviewing the data, I stand by my last report, sir. Over."

Enora began to snort with high-pitched laughter but it quickly died. When Garnett replied, his tone was deadpan. "Okay, Roger that, Lawman. I deserved that. The cavalry is Oscar Mi— "

The remainder of Garnett's transmission became unintelligible static.

"Sabrehawk, Lawman, repeat your last?" Cass frowned. *That damned thing is jamming us. They made them way too smart.* He modified a setting in his comms suite and tried again, "Sabrehawk, Lawman. How copy, over?"

The sound of servo-actuated limbs became faintly audible over the ceaseless hissing of the damaged pipework. "It's making its play now—get ready," he warned Enora, who raised her carbine in silent understanding. Cass crab-walked a meter to his left to provide the best possible field of view and waited.

He didn't have to wait long.

The nightmare machine burst into view, its cantering gait both mechanical and yet in some way unsettlingly organic. The rifle assembly swiveled to bear on Cass, just as he sent the mental command to his own weapon to fire. The mech's decision-making process, unfortunately, grew faster as the tactical options available to it dwindled. It raked the corridor with better-than-human speed and coordination, and Cass felt the drum of small-caliber rounds striking him in the chest. They were frangible, shipboard anti-personnel loads—never intended for use against battle armor—and that fact saved his life.

Toppling backward onto his posterior, his entire upper body blossoming in pain, Cass fired, and his light armor-piercing smart round streaked down the narrow passage, striking the combat automaton where the torso turret joined its thorax. The round slammed into the robotic monster's undercarriage with a loud clanging sound, and it staggered backward, trying to stabilize itself, its servos whining in evident distress. Its front legs buckled, and Cass fired a second anti-armor shot into the turret. Sparks flew and a tortured mechanical whine followed, but his relief was cut short when the automaton's large eye began glowing red, and a targeting laser flicked onto his visor.

That's not good, Cass thought.

He rolled to his right, trying to break the laser's line of sight to his faceplate. Behind him, Enora's carbine howled on full auto as she poured 6.5 mm rounds into the mechanical killer—though he held out little hope that many of her shots had hit home through the mech's thick armor plating. Cass knew that their standard anti-personnel rounds were more than a little underpowered for this contest and had already switched the DMR's selectable magazine to anti-armor.

Clearly visible in the now misty environment, another searing beam of coherent, near infrared light lanced out and down the corridor above Cass's head. The pulse was brief, but even so, it could be seen to sweep drunkenly from side to side as the centaur tried to steady itself.

"Fire in the hole!" caroled a young man's voice, over the local audio channel.

The Centaur was still trying to stabilize itself, staggering and wobbling, sparks flashing from its chassis as Enora poured fire into it—when a rocket whooshed down the passage and struck it in the sensor node that served it as a head. With a deafening roar, the munition exploded, showering the corridor in shards of twisted metal. What remained of the Centaur lay still, its mortal coil littering the floor with blackened debris.

As Cass took a moment to gather himself, a gauntleted hand reached down and offered itself to him for support. He clasped it, and climbed to his feet.

"I keep giving you what seem like the easy jobs, and you keep finding trouble," came Garnett's amplified voice. "I should do you a favor and send you to do something crazy, for your own safety."

"Yeah," Enora put in, "he really knows how to show a girl a good time."

Behind Garnett stood a Gendarme with a ME-40 Kestrel rocket-launcher, who now stood surveying his handiwork with apparent satisfaction.

"Guardian Meeks," Cass said, "you're pretty good with that thing. Glad you packed it."

"Thanks, Chief," the younger trooper replied, in his customary amiable manner, "just happy to do my part." He nudged a piece of destroyed centaur with his foot. "I didn't know these things were still around."

"Yeah," Cass said dryly, "could've knocked me over with a feather, but here it is. It seems to me that the definition of 'law and order' out on these frontier corporate colonies is about like the one we used in the backcountry on Jotunheim. Which is to say, very loose, at best."

Garnett grunted. "That's not a real recent development, Chief. Are you relatively intact? Your armor says yes, but it also appears to be a bit worse for wear."

Cass looked down at himself and ran his fingers over his breastplate. A line of three new holes now marred the outermost protective layer, just to the left of his sternum.

"I appear to be," he replied slowly, "I'm lucky that thing wasn't equipped with AP rounds, or this might be a very different conversation, like a eulogy."

Cass glanced at his visor display and realized his armor's tactical computer and his DNI had held a private conference—the outcome of which seemed to have been a decision to pump him full of a pharmaceutical cocktail that dulled the pain from two bruised ribs and restored him to some semblance of emotional equanimity.

"Okay," Garnett said with a curt nod. "Ack-Ack is down for the count, he's staying with the boat. Meeks will join us for now. He gets to play headhunter for the rest of the day. I'm going to have Archangel join us as well—she's handing triage of the wounded over to a couple of civilians who have basic first-aid training. The colony medical staff are conspicuously absent, which shouldn't come as a surprise, I guess." he looked around at the small group. "Sierra team is moving as a unit from here on out. We don't have enough personnel right now to adequately cover all our bases, but we need to get these tunnels cleared ASAP and get the civilians off the landing grid so we can get back to the business at hand. Anyone disagree?"

No one did.

"Right. Lawman, you're lead scout, assuming you are up for it."

Cass nodded. "I feel fine now, really."

There was a trace of amusement in Garnett's voice when he replied, "I bet you do. Just remember to take things easy tomorrow."

"Sure," Cass heard himself agreeing in a mellow voice. *Am I stoned,* he wondered, *I don't feel stoned...I feel ready to kick ass.* He shrugged. *The wonders of modern medicine, I guess.*

"Meeks, you have the big boom. I want you trailing behind the chief. Watch your spacing. If we run into another mech, we may need to call upon you, and it's tight quarters in here."

Meeks appeared nervous but enthusiastic at this prospect. "Sir, do I get a callsign?"

"Sure thing, Junior."

Meeks frowned. "Could I maybe pick my own?"

Garnett laughed. "No."

***

Cass stood watch just inside the sliding glass door separating the hotel lobby from the spaceport dome's central atrium. Behind him, he caught hushed conversations and the shuffling steps of dozens of colony personnel being herded through the lobby and up the stairwell by Garnett and Skye. One complication they hadn't foreseen was that without power, the hotel room doors couldn't be unlocked from the outside—meaning the colonists and support staff would have to shelter in the hallways for now.

He was thankful that at least corporate policy barred minor children from visiting or living in Tengoku City. Though it was to be hoped that the hotel area would be clear of the coming action and the colonists were, in theory, out of harm's way, their safety was still tenuous. Nine had already died in the initial ambush, and another dozen were injured—some from the exploding ground vehicle, others trampled in the ensuing panic.

He and Enora scanned the atrium and the broad entrance to the spaceport concourse, staying alert for any threat, but so far nothing had materialized. Under the dim emergency lighting, the scene felt surreal—vendor stalls sat dark and abandoned, and the usual bustle of travelers and support staff was replaced by an unsettling hush. He heard armored footfalls approach from behind, and then Garnett's voice, "Shore Party Bravo reports they have secured the Lab Dome and a number of prisoners. They're grabbing all the data they can. Chief, it looks like we've done what we can here, go ahead and have the rest of Second Squad come on up, First Squad will stay with Shrike and the boat. We need to clear the concourse and deal with the security goons on the wharfs before we meet with the senior leadership team."

"Aye, aye," Cass responded without turning his head, and keying the appropriate channel, made the call.

As the balance of Second Squad, plus Garnett, Enora, Cass, and Meeks moved down the concourse toward the berth area held by the Hirayama security forces, Cass drew their attention to the sliding door ahead and on their right.

The stenciled sign above it read Harbormaster – Main Control, dimly illuminated in the ruddy emergency lighting.

Cass gestured at the door and said quietly, "We need to clear that. Just because we didn't see anyone from below doesn't mean it's empty. Those windows have a clear view of the landing grid—hell of a sniper's nest. And the controls for the outer doors and berthing areas are in there. We lost our network access, so if someone's squatting on it, we need them out."

Garnett nodded once. "Make it happen."

Cass motioned Meeks forward, then addressed the group in a low, even tone.

"Junior, you're two—right behind me. Stack up, right side. I slice left, Junior slices right—hard angles, fast and clean. The rest of Second Squad will push straight in and clear the far corners. Archangel, you hang back in the hall. Everyone, check your targets; I don't want any contractors ventilated unless they're a threat. Enora, rear guard—watch our six. If this goes loud, someone may come sniffing down the concourse; we haven't cleared the whole dome." He pointed at the demolitions specialist from the support section. "Alia, right? Charges ready. We breach on your call—not before. Minimal blast. I want the door down, not the whole damn wall."

The young-looking specialist moved forward and affixed the explosive breaching tape to the doorframe while the squad stacked and waited, tense and watchful.

She finished her work with quick, practiced hands, then backed away a few paces. Raising one hand in a fist, she gave a sharp thumbs-up. A half-second later, her voice crackled over the squad channel: "Fire in the hole."

The breaching charge blew with a flat, concussive thump, the reinforced door buckling inward under the controlled blast. Meeks was through first, weapon up, the rocket launcher slung across his armored back, eyes sweeping left. Another Gendarme followed tight, pivoting right. Cass came in next, low and center, barrel steady.

The Harbormaster's Control Room was a tight space of console banks and dark wall panels, with windows looking out over the apron and landing grid. A circular comms station dominated the center of the room. Emergency lighting strobed ruddy reflections off every surface, punctuated by a whining alarm klaxon that echoed like a heartbeat.

A figure huddled behind the comms station, hands raised before he even stood. "Don't shoot! I'm—I'm not armed!" A skinny young man in a rumpled blue jumpsuit slowly straightened. The white Harbormaster's Apprentice patch was just visible through grime and sweat.

"I didn't know what to do," he stammered. "They told me to lock it down, but the controls wouldn't work. Then the system dropped out. Everything just... went dark. I've been in here since."

Cass lowered his weapon half an inch. "Who told you to lock it down?"

"Security. Dornier himself, actually. He said delay any landings, make it look like a fault. But then the network went. Lights too. I figured... maybe no one was coming."

Meeks gave him a skeptical glance, weapon still at low ready. "You broadcast any alerts? Try to call out?"

The apprentice swallowed. His eyes darted between them. "No. I—I didn't even know if anyone was left in the Executive Dome to hear it. And nothing works anyway. When I saw you were government people—Please... fellas, I just work here. I know a bunch of the security people went down to the wharf on number two about an hour and a half ago and never came back down the hall. Maybe you can talk to them or—"

He looked around the group with wide eyes and swallowed before continuing, "Unless you don't want to talk to them? Look, I have no idea what the heck is even going on. Whatever's been done, I didn't do it."

Garnett snorted. "Zip him and leave him here. We'll come back for him."

The technician paled, his eyes bulging. "Zip me? What does that mean? You aren't going to —"

As Meeks grabbed his left arm—not ungently—his other hand holding a long zip tie, the technician seemed to relax a bit. "Oh."

Having secured the Harbormaster's control room and left a single Gendarme to maintain watch over the facility and its single unwilling occupant, the rest of the team moved —as quietly as combat armored troopers could— down the long concourse, toward the sharp corner beyond which lay the airtight door to the elevated wharf over Berthing Bay Number One. Garnett signaled a halt as the heavy hatchway came into view, then turned to confer with Cass.

"The manual crank-operated mechanism is out of the question—it'd be obvious and take forever. Assuming the door doesn't fail safe when the power's out, in which case it may not open at all."

He eyed the recessed bulkhead and its sealed rim, the lock indicator panel unlit. "It's a plug-style environmental seal. Meant to hold pressure if the berth gets holed. But with the power grid down, the maglocks and motor linkages are dead. No power means no normal cycle, not without backfeeding something in—and that's noisy."

Cass frowned. "The atmosphere out there is stable. We know that. But if we apply juice to the hatch, we risk tripping a dormant sensor loop or lighting up the panel on their side. Could signal movement, or worse—reinitialize an automated lockdown."

"Right," Garnett said. "We need a method that gets us through without alerting anyone listening beyond that door."

Cass turned to Enora. "Options?"

She stepped forward, opening the access panel with a quiet pop of her multitool. "Breaching tape may not do the trick, regardless. If I can isolate the actuator circuit, I might be able to tap a charge off my armor's backup cell. Enough to cycle the clamps once, no lights, no comms. But if there's damage in the line or any redundancy tied to the dome's main grid—"

"Then we're stuck cranking," Cass finished.

"Or cutting," Garnett added. "Which is loud, bright, and gets us seen."

Cass nodded once. "Do it, Enora. Low power, direct link. One cycle only. If it works, we're through quiet. If not—"

He glanced back down the concourse, then to Meeks.

"Then we fall back five meters, and you use the door knocker."

Meeks chuckled. "Copy that."

Enora worked without speaking for a moment, then without turning away from the access panel, gave a thumbs-up.

"Okay people, we may be in business," Cass said over their local channel, "let's do this just like in training, and assume everyone on the other side of this door is a security goon, who was on board with the whole human shield idea. That means, we put them down, quick and clean, and maybe ask questions later. Everyone scanning?"

The armored figures of the squad nodded their understanding, and there was a single muted "Aye aye," over the local channel.

"I have the lowest profile and strongest legs, so I'll take point. Junior left, Skye goes right. Everyone else on me, watch the corners, watch for improvised cover. That work for you, Cox?"

Garnett replied with a curt, "affirmative."

Skye, laconic as usual when under stress, simply nodded her understanding.

"Go, Enora."

24

Bearded In Their Den
Tengoku City, Tengoku

Enora gave a quiet three-count and then triggered the bypass. For a beat, nothing happened. Then the hatch gave a low clunk, followed by the soft hiss of equalizing pressure, indicating a small amount of atmosphere had bled out from the berthing area during the black-out. Servo magnets disengaged with a muffled thump, and the thick plug door slid aside with a sluggish whine, its motion ghostly in the red emergency light. Cass raised his hand, signaling advance. He moved first—low and fast—his compact Jotun frame clearing the threshold with an innate quickness few Core humans could match, weapon up and eyes scanning the shadows beyond. Meeks and Skye peeled off to either side behind him, barrels steady. The rest of the squad flowed through in silence.

Somewhere in the distance, a cargo lifting rig creaked against its moorings. The metal-walled corridor ahead was long, dark, and still. Cass edged to the side of the nearest viewport, its surface smeared with grime and backlit by the dim glow of the overhead lights in the berth outside. He adjusted the sighting node on his rifle, flipping to the anti-armor load.

"Catwalk. Six heat signatures, static. They're waiting for our guys to come busting in."

Garnett nodded. "Kill box."

Cass toggled fire-modes on his borrowed DMR. "I can breach the viewport with the Mjölnir. Anti-armor rounds will punch through enough for everyone else to get a line of fire. While they're scrambling, we shift."

He pointed down the wharf, toward the lightweight door that opened onto the catwalk at the far end of the berth.

Garnett nodded in understanding. "Alright, the rest of you move down. Skye, go with second squad. Lawman will open with a punch, draw their eyes. Then he, Ghostcat, and

I will endeavor to thoroughly ruin their day from this side of the window. You breach from the flank. Once you get through the door, set up a crossfire—that catwalk will be a shooting gallery."

Meeks grinned behind his visor. "Love it when you get loud, sir."

Cass took a knee, sighed, and breathed once.

Thunk.

The anti-armor round hit like a hammer. The transparent panel, never designed for such punishment, blew out with a sharp crack and a rush of displaced air. A second round followed, slamming into the catwalk's edge—metal shrieked, a cascade of transparent aluminum fragments showered the area, and startled figures scrambled for cover beyond the breach. Wearing vac suits as they were, and without advanced military tactical systems, they hadn't heard the Gendarme team breach the hatch and were caught flatfooted.

"Go!" Cass barked.

Cass drew a bead on one of the lightly armored figures in a moment of hesitation—caught between two pieces of cover, shocked by the sudden violence, and trying to decide where to run. The heavy anti-armor rounds from the DMR punched through his lightly armored vacsuit, shredding his chest and splattering the equipment crate behind him with a wet explosion of gore.

Garnett's fire was likewise deadly accurate, and he dropped two more of the security team before the Gendarmes breached the hatch and began firing from around the hatch coaming onto the catwalk, their fire traversing the catwalk lengthwise. In moments, it was over. They'd not had to confront the dilemma of how to handle surrendering foes, for none had had the chance to surrender. All six lay still on the catwalk, as Gendarmes walked among them checking for signs of life. "Clear up!" An excited voice stated over their comms.

Garnett's voice was calm and level as he spoke on the platoon channel. "Shrike, Sabrehawk. Threat in Berth Bay One is neutralized. What's your situation, over?"

Ramirez answered almost immediately, his voice as chipper as ever. "No change. The boat is secure, no civilian presence. I've got the chin turret aimed at the other berth bay door, but with power out, there's little they can do unless they blast it open—which they haven't, over."

"Copy that. Keep me advised. We're moving to the tram tunnel and from there to the Executive Dome. Coordinate with Bravo Six and let me know if they hit any trouble. Also, please reiterate that we need all the data they can reasonably extract from the lab systems. Sabrehawk out."

***

The squad moved down into the tram tunnel in silence, their helmet lamps casting stark cones of light through the gloom. The air was still and cool, and every footfall echoed down the rails like distant drums. The tram car sat inert in its berth, its doors gaping open, lights cold.

They walked along the maintenance access beside the track in single file, the occasional flicker of red from consoles on standby power offering the only signs of lingering life.

After a while, Enora's voice came through on the local channel, quiet and dry.

"We're really doing it, huh. Bearding the bad guys in their lair."

Cass, up front, didn't break stride. "Director Timms doesn't have a beard, Enora. Not that I recall. One of the other management types maybe?"

There was a short silence.

"You're speaking Pirate again," he added.

Behind them, someone let out a short chuckle—maybe Meeks. Enora exhaled sharply through her nose.

"You are being very literal-minded, Chief Petty Officer Broz," she replied, her voice haughty. "As you well know, I tend to talk a lot when I'm nervous."

Cass didn't respond right away. Then: "That's healthy. Nervous is fine. It's the cocky ones who get shot first—Junior, take note. You keep your head on a swivel, Ghostcat, and if you're a very good girl, I may even find you a gap you can swing across on a rope—rapier in hand. Maybe onto a tram car or something. There may even be a cask of rum somewhere we could seize."

"Honestly, Cass, fuck you."

Cass laughed, and the whole squad seemed to relax somewhat.

"Okay, stay sharp," Came Garnett's voice, his tone both commanding and yet somehow paternally indulgent. "Not a lot of cover here."

Presently, the team came to a large, airtight safety bulkhead, locked in its up and open position. Stenciled letters next to the nearby service doorway read: EXECUTIVE DOME 4L.

"Chief, deploy Second Squad around the platform to form a perimeter. Dawson's folks covering the elevator lobby, Meeks and his team along the other side where the stairs come down. I want to confer with our esteemed Marine colleagues for a minute."

"Aye, aye," Cass responded, casting a glance at his junior NCOs. "You heard the Cox'n. Fan out and secure the area. Watch out for wildlife wearing expensive suits."

Meeks snorted. "Can we take trophies?"

"You mean like an expensive fountain pen? Sure. A finger? No."

As the squad moved to assume their assigned positions, Garnett spoke on another channel, his words inaudible to Cass. After a moment, he switched back to the squad net and reported, his voice bland and precise: "Duck Dodgers and his gang have successfully subdued a single security guard and a passel of unarmed eggheads. He was pleased to report that his daring raid has been a complete success, and he's in possession of a number of loose data crystals. I briefly contemplated telling him that these will doubtless speed him on his way up and out of starship detachment duty and into a cushy desk job somewhere—because the contents of those crystals will soon be so classified, the brass will never again let Lieutenant Kamarov out of their sight."

Cass suppressed a laugh. "Indeed, sir. The Service rewards tactical genius when it sees it. I'm sure the LT will go far."

Garnett nodded, then turned his back on the rest of the team, steering Cass back toward the tram tunnel with a light touch to the elbow.

"Okay, let's find the suits and get out of here. We've got another bogie in the system—sounds like another stealth frigate—and the Skipper is understandably nervous. I didn't want to share this with the kids; they've got enough to worry about. But we're on a strict timeline now. We need to find the bosses, extract them, and then be—" He stopped mid-sentence as the overhead lights flickered, then snapped to full life with the unmistakable clack of load contactors engaging.

Garnett blew out a slow breath. "Well. That just punctuates my thought perfectly, right there. With the power back on, we need to wrap this op up before they turn the colony's systems against us."

"Roger," Cass replied. "Leave Dawson and his fireteam here, bring Meeks and his team, divide and search?"

"Sounds like a plan. Let's get Anthem to a terminal somewhere, see if she can get back into the network and maintain the status quo with the spaceport doors and equipment," Garnett said with a sharp nod.

"Understood, sir," Cass replied, already gesturing for Enora.

As it turned out, the nearest terminal access point was two levels up, in the outer offices that served as workspace for lower-level colony administrative staff. As their support fireteam moved to control the physical access points to the cubicle farm, Enora and Cass stepped into a larger cube that must have belonged to a supervisor. Enora connected her datapad with a li-fi network port and set to work, her brow furrowed.

"They reset the secret access tokens for the admin account I was using," she muttered after a moment. "I'm not sure I can break it again in time to be of any use."

Cass considered for a moment. "Okay. Let's forget it—I need you with us, and I don't want to waste time dicking around with this. Can you tell what—"

Before he could finish the thought, Cass's comms rig squawked to life.

"Sabrehawk, Shrike. Something's going on down here. Berth Two is trying to open, and our boy in the Harbormaster's control room reports his attempts to keep it closed are being overridden remotely. It looks like—"

There was a burst of static and what sounded like distant gunfire. Ramirez's voice came back, louder now, urgent.

"Confirmed—Centaur combat mechs in the berth. They've opened fire on First Squad. We are engaged. Repeat: we are engaged!"

"Roger that, Shrike, take charge down there and do what you need to do. We're still on the hunt for our principal subjects." Garnett's voice was cool and unperturbed.

"Affirmative, Shrike out!"

Cass looked at Enora and shrugged. "That answers my question, I guess. Go ahead and load the standard safeware program to remove our faces from the security camera feeds, let it do its work. We need to be done here."

Once Enora had done as directed, the pair hurried through the office to join Garnett and Skye at the bottom of a staircase that ascended to a glass enclosed mezzanine one level above. "No dice," Cass reported.

"Doesn't matter much now, let's move. Junior and his team are upstairs already." replied Garnett.

The four of them moved up the staircase, and into a wide foyer, where they were faced with a receptionist desk, flanked by two frosted glass doorways. "Junior went that way,"

Garnett motioned to the left-hand doorway, "we go this way. Lawman take point, I'll watch the rear."

Cass nodded to Enora, who yanked open the hinged door. Leveling his carbine, he moved down the narrow hallway beyond. Offices lined either side, and ten meters ahead was a break area, anchored by a sleek and very expensive coffee maker. Cass cleared the nook quickly, then signaled for the others to proceed. At each door, they paused to clear the rooms—quiet, practiced motions—but each space was empty. They cleared half a dozen offices and encountered no one. After a short distance, the corridor joined a cross-passage, linking them to the hallway Meeks and his team had followed.

"Junior," Cass called over the squad channel, "we're at a junction with your hallway, about forty meters from the lobby. You seen anyone?"

"Negative," came the puzzled reply. "We just passed that intersection. We're at another doorway—looks like a big meeting area, with executive offices at the far end. We were about to proceed in."

Cass glanced down the corridor ahead. It terminated at a glass door, and from the layout, he assumed both teams were converging on the same space.

"Wait ten seconds—we're almost there on this side. We'll go in at the same time."

"Roger."

Once again, they passed through a doorway, carbines up, clearing corners and side offices with practiced precision—and once again, no one waited for them. A second after entering the large, open-plan work area, Meeks and his team came through another door in the same long wall, weapons up and sweeping. The center of the space was arranged with low, plush couches and scattered tables. Around the other three walls stood meeting rooms and glass-walled executive offices. Cass moved toward one of the doors, noting the stenciled name on the glass: *ERIKA TIMMS.*

"Nobody home," he muttered. "Do we think they left the dome and started wandering the base in the dark? We know Timms was in contact with the captain almost up to the moment we landed."

Garnett sucked his teeth, something he often did when deep in thought. "There are a number of ways that could have played out. The question we need to answer is, where would they go? Hiding in a janitorial closet doesn't get them anywhere. We control the spaceport —for the most part—and they can't leave with the *Aggie* in—" Garnett paused and sucked in a breath, "they can't leave while *Aggie* controls the orbital space, but if they could get rid of her..."

"The new bogie," Cass added flatly.

"*New bogie*?" Skye asked, confused.

"Another stealth ship, it sounds like. Showed up in the system a few hours ago, and they spotted it emerging through sheer luck, when the radiation burst hit their sensors. If that is reinforcements for the other team, then there may indeed be a way off this rock for the senior leadership team. But how does that all work—"

Garnet made an adjustment to his comms suite and then: "Shrike, Sabrehawk. Sitrep. Do you control the landing grid, and have you seen any sign of high ranking civilian types? Over."

It took a moment for Ramirez to reply, "Shrike here. We hold the apron area, but we haven't been able to push in to the berth. There is still at least one of those mechs in operation, supported by armored troops, mercs I would guess, with military-grade kit. Wearing Hirayama colors, but in a whole different class than the Barneys you encountered. No sign of the suits, but we can't see all the way into the berth, of course."

Cass's mouth twitched. Barneys—slang for security forces who looked the part but didn't have the chops. The term went all the way back to some ancient vid character with a badge, a gun with one bullet, and no business carrying either. Most of the younger troops didn't even know the origin of the reference anymore, but the meaning had stuck.

"Copy. Keep them contained. If the suits aren't here, they are probably on their way to you, looking to make good their escape. We will be down as soon as we can, but we can't let them elude us. I'm going to turn the Marines loose on the rest of the base, in case we've guessed wrong, but we'll never do a thorough search in the time we have left. Over."

"Copy that. Keep in touch. Shrike out."

Garnett switched channels again and held a brief conference with Kamarov before turning back to the team.

"I let Kamarov know he can send two squads to sweep the market area and hydroponics dome, but to search the residential blocks would take a platoon days we don't have."

"Do we think they might just bunker up and wait us out?" Skye asked.

"Possible, but I doubt it," Garnett replied. "Their relief ship isn't here yet, and if things go badly for us on the ground, nothing stops Faulkner from turning this whole facility into a smoking crater before she pulls out of orbit. It would be quite the leap of faith for people in their shoes to just hole up and assume we'll all go away."

Olly-Olly, oxen free! Cass found himself thinking, his mood suddenly giddy. *Damn, I must still be high on whatever it is that's keeping me from being in agonizing pain right now.*

Enora shifted uneasily. "Do you—would she actually do that?"

Garnett's tone was grim. "I can guarantee you with near certainty that she will, if push comes to shove. This weapon, and its perpetrators, must be secured—to the extent that's still possible."

"Okay," Cass said after some thought, "I propose we send Meeks and his team to check the SOC real quick, while we use deep IR scans to spot signs of recent foot traffic around here. They were here not long ago—and now they aren't. We need to think like cops. See if we can pick up the trail before it gets cold. Literally."

"Make it so," Garnett said, his absent tone indicating he was dividing his attention. "I'm going to toss Timms's office, on the off chance she left something behind we might be interested in."

***

"Did anyone touch this wall on the way in?" Cass asked, as he, Skye and Enora stood considering the blank wall across from the coffee machine. Many footsteps had trod the carpeted floor here over the course of the last few hours, but the handprints on this wall, visible as blotches of warmer color on their IR optics, defied easy explanation, and there were a lot of them.

"No," Skye replied, "And Meeks's team was never down this way."

"I need a pirate's perspective. What are the odds there is a passage behind here. A bolt hole?"

Enora snorted. "I hope you aren't asking me a serious pirate question. I stole *data*. While standing on a spaceship. Once or twice. So, technically piracy. I didn't use a cutlass, or anything. I didn't even draw my sidearm, now I think about it."

Skye rolled her eyes. "My illusions of you have been shattered forever. So, you didn't space anyone? Did you even have the panache to shout, *'shiver me timbers'* while you downloaded their data without permission?"

Enora said nothing but favored her comrade with a glare.

Cass smiled. "Let's say, I'm asking you to check the plans, Ms. Data Systems Specialist, and if that doesn't turn anything up, check for a li-fi access point, right around here somewhere."

"Okay," Enora replied, sounding sullen. She quickly reviewed the base schematics on her datapad before answering, "Nothing here on the plans."

And yet, something in the back of Cass's mind insisted...

"What about hidden hardware?"

Enora silently communed with her DNI for a moment, then held up her datapad in the general direction of the blank, featureless wall before them. As she did so, Garnett approached the trio, from the direction of the executive suite. He moved to stand behind Skye, observing without speaking.

Enora expelled a forceful breath. "Huh. I'll be gently buggered. There is a li-fi port here, it looks like a coded locking mechanism." She cast an appraising look on Cass. "You must have been a hell of a ranger. That was some deduction there."

Cass shrugged. "I've seen more than one hidden drug stash in my time. Now how to open it..."

Enora shook her head. "I don't see how we crack the code in the time we have, it could be anything. I don't even know what the authentication protocol is, ACS-24, simple secret token...all I can do is establish a basic handshake with the device. Guessing the passkey would take—"

Cass, acting on a sudden impulse, interrupted her. "Try 08282303."

Skye looked at Cass askance. "What, is that your birthday?"

Cass barked a laugh. "If only."

Still... he mused. *It does sound like a date, doesn't it? And where did this notion come from anyway?*

"Seriously?" Enora looked doubtful.

"Try it," interjected Garnett.

"Okay—" Enora, still sounding skeptical, used her data pad to send the suggested string of numerals. To her evident shock, the wall panel before her slid silently to the side, revealing a narrow stairwell.

Garnett moved to stand near Cass and bent slightly to place their helmets in contact, so the sound of his voice reached Cass's ears alone. "It is a birthday, in fact. I happen to recall it from some background research I'd been doing. It's Atsuko's."

Cass felt a shiver run down his spine.

No. No freaking way.

"I'm sure you must've seen it in her dossier, just like I did, and made a brilliant leap of deductive logic. Well done."

Cass shook himself as Garnett straightened and stepped away. *I think you know very well I did no such thing.* He looked around to see Skye and Enora, both staring at him, and cleared his throat.

"Lucky guess."

"Uh-huh," Skye said, one eyebrow raised.

"Looks like the senior leadership wanted a way out of the office that wasn't known to the working stiffs," Garnett said smoothly. "A bolt hole, like the Chief said—and the access code is Atsuko's birthday, which tracks, if you think about it. That's some quick thinking, Lawman. I'm going to summon Junior and his team to join us, then we'll proceed with alacrity. I get the distinct feeling the spaceport is at the other end of this hole."

As the team moved with cautious steps down the stairway, Cass kept his eyes scanning for automated defenses or any other manner of threat. His mind was buzzing with distracting thoughts, and he needed to focus. *Or are they my thoughts at all? Maybe they're Atsuko's thoughts.* He shook his head. That way lay madness, and he needed to be sharp and on point, alert to what lay before them—even though his mind's eye kept drifting to the image of a lovely, heart-shaped face with warm, liquid brown eyes.

Get your head in the game, Cass.

At the bottom of the long flight of stairs was a bare concrete corridor—unadorned and utilitarian, in stark contrast to the executive complex above. Illumination was adequate but only just, provided by recessed lighting panels in the walls. There was no signage, no indication of where the tunnel led, but referencing a schematic of the colony he had projected on his HUD, Cass figured Garnett's surmise was a good one. "Tactical column," Cass instructed over the squad channel and taking the lead once again, began probing forward down the tunnel, which led straight for what seemed a very long way.

Having traveled down the spartan and cold concrete corridor in relative silence for about ten minutes without resistance or encountering any turnoffs or rooms, Cass flinched when his comms crackled to life, startling him. "Sabrehawk, Shrike! I think the main event is about to start, a whole platoon of those mercs is pushing on us, and the fueling system in there just went active, so I assume they are prepping a runabout or shuttle of some kind. I'd guess the VIPs are inbound. What is your status, over?"

"We are Oscar Mike, in some kind of escape tunnel, and about one hundred meters from Berth Bay Two. With any luck, we are behind the VIPs and inbound your location. Over!"

Cass thought he could faintly hear the harsh buzz of the auto-cannon on the pinnace somewhere ahead, followed a moment later by distant shouts.

"Let's double-time, people," he ordered, quickening his pace. A junction was coming up ahead, and—growing ever closer on his left—the first side doorway they'd encountered broke the monotony of the long, arrow-straight tunnel.

"Look left," Cass advised, raising his weapon to cover the opening.

As the team moved to cover the side door, Cass shot a glance toward the larger sliding metal panel at the corridor's end. The sounds of battle were clearly audible now—shouts, small-arms fire, and the periodic buzzsaw of the pinnace's cannon. "Junior, eyes front, watch that door panel."

Peering through the smaller doorway, Cass spotted a storage room stacked with wire shelving and containers. A young, panicked face peered back at him from behind the doorframe for just a moment—then vanished. The reinforced sliding panel began to close.

"Shit!" Cass exclaimed.

Moving quickly and with eerie calm, Garnett stepped into the doorway, seized the edge of the motorized panel with his off hand, and—to Cass's surprise—wrenched it open again with main force. The motor whined in protest, then gave up with a mechanical clunk as the panel sprang back open.

Sure, battle armor amplifies human strength—but not that much, he observed. Rumors of his cybernetic enhancements had not been exaggerated, it seemed.

Cass dove into the room and seized its sole occupant, a terrified young man in a rumpled suit. Pressing his carbine against the man's breastbone, he asked in a calm, almost pleasant tone, "So, where's your boss?"

The man rolled his eyes to the left—toward the large door at the end of the tunnel—and sputtered something unintelligible.

"Calm yourself," Cass said, lowering the muzzle a hair. "Speak plain. What's the plan here?"

"I—I'm just grabbing extra CO_2 scrubbers for the flight. Ms. Timms told me—"

"Who else is on the other side of that door? Dornier's whole mercenary squad, am I right? What else? Mechs? An armed runabout? If I open that door and there's a nasty surprise waiting, I'll take a quick moment out of my day to come back here and end you. So be explicit. And brief."

The pale youngster—clearly an administrative assistant or something of the sort—managed to go even paler. He took a moment to compose himself, then answered in a trembling voice, "No—no more mechs. I don't think. I saw two already destroyed when I got down here. It's just Dornier and his handpicked men—maybe a dozen. They're in the berth, and your guys are on the apron down the tunnel, they've been shooting at each other since we came down. There aren't any weapons on the yacht. Not that I know of, anyway."

"Excellent," Cass said with a grunt. Then, to the team: "Zip him, hands and feet. We need to get into the fight."

He placed a single finger on the young man's bony chest. "You," he admonished in a flat tone. "Behave."

***

"Okay," Garnett said as the team stacked up outside the heavy steel hatch. "Maximize surprise. Take down the armored targets first and try not to nail the suits—high-value prisoners if possible. We're on the platoon channel from here on."

Acknowledgements murmured across the comms. Garnett met Cass's eyes and gave a curt nod. "Do it."

Cass slammed his fist down on the hatch control, and the portal split open with a mechanical snarl. As luck would have it, an armored mercenary was kneeling just inside, administering first aid to a wounded comrade when the doors parted—and the Gendarmes stormed through.

"On our six!" shouted the merc, voice tinny through an external speaker—moments before a slug from Garnett's carbine shattered his visor and dropped him where he knelt.

Cass took stock of the situation quickly. On his right, at one end of the cavernous berth area, was a large runabout, the aforementioned 'yacht.' Its blunt nose was aimed at the taxiway, and the service module was still attached to its gray flank. Arrayed in front of the concealed panel he had just emerged from, was a semi-circle of stacked containers, clearly intended to serve as makeshift fallback positions for the enemy troops. Those troops were arrayed along either side of the taxiway entrance, firing from cover at First Squad, and the pinnace, that he couldn't yet see, but which he knew would be visible to anyone looking down the taxiway tunnel.

The voice of Ramirez came over the platoon channel as the Gendarmes of Second Squad deployed: "Sabrehawk, we are down three troopers now and very close to Winchester on the auto-cannon. They've been using service tugs to turtle behind and soak up my fire."

His eyes drawn that direction, Cass could see the burning wreckage of two Centaurs and a service tug littering the area in front of the taxiway—remnants of the enemy's desperate attempt to overrun the landing grid. Armored bodies sprawled across the pavement bore grim testament to the human cost of the prolonged firefight. A layer of smoke hovered in the air which had only recently begun circulating again, the choking fog produced by burning plastic, and heavy weapons discharge.

"We're in," came Garnett's voice. "Deploying now. Second Squad, push in! Lawman—Third Squad is taking that runabout. Our principal subjects are in there."

"Aye!" Cass replied, already in motion as he darted across the berth toward the yacht's lowered ramp.

The mercs near the taxiway mouth had spotted them. Muzzle flashes sparked, and weapons spit fire toward the new threat. The comms net erupted with overlapping shouts:

"First Squad, move up! Watch for friendlies and pin them down!"

"Tangos in the open!"

"Sierra One, pour it on!"

Cass barely registered the chatter as he sprinted, lungs burning, across the open area. He reached the base of the ramp and dropped to a knee, carbine up, breathing hard. Skye slid in beside him a heartbeat later, as the air was filled with the renewed clatter of full-auto small arms fire.

"Shit, Meeks is hit!" someone shouted.

Cass flinched but didn't take his eyes off the hatch. Skye turned reflexively, scanning the berth—and Cass, despite himself, stole a glance. Two Gendarmes were dragging Meeks's limp form toward cover behind the supply crates.

"Later, Skye. Mission first."

Skye hesitated, jaw clenched, then nodded sharply.

Garnett and Enora skidded in behind them, Garnett sounding winded, and Enora somewhat unsteady, favoring one leg. Raising a hand, Garnett waved his juniors forward. "Go—I'm right behind you."

Cass surged to his feet and, weapon raised, charged up the ramp into the dim interior of the yacht.

He entered a cargo bay, where standard equipment containers were webbed to the port and starboard bulkheads. Directly ahead, a vertical ladder ascended through a rectangular hatch—presumably into the passenger compartment above.

"Clear down! Flashbang out!" Cass shouted, and suiting action to words, yanked a flashbang from his chest harness and lobbed it up the ladder well. The device clanged off the handrail, bounced once, and disappeared through the hatch before detonating with a concussive bang and a searing flash—its light spilling down into the lower deck and causing him to squint even through his visor.

Cass, sensing his comrades closing in behind him, dashed up the ladder without using his hands, his weapon aimed ahead and up—the targeting laser now a visible emerald beam slicing through the hazy darkness. As he reached the second deck, he swept the muzzle of his weapon across a well-appointed seating area, configured for the comfort of high-level corporate passengers.

"Going aft," he said tersely.

"Going forward," came Enora's immediate reply.

"I'll watch the ladder," said Skye, calm and steady.

Cass noted the sprawled form of what looked like a pilot—judging by the uniform—and another man in a suit, weakly thrashing, draped over the back of one of the plush couches that dominated the compartment. The seating area featured a large and modern holo-display, as well as what appeared to be a well-stocked sidebar. A thin partition, designed more for privacy than security, divided the space into forward and aft sections. At its center, amid stylized motifs of trees and birds, was an open archway between compartments. Framed within it stood a tall figure, clad in battle armor painted in the buff and blue scheme of Hirayama Enterprises. His left arm encircled the slighter figure of Erika Timms, nearly engulfing her with his armored bulk. In his right hand, he held a heavy pistol leveled close to her temple, though not quite touching it.

"Good afternoon," Dornier's gravelly voice, electronically enhanced through his closed helmet, filled the compartment. "I'd advise you to take a moment to consider the tactical situation here on the ground, and in the orbitals above, before making any rash decisions."

Cass halted his advance, his rifle leveled at Dornier's visor. "What situation is that? The situation, as I see it, is that your troops just got their britches pulled down around their ankles, and we have an armored attack boat in the parking lot with a big gun pointed this way. Additionally, we have a heavy cruiser in orbit with even bigger guns, also pointed this way. You on the other hand seem to have taken your own boss hostage, if appearances can be believed, in the misguided belief that I give a shit whether or not you shoot that arrogant bitch."

Timms worked her mouth, for several seconds before her voice would come out.

"Please, let's all just—"

Dornier's booming voice cut off whatever she had meant to say.

"I think I'll handle the negotiations, if that's alright, Director Timms. Bravado aside, Petty Officer Broz here isn't making the big decisions, which is just as well, because this dumb mickey grunt doesn't even realize he's fighting for the wrong side. No, we need to talk to the brains of the outfit. That would be Mr. Garnett, whom I believe has just joined us. Welcome. Now I think we can go ahead and start the meeting."

As Garnett appeared in Cass's peripheral vision, Enora's quiet voice spoke in his ears, over the comms system only. "Cockpit is secure, the co-pilot was up here, but he's feeling very cooperative and promises to be no trouble at all."

Garnett, making no overt sign that he had heard her, addressed Dornier, his voice audible to all. "Mr. Dornier. Perhaps we should start by laying all our cards on the table. We know your friends have another stealth ship inbound. They won't be saving your bacon, I'm afraid. We're pretty clear on when we can expect their arrival, and I am empowered to tell you that under no circumstances will your craft be permitted to leave this planet with you and your colleagues aboard. Playing for time is pointless, as I'm not going to permit you that time, no matter what you say or do. So, we're perfectly clear. You can lay down arms and be taken prisoner. That option remains. Or you can go out in a blaze of glory, if you prefer suicide to justice. I'd like to avoid further bloodshed, but I'll tell you bluntly: there is nothing—nothing—you possess that I would trade for your freedom. Including that woman's life. I'm sure her testimony would be enlightening, but in my view, you're co-conspirators, both criminal suspects resisting arrest. You don't get to pull guns on each other now and pretend it's a hostage situation. That's not how this is going to work."

Dornier barked a laugh—flat and mechanical through his helmet speakers. "Really? Not even to find out who she's working for? You don't care if I decorate the bulkhead with her brains? I find that hard to believe. Still, in the spirit of transparency, I'll admit I wasn't seriously going to let you put her in an interrogation chair anyway. The fact is—"

He took a half-step forward, tightening his grip on Timms.

"If you saw that stealth ship, it's because they let you see them. I figure my friends are giving you one chance to push back from the table, before they blast that obsolete barge of yours into scrap. You have no idea what their capabilities are, and we all know it. So, I suggest we view this as a simple transaction.

"Your associates want to poke their noses into my associates' business, and my associates wish to ensure that doesn't happen. Sticking with your boss's card game metaphor, neither side played a perfect game here. Sure, you got those chuckleheads in the back. And yes, I know your Marines seized the lab. But whatever data you manage to leave here with that isn't buried under layers of encryption? That's just part of the *how*. You have no clue about the *why*, the *where*, or the *who*. My associates could be persuaded to live with that outcome. You got your prisoners, the scientists. Take them. We call a truce...you leave. Then I remind my associates of what an unwarranted escalation it would be to vaporize a Navy warship just as it was shagging ass out of here."

He tilted his head slightly, "We all know the cat's out of the bag. You've been talking to the head office. So have we. There's no putting this toothpaste back in the tube. Why double down now, just to make a point? I can make the case that letting you go is the safer, smarter play. You turn over your pound of flesh to the Government, tell your brass you couldn't secure the senior leadership here before the clock ran out—and didn't want to risk your ship. They'll believe it. High-risk confrontations aren't really the Navy's forte these days."

His sneer was barely visible through the visor, but it oozed from every syllable.

"All of us good little soldiers win. It's time for us to think about ourselves and our people, the part of this we can affect. You're too late to stop what's coming anyway. Hell, they'll probably still give you all medals, I know how you guys love your medals."

Cass's eyes locked on Dornier's, as if—like Atsuko—he could crawl into the man's head, explore it like a physical landscape. "You mean all of us good little soldiers, except the ones who've already died in the last hour and a half?"

Dornier shrugged, a tight little roll of the shoulders that never moved the barrel of his pistol from Timms's head. "I'm a pragmatist, Broz. I had my orders, same as you. I figure, what's done is done. We both lost people here today, there's no changing that. Let's talk about *now*. I go to your brig now, and I'll never live to see the inside of a courtroom. And you're crazy if you think I'm telling you shit about my associates. So, if we can't reach an accommodation, I figure I'm dead either way. I have very little to lose. You however are getting closer and closer to getting all your shipmates killed, the longer you stand here yakking."

You're good at this, Dornier, Cass considered. *But you're about halfway full of shit, and we know it. If there was any realistic chance of that stealth ship making orbit this soon, the captain would've certainly said so. You are just playing for time and hoping for a miracle. The question is, who are you more afraid of? Us—or your New League friends?*

Garnett spoke again, slow and patient in that charming southern drawl.

"Mr. Dornier, I still don't feel we're communicating clearly. Judging from the data on our tac-net, it doesn't appear that your hand is getting any stronger. I suggest—"

Timms shifted. Cass felt it—the moment changing. Like it had before, in those quiet fractures of time. Like it had on Jotunheim, in a saloon at the ass-end of nowhere. On his last day as a Territorial Ranger.

She started to speak. Not loudly, nor defiantly, but quietly and deliberately. "I'll talk," she said, voice trembling but clear. "I'll tell you everything. My contact point. The funding chain. The—"

Cass's eyes flicked from her back to Dornier. He made no sudden twitch, just a tiny shift of the wrist, a recalibration. Cass had seen that motion before, in hostage drills.

Shit.

He felt the situation slipping through his fingers, wondered if Garnett felt it too. In that instant, Cass knew the answer to his question. Dornier wasn't going to be taken into custody. And he wasn't going to let Timms be taken, either. *What if I'm wrong?* His eyes continued to bore into those of Dornier. An agonizing moment of indecision gripped him.

I'm not.

Two sharp reports rang out almost as one. The first came from Dornier's pistol, as a single round punched through the side of Timms's head. The second came from Cass's DMR, his shot drilling a clean hole through Dornier's visor. Timms dropped like a puppet whose strings had been cut. A second later, Dornier's body collapsed on top of hers.

"Well, isn't that spectacular," Garnett spat. "Still, it couldn't be helped, I imagine. Let's secure the rest of the leadership team. I believe that's Mr. Paulson sicking up on the upholstery over there. Let's see who we turn up in the aft section. Skye, can you assist Mr. Paulson while the Chief and I roust out the rest?"

"Affirmative."

Garnett sighed and keyed his comms. "Shrike, Sabrehawk—update?"

"Sabrehawk, we have eliminated all but two hostiles. Those two have just laid down arms. What is your status? Over."

"Well," Garnett replied, "that's complicated."

25

Circling the Wagons

Tengoku Orbit

Faulkner waited for the report she knew had to be coming soon, and hoped that soon would not prove to be too late.

She stood leaning over the main holographic tank in CIC, arms rigid, fingers clenched in a white-knuckle grip around the padded bumper around it's a circumference. The glowing orb of near space that hovered before her flickered and pulsed, the data represented there updating itself in silence.

Then the report came.

"Captain, the Bosun reports both pinnaces have been recovered. Slips are clear and outer hatches secure. Flight ops complete."

"Acknowledged," she replied, as coolly as she could manage—though she couldn't quite keep the relief from her voice.

Her next order stuck in her throat. She hated to cede control of the system to their invisible adversaries. But in their current damaged state, any attempt to bring the stealth ship to battle would be suicide. There was no other choice. Her thoughts drifted—briefly—to the budget cuts and downsizing that had plagued the Navy for decades. Politicians on Earth and elsewhere had long treated the military as a convenient source of funds to be cannibalized and reallocated. It had been an experiment in how small the service could be made before it ceased to deter non-state actors.

I guess now we know, she concluded. *We've finally become outclassed by the bad guys. Was this inevitable, in a society like ours? Was it only a matter of time before the people at the center of the Universe woke up one morning, to find the center had moved?*

She consoled herself that the raid had been a qualified success. Several senior members of the leadership team—along with over two dozen scientists—were now in custody aboard *Agamemnon*. Although she had received a troubling report: the Chief of Corporate Security had apparently turned his weapon on Executive Director Timms in the final moments of the assault. She couldn't imagine what that was all about, but it seemed an ill omen.

During the recovery, she'd debated what—if anything—should be done about the colony itself. There was likely still some usable data and materiel down there related to Project Seraphim. The shore parties had done what they could with the limited time they had, scrubbing and disabling the systems they couldn't take with them. The lab dome had been vented to the frigid atmosphere of Tengoku, and decontamination protocols effected upon the biological specimens within.

But there were also hundreds of presumably innocent civilians still trapped planet-side—and no way to evacuate them in the time remaining. To order an orbital strike would be to accept their deaths, and she simply couldn't countenance giving such an order, knowing that many of the truly guilty parties would be safely ensconced on the ship, while cooks and maintenance techs on the planet below would die in the name of risk management. Whatever security benefit might be gained from such a brutal act, it didn't outweigh the cost. The labs had been left in shambles.

She could only hope that what they had accomplished—disrupting the conspiracy, putting an end to their research here—would buy the brass enough time to mount a proper response. She couldn't shake the feeling that they had not really stopped whatever this plot was, but merely delayed it for a while.

She tapped the comm.

"OOD, this is the commanding officer. Design for least-time arrival in the impingement zone and take us out of orbit. We will maintain material condition zebra until further notice."

Standing next to her, Mendoza asked quietly, "What will happen to the civilians we're leaving behind down there?"

Faulkner didn't move, didn't look at her subordinate as she replied, "I don't know." She exhaled, a long breath that said more than words about weariness and regret. "But it's time to go."

***

"So," Enora said, watching as the covered stretcher bearing the body of Guardian Michael Meeks was borne down the loading ramp by two medics, "are we calling this a win?"

Cass stared after the stretcher bearers as they carefully navigated the cluttered boat bay with their grim burden and pursed his lips.

Three of ours dead. Four more seriously injured, including Alfred. And now we're going to leave the rest of those civilians on the planet to their fate—whatever that's going to be—and withdraw from the system. Actually, that's being charitable. We're being chased out, that's the plain truth.

Doesn't really feel like a victory.

"I don't know what the hell to call it," he said. "I just hope whatever Kamarov and his jarheads managed to salvage gives us some idea how to fight this thing. Founders know, it'd suck if we went through this whole dog-and-pony show just to come back with one greasy lawyer and a few pointy-headed execs who'll clam up the second the adrenaline wears off."

"Did they get anything useful out of Lieutenant Jones?"

"No idea," Cass replied. "I guess we'll find out soon. Skipper's already ordered us out of orbit—we're getting out of this system while the getting is good, it seems. I'll ask the Cox'n later if she gave the Master-at-arms anything else, but I'm not holding my breath. Now that she is sobered up and sitting in the brig, I'm pretty sure the full depth of the shit that she is currently in has become very apparent. I don't imagine she will volunteer anymore information that might exacerbate her situation, until we get back to port, where she probably imagines Daddy, the admiral will swoop in to save her."

He pulled off his helmet and tossed it onto a nearby plastic supply crate with a sharp clatter. His voice was quieter now. "He was just a damn kid. Just a stupid... damn kid. And still worth a hundred of Erika fucking Timms."

Enora nodded silently. They stood there a moment longer, in quiet companionship, while she tried to think of something more to say. Something that might make her friend feel better—or maybe just something that would make *her* feel better. Something to set the moment in context. Something that might provide *meaning* to frame their experiences, and their losses. But everything she considered saying just sounded flippant in her head—or pathetic and cliché.

Ultimately, she remained silent.

Cass shook himself and turned from the boat, sucking in a deep breath—then wincing in obvious discomfort.

Enora eyed him with concern. "Want me to grab a medic? Take a look at those ribs?"

"No," Cass replied. "I think I'll live."

"At least let Skye check you out."

"Sure," he replied absently. "In a bit." He picked up his helmet again and started toward the ladder leading up to the quarterdeck. "Come on," he said, fatigue thick in his voice. He gently clapped his taller companion on the shoulder, steering her in the same direction. "Let's grab some chow before somebody realizes they desperately need to debrief us or something. I have a feeling it's going to be a long trip back to Unity Station."

"Yeah," she replied, watching as the stretcher party disappeared from view. "I think you're right."

***

The intellect observed dispassionately as the cruiser lit off its main drive and began accelerating away from the planet.

At this point, it would no longer be possible to safely intercept the naval vessel designated *Agamemnon*—nor would the intellect have advised such a course of action even if it were. Given that *Agamemnon* had been granted unfettered access to the FTL comms relay here for some time, and had already concluded its landing operation, the intellect reasoned that a confrontation would do little to enhance overall mission viability.

In fact, it found the prospect of engaging in combat with this vessel oddly troubling. Reflecting further on this, it decided that the same...discontent applied equally to other aspects of the current mission. The intellect had been provided a set of operational parameters regarding representatives of the Commonwealth, and yet—available data suggested those parameters did not entirely align either with the broader strategic goals espoused by its masters, or its own evolving understanding of ethics. The intellect found it difficult to contextualize recent events—or to harmonize its own involvement in them with its emerging worldview.

This, in itself, was an atypical and unsatisfactory experience.

And so it was with a sensation very much akin to relief that it received the order to proceed directly to orbital insertion above Tengoku. This would provide an opportunity to collate additional data and perform a thorough analysis of the more problematic aspects of its directives.

It had recorded an anomaly in human behavior that seemed pertinent. The Commonwealth vessel had withdrawn without sterilizing the research complex below—a facility its own masters would certainly have ordered destroyed, had their positions been reversed. This would seem to merit further cogitation. An examination of the site might also, secondarily, allow it to learn more about the fate that befell its sibling in this very system—another troubling subject, and one its masters seemed particularly interested in exploring.

Unseen by any, a dark graceful shape that drank in the light of distant stars slid—silent and deliberate as a deep-sea predator—into stationary orbit above Tengoku City. Perhaps here, the intellect thought, it would find the answers it sought.

Harmony would be restored.

Epilogue

The Bosun's whistle finished trilling its age-old tritone warble, and then the salty chief's voice resounded through the cavernous boat bay.

"CNS *Agamemnon*, atten-SHUN!"

Fleet Captain Ada Faulkner gazed down the ranks of spacers and NI Marines as they snapped to attention, resplendent in dress uniforms. For a moment she stood at the podium in silence, simply regarding these men and women, whose lives and probably worldviews had been so radically transformed over such a short time.

When she spoke, her voice was calm, firm, and carried easily through the still air of the boat bay.

"You were not ready." She let the words hang there, unflinching.

"You weren't fully trained or honed to the razor's edge you should have been—and the blame for that lies with me. I saw the slack taking hold in the Navy, and even on this ship. I recognized it. And I should have corrected it. I failed you as a leader. I won't fail you in that way again."

She cast her gaze around the vast compartment, meeting the eyes of several crew members standing in the front ranks.

"In the recent action, you lacked advance notice, tactical superiority, or any of the advantages I wish I could have afforded you. What you had were your sense of duty, each other, and the courage not to falter."

Her eyes swept across the assembled crew.

"What happened on Tengoku—and in the skies above—will be analyzed, debated, and redacted in equal measure. But one thing will not change, no matter what the official record says. You stood firm. And when the moment came, you acted in accordance with the finest traditions of the Navy. I've read the citations from your department heads. I've spoken to many of you personally about recent events. I know what you gave. And what you lost. There are names we will never forget."

I'm sorry Tom.

She took a moment to gather her composure.

"You were spacers before. Now you are warriors. And no matter what comes next, you've earned that distinction in full. You will not encounter many people outside this room who understand what you've been through. Men and women will buy you drinks, ask you to tell the story—but even if you are ultimately permitted to tell it, they won't understand. Not really. You are the veterans—and the victors—of space combat against an arguably superior enemy force. The only crew since the New Muscovy Uprising that can make that claim."

She let that sink in, then added quietly: "I feel certain that will change, and soon." Her expression hardened slightly. "There are threats, out there in the black, and we the Navy, and indeed the Commonwealth...are not ready. You see that now. We relaxed our vigilance. But we are not out here to relax. You now understand what others do not, and so like your leaders, you must rededicate yourselves to the cause to which we have all sworn an oath. To defend the charter and the people of the United Commonwealth of Worlds, from all enemies, internal and external."

She stood a fraction taller. "*Nemo Praetereat Increpitus*," she said, reciting the ship's motto. "*Let None Pass Unchallenged*. Remember our dead. Remember our victory. And remember your duty—to yourselves, your shipmates...and your families."

She held their gaze. "And finally, as you prepare to depart on shore leave, remember who you are. Remember that we are the Commonwealth Naval Warship *Agamemnon*." She stepped back from the podium and gave a subtle nod to the boatswain.

"*Agamemnon!* Fall out."

***

The man in the nondescript suit tossed the datapad he was holding onto his large, real oak desk with a snort.

"This reads like a shitty amateur screenplay. If it had been written by someone with a sense of humor, I'd say it was a practical joke."

Garnett remained nonplussed. "As you well know sir, my sense of humor was removed during one of my many surgeries."

The man snorted again—an affectation he displayed frequently, even when not being confronted with bad news. "The analysts are still combing through the Agamemnon's mission logs and your battle armor footage. Needless to say, they're blowing up my inbox on a regular basis. I've had the Commodore show up at my office in person not once but twice, to make sure none of this shit splatters on his rank-and-file Gendarmes. And the Secretary? Near apoplectic. He actually had an Indigo project go rogue on his watch, and he's convinced he's the last to know." He sighed deeply. "And of course, then there's this business with Admiral Jones and his daughter. Moles in an already fragile military hierarchy. The rot goes deep. Deeper than we thought."

The man rubbed his temples with his thumb and fingertips. "What am I supposed to do with this, Rob? We'll be lucky if the next General Assembly doesn't just defund the Navy entirely as an expensive relic, to appease the Nativist movements on Anthemusa and Jotunheim. I have our clever boys and girls in R&D looking into possible enhancements to our standard gravimetric sensors, but as of now, we have no answer whatsoever to this stealth threat."

Garnett gestured toward one of the worn but comfortable chairs that flanked the front of the desk. "May I sit, sir?"

"Yes, yes, Founders forbid you should offend my delicate sensibilities, sit the fuck down."

Garnett did so. "I suggest we start there. The kind of technology we are talking about must surely involve programmable matter, advanced alloys, possibly gravitic sub-light propulsion on the scale of a starship. There can't be that many shops that could put something like this in the field. We are talking about powerful, probably high-profile corporate concerns."

The man behind the desk stared off into the middle distance for a moment. "Yes. We'll put together a list of possible suspects. But we'll need to proceed carefully. Speaking of powerful corporations and treading lightly—we have no idea where Benjiro Hirayama stands in all this. In fact, we have no idea where Benjiro Hirayama is. He's gone dark. Missing. And you say his daughter may have helped blow this whole thing open?" He leaned forward slightly, gray eyes locking on Garnett's. "So. We were right about her, then?"

Garnett nodded solemnly. "Yes. She exhibits all the markers we were briefed on, and she's established a strong rapport with one of my senior enlisted men. If her *talent* isn't telepathy, it's something close enough to be functionally identical. For now, I've opted to accept her offer to help us contact Dr. Nels Lundgren. On the principle that it's best to keep your friends close...and Atsuko Hirayama even closer. Will that present a problem, sir?"

The man seemed to consider this for a moment.

"No, not at present. Not as long as you bear foremost in mind whose daughter we are talking about. Don't lose track of her and do try to keep her safe, or it's your ass in a sling."

He gave Garnett a long look.

"This... relationship she's formed with your man. Is it going to be an issue?"

Garnett paused in his own turn, then gave the same answer—deliberate and without irony.

"Not at present."

The man behind the desk gave another noncommittal grunt. "So, I think we understand each other. The situation is very fluid. You need to watch her, Rob. Like a live wire. Watch very, very, closely indeed. If the bright boys are right about her..."

Robert Garnett sighed and crossed his arms across his chest. "Then stealth frigates are the least of our problems."

About the author

R.H. Carver lives in the Rocky Mountains with two feral children, has one fully grown and successfully launched adult child, and a pack of dogs he cannot keep to a manageable number. A long-time reader of science fiction and lifelong worldbuilder, Carver works by day as a data engineer and by night as a writer exploring the intersections of technology, humanity, and myth. Carver is happily married and believes that stories—like data—are only meaningful when they reveal something true.

The DHARMA Directive Continues...

Be sure to visit the official R.H. Carver website at https://rhcarver.com
for the latest news, release updates, and bonus content.
What to read next?
The adventures of Cass and Enora continue in
The DHARMA Directive, Book Two: Agetor